PROLOGUE

The red sandstone walls and slate roof of the thirteenth-century church stood out against a bleak sky, with rain falling steadily as the mourners followed the coffin towards a large hole dug in the ground. The faint echo of an organ's notes reached the woman standing under a tree, just close enough to see proceedings but far enough away not to be included. She pulled her hood up and shivered, partly with cold, partly with grief, as she leant up against the trunk, noticing the wonkiness of the church, which tilted lopsidedly as if half of it was sinking into the ground below.

The engraved lettering of the gravestones had faded over centuries, and they were now covered in lichen.

The woman watched the small group of no more than ten or twelve people surrounding the grave, all with ruddy faces, battered over decades by wind and rain. There were no children. A small, wiry woman held a dog with one hand, blowing her nose loudly with the other, as the vicar intoned a blessing before the coffin was lowered into the ground.

The dog pulled hard at the lead and tried to jump in after it.

'No, Jiffy, no.' The woman's voice carried as she struggled to restrain the Welsh terrier.

'Here, Gwen, let me take him. He'll pull you in there with

him if you're not careful.' A big, muscular man with broad shoulders, and arms as wide as thighs, scooped up the dog and held him tight.

The woman under the tree watched and waited. She noticed a tall, harassed-looking man in riding boots arrive late. He nodded at the mourners and took off his cap, bowing his head momentarily before raising his impressively prominent cheekbones to gaze out into the distance. His lips moved, mouthing words no one could hear. Perhaps a prayer, perhaps a last goodbye or a final rebuke. It was indecipherable. Then, a couple of minutes later, he walked away. The dog growled.

'You're not wrong, Jiffy. I'm surprised he bothered.' The huge man holding the dog tutted.

The woman next to him wiped tears from her eyes with a handkerchief. 'Oh, he's not as bad as his father. They may not have spoken a word to each other, but there wasn't as much anger between them as in the old days.'

Family grudges lasted generations in these parts.

The mourners started to move away. The man carried the dog and guided the woman with the hanky to the car. The woman under the tree waited.

She watched the gravediggers fill in the grave. When she was sure they had all departed, she walked carefully across the sodden turf towards the spot where he lay. Or at least where his body now lay. He had long gone from her life. She crouched down and touched the damp mound.

The mourners didn't know the William she knew. They had met only the gruff, fierce farmer who worked long, hard

Pastures New

Clare Balding grew up in the countryside surrounded by horses and dogs. A keen reader, she devoured the books of everyone from Jane Austen to Gerald Durrell. After an English literature degree at Cambridge she became a journalist and broadcaster, but always itched to write a book. She has now written nine, including her autobiography, *My Animals and Other Family*, which won the National Book Award for Autobiography of the Year. Encouraged by Jilly Cooper, she took the leap from her series of children's books and *Pastures New* is her first adult novel.

Alongside her award-winning sports broadcasting and coverage of major royal events, Clare hosts her much-loved *Ramblings* series on Radio 4, exploring Britain's landscape and its storytelling.

To find out more about Clare Balding:

www.clarebalding.co.uk
📷 @clarebalding
𝕏 @clarebalding

Also by Clare Balding

Non-Fiction

My Animals and Other Family
Walking Home
Heroic Animals: 100 Amazing Creatures Great and Small
Isle of Dogs

Children's

The Racehorse Who Wouldn't Gallop
The Racehorse Who Disappeared
The Racehorse Who Learned to Dance
The Girl Who Thought She Was a Dog
Fall Off, Get Back On, Keep Going
*Animal All-Stars: Incredible Facts for Kids Who
Love Animals and Sport*

CLARE BALDING

Pastures New

HarperCollins*Publishers*

HarperCollins*Publishers* Ltd
1 London Bridge Street,
London SE1 9GF

www.harpercollins.co.uk

HarperCollins*Publishers*
Macken House,
39/40 Mayor Street Upper,
Dublin 1, D01 C9W8
Ireland

First published by HarperCollins*Publishers* Ltd 2025
1

A catalogue record for this book is available from the British Library.

ISBN: 978-0-00-860701-2 (HB)
ISBN: 978-0-00-860702-9 (TPB)

This novel is entirely a work of fiction.
The names, characters and incidents portrayed in it are
the work of the author's imagination. Any resemblance to
actual persons, living or dead, events or localities is
entirely coincidental.

Typeset in A Caslon Pro by Palimpsest Book Production Ltd, Falkirk, Stirlingshire

Printed and Bound in the UK using 100% renewable electricity
at CPI Group (UK) Ltd

This book contains FSC™ certified paper and other controlled sources to ensure
responsible forest management.

For more information visit: www.harpercollins.co.uk/green

For Sue and in memory of Ed

days – and most nights too during lambing season – who wore the same jumper every day and who never took a holiday. As far as they were aware, he'd never been out of the village, let alone crossed the River Severn or flown out of the country.

They hadn't seen him in a jazz club in Paris, laughing uncontrollably, or climbing a mountain in the Dolomites, singing at the top of his voice. They hadn't felt the flame of his passion or the tenderness of his kiss, and she was certain they had never seen him cry like she had.

She felt a sharp pain in her chest, as if her heart was physically splintering. She filled her hand with heavy, wet earth and threw it onto the grave. The breath was knocked out of her. She looked up to the sky to let the rain fall on her face and mingle with the tears flowing down her cheeks.

CHAPTER ONE

Alex quickened the pace because a tube train was due in two minutes, according to her app. The sky was grey, and mizzle lay thick in the air on this cold December morning, but at least it was only two days until the Christmas break.

Alex and the other flat-owners had done their bit outside the front door, but they couldn't make the whole street safe; it was littered with slippery wet leaves that the council had failed to sweep away. A jogger in a neon beanie hat came by and skidded on one as he swerved to avoid a woman holding a toddler on one arm and pushing a baby in a buggy with the other.

'Shit,' he muttered to himself.

The toddler turned to his mother. 'What's *shit*?' he asked.

'No.' She shook her head. 'Not a nice word.'

'Shit, shit, shit.' The toddler started to sing the words to a tune he had created.

Even on a grim day like this, Alex enjoyed the walk to the tube station. There was always something to see in London. People to observe, houses to stare at, now with their oversized seasonal wreaths hanging from the front door, cars to check out and, best of all, dogs to watch and greet as they headed towards the park for their morning walks.

A miniature schnauzer with comical white eyebrows on a steel-grey face was straining at the lead as it recognized Alex.

'Hello Monty!' She grinned, bending down as Monty's whole body danced with joy.

'I'm so sorry. He'll make your trousers dirty,' Monty's dog walker, clad head to toe in waterproof clothing, warned.

'Oh, don't worry about that. I'd rather have a cuddle than clean trousers. Are you picking up a few others?'

'Yeah. I've got a noisy dachshund called Dave and a cockapoo called Kevin on this road, then Pip the Cavapoo on Devonshire Road. Four is the max, so that'll keep my hands full for this morning.'

Not for the first time, Alex thought how blissful life as a dog walker would be. Endless fresh air and exercise, with different dogs to share it with, all of them treating you as if you were the most important, joy-giving person in their life. She relished the freedom of walking without a care in the world.

As a child, she had been asked at school what her idea of success was. Where other pupils had talked about earning millions, owning a racehorse or a super-yacht, buying a football club or running a huge business, she had answered 'having no responsibility'. To her, that would mean she was winning at life.

Until that dream day, there was a career to manage in a job that didn't always leave Alex wagging a metaphorical tail, thanks to a demanding boss and unsociable hours.

She heard the tube rattling over the bridge and ran up the stairs, but she was just too late. The train doors closed in her face. Bollocks. She looked up and saw the next train wasn't due for six minutes. Ah well. It had been worth the delay for the cuddle with Monty, which was always a highlight of her day. She sat on a bench in the middle of the platform, tucked her shoulder-length brown hair behind her left ear and made the best use of the time, scrolling through the social media posts of the infamous, taking screen grabs when something piqued her interest for a potential story.

Being a freelance society reporter for *Rizz* magazine had its benefits: travelling the world, discounts on clothes, free food at parties, an endless carousel of new people to meet, some of them interesting, some of them beautiful, some of them beddable even.

It was supposed to be the perfect life for someone who had made it her mission to have no ties and no responsibility, to ensure there was nothing to worry about. Best to enjoy it, thought Alex, and ignore the voice that sometimes whispered, *Is this it?* It had certainly been enough through her carefree twenties and most of her thirties, but now, as she approached her fortieth birthday, the world around her looked very different, and it didn't feel as satisfying as it once had.

Her friends were married, and most had children now. Her younger brothers were also settled at home with well-paid jobs. Meanwhile, Alex had no relationship and a one-bedroom flat with a mortgage. Paying that off was her only motivation to keep working in a job that required little emotional or intellectual investment, and which she no longer enjoyed like she once had.

Still, there was only another couple of days to get through, and then she could head home to her parents' for Christmas.

The *Rizz* office was part of the new development at White

City, where BBC Television Centre had stood for decades. ITV had since moved into the new studios, taking over the iconic horseshoe and reaping the benefits of a recognizable hub, as well as the new restaurants and shopping centre. There was even a swimming pool up on the roof of a private members' club. It was all very LA, although looking out at the cars streaming into town on the Westway didn't have quite the same cachet as the view of a Californian sunset.

When Alex had been here as a trainee, the area had been very different, even a little seedy. Now, it was full of hipsters in spotless white trainers wandering around with wireless headphones and backpacks.

Rizz magazine fed off the social posts that the notorious, the illustrious, the fêted few shared with their fanatical followers. It was easy work for Alex to sift through the updates and photos, harvesting interesting information and working it into her weekly column. The small team of reporters all thought of themselves as farmers, cultivating the seeds they were offered and turning them into a crop upon which the readers could feast.

It always amazed Alex how these same individuals who always talked about protecting their privacy would willingly share so much online. It was like a jewellery store paying a fortune for an alarm system and then leaving its best gems out on the pavement for passers-by to stick in their pockets.

The real skill of a society reporter, like a good detective, was not just to follow the accounts of famous people but also those of their siblings, children, friends and associates. That was where the gold dust lay. Celebs might be careful in their own feed, but their friends were never quite so disciplined, particularly at the end of a fun night out, which could make for much more candid material. Scanning the feed in the hour around and after midnight was always worthwhile, jotting down details and taking screenshots before posts were deleted in the cold light of morning.

Some of Alex's best stories had come from late-night detective work, including discovering a treasured and supposedly happily married political correspondent approaching young men at a nightclub, and a celebrity chef surrounded by girls younger than his daughters. For all the celebrities who might want to edit their lives into the perfect Insta story, *Rizz* could see through the sepia-tinted glow. It was the magazine that no one wanted to be featured in but everyone wanted to read; it wasn't sycophantic like some of the other glossies, and that was what gave it its edge.

As Alex walked through the large foyer towards the security gates, she realized that trying to wipe Monty's muddy pawprints away with a tissue had only created a grey smudge. She would just have to style it out.

Alex's phone buzzed as the lift doors opened. It was a text from the parentals.

What time you home tomorrow?

There always had to be a bloody timetable with them. She put her phone back in her bag as she walked into the office. She looked around for someone to greet, but seemingly everyone was either away or 'working from home'.

9

The office was supposed to be all hot-desking, but she flung her bag onto what had become hers by virtue of regular use and keeping a few personal items – mainly chewing gum and a notepad she'd taken from a hotel room – in the accompanying drawer.

As Alex rummaged around in her handbag, looking for the phone she had put in there only seconds ago, she wondered again why anyone paid hundreds of pounds for a designer bag that barely fitted a phone and a set of keys. Hers was a multi-coloured large tote she had picked up for cheap in a market in Guatemala City. It had endless space, although that did mean everything always got lost at the bottom.

'Oh god, I'm turning into my mother,' she said out loud.

It was the fate she dreaded most of all.

Having retrieved her phone, she typed her reply.

About 6 I hope. Slightly depends on a deadline but I'll do my best. Can't wait to see you. Any last min purchases you want me to get?

Alex knew better than to stand there waiting for a reply, even though she could see the message had been read. It wouldn't happen. One thing she always agreed on with her brothers was that their mother must think that texts were charged by the word. They were rare, short, one might even say terse. Alex pictured their mother in the kitchen, surveying the contents of the fridge and trying to work out whether she had enough food to get through the oncoming family avalanche.

'Save the pennies, and the pounds will take care of them-selves' was her mother's favourite saying, which didn't even make sense now that no one carried cash.

Alex had inherited traces of that presbyterian outlook but tried hard to suppress it.

She wandered to the coffee machine with her Thermos mug, grateful that one of the perks of coming into the office was limitless free caffeine to help her get through the day. Jack, the only other person at work this morning, greeted her with a cheery smile. He was wearing a tight red jumper featuring a reindeer whose antlers and nose sparkled with sequins. On anyone else, it would have looked ridiculous, but somehow on his twenty-something muscular frame, it was fashionably ironic. He was the photo editor for *Rizz*, and Alex loved providing the copy for the photos he found. It took so little effort, with the shots already telling the story themselves.

Jack asked Alex about her plans for Christmas.

'Oh, just the usual. Heading down to the family to be infantilized,' she replied.

'I know what you mean.' Jack sighed. 'My mother still offers to put name-tapes in my clothes so they don't get lost. But hey, it's useful to get the washing done and have my shirts properly ironed, so I can't complain. And she spoils me rotten, cooking all my favourite things.'

'Mums and their boys, eh?' Alex mused, filling her cup with black coffee then opening the fridge to find the oat milk. 'Unconditional, never-ending love. Lucky you.'

Jack laughed and headed back to his computer to download the latest set of celeb Christmas party photos.

11

'I've got some good ones for you,' he shouted back over his shoulder.

Alex stirred her coffee and felt vaguely nauseous as she wondered which celebrities she would be ordered to roast on an open fire.

CHAPTER TWO

Christmas Eve Eve or, as some people might call it, the twenty-third of December, was a dank day in Hampshire, with only the dark filigree of tree branches providing context and shape to the milky-grey sky. Any hope of a white Christmas had disappeared in a sticky mess of mud, after a thoroughly miserable December during which rivers had burst their banks, causing untold damage to thousands of houses, and a permanent thick grey smudge of fog had hung around like the last guest at a party, refusing to go home.

The kettle bubbled in the kitchen of a large 1970s red-brick house, situated high enough to have avoided the worst of the flood damage but close enough to the river to be wary of the power of the raging torrent. Alex's parents had lived at the grandly named Riverview Manor for over forty years, and all three of their offspring had spent their childhoods being warned not to mess about near the river. Even though they had all ignored the instruction, they had lived to tell the tale.

Isobel and David had talked for years about modernizing the house, putting in patio doors from the kitchen to make use of the generous south-facing space at the top of the garden, but they had never got around to it, nor had they changed the butter-lemon colour of the walls inside. Isobel had got more paint than she needed in a sale at B&Q and topped up as and when required. There were brushmarks all over the place, as every new patch-up was a bit stronger in lemon colour than the rest of the wall, but she didn't see the point of paying a decorator when she could do it herself.

The shop assistant had told her the paint would make her feel as if the sun was always shining; although that definitely wasn't true on this grim December morning, Alex's mother liked it well enough, and she couldn't see the point of change for the sake of it. After all, who really noticed interior design apart from interior designers – and they were paid to care about it. The upheaval would be a pain in the arse and would just make David even grumpier than usual. As she poured boiling water into the teapot, he was already complaining.

'Honestly, I don't understand why we have to invite the Palmers for dinner. Can't it just be drinks? That way, we can get rid of them by eight o'clock latest and I can watch the Attenborough documentary,' David chided, breathing heavily through his nose and inhaling coffee through his mouth, seemingly at the same time.

Isobel opened the day's Christmas cards with a knife, resisting the temptation to stab him for slurping. The noise was unbearable. There were many reasons to kill him, but she concluded a defence plea that 'he was breathing, m'lud, and I just couldn't stand the racket any more' was not likely to spare her jail time.

Isobel had sent Jacquie Lawson email cards, which were much better for the environment, and postage was just a rip-off these days. You couldn't even guarantee it would arrive in time, and she was damned if she was going to spend over a pound on a stamp and then worry about whether it would actually get there. She hand-delivered to the locals from a stash of cards she'd bought years ago in a post-Christmas sale.

The Palmers, who were coming to dinner that night, had switched to email long ago, as that way they could write their godforsaken updates on their grandchildren and send them to as many people as possible, as if people had willingly subscribed to this family newsletter. Isobel was always tempted to write a truth bomb Christmas update in return, detailing her daughter's series of failed relationships, her elder son's naked ambition, her younger son's jealousy, plus her own daily frustration with being married to a man she increasingly could barely tolerate.

She adjusted her navy-blue woollen jumper so that it fell just over the waistband of her Marks and Spencer jeans. She worried that she was technically too old to wear jeans, but this new high-waist cut was the most comfortable she had found and didn't have the ridiculous flared bottoms that seemed so popular. She rather regretted that it had taken her six decades to find a pair of jeans that she liked.

She watched David reading the newspaper, grunting and tutting at regular intervals. His thick salt-and-pepper hair was flopping forward. He had just celebrated his seventieth birthday, and she was a couple of years younger, although the wrinkles on her face betrayed the years of worrying about things that never seemed to bother David. He lived life while she had to deal with it; that was why her hair was greyer than his and why she found increasing grooves either side of her eyes, on the corners of her mouth and even across her cheeks. Her pale-blue eyes scanned the lengthy shopping list.

Isobel had to cajole her husband through Christmas. She knew he hated the large gatherings, as it meant too many people, too much chat about children, too many mince pies, and she had to suffer the after-effects of turkey and Brussels sprouts on his digestive system.

'Father Christmas is basically an overweight alcoholic given free rein to break into the house,' he had told the children when they were still young enough to believe in the global benefactor. They were terrified ever after, and Isobel had had to reveal her own role in filling their stockings long before she wanted to destroy the harmless fantasy.

David flicked from the back of the paper to the front and paused.

'Jeez Louise,' he huffed.

'What is it, darling?' Isobel paused opening the envelope.

'"CEO in charity fraud scandal",' David read aloud. 'People think they can get away with anything. All that money raised by good honest folk, running and making cakes and setting up auctions, and this sharp-suited wide boy decides he'll use it to build a swimming pool. The bloody cheek.'

Isobel noticed her husband's face was turning a brighter shade of pink and sighed. He had a problem with his blood pressure, but he ignored her protests not to stress himself out.

'That's why I never give to charity.' She shook her head. 'Those CEOs are all on six-figure salaries, you know. It's a disgrace. It's not like it used to be when we were out there shaking tins for the Guide Dogs. We did that for love, not money.'

She glanced at the plastic pill box. It had little dividers in it to mark the days, and she could see that David had not yet taken his pills for today. She popped the multi-coloured collection into her hand and took them over to the kitchen table.

'Take these with your coffee. It'll help swill them down,' she reminded him.

David rolled his eyes and huffed even more noisily.

'Yes. I know you're not a child.' Isobel tried to sound warm and encouraging. 'And I am not your nanny, but the doctor said you mustn't forget, especially if you know you might get stressed.'

David's face started to turn even redder, and she realized it was another losing battle.

'*I do not get stressed!*' David said tersely, as he stood up too quickly and banged his knee on the table. 'Coco!' he called. 'We're going for a walk.'

Their caramel-coloured Norfolk terrier obediently trotted towards him, tail wagging. She stopped and cocked her head on one side, looking towards Isobel with an expression that, if you thought dogs could show emotion, suggested sympathy. Coco turned to follow her master, who had stomped towards the back door and was now pulling on his boots, grimacing.

Isobel opened the fridge and took out a large dish of chicken in a sauce.

'Married the wrong one,' she muttered under her breath as the back door slammed shut.

'What's that, Mum?' Alex had appeared behind her in checked flannel pyjamas. Her dark hair was sticking up as if she'd had an electric shock, and she had smudges under her deep-brown eyes where she hadn't taken her mascara off properly. She shuffled towards the kettle.

'Marinaded the wrong one.' Isobel pointed at the chicken.

'Oh well, never mind. I'm sure it'll be delicious. I'm starving.'

'You look tired,' Isobel told her.

'Thanks, Mum. Always useful to know.'

Alex had arrived too late for supper last night, and Isobel had been so keen to go to bed that she'd turned off the downstairs lights as soon as Alex had got her bag inside, so she hadn't seen her properly.

She watched her daughter put two pieces of bread in the toaster and yawn at the same time as asking, 'Who's coming tonight?'

'The Palmers. Your father is in a huff, but I thought it would be good for us to have some company. I read an article that said it's important to keep stimulating the mind with different conversation.'

'Right.' Her daughter pulled out the teabag and left it crushed on a spoon on the counter. 'Well, I'm not sure how "different" your conversation with them will be. I can give you the list of topics you'll cover now: pension funds, inheritance tax, Brexit, where the grandchildren are going to school, and – for a bit of light relief – a long discussion on why England keep kicking every time they get the ball. What's happened to free-flowing rugby, eh? I can draw up an agenda if you like,' she teased.

'Very funny.' Isobel rolled her eyes as she automatically scooped the teabag into the food bin and slammed the lid, hoping her daughter might notice.

'When are you back to work?'

'It's Christmas, Mum. I've got four days off, but don't worry, I can tell you want rid of me even though I've only just got here. I'll be out tonight, and I'll make sure I've left long before the Palmers get here. I don't need Daphne's disapproval and Michael's over-friendly greeting as he pats my bum and then holds me at arm's length to stare at my tits.' She shuddered. 'That might have been acceptable in the Seventies,' she added for her mother's benefit, 'but now it's classed as harassment. You really ought to tell him.'

Isobel sighed. Honestly, in her day she'd have taken it as a compliment, but Alex was so sensitive about these things. She'd add 'woke' to the list of topics to discuss tonight.

'I will have time to go through your fridge and larder if you like? Check those sell-by dates and chuck out anything that's a year or more over . . .'

'Don't you dare. No one will die from eating marmalade that's a month or two over. Anyway, those dates mean nothing. It's just a guide.'

'Yeah but three years, Mum. That's a bit much. Remember that time I found a ketchup bottle in there from 1997?'

Isobel tutted her disapproval, knowing that she had got the tomato ketchup in a job lot, and it was discounted so heavily it was virtually free. If one of her children got a little runny tummy because of it, who was going to complain? A bargain's a bargain.

'Before you disappear, Miss Best Before, this one's for you.' Isobel handed her a letter addressed to Alex Roberts, Esq.

'Another one who can't work out if I'm a boy or a girl.' Alex sighed as she examined the shape of the envelope. It didn't look like a Christmas card.

'I thought you'd told me that in this day and age, gender should not define anyone?' Isobel challenged her daughter.

'Well, yes, that is what I said, but that doesn't mean I want to be mistaken for a man. I am quite happy with my identity, thanks very much.'

Alex was studying the postmark – Monmouth. She ripped it open while taking bites of toast. It had some kind of official letterhead. Davies and Davies Solicitors. Alex quickly scanned the contents.

'Holy shit,' she said. 'Who the hell is William Griffiths, and why would he have left me a farm?'

CHAPTER THREE

'This has got to be a prank.' Alex read the letter again and laughed. 'I'm going to call Ethan right now. That's just the best joke ever.'

Isobel stared out of the window and watched a robin sitting on the ledge looking back at her. It nodded its head. The back door swung open, and Coco dived straight towards Alex, who scooped her up into her lap and started kissing her face while Coco happily wagged her tail.

'Oh, please don't let her lick you. We've been trying to stop her doing that,' Isobel implored.

'I don't mind. It'll save me having to wash it, won't it, Coco Pops? Clever girl. Have you had a nice walk with Daddy? Have you?' Alex lavished her love on the Norfolk terrier. 'You don't care if I look tired, do you? No you don't, because you love me just as I am. Good girl,' she fussed.

David slammed the door shut as he stomped back in.

'That was quick,' Isobel said.

David was flushed from the exertion and the biting cold wind outside. He leant on the counter for support.

'Coco seemed to know Alex was up and about,' he explained, between laboured breaths. 'She turned around up by the woods and just started heading home, so I had to follow.' He checked his watch. 'About time too. You never were an early bird.'

'Morning to you too, Pops. It's so lovely to be home and to feel like a teenager again.' Alex smiled at her father, and it had the desired effect of calming his bad mood.

He ruffled her hair and sat down at the kitchen table next to her. Despite the mop of dark-brown hair on her head, the sleep in her eyes and the lack of make-up, she still radiated warmth and light. Alex had never been as thin as she would have liked, nor as tall and certainly not as elegant or as beautiful. To her own eyes, she was average in every regard, but to her father, she was luminescent.

'So, tell me all your news. How's work? How's Ethan? Any wedding bells I need to hear about?'

Isobel started making a list of the things she needed for tonight's dinner party, but she stayed in the kitchen, listening to Alex's answers. She never asked her personal questions, mainly for fear of the replies, but she stalked her daughter on social media, so she knew as much as anyone about the stories Alex chose to tell.

'Work's fine, although my editor is on my case. I've got a trip to Dubai coming up in January. That footballer you say is dodgy is opening a restaurant so, you know, that'll be fun.' Alex's updates flowed easily with her father. He listened and occasionally smiled or laughed to encourage her. 'I got a Christmas bonus, so that was good. They particularly liked my story about that politician – you know the one – taking cocaine in the kitchen with the daughter of the host who caught them both and kicked him out.'

David laughed and confirmed that he had indeed seen the story, albeit its second iteration in a respectable broadsheet where a journalist had picked up on Alex's scoop and rewritten the story, without crediting her. He tried not to read magazines like *Rizz*.

'And what about Ethan? You two going on holiday or moving in together or anything like that, hey hey?' David winked at his daughter, always teasing her about him.

Isobel could never have that sort of conversation with her daughter without Alex accusing her of being 'judgy', or taking umbrage at some perfectly well-meaning bit of advice. She never knew why Alex reacted that way.

'I've told you before, Ethan's gay,' Alex admonished her father.

'Ah, but that never stopped anyone. I know lots of gay men who are happily married to women.' David's eyes shone with a naughty twinkle.

'Yes, Dad, but that's because they had to. We've got equal marriage now, you know. It makes far more sense to live as a same-sex couple, to be honest.'

Here we go again, Isobel thought, raising an eyebrow but deciding it was best to stay quiet as Alex eulogized on her favourite subject. She let the words float as bubbles above her head, because she'd heard on the radio that if she imagined them that way, they couldn't annoy her.

'Society sells us heterosexual relationships as the ideal, but they're really not. Men and women don't like the same things.' Alex was just getting started. 'Most of the time, they don't even want to be in the same room, let alone live together, so it's a conspiracy to keep the world in a wretched state of constant frustration.'

Some of us, Isobel thought, *have to make do with our lot.* Lucky old Alex to have the choice of how she wanted to live her life.

Isobel was hardly some kind of secret lesbian who hated her husband and would rather be living with Muriel down the road. She did like Muriel, even quietly considered her rather attractive when she was wearing dungarees, but the last thing on earth Isobel would ever do is be the subject of village gossip for upping and leaving her husband. Far better to soldier on, put on a good show and be secretly miserable than to be a happy non-conformist.

She finished her shopping list by underlining *Lemons*.

'Right, you two, I'm off to the supermarket. Anything you want?' Isobel asked.

'Oat milk please, Mum.'

Isobel could swear she saw Alex smile at David as she made her request. Was she doing it deliberately to wind her up? That's what came of Alex living twenty years in London, soaking up all its stupid bloody fads when, before, old-fashioned dairy milk from an actual cow had been good enough.

'I'll try, but I don't know that they'll have it.' She stretched her lips into a thin smile, not voicing any of this.

'Well, almond or soya would do if they don't have oat,' Alex replied, quick as a flash.

Isobel tried to stop herself from swearing out loud. Next she'd be asking for vegan cheese and stevia instead of sugar. Alex really could push all her buttons.

'You all right, Mum?' asked Alex.

'Fine. Just fine,' Isobel replied, without even moving her lips, and tried to suppress the heat from her cheeks. She rolled her shoulders and stared out of the window again. That robin was still there, watching her and bobbing its tail up and down.

'Don't you start,' Isobel muttered.

'What?' asked David.

'Nothing. Just talking to the robin in the garden.'

David looked at his daughter and waved his forefinger in a circle by his left ear. Alex giggled.

'Right, I'll leave you two to laugh at each other's jokes while I go and do something useful. Alex, try to be dressed by the time I get back. You look an absolute mess.'

'Sure thing, Mum. Anything you say, because I'm not at all a grown-up woman with my own life and old enough to make my own decisions. Can I have some sweeties if I'm a good girl?'

Isobel carried on her breathing exercise as she shut the door firmly behind her.

David sighed. 'Honestly, you two. You just wind each other up.' He was a little short of breath so took a sip of coffee before speaking again. 'For all that stuff you say about men and women not being able to live together, you and your mother . . .' He paused again. 'You two would kill each other if you were left on your own for more than an hour.'

'Well, at least the boys will be home tomorrow and it'll take the pressure off me.' Alex sipped her tea with one hand and held the Norfolk terrier with the other. Coco let out a little mumbled bark, having made herself comfortable in Alex's

25

lap and fallen asleep, dreaming of chasing imaginary bunny rabbits. Alex couldn't move even if she wanted to. 'She won't notice me once Kit and Hugh arrive.'

She noticed her dad looked a bit peaky, so decided to show him the letter to cheer him up. 'Anyway, I've got to ring Ethan and congratulate him on the best prank *ever*. Look at this!'

She passed the letter from the Monmouth solicitors to her father, who wheezed and coughed loudly while she dialled her best friend. There was no answer, as always, so she left a voicemail telling him how clever he was. Next to her, her father read the letter slowly in silence but, rather than perking him up, the contents seemed to make him look even more off-colour.

'Dad?'

Coco jumped off her lap and went straight to David, nudging his leg. David's breathing rate increased, and his eyes lost focus.

Alex looked up from her phone. Her father's face was now the colour of an overripe beetroot.

'Dad, what's the matter? What's happening?'

David grabbed his chest with his right hand and started rocking back and forth. His left arm was hanging limply. Alex followed Coco's lead and knelt by her father's side.

She put her hand to her father's forehead. It felt cold but clammy.

'Shit, how do I know if it's a stroke or a heart attack? Hey, Siri,' she shouted at her phone. 'Google symptoms of a stroke.'

Her phone started talking to her.

'Keep looking at me, Dad. You're going to be OK. Just stay with me.'

Alex reached for his wrist to take his pulse.

'Siri, call 999,' she ordered.

'Calling Fine and Dine,' Siri replied.

'No. Fuck. No. Stop.' She dropped her father's wrist and grabbed the phone.

Alex punched in the numbers 999, cursing voice recognition and her obsession with Fine and Dine caterers.

A female voice answered the call and asked Alex various questions.

'It's my father,' Alex explained, trying to stay calm. 'I think . . .' Her voice cracked as she said the words. 'In fact, I'm pretty sure . . . he's had a stroke.'

CHAPTER FOUR

The paramedics, who came surprisingly quickly to the house, were efficient and capable. Isobel had turned the car around once she'd ensured Alex wasn't making a fuss over nothing, and she climbed into the ambulance with David, leaving Alex to follow.

When they got to Accident and Emergency at the hospital, Isobel groaned. It was chaos.

The waiting room was crammed full of people of all ages, with more arriving every minute. A man was shouting at reception, complaining about his four-hour wait without seeing a doctor, and from the pained look on the faces of the nurses, it was clear he wasn't the only one.

The paramedics carried David into a side corridor and magically turned the stretcher into a bed. There was no chair, so Isobel stood with him. She didn't hold his hand or do anything that might be interpreted as a public display of affection. Instead, she paced up and down the corridor as they waited for a doctor, occasionally walking into reception just to make sure they hadn't forgotten all about them.

One paramedic came back half an hour later to explain that she had filled out the paperwork but they were at capacity right now. If nothing had happened within another half an hour, she promised to take him to the MRI scan herself.

'We need to see what's happened up there.' She pointed

to David's head. 'There could be a blood clot but, don't you worry, we've seen all this a million times and we've got the best doctors in the world. They'll sort him out, and by New Year's Eve, he'll be right as rain and ready to party.'

'I doubt that,' Isobel said in her iciest tone. 'Even on a good year, he struggles to make it past ten o'clock.' Isobel leant into the stretcher and addressed David. 'You always said you'd rather be in A & E than face roast turkey with all the trimmings, so well done on that score.'

She saw the side of David's mouth twitching, which gave her hope he could hear her.

Isobel heard a kerfuffle in reception and recognized the voice.

'But I organized a fundraiser for this building only last summer, and I think you'll find that if you call your senior consultant he knows exactly who I am. Diana Roberts-Cooper.'

Moments later, in a blaze of brightly coloured cashmere, David's older sister Diana appeared, dragging by the hand a doctor who looked too exhausted to protest.

'Darling! How are you? You look wrung out.' Diana enveloped Isobel in a citrus-scented hug and loudly air-kissed each cheek. Her suspiciously grey-free hair was blow-dried and hair-sprayed into a perfect dark curve that framed her face and stopped just before the turned-up collar of a starched white shirt. Isobel could have sworn there were frown lines around her eyes and deep grooves in her forehead last week, but now the surface of her face was as smooth as the skin of a nectarine. Other than a slight sheen, she was flawless, and her large eyes were framed by long dark eyelashes and perfectly curated eyebrows.

Isobel explained her frustration at the lack of progress, and Diana turned to the doctor to issue a charming yet chilling rebuke.

'It's been two and a half hours since the episode. You and I both know you need to move fast here or – and yes, you can write this down if you like – there will be consequences.' She smiled her most winning smile before adding, 'For my dear brother and for you.'

The poor man looked terrified as he consulted the notes attached to the end of David's stretcher-cum-bed. Isobel wanted to berate Diana for bullying, but she was simply relieved that someone who cared less about making a fuss had taken over to get David the attention he clearly needed.

'Have you seen, he's got lovely eyes?' Diana whispered in Isobel's ear, pointing at the doctor.

Isobel shook her head in disbelief. 'Honestly. This is hardly the moment.'

'Are we making progress?' Diana smiled at the doctor again.

Flustered but stung into action, he dived into a side room and returned immediately with a nurse.

'Well done,' Diana said. 'I knew you looked the sort of man who would get things moving.'

'Stop it,' Isobel hissed.

'We'll take him for a scan now and get him comfortable on a proper bed if we can find one,' the nurse explained, pushing the trolley towards the lift.

'Got results, didn't it?' Diana winked.

Diana lived about five miles away in a crumbling but classy Georgian mansion. She was due to be hosting the family

Christmas Eve gathering tomorrow. They always played party games, and the evening usually ended in a drunken row, with someone accusing someone else of cheating. Everyone said the Roberts family were competitive, and there was nothing like party games to bring out the worst in them.

'We'd better leave them to do their job,' Diana said briskly. 'You look like you need a strong cup of coffee, so let's do that while we wait for the scan. You're probably in shock, darling. It happens to the best of us.'

Not normally one to sit and have coffee with another woman, Isobel was strangely happy to be led. She could listen to Diana's stories and let the words just wash over her while she thought of anything but the events of this morning and her husband now lying on a cold hard surface, being shoved into a noisy, beeping tunnel.

CHAPTER FIVE

Having thrown on some presentable clothes and left messages for her brothers to explain what had happened, Alex drove to the hospital.

In the car park, she spotted Aunt Di in a cloud of vape smoke next to her mother, paper coffee cup in hand, looking as if her patience was wearing thin. Diana raised her hand with a flourish to signal the end of a story just as Alex drove into a parking space.

There was something about Aunt Di's combination of drama and decadence that felt like a throwback to the 1920s. She was willowy and elegant, always wearing a scarf with its designer label arranged to be seen, or a pair of shoes that cost more than Alex's monthly mortgage payment. Alex loved being around her, hoping some of her golden glow would rub off. She embraced her favourite aunt warmly.

'What's the latest?' Alex asked.

She was encouraged to hear that her father had been taken for an MRI scan. Now they were waiting for the results.

Her mother was factual and unemotional as always, swiftly changing the subject.

'Are you OK?' Alex asked her.

'Me? Nothing's wrong with me. Of course I'm OK.' Isobel seemed almost offended by the question, to the point where

Alex regretted trying to be nice. 'Your aunt was telling me about her latest date. You must hear about this one.

Alex wondered if her ability to divert and distract was a coping mechanism.

'You're better at it than me.' Alex turned to her aunt. 'Tell me everything.'

'Oh, he was called Bill or Bob or Balthazar. Something like that. He looked nothing like his profile picture, and I'd suggest that using adjectives to describe himself like "fun", "fearless" and "fascinating" broke all the rules of the Trade Descriptions Act.' Aunt Di took a long suck on her vape.

'You met him on a dating app?' Alex was intrigued. She'd never been brave enough to try any of them for herself and was still relying on the age-old method of meeting someone in the flesh to see if there was a spark.

'It's called Nifty,' Aunt Di told her. 'It's for the over-fifties. Nifty at Fifty, I suppose it's meant to mean. I lie about my age, obviously. No one has challenged me yet.'

'I bet they haven't,' Alex said, her mind wandering to her dad.

Even at seventy-two, her aunt barely looked out of her forties. She'd had a few little lifts and tucks here and there. Nothing too obvious, and only if you looked at the papery skin on the back of her hands or the slight tortoise texture of her neck could you tell that she was older than she admitted.

Alex's phone pinged.

Heard yer message. WTF? Not me, babe.

Her father's sudden seizure had rather distracted her from the letter. If Ethan said it wasn't him, then who else would've constructed such an elaborate joke?

'It wasn't Ethan,' Alex announced.

'What wasn't?' Aunt Di asked.

'The letter from the solicitors this morning.'

'I'd better head back in,' Isobel interjected. 'I'll see if Dad's back from the scan. I'll text you if he's out.'

'He'll be a while yet, and I haven't finished telling you about my date,' Di offered.

'I'll be there in a minute,' Alex shouted after her mother as she went back inside, clearly more worried about her dad than she was letting on.

'Aunt Di.' Alex leant towards her aunt as if she were a spy trying to elicit secret information. 'Have you ever heard of a man called William Griffiths?'

Aunt Di paused, as if straining for a memory.

'I don't think so, darling. Not unless he's one of the ones I met on the singles cruise. There were a lot of dancing partners on that one. There might have been a "Will", and I'm not sure we even bothered with surnames!' she replied.

'No, he was named on a letter I got this morning from a solicitors in Monmouth. It says he's died and he's left me a farm.'

'Oh, well done, darling!' Aunt Di exclaimed, embracing Alex with such a forceful hug that she nearly fell over. 'There's nothing better than a gift from beyond the grave. They can't chase you for a thank-you letter, and you don't have to provide them with anything in return, if you know what I mean.' Aunt

Di patted her on the back as she released her. 'Honestly, well done you!'

Alex hadn't thought of the letter as some kind of winning lottery ticket. It was clearly a mistake. And if it wasn't a mistake, then she had a massive problem on her hands, given that the last thing she needed was to be responsible for a farm. Besides having to pay a mortgage on her flat, Alex had very few commitments in her life, and that was exactly the way she liked it.

She thought about the money that Aunt Di had made over the years from minor roles in film and theatre; these always seemed surprisingly well-paid, despite the fact Diana Roberts-Cooper had never been the star of anything. Or maybe they hadn't been her main income source, and the big house, the designer clothes and the flash cars were all provided for by long-gone lovers. And, although horrifying, perhaps that was not so unusual a way to build your fortune.

'It's not that sort of a bequest,' Alex said firmly. 'I have never met the guy. Never even heard of him.'

'Even more impressive if you didn't have to – you know – service the loan,' Aunt Di remarked.

Alex tried very hard not to visualize her aunt in any sort of servicing role.

'The only Will I remember was a friend of your dad's from uni. I didn't see a lot of him in those years. I was off on tour doing Shakespeare in the provinces. Gosh, those were wild days, let me tell you.' Aunt Di took another puff on her vape.

Alex's phone buzzed.

'He's out of the scan,' she reported to her aunt, frowning down at the text from her mother. 'It's good news by the sounds of things, but there's not a lot of detail. She just says, "Not as serious as feared. Ward F".'

Her mother maintained her relentless economy with her texts, even in a situation like this.

'Are you sure you don't want to hear about my time touring Shakespeare?' Aunt Di offered, seemingly happy to distract Alex for a bit longer.

'No, I'd better go see Dad,' Alex replied.

'I'll leave it to you, darling. Anyway, I've got things to be getting on with for tomorrow night!'

Alex paused. 'Are we still going to do Christmas Eve?'

'What? Of course we are. Wild horses and wars wouldn't stop us, let alone a mild stroke. Your father will be fine, and he'd hate to think we missed out on all the fun just because he couldn't be there. What are we going to do instead? Gather round his bed and sing carols? That would be as quick a way as any to kill him.'

Alex headed into the hospital and found her mother on Ward F. Her father was finally in a proper bed and was attached to various machines, wearing an oxygen mask, with a tube coming out of his left hand, connected to a drip. The heart-rate monitor beeped regularly, and she thought he looked strangely peaceful.

Alex held her father's hand, relieved she'd been there when it happened and had been able to respond so quickly. She exhaled as her mother relayed the doctor's update: the scan had shown a clot that was now being treated, rather than a much bigger stroke. She knew her dad hadn't looked right, and her mother was always going on about her dad needing to lower his blood pressure.

She leant forward and kissed her father's forehead, then stroked his hand and uttered a silent prayer. She didn't believe in God but, at moments like this, prayer seemed appropriate, if only to thank whichever higher power had saved him.

'You can leave him in our hands.' A flustered nurse bustled in. 'I promise we will look after him. You can come back in visiting hours this evening or tomorrow morning when he should be more responsive. He just needs a bit of time. The doctor is confident he'll make a full recovery, so you can go and get ready for Christmas.'

'Thank you,' Alex said, patting her father one more time on the hand. Isobel flicked her head sideways, indicating *let's go.*

'That's one way of avoiding tonight's dinner party.' Isobel rolled her eyes as she jabbed at G for the ground floor in the lift. 'Typical. I've told the Palmers what's happened, but they still want to come, so I've asked Muriel to make up the numbers. She's on her own, and it's a kind thing to do at Christmas.'

'Wow, Mum. Priorities, eh?'

Her mother's capacity to soldier on was legendary, but Alex couldn't believe she was contemplating hosting a dinner party when her husband was in hospital after a stroke.

'When you plan something and make a promise to people, it's important to go through with it,' Isobel said firmly, before adding under her breath, 'You wouldn't know.'

38

Alex bit her lip; it was just another barbed comment from her mother that always made her feel like the wild child, just because she hadn't conformed to the rules of polite society. By her mother's standards, she should have been married by the age of thirty and dragging around two children by now. There were so many things she wanted to say, but she had learned the basic rule of *don't say what you can't recover from.*

'Bit judgy, Mum,' was all she managed.

'You're thirty-nine, for god's sake. You shouldn't be behaving like a teenager any more, as if sticking with anything is a weight around your neck.'

Isobel motioned her right index finger from left to right, to signal the hand of a clock, adding a 'tick-tock' for good measure.

As the lift doors opened and Isobel strode on ahead, Alex hung back, taking a deep breath to compose herself. She would give her mother the benefit of the doubt. Maybe her dig was just a way of releasing the stress and worry about her father. It had been a frantic morning – and she still had to go to the supermarket.

CHAPTER SIX

Monmouthshire

The skies had finally started to clear after weeks of persistent rain, so at least Christmas week was a little brighter. Gwen swept the floor of the kitchen, even though there was no one making much mess and no one for whom to keep it clean. Jiffy, the Welsh terrier, was curled up in the armchair, lying on William's sweater. Gwen had tried to move him so that she could fold up the jumper and put it somewhere safe, but Jiffy had growled at her, which was something he'd never done before.

She was worried about the dog. He wasn't eating properly, and he would only leave the chair (and the sweater) to go outside and do his business. As soon as he got back inside, he hopped right back onto it and shoved his long nose so far into it that she was surprised he could breathe at all.

He wouldn't come for a walk, he hadn't wagged his tail once, and he hadn't offered his head for a stroke or jumped up next to her on the sofa for a cuddle since William had died. He was officially and committedly in mourning.

The kitchen was the only room in the house that was warm, thanks to a log burner that needed constant feeding from the wood in the store. The brick floor was cold and, no matter how much she washed it, stubbornly remained stained. There

41

was a wooden kitchen table, scarred with decades of cracks, a farming magazine tucked under one leg to stop it wobbling. The kettle needed two hands to lift it from the sink to the Aga and had a crust of limescale around the spout. Pots and a frying pan hung from pegs on a contraption that lowered with a pulley system.

Gwen shivered and made a mental note to ask Owen Odd Job to chop some of the big branches into logs small enough for her to carry. They'd been drying out for more than a year, so they should be ready. Longer term, someone would have to fell more trees, but that wouldn't be her problem. It would be a job for Alex Roberts to sort out, whoever he was.

Gwen had been asked to go to Davies and Davies Solicitors in Monmouth a few days earlier, and she had dressed up especially for the occasion. Two men in moleskin trousers and pale-blue shirts had shared the details of the estate of William Griffiths. As far as she had known, he was the last in the long line of Griffiths men to own Tir Glas Farm. She had begun to run through the options and the help she would need in case she were left in charge. To call her a housekeeper would not quite do justice to the myriad responsibilities she fulfilled and the things she did before she was even asked. She was as much a part of the estate as the walls, the roof and the grass that grew all around, after being part of its daily existence for over twenty years.

There were 100 acres of land; some of it was used to grow crops for animal feed, but most was pasture for 200 ewes to graze. Winter into springtime was busy with lambing, and William barely slept for the best part of a month every year during that time. Owen Odd Job lived in a caravan on the edge of the furthest field and helped out when he was needed, especially as the ewes tended to set their birthing alarm to two in the morning. Owen never said much, except to his Border collie, who responded to a myriad of commands issued in whistles and shouts.

William had done the rest, acting as part vet, part crop expert, part nutritionist, part accountant, part salesman. He'd even tried for years to do the shearing himself to avoid paying contractors, but when his back had given in, he'd finally agreed to get two strapping young lads in to rid the sheep of their woolly coats. The ongoing, ever-changing edicts from the Welsh government were the biggest problem to contend with – it was a migraine, rather than a headache.

The politicians had no idea of the reality of farming and how hard it was to get the fields in good shape to be decent pasture and keep them that way. They'd be captivated by some hare-brained scheme that would change the following year when they listened to the feedback from a different focus group. When William got around to looking at the paper-work, which he hated, he'd tell Gwen that he wished he could hand it all over to the bloody politicians for a single day to make them understand how hard it was for farmers trying to produce high-quality food for the nation. No doubt all they'd see would be playful lambs skipping about, and they'd think it was a glorified petting zoo.

Gwen knew the reality would be five to six months of hard work keeping the lambs and the ewes healthy, checking feet, eyes and noses, hoping beyond hope that they didn't pick up some awful disease before the inevitable trip to the abattoir. 'Sheep have two missions in life,' William used to say: 'one is to escape and the other is to kill themselves, and they'll try their best to do both at the same time.'

The farmer's constant duty was to keep them alive with love and effort and then hope they would make enough money from their meat to do it all again, reinvesting what meagre profits they got these days back into the farm.

As the first man in a pale-blue shirt started to read the details of the will that day, Gwen realized that she had let her imagination run wild. The responsibility for running Tir Glas would not be hers, after all. Some bloke called Alex Roberts had been left the farm, under condition that he didn't sell it for five years. William had clearly wanted to ensure that it didn't get passed on like a rugby ball to a stranger by putting it up for sale or, even worse, to a rival neighbour.

He had never liked that underfed, useless racehorse trainer Dickon Jones and wouldn't have wanted him getting his hands anywhere near the land, just for his precious thoroughbreds to gallop all over it. William had fallen out with Dickon's father in a massive row about oilseed rape. The government had offered a tidy grant on it, so William planted out a few of the big fields near the boundary. As soon as the bright yellow flowers started to appear, old man Jones had come round, shouting his head off about the horses not being able to breathe and how William was deliberately sabotaging his season. He demanded the oilseed rape be dug up immediately. William refused. The trainer didn't have a single winner for over a year, and they never spoke again.

'Where there's a will . . .' Blue Shirt 1 had explained, 'there's an inheritance.'

William's most prized possessions: his shotguns, his watch and his dog, Jiffy, were all bequeathed to Gwen. He had also given her ten thousand pounds' worth of premium bonds.

'Turn up for the books, that is.' She rolled her eyes to Blue Shirt 2. 'I never had William down as a gambling man, see.'

'Well, it's not technically gambling,' Blue Shirt 2 explained. 'You can't lose your lump sum, so it's not a bet. It's more of a random thing. Sometimes you'll get a pay-out, and it could be small or big, and sometimes you won't get one at all.'

'And how do you know if you've won?' Gwen asked.

'They'll email you,' Blue Shirt 1 told her. 'We can update the details so that they know you're now the owner of the bonds. There's an app that has a prize checker so you can look at that every month but, either way, the money will be sent to your account automatically.'

Gwen didn't understand apps and, although she had an email address, she hardly ever looked at it. She didn't want to look foolish in front of these clever chaps in their moleskin trousers, so she nodded and said, 'That's very kind of him. Thank you.'

Now, Gwen made herself a pot of tea in the kitchen, still wondering about this mysterious Alex Roberts. Who was he, and how was he related to William? She'd never seen pictures of him or heard the name mentioned. William wasn't one for sending Christmas cards or letters, but it was odd that he'd never got any from this Alex if they were close enough for William to leave the farm to him.

45

Maybe this would be her last Christmas here at Tir Glas. Best to enjoy it while it lasted, she supposed.

She had made a promise to herself and to Owen Odd Job that she would never leave the farm to rack and ruin, so she'd stay there and make the best of it until this Alex Roberts turned up. Then she'd see what was what.

CHAPTER SEVEN

Isobel examined herself in the mirror of the downstairs loo, fixating on the skin that had started to droop around her jawbone and neck. As for the wrinkles – well, whoever said they were a road map of your life had been sugar-coating aniseed. She did not care for the 'lived-in' face she saw staring back at her.

The bags under her eyes were now permanently grey, thanks to sleep that was regularly interrupted by David's snoring. Although concerned about his well-being, she was relieved that she would be spared that for a few nights. Instead, the man in the next-door bed on Ward F would have to deal with David's nocturnal noises.

A wedding photo hung on the wall, to be admired by visitors as they washed their hands. Isobel had never allowed herself to think she was beautiful, but she had certain attributes: piercing blue eyes that had now faded with age, a strong jawline and fine cheekbones. What she didn't have was swagger. If she walked into a room, no one noticed.

David, on the other hand, always attracted attention. He was more conventionally handsome, with a face that was perfectly in proportion. Everyone said how well he had aged, with his bright eyes and perfect teeth. A smattering of grey hair ran through the thick dark-brown mop, adding gravitas to his appearance.

It might be that the passing years had all caught up with David now. Who knew what he'd be like when he recovered from this inconvenience? Perhaps she should say 'if' rather than 'when' because, seeing him hooked up to all those awful machines, his future seemed less certain. It had given Isobel quite the scare.

Realizing that the Palmers would be arriving in an hour, Isobel laid the table and put out wine glasses. She had bought a couple of nice bottles of Pinot Grigio on offer at Waitrose. Only two, mind you. And one should really be plenty for four of them, because one of the Palmers would be driving – probably Daphne, as Michael always liked a drink. She remembered Muriel having a bit of acid reflux at one of their book club meetings and wasn't sure she cared for wine. Maybe it had been one of those ghastly tart Sauvignon Blancs from New Zealand that everyone seemed to have switched to when they decided Chardonnay was too oaky.

Isobel was glad Muriel had accepted the last-minute invitation – she was a bit like a submissive golden retriever, biddable and reliable: the ones that roll over as soon as approached and ask for a tummy rub. She had to stop herself from saying 'good girl' on the telephone when Muriel said she was free and would love to come.

It would have been a shame to have let down the Palmers when they had had the date in their diary for six weeks. Whatever had happened this morning, it was important that the Christmas spirit should win through.

Isobel had thought about going back to the hospital during evening visiting hours but was relieved when Alex offered to check David was settled onto the ward before meeting her friends at the local pub.

Isobel would host this dinner party, would try to enjoy herself and would look forward to seeing her sons tomorrow. They could come with her to visit David then. Hopefully it would all be fine by the time the New Year came around, just as the nurse had promised – a minor blip he would get over.

'Why can't you tidy up after yourself?' Isobel muttered as she cleared things from the kitchen island that Alex had left scattered around, including the letter from Davies and Davies.

Isobel finished laying the table, planning to take Alex's things up to her room later.

By the time Alex returned at 10.30 p.m., hoping the Palmers would be putting on coats to leave, the dinner party was still in full swing. Michael was regaling the three women with stories of his life as a diamond expert, when he used to be flown first class to Nigeria or South Africa to value the huge chunks of mineral they had dug up. Daphne laughed along with the others, despite knowing that some of these friendly encounters with various flight attendants must have happened after they had been married.

'Well hello, stranger!' Michael stood up as Alex came into the room, smoothing his lacquered hair. He moved around the table, putting both hands on her shoulders, kissing her on each cheek before holding her at arm's length. Alex tried to wriggle free.

'I remember when you were just a little girl, this high, and you were so cheeky.' He chuckled as Alex shook him off. 'You used to sit on my lap and pretend I was a horse you were riding. You loved that game.' His eyes scanned her from top to bottom, staying a little too long in the chest area. 'We can always play it again, if you like!' he suggested with a smirk.

Alex was about to tell him to fuck right off when her mother intervened.

'Oh, Michael! You are such a card. Now tell me, darling, how was Dad?'

'You were so right to go and see him this evening. It's vital you keep on top of his care. The NHS is broken, you know. It's lucky you're home and your mother could rely on you. Otherwise, who knows what would have happened,' Daphne butted in.

Alex forced herself to bite her tongue. She would have loved to correct them for slagging off the state of the country without recognizing the consequences of years of under-investment in public services, but her brain didn't have the energy for the fight. Not tonight.

Isobel started to usher her daughter towards the door, clearly eager for her to leave before she went on one of her left-wing rants.

'It's been a long day for you, and I know you'll want to be at your best for tomorrow when the boys get home.' She smiled. 'Thanks so much for seeing to Dad this evening. I'll go again first thing in the morning. Well, as soon as visiting hours allow.'

Alex mentally rolled her eyes, poured herself the last of the wine and took the glass with her.

'Lovely to see you all,' Alex nodded, hoping they wouldn't detect the sarcasm in her voice.

She could hear Michael Palmer asking if there was any more wine as she closed the door of the bedroom she had called her own since childhood.

You'll be lucky, mate, she thought.

That man really was insufferable.

She placed her wine glass on the bedside table and stretched out on her bed. It was a place that was so familiar and yet seemed so distant from the person she was now.

One wall was covered in photos of ponies and rosettes, the other with a montage of photos from her teenage years, when she'd left the ponies behind and discovered parties. Looking at it was like being in the midst of a rave, surrounded by her closest friends from that time, when they were all fit and beautiful, often pissed, and laughing with the freedom of youth. No family or jobs to worry about, no mortgages to pay and no accountability, unlike the group of local friends she'd just caught up with in the pub this evening after swinging by the hospital.

They had big grown-up lives, with kids at school and careers they cared about. They discussed promotions and pension plans, affordable holidays and after-school clubs, while she countered with the latest celebrity gossip. She thought she was being entertaining with her liberal name-dropping and her talk of fancy trips and Michelin-starred restaurants, but she felt rather feeble in comparison.

'I'm surprised you're still in that job,' her childhood neighbour Frankie had said. 'I had you down as a serious writer.'

'She doesn't mean it like that,' Frankie's husband had stepped in, although Alex knew that she absolutely did mean it like that. 'She's had a few too many. We really ought to be getting back. The sitter will start to charge us overtime in a minute.'

'Lucky you, not to have anything serious to worry about,' Frankie slurred as she and her husband departed.

He had laughed to cover the awkwardness, but the drunken rebuke stung. Alex felt frivolous and shallow with her trivial concerns compared to theirs. The criticism hurt even more because she knew it was true. She wanted more out of life, but she had no idea where or how to find the magic ingredient that would make her feel worthwhile.

Alex opened her WhatsApp and saw that Ethan was online so called him, in need of a friendly face.

'Babe, you wouldn't believe the evening I've had!' he gasped as soon as he picked up, his face lighting up the screen.

'Oh me too, Eeth, me too.' She was so relieved to hear his voice and see him that she nearly started crying.

'You first, babe. I'm all ears.' He settled his phone on his knees so that she could only see the top of his head and the ceiling of his sitting room.

'I'm not sure that's your best angle,' she teased him.

She filled him in on her father's seizure, the dreadful dinner party guests, and Frankie's veiled criticism – all of which had happened in the whirlwind twenty-four hours since she'd seen him.

'Oh, and my mother keeps telling me how tired I look,' she added. 'As if that's helpful. At all.'

'Your mother just has a funny way of showing her love,' Ethan assured her.

'Too right. So come on, what's been going on in your world?'

Ethan had been organizing the last of the Christmas parties for people with too much money and not enough time.

'You should have seen the tree!' he shrieked. 'In fact, all three of them. They had to have a crane to get the one up on the balcony above the front door. It was insane.'

Downstairs, they still had the same fake tree they'd had for the last thirty years, so Alex could only imagine how her mother would react to such decadence. To cover the increasing crookedness of the branches, her mother had drowned it in multi-coloured tinsel and an assortment of random baubles. It looked as if a child who'd eaten Neapolitan ice cream and three packets of Liquorice Allsorts had vomited all over it.

'And then . . .' Ethan paused dramatically, carrying on with his story. 'The most handsome man I've *ever* seen walks in. Like Harry Styles but taller and without the frilly collars. Drop-dead gorgeous, and I swear he was giving me the eye.'

'So what happened?' Alex asked. Ethan's life was full of chance encounters with good-looking men. He usually got off with them too.

'Turned out he had a *wife*. I mean, honestly. She was gorgeous too, so there was no hope for me. I've been crying into my champagne ever since.'

He wiped away an imaginary tear, but Alex knew he'd be fine. He was always falling in love, getting his heart broken and bouncing back for more. She, on the other hand, protected her heart as if it were the crown jewels. No one was stealing it without an alarm system going off.

'Oh, I wouldn't give up. Dad was telling me only this morning that all the gay men his age are married to women. How he knows that I have no idea, but he was very sure of it.'

'Good old David,' Ethan replied. 'Is that what gave him a stroke?'

Alex took a sip of her mother's bargain-basement Pinot Grigio. It didn't taste as bad as she'd expected.

'He didn't look right all morning, and Mum is always going on at him to lower his blood pressure, but she probably makes it higher.'

'He'll be fine; your dad is strong enough to have put up with your mother for all these years,' Ethan reminded her, which buoyed Alex up. 'Anyway, tell me more about this strange letter.'

Alex saw that her mother had left it on her bedside table and waved it up to the phone.

'It's not a prank. That's a proper letter, and it's a proper farm. I looked it up. It'll be a sheep farm. Most of them are. And it'll be very green, lots of grass, but also with a blue tinge.' Ethan raised an eyebrow.

'What do you mean?'

'Tir Glas means greeny-blue or blue. It means blue land in Welsh.'

'Thank you.' Alex smiled, grateful that he'd somehow found time in his busy day to do some snooping on her behalf.

'For what, babe?'

'For cheering me up and for giving me such a lovely view of your forehead.'

He adjusted his phone so that she could see his whole face. He had recently restyled his hair to grow the top a little longer and to allow his natural strawberry-blond colour to emerge. A light smattering of ginger stubble covered his jaw. His blue eyes twinkled as he raised his champagne glass to her.

'Impressively wrinkle-free, I think you'll agree.' He grinned. 'Now, you'd better pay me back by taking me with you down to Wales. I'm not missing out on the chance to meet a fit rugby player or three.'

'It's a deal.' Alex raised her glass in return, drained it and blew him a kiss goodbye, thankful that – despite all the chaos – she had a brilliant best friend always by her side.

CHAPTER EIGHT

Monmouthshire

'Have it your way then.' Gwen left Jiffy on the chair, curled up in Will's jumper. He had lifted his head and looked at her with disdain and then stuck his head back in the jumper. She noticed his curly hair was starting to matt. It needed a good brush, but she didn't dare try, in case he growled at her again. She headed to the Black Prince pub for the traditional pre-Christmas gathering.

For most people, it meant the beginning of a short holiday, but for all the farmers, holidays didn't exist, so Christmas Eve was an excuse to feed the animals early and give themselves permission to enjoy an evening off. The vet would be there, along with the local farrier, the feed merchant and the mechanic, so if anything went wrong at home, there wouldn't be anyone to come and help because they'd all be at the pub.

Owen Odd Job was the only one who never came. He preferred to stay in his caravan with his Border collie. Being out with people would have required changing clothes or having a wash, and he didn't want to do that; after all, he'd never been one for company.

Gwen, however, liked being with people, and she particularly enjoyed the Black Prince. Rhys was behind the bar, pulling pints and smiling at all-comers. His shoulder-length mane of brown hair was pushed back behind his ears, a soft brown beard framed his mouth and jawline, and eyes as black as a pint of Guinness, so dark and deep you could barely identify where the pupil started and finished, missed nothing. A short-sleeved woollen polo shirt revealed his biceps and that tattoo of a tiger on one arm. It was an exact replica of one his grandfather had worn during the Second World War when he was part of the Second Battalion Welsh Regiment deployed to Burma. Rhys's grandfather had survived when many of his colleagues had perished in the bloody jungle combat with the Japanese.

Rhys used to tell the tale of when his grandfather came face to face with a tiger and how it was the most scared he'd ever been in his life as he stared into its eyes. Luckily, it had only just finished eating and it slowly padded past him.

'Never,' they used to say in mesmerized disbelief, when he'd brush by people to show how close the tiger had been.

'On my life,' he'd swear.

Not surprisingly, Rhys's grandfather had been known ever after by the nickname of Tiger.

At six foot five, Rhys could reach the bottles at the top of the shelves easily, but he had to stoop slightly to nod at Gwen as she came in, quickly shutting out the wind and the cold. He started to mix a vodka, lime and soda before she even got to the bar to order.

'Thanks, Rhys.' Gwen smiled. 'You know me too well.'

'How goes it?' he asked, his deep-brown eyes fixed on her, aware that they hadn't caught up since the funeral. 'You doing all right out there?'

She nodded, taking a sip of the drink.

'And Jiffy?'

'Not so good.' She shook her head. 'He's barely eating, and he won't leave the chair.'

'I'll come by later, if you like, and take a look at him,' Rhys offered, reaching across and patting Gwen's hand before turning to serve the farrier and his son. Rhys was big and strong, but underneath it all, he was as soft as a Labrador puppy.

'It's hard, y'know. The house is cold as hell, and Jiffy, well, I'm dead worried about him.' Gwen sighed as Rhys turned back to her, wiping the bar with a cloth.

Rhys nodded sympathetically. The bar gave him protection, but it was also like a stage. He could start any conversation, ask any question, and people would talk to him. He could also move away if he felt anyone was getting too close. He had plenty of acquaintances and a few good friends, but he was a private man, and there were secrets he kept, even from them.

'He's grieving,' he said softly. 'You both are.'

'I was just the housekeeper.' Gwen looked down at her glass. 'I have no right to any grief. Or to anything that was his.'

'I'll not be having that.' Rhys waved his hand. 'You have more right to grieve than anyone. He didn't have time for many people, did William Griffiths, but he always had time for you. Now come on, Gwen, let's get a bit of Christmas spirit inside you.'

He started to pour her a small glass of mulled wine to warm her up.

'It's on the house. If you need some advice on Jiffy, Tony's coming later when he finishes his last call.'

Tony was the local vet, although he covered a vast area of

Monmouthshire and sometimes strayed over the border into Herefordshire. He was meant to be a sheep and cow man, horses too, but he often 'had a quick look' at a dog when asked. He knew the farmers didn't have time to take their dogs into the practice if something was amiss, so was always happy to help – after all, that's what people did around here.

Gwen took a sip and felt her shoulders drop. She was barely sixty but had been ageing by the minute as she grieved. She hadn't been eating properly since William died, and she had lost at least a stone from a body that had never had much to spare. She wore her dark hair scraped back into a ponytail, with some strands of pure white that had multiplied in the last few weeks. She had a small button nose and a mouth that looked large by comparison and, when she smiled, revealed a perfect row of small white teeth. Rhys was kind to help her, and she could chat to Tony about Jiffy. It was better to be here with everyone rather than stuck on her own in the middle of nowhere with only Owen Odd Job close by. Slowly, she relaxed and started to enjoy herself. She knew everyone in the pub and, when the singing started, she was right in the midst of it.

'Voice of an angel,' Rhys commented to those sitting at the bar. They all agreed, whooping and hollering their approval at her performance.

Tony advised trying fresh chicken to tempt Jiffy to eat a bit more.

'Any friends he would enjoy seeing? Might help him get out and take more exercise,' Tony suggested.

'Not any I can think of,' Gwen mused.

'Like his master, eh? Not one for making friends.'

Everyone was a bit loose-lipped tonight and, even though it was a bit harsh, she knew Tony meant no harm by it. A lot of people didn't know the same William she did.

Gwen hadn't planned to stay long, but suddenly it was closing time and she found herself helping Rhys clear up. He was ten years younger than her but took the role of paternal guidance.

'You'd best not be driving back,' he told her, as she passed him glasses to stack in the dishwasher.

She tried to argue the case, but he wasn't having it. He backed up his big old noisy Land Rover, and she hopped in beside him. The seats had no cushion left, and the floor was covered in mud, crisp packets and empty cans of Diet Coke.

'Are you banking on one cancelling out the other, Rhys?' She laughed.

'It's my one sin,' he admitted. 'I'm a barman who doesn't drink; I own a pub with a covered smoking patio, and I don't smoke; I have the racing on all the time, and I only bet once in a blue moon.'

'Any other sins you *do* partake in?' Gwen asked coquettishly, as the Land Rover bumped along the drive to Tir Glas Farm. She put her hand on his left thigh and gave it a squeeze.

Rhys kept his eyes on the road. It was late, and Gwen was clearly drunk, plus she was still in mourning, needing a shoulder to cry on. What could he say that was true and kind, or at least not untrue and not unkind? The fragments of a Philip Larkin poem came back to him. He was not a well-read man, but what he had read he remembered, and he'd always liked Larkin.

'I love you, Gwen, but not like that,' Rhys said with a tenderness that softened the sting of rejection. 'Let's get you back safe and sound, and I'll say hello to Jiffy.'

Rhys had been worried ever since the funeral. He'd known dogs so loyal to their owner that they'd chase after their car, wait for them all night if they went out, and stick by their side like a limpet, but he'd never seen a dog try and jump into a grave before. Welsh terriers were renowned for their faithfulness to one person. That dog knew his master was in the coffin, and he wanted to go with him, not wanting to be left behind.

No wonder the Neolithic farmers had tombs for the whole family, including the dogs. He'd heard of the tombs being excavated and dog bones being found in the side chambers. It made perfect sense.

'"Talking in Bed",' he muttered to himself. 'That's the poem.'

He remembered a line about lying together in bed being far from isolation, and he thought about the last time he'd had someone in his bed he'd wanted to talk to. He might have wanted other things, but talking was the most intimate act of all. He felt a little sad that he'd not found that – not for a long while anyway.

'I'm so sorry,' Gwen mumbled as Rhys helped her to the farmhouse door. 'Totally misread the situation, and you're much too young for me. Please can we forget it ever happened?'

'I have no idea what you're even talking about,' Rhys pretended, as he ushered her into the hallway, which was as freezing as the temperature outside. The fire was nearly burnt out in the kitchen, so Rhys piled some logs on the embers and blew until the flames caught. Jiffy looked at him suspiciously.

'C'mon, lad,' Rhys said firmly. 'Let's get you outside. You can't sit here all day, every day, moping. He's not coming back. I'm sorry to be so blunt, but that's the way it is.'

Jiffy cocked his head on one side and looked at Rhys. He let out a huge sigh for a relatively small dog and hopped off the chair, obediently following Rhys out through the front door. Once he'd sniffed around for a bit and done what he needed to do, he came back inside. Gwen had taken some of the chicken leftovers from the pub and put the meat on top of Jiffy's biscuits. His nose twitched and then, tentatively at first, he started eating.

'That's more like it.' Rhys smiled. 'Now then, if you're all right, I'll be leaving you both. Best get back before I catch Father Christmas trying to steal all my sherry. He's a bugger for that. Happy Christmas.' He kissed Gwen lightly on the cheek and gave her a warm hug.

'Thank you,' she said. 'For everything.'

'Nothing to thank me for.' Rhys shrugged.

Gwen settled on the sofa and, after Jiffy finished his dinner, he suddenly appeared at her side. She reached out an arm for him and held him tight, his softly curled hair a comfort like no other. She ruffled his ears, and he leant in closer to her side.

'What a pair we are, eh, Jiff? You're mopey and moody, and I tried it on with a friend. Bloody 'ell, what a fool I am. Thank god he's a gentleman, eh? Otherwise, what a mess we could have made of life.'

Jiffy let out a sympathetic sigh and settled in across her lap. They stared at the fire until tiredness overwhelmed them both.

CHAPTER NINE

It was nine o'clock in the morning, and Isobel hadn't heard a creak on the floor above. What on earth was her daughter doing sleeping so late? That was the sort of thing teenagers did. Not thirty-nine-year-old women on Christmas Eve. She wouldn't be able to do this if she had children of her own. Or a dog. Or anything in the world that might actually depend on her being a responsible adult. Isobel caught herself grinding her teeth in frustration.

Her phone pinged, and she saw she had a text from Kit, her eldest. She'd spoken to both of her sons very briefly yesterday, but she hadn't got around to ringing them back.

How's Dad doing? Alex has kept me in the loop. I'll visit him before the party. Kids are playing up but really looking forward to seeing you. Anything I can bring? Anything particular you want for Christmas?

Good. No. Not a candle, she typed, thinking of the expensive Jo Malone candle Muriel had brought her last night. It was too nice to even regift, as Muriel would notice if she didn't have it on display.

Message delivered, she rang the hospital, which she'd so far been putting off.

The update on David was vague. He was stable, but he'd

need to stay in for a few days at least, so she'd definitely have to go and see him today. She hated hospitals. It was the smell more than anything. And the sound – the way it echoed off all the hard surfaces. Horrible places.

She heard footsteps, which meant her daughter had finally surfaced.

'Morning.' Alex's voice was barely a croak. She had overdone it last night with her mates, and the glass of wine she'd had when she came back home had tipped her over the edge. She was craving a glass of water, and her head hurt.

'Got any paracetamol?' she rasped.

'Cupboard.' Isobel pointed above the kettle, annoyed that her daughter didn't seem to know her way around the kitchen of a house she'd lived in most of her life.

'That explains your rudeness last night to Michael. There was no need for that sort of behaviour,' Isobel chided, her rage simmering just under the surface.

Coco hopped up from her bed and wagged her tail. Alex made a fuss of her.

'You love me, don't you, Coco, and you know I'm right. That man is complete tosser, isn't he? Yes he is.' She crouched down to Coco's height and was given the full face-wash.

Alex and her mother often had a conversation through the dog rather than directly with each other. It was easier that way, for both of them.

'How's your daddy?' she said to the dog. 'Shall we go and see him today and find out? Yes, we will.'

'No dogs allowed at the hospital,' Isobel said tersely. 'You know that. I've just called, and they say he's stable. I was going to go in this morning, but if you want to pop in then do, and I'll go this afternoon instead. Kit says he'll meet me there. I've got wrapping to do.'

Alex took two pills with a glass of water and put the kettle on for a cup of tea. That would see her right.

'Don't forget we're going to Aunt Di's tonight,' her mother reminded her. 'All of us. Wear something suitable.' She waved a hand at Alex's pyjama bottoms and T-shirt in mute disgust. 'The boys will be there.'

'Oh well, then I must make an effort if my perfect brothers are putting in an appearance.' Alex's voice dripped with sarcasm. 'God forbid I show them up or do anything to let the side down. Aunt Di's got a new man, by the way. She told me all about it yesterday. He's an actor.'

Isobel kept quiet. Of course her sister-in-law had a new boyfriend. She changed them with the seasons. Isobel used to be fascinated, but these days, she had little interest in the constant rotation of Diana's leading men.

'I talked to Ethan last night,' Alex said as she took her teabag out and, once again, left it on the sideboard.

Isobel picked it up and flung it in the food recycling bin. 'Teabags go here,' she muttered under her breath.

Alex moved to the breakfast table, unaware of her mother's frustration. 'He said Tir Glas means blue land in Welsh. Did you know that?'

Isobel moved things unnecessarily on the kitchen island to calm down.

'I mean, the land isn't really bright blue like a Smurf, is it? Maybe it just has a blue tinge on a misty morning. Ethan

67

reckons it's a sheep farm. He says he'll come with me when I go down there.' Alex blew on her tea and took a careful sip. 'Mum, are you listening?'

Isobel looked up with a jolt. Yes, she had been listening.

'That's nice,' was all she offered.

Alex was confused by her mother's lack of interest in the mystery bequest, but she assumed she was just distracted by her dad's condition and their Christmas plans being disrupted.

Alex began checking her emails as she drank her tea, although she didn't imagine there would be anything important on Christmas Eve.

'Oh bollocks.'

'Language, Alexandra.' Her mother issued the rebuke on reflex.

'Oh, Mum, come on. There's no one here, and you've heard worse. Coco certainly doesn't mind, do you, little one?'

Coco looked up at her and squeaked a reply.

'See?'

Alex scrolled through the email from her editor, asking for a rewrite on the piece she'd submitted before she left London. *Honestly, doesn't she know that the holiday has officially begun?*

'Dammit, I've got to do some work before I go and see Dad. Sophie is on my case, and I've got to file this article before midday.' Alex rose from her chair and headed for the stairs. 'I'll do it as quickly as I can and then go to the hospital.'

Alex was annoyed. She had thought the article was fine as it was. It was funny, gently poking fun at a television presenter who had posted photos of himself in fancy dress. Sophie, the editor of *Rizz* magazine, wanted it to be punchier, more critical and acerbic. She wanted it to mention the perilous state of his marriage and the affair he was rumoured to have had with a co-host. It wasn't Alex's style to be malicious, but if that's what her editor wanted, then that's what she would give. She felt increasingly that she'd had to make these kind of compromises recently, because it wasn't worth pushing back.

She sat at her old dressing table with her laptop squeezed between a hairbrush and an eyeshadow kit.

'Is this what I've become?' she asked her reflection as she bashed away on the keyboard.

She completed the task as quickly as she could and fired it off to Sophie before making herself presentable for her hospital visit.

Driving towards the North Hampshire hospital, she wondered again about the letter and the identity of William Griffiths. She wanted desperately to discuss him and his farm with her father, and maybe even her brothers when they arrived.

She knew her way around the hospital fairly well. She'd been in a few times with cracked or broken bones as a child, and it hadn't changed much in the intervening years.

Her father was sitting up in bed with various tubes coming out of him. A monitor alongside the bed was beeping away. His face was a little lopsided, and his hair was a mess. He looked at Alex as she approached him, and she was sure there was a flicker of recognition in his eyes, but when he tried to speak, it came out as a grunt.

Alex tried not to look shocked. She had expected him to

be much better than this, and even the nurse had said he'd be home in a few days, so she thought it was just a minor stroke. She pulled up a chair next to him and took his good hand, stroking it gently, not knowing what to say. She had brought in a hairbrush along with a few other essentials and, as she softly brushed his hair, she found her voice and decided to tell him about the previous night's dinner party.

'You did well to avoid that one, Dad. Honestly, that Michael Palmer is the biggest prick I've ever met!' Definitely a flicker of a smile on her father's lips. 'And poor Daphne just sits there and has to listen to it all. Mind you, she's right of Attila the Hun so it's best if she doesn't share her political opinions. It makes me sick that he retired on a big fat pension when he should have been in jail for sexual harassment. Those poor interns – and as for his PA, she deserved the biggest pay-off of the lot. I bet she didn't get one. It's so unfair.'

She looked at her father to check he was following and, reassured, she carried on, hoping this was entertaining him.

'Muriel filled in for you, and she's very sweet, if a bit – you know – wet. She was trying to persuade Mum to do Pilates with her, but you can imagine how that went down. Mum's friend Karen told her once about the yoga teacher who'd asked them to pair up and she'd ended up with her legs around the waist of a complete stranger.'

She noted the smile on one half of her father's mouth and a twinkle in his eye. The very thought of being in close physical contact with anyone, let alone someone she didn't know, would horrify her mother. Alex continued talking, hoping she was stimulating her father's brain.

'You know how yoga tends to bring out the wind in you?'
She paused, stifling her giggles. 'Well, that's what happened,
and Karen hasn't been able to go back since. Remember how
Mum stopped going to church because the vicar was asking
everyone to shake hands with the people behind them? That
was too much intimacy for her. She was thrilled when Covid
came along and no one could touch anyone else. Her idea of
heaven.'

Alex looked again at her father. There was a sharp pain in
her chest, or maybe it was her heart. She carried on talking;
it was the only way to distract herself from the reality of the
shell of a man who lay in front of her. She would be glad
when Kit and Hugh were here to come and visit as well,
rather than it falling just on her.

'She thinks yoga and Pilates are the same thing, even though
I've tried to explain they're not, but it's a million-to-one shot
that she'll ever go.'

Alex shuddered at the thought of her mother in her gym
gear in a room full of the local women of a certain age and
yummy mummies. Her father made a noise that sounded like
a laugh but turned into a cough. She stroked his hand and
waited for him to catch his breath, hoping she hadn't agitated
him or made things worse.

After half an hour, Alex had exhausted her supply of one-
way chat. In any case, she was concerned she might tire him
out. She kissed her father gently on the forehead as he tried
to say something to her. It sounded like 'far', and she guessed
he was trying to say thank you but couldn't get his tongue
around the 'th' sound.

'It's OK, Dad, you'll be fine. Give it time. Mum is coming in this afternoon with Kit. They'll talk to the nurse and make sure you're on the mend. It's all going to be all right, I promise.'

She reluctantly got up to leave. He looked so sad lying there on his own, unaware of what was happening, unable to converse. She had always relied on her father, and she wanted his advice, his guidance about the letter from the solicitors, but for now, it was her turn to care for him. His counsel would have to wait.

CHAPTER TEN

When Alex got home and checked her emails, she found a one-word response from Sophie, her editor at *Rizz*: *Better.*

She quickly scanned the *Rizz* website and saw that the article was already live, with pictures of the television presenter and his co-host laughing together on the sofa, alongside one of his wife looking forlorn and him dressed as a vampire in full make-up, with fangs and fake blood running down his chin. The headline above the pictures ran:

BEWARE: COUNT DRACULA BITES

It was classic click-bait. The pictures suggested a story, and her words were vicious enough to ensure that the readers reacted. Looking at the comments below, she could see that it was working. Once, she might have felt satisfaction that a story she had written was catching people's interest, but this piece was so far from what she had intended when she had started it that she hardly recognized it – or herself. Frankie's words from last night came into her mind – that she was surprised Alex wasn't doing something more meaningful with her life as her forties loomed.

She went to the bathroom and scrubbed at her face, trying to wash away the sensation of feeling dirty. She applied a bit of make-up before changing into an outfit she hoped would not cause her mother to look at her with disdain.

'Come on, we're going to be late!' her mother shouted up

the stairs as Alex grabbed a jacket and hurried down. Her brothers were on their way from different directions, and her mother was clearly keen to see them. Isobel had caught up briefly with Kit at the hospital when they'd both visited David in the afternoon, but they hadn't had a chance to chat properly.

Isobel drove carefully on the winding country roads, keeping both hands on the steering wheel in the advised ten-to-two position.

'Do you want me to drive?' Alex offered after her mother pulled into a layby to let a car pass after seeing its lights approaching from a distance.

'No,' her mother replied. 'Why would I?'

'I know you don't like driving in the dark, that's all.'

'I'm absolutely fine. Just being careful. Most accidents happen on country roads – I read that in an article. I don't need any more of us in hospital this Christmas,' she tutted.

Alex stared ahead, eyes alert for wayward rabbits crossing the road, and tried to ignore the image that kept appearing in her head of her father lying helpless in his hospital bed. It had been a shock to see him so incapacitated this morning, and it felt wrong to be carrying on as if nothing had happened, on their way to the party.

Diana opened the heavy oak front door as they approached, a vision in cream silk. The dress coat hung down to her ankles, and the silk turban around her head kept her hair hidden.

'Darlings, how utterly wonderful of you to come! How was David this afternoon?'

'He's doing well. The nurse says he's stable.' Isobel leant forward to kiss her sister-in-law. 'Are we early?'

'What? No, you're bang on time.'

Alex elbowed her mother to stop her saying what she knew would come next.

'Loving the kimono look, Aunt Di,' she interjected. 'It's all the rage in London. Complete with the turban – that's so elegant.'

'Well, you both look . . . simply divine.' Diana looked them both up and down, noting Alex's bomber jacket over a wide-legged trouser suit, and the calf-length skirt with cardigan that Isobel had chosen. Neither were showstoppers, but they'd do and, after all, it meant their outfits wouldn't upstage her own.

Diana floated through the vast hall, past a Christmas tree decorated simply with white lights and minimal white baubles, her vape leaving a trail behind her.

'I thought we'd caught her just out of the shower,' whispered Isobel to her daughter.

'I know you did.' Alex suppressed a laugh. 'It's high fashion. Costs a fortune.'

Isobel tutted. 'Looks like she's wearing a dressing gown and a towel round her head.'

The curtains were open in the drawing room to show off its floor-to-ceiling bay windows overlooking the garden. Outside, the trees were festooned with strings of Christmas lights, and lanterns had been placed along the edge of the path that led to a Christmas grotto.

'I've hired a magician as well. She's setting up in the grotto,' Aunt Di explained, pointing out of the window. 'To keep the children amused.'

'To keep them out of here, more like,' Isobel muttered. She resigned herself to not being able to play indulgent grand-mother, unless she decided to brave the chill of the garden.

'Luigi has sweetly agreed to play for us this evening. He'll take requests, the darling boy.' Diana exhaled a cloud of her favourite bubblegum-flavoured vapour as she nodded towards a man in a dinner jacket and bow tie, who was sitting at the baby grand piano in the corner, playing Christmas carols.

'Dad will be so sorry to be missing this,' Alex lied to her aunt as she sipped her champagne, the bubbles dissipating on her tongue. She felt fully recovered from this morning's hangover.

'Ah, muffin, there you are!' Diana hailed the entrance of her latest beau, who had appeared in the doorway, clearly dressed to impress. His hair was slicked back and his face glowing with a faint sheen, as if he had rubbed it with baby oil or maybe furniture polish. The trousers were perfectly tailored and met the edge of a pair of blue suede shoes that toned with a midnight-blue velvet smoking jacket. A triangle of pale-blue handkerchief poked out of the breast pocket, identical in colour and pattern to the silk cravat that fell softly into an open-necked shirt. He was undoubtedly attractive, and at least ten – maybe even a good twenty – years younger than Aunt Di.

He strode into the room with the air of a man who was used to being looked at. He gave a cursory glance to Isobel and Alex before moving towards Aunt Di, holding her face in both hands and kissing her full on the lips.

'Bit much,' Isobel chuntered, a little too loudly.

'Rude not to.' He pointed at the mistletoe hanging from the chandelier above, before smoothing hair that didn't need to be smoothed.

'Darlings, this is Orlando.' Aunt Di flushed with excitement. 'The love of my life.'

Alex and her mother both raised their eyebrows, sharing a look with each other. Orlando took Isobel's hand in both of his, kissing the top of it while staring into her eyes. Alex avoided the same fate by grabbing his hand and shaking it firmly.

'I wish my gorgeous brother was here to meet you,' Di gushed. 'He'd have adored you, and you'd have so much in common.'

'Doubt that,' Alex whispered to her mother.

'What?' she hissed back.

Alex wondered if her mother was going a bit deaf. She pulled her face into a full gargoyle grimace to show how much her father would dislike Orlando. That made Isobel smile, bonding them with mutual disapproval. Alex often felt she and her mother were polar opposites, so it was nice to be on the same side for once.

With Diana preoccupied in the hall, greeting her brothers and their over-excited children, Alex took the opportunity to find out a bit more about Diana's new beau.

'So, Orlando, what do you do?'

Soft opening serve. All three of them knew that what she was actually asking was: *Do you earn your own money, or are you intending to fleece Diana?*

'I'm an actor.' Orlando shifted his stance so that the light fell in a more flattering manner on his face. He spoke loudly, as if on stage, which Alex knew would please her mother. She was always complaining about people who mumbled.

'Of course you are,' said Alex encouragingly. 'Haven't I seen you in something?'

'It's been a bit quiet since Covid, obviously. Everyone's in the same boat.' Orlando spoke in a deep baritone, seemingly enjoying the sound of his own voice. 'But you might have caught me in a recent episode of *Casualty*. Then I did *Vera*, and I've got a big advert in the pipeline. My agent is very excited.'

'An agent,' Isobel gasped. 'Gosh.'

'They all have one, Mum.' Alex couldn't disguise how unimpressed she was. 'Standard.'

As Orlando started to talk about the art of playing a corpse, Alex zoned out and sidled towards the pianist. She asked him if he would play 'You're So Vain' by Carly Simon, catching her mother's eye at the sound of the opening bars. They both grinned.

Orlando's monologue was finally halted by the entrance of Alex's brothers, sisters-in-law and children. Isobel visibly glowed with joy as she embraced her sons, seemingly in awe of their magical transformation from muddy, naughty little boys into fully grown adults with children of their own.

Isobel attempted to engage with her grandchildren, but they were distracted by the promise of the grotto. Diana soon swept them outside down the beautifully lit path. 'There's a very special place for you out there,' she promised.

With the arrival of Kit and Hugh, Alex saw that Orlando had already identified a new captive audience. Her brothers' responses were polite, if a little distant, while their wives,

Sukie and Fenella, seemed entranced by Aunt Di's dashing boyfriend. They were enthusiastically admiring his dapper outfit, which was a far cry from their husbands' casual dress, laughing loudly at Orlando's anecdotes and eagerly asking him about all the famous people he'd worked with.

Alex happily accepted a top-up of champagne, thinking she'd need it. Her sisters-in-law were identikit wives who both wore flower-printed dresses that looked as if they had come from the same Boden catalogue. Their favourite conversation topics were discussing best use of an Aga, whether it was worth getting an air fryer, and whether a 'feature wall' was a passing phase or something they should adopt in the sitting room. Alex liked them both and wanted to get along with them, but she didn't know anything about cooking, and her views on interior design were limited. When they got on to celebrities, she would be in her element.

'I'm going to take him to Firenze.' Aunt Di offered Alex a plate of smoked salmon blinis, complete with sour cream and a touch of caviar. Alex remembered that her aunt was always like this in the early weeks of a new romance and wondered what it would feel like to be swept off your feet.

'Do you mean Florence?' she asked.

'If you want to be prosaic, then yes, but I prefer to call places by the names they were given.' Diana waved her left hand theatrically. 'We may move on to Roma or Venezia, but it all depends on whether Orlando's agent gets him a job and he has to come back for work.'

'Oh, I think you'll be safe enough.' Alex spoke before she'd engaged her brain, and Hugh dug her in the ribs.

'I'm so sorry, Aunt Di, I didn't realize we were meant to be smart tonight,' Hugh apologized, quickly changing the subject. He was a younger version of David, his dark hair falling forward in a floppy fringe and his eyes a lively light hazel. He wore faded beige cords and a cashmere jumper, while Kit, who was taller and broader, was in a blue blazer over jeans with an open-necked check shirt.

'Not at all – there's no dress code. Just family, as always on Christmas Eve, and you know you can wear whatever you like here. If your father was here, he'd be the scruffiest of the lot, poor thing.' Diana laughed sympathetically.

'How is Dad really then?' Hugh turned to Alex.

'Mum's obviously behaving as if nothing has happened. Keep calm and carry on – the usual bollocks.' Alex swallowed the last of her smoked salmon blini. 'I was pretty shocked when I went in this morning. Dad couldn't talk, but I'm pretty sure he understood what I was saying. The doctor has been very positive, and the nurse said he should make a full recovery. We've just got to give it time.'

'Should?' Hugh was struggling to take it in.

'Well, it's never a certainty with things like this,' Alex said, with a knowledge she'd only gleaned from her recent hospital visits. All she knew was that their father still had his sense of humour – and that was vital, with their family.

Feeling out of her depth, she waved Kit over to find out from him how their father had seemed that afternoon.

'The staff seem to be giving him excellent care, and it sounds like it was a mild stroke,' Kit reassured them both.

Hugh wanted to know a whole lot of details, and Alex

80

listened carefully, knowing that Kit would have asked the right questions of the nurse. She was comforted by his confidence that their father would be home soon and that, with the right care, he would be back to himself in no time.

Alex was more worried about what would happen in the short term, when David needed her mother. There would be a lot of patient supervision required, which could prove to be a challenge for Isobel. She didn't have the best bedside manner.

As Hugh stepped away to find more champagne before checking on the kids in the grotto, Alex seized her chance to get some legal advice from Kit. She beckoned him to follow her to one of the bay windows and moved aside some perfectly wrapped presents to perch on the window seat.

'I assumed it was a joke, but I thought you'd know if it's genuine.'

'I'm a criminal barrister, Ali, not a solicitor.' Kit could be pompous when warranted, but his face softened when he saw his older sister's confusion. 'I know you think I know everything.'

He paused, and she gave him an imploring look, making it clear it wasn't time for his ego when she needed some sound advice from her younger but more grown-up brother.

He issued his judgement with due gravity and sincerity: 'It seems to me that you are now the proud owner of a farm – and you'd better get yourself to Monmouthshire as soon as you can.'

CHAPTER ELEVEN

Alex leant back towards the window as the truth hit her. What on earth was she going to do with a farm? What with her father's stroke, there was too much else going on for her to properly digest the news, but it seemed there was no doubt that the letter was real and that she was the beneficiary in a stranger's will.

'What are you talking about?' Hugh asked, reappearing with a refreshed glass.

'Ali's been left a farm,' Kit explained. 'In Monmouthshire.'

'How? Who?' Hugh laughed as he rattled off questions. 'And most of all, *why?*'

'I have no idea.' It was the only honest answer Alex could offer. 'I've never heard of William Griffiths, I've never been to Wales, and I certainly wouldn't know how to run a farm.'

'Well, here's to you and a brand-new life!' Hugh toasted his sister and smiled broadly. 'Farmer Alex, eh? You can get a whole column out of that, I bet.'

'What was that name again?' Diana swooped over; she had hearing like a bat.

'William Griffiths,' Alex reminded her.

Diana tipped her turbaned head to one side. 'It's come back to me now. He was a rugby friend of your father's,' she announced. 'That's how your parents met. William Griffiths introduced them.'

Alex looked towards her mother, still trapped at the fireplace by Orlando. It was odd that she hadn't said anything and yet so like her mother not to offer more than was necessary.

'Watch out, Aunt Di, children incoming!' Alex warned, seeing a swarm of children running back towards the house.

The children were allowed in the drawing room for precisely ten minutes, under strict instructions not to touch anything. It allowed time for them to sing a few carols, play one game of charades, and pose for a photo that would make the whole evening look like the perfect family gathering without them ruining Diana's fun.

Alex moved to the back of the room, away from the chaos of the sugared-up children, and felt a figure move alongside her. The woman who had ushered the children back into the house helped herself to the last glass of champagne and smiled with relief.

'God, I need this.' She sighed.

'Were they a handful?' Alex gestured towards the children.

The woman sipped the champagne and gave Alex a sideways smile. She had a deeper voice than Alex had expected, a rich tone that was instantly calming, and her skin was radiant. She had short, very dark hair slicked back behind her ears, and she stood confidently at her full height of five foot seven, her slender legs crossed one in front of the other as she leant back agains the wall. She wore a dinner jacket with huge pockets, over a white shirt and black jeans. Her eyes were bright blue, deep set with a smudge of kohl accentuating their brightness.

'No worse than any others. Luckily, they are young enough

to believe in magic and not try to catch me out.' She offered a hand. 'I'm Mandy, by the way.'

'Nice to meet you, Mandy. I'm Alex.'

'They just take a lot of energy to keep them entertained. That's all.' She took another sip of champagne. 'My girlfriend thinks I prefer the company of children to adults. I don't, but they pay the bills.'

The pianist started to play 'Away in a Manger', and the children opened their throats, singing with all their might.

'Brave,' Mandy offered as a review.

'Enthusiastic,' Alex countered.

'Original.' Mandy grinned.

'Fresh.' Alex laughed as they played verbal tennis, swapping the adjectives easily.

She leant towards Mandy and whispered conspiratorially, 'Truly awful.'

Mandy clinked glasses with her and leant back against the wall.

The children had got to the last verse of 'Away in a Manger'.

'Please god don't let them do another one.' Alex winced.

Mandy looked at her watch.

'Have you got far to go?' Alex asked. 'I expect you do a lot of these sorts of parties, do you?'

She wasn't asking out of politeness; she found she suddenly wanted to know all about this magician and her working life. She was so different from the usual crowd Alex met.

'Oh, it keeps me out of trouble, although the dads can be a problem, you know?'

Alex nodded. She could see why Mandy would be a victim of unwanted attention with her natural, striking beauty.

'How do you deal with that?' Alex probed.

'Oh, I just make their watch disappear. That usually sends them into a right spin. I've got a stash of Rolexes to keep me comfy in old age.'

Alex wasn't sure if she was joking or not, but she admired the chutzpah.

'Do you do magic for adults as well?' Alex immediately regretted the question. It made her sound like one of those creepy dads. She blushed and tried to recover. 'It's just in case, you know. I'm having a big party next year, and I suddenly thought it would be fun to have a magician – that's if you're free, of course.'

'Well, I'm not free,' Magic Mandy teased her. 'I do charge, but I'd happily give you mates' rates.'

'Yes, yes, of course,' Alex blustered. 'I wasn't suggesting you do it for nothing. Oh god, what must you think?' Alex was generally confident when speaking to strangers as part of her job, but right now, she wished that the ground would swallow her up.

Magic Mandy reassured her it was fine before wandering off to round up the children.

Alex had always been desperate to be more laid-back in social situations, but that in itself was counter-productive. You can't be casual and self-composed if you're trying too hard. Instead, she just turned into a purple beetroot, as she did now. The conversation had confused her.

Mandy definitely wasn't flirting. Was she? Alex didn't really know. The awkward teenager in her had never really disappeared, and she often felt out of her depth when she met strangers who she actually liked. She needed adults to play

86

with, but the ones she'd known all her life had grown up rather too fast, especially now her friends were married and had disappeared into a sea of nappies. Mandy and her magic wand seemed kind of cool, being so carefree and fun.

'Can you take care of Luigi, darling?' Diana asked Orlando once the carols were finished.

Orlando patted his velvet smoking jacket, turning his hands outwards to signify that he had no cash, as if he'd forgotten his wallet. 'I never need it,' he explained.

'Bet you don't,' said Kit sharply. 'I'll sort it, Aunt Di.'

He ushered Luigi to the front door with effusive thanks and gave him two crisp notes as a tip.

'Cheers, mate,' Luigi said, sounding more Tooting than Tuscany.

'We'd better be off, Alexandra.' Isobel appeared beside her, clearly having had enough. 'Father Christmas may not be coming for you, but I need to be up early in the morning to put the turkey in the oven, so chop-chop.'

Alex prickled with embarrassment. It was bad enough being treated like a child at home when no one was watching, but in full sight of her brothers and the magical Mandy, it was mortifying.

Aunt Di held Alex tight as she kissed her goodbye, before handing her a present wrapped in luxurious paper and topped with a huge bow.

'Such good news about your farm, pumpkin,' she whispered. 'You'll have to grill your mother about Will Griffiths. He was a handsome young devil, and I know she had a soft spot for him back in the day.'

Giddy from the party, the champagne and the confirmation of her inheritance, Alex slumped into the passenger seat of the car as her mother started the engine and crunched down the gravel drive.

She spoke loudly and slowly so that her mother could not mishear. 'You could have told me when the letter came that you knew William Griffiths,' she began, although it sounded more accusatory than she'd intended.

'I hadn't seen him for years,' her mother answered, keeping her eyes firmly ahead and both hands on the steering wheel. 'He was more your father's friend than mine.'

That wasn't what Aunt Di had said, Alex mused, but she could tell her mother was in oyster mode. The shell was clamped shut, and no amount of prising was going to make her offer up a pearl tonight.

'What did you make of Orlando?' Alex asked, deciding it was better to head for safer ground rather than be in danger of digging up a land mine.

'Narcissist nonpareil,' her mother tutted. 'Or to put it in more colloquial terms: first-rate tosser.'

They laughed together. Maybe they were more alike than Alex cared to admit.

'Did I see you speaking to a magician?' Isobel glanced momentarily sideways at her daughter.

'Yeah,' Alex said. 'I was.'

She hadn't left her any form of contact, so Alex would have to do a bit of digging online. Mandy was bound to have an Instagram account she could follow. At least, she hoped so.

CHAPTER TWELVE

Monmouthshire

Jiffy had finally consented to go for a walk, and Gwen wandered alongside him through a field of pregnant ewes, checking the water troughs and the fence-line, making sure they were secure. She could see Owen Odd Job in the distance, his Border collie working his way from left to right, looking back at his master for instruction. William was the one who always called him that – 'Owen Odd Job', as if it was his full name.

'It's so you know which Owen I'm talking about,' he'd always explained. 'And so that when I ask him to do odd jobs, he feels he can.'

Gwen had caught the habit, even though she hadn't required him to do an odd job in weeks. She had long ago given up asking him if he wanted a cup of tea, because he never did. He preferred his own company up there in his caravan in the woods. She'd once offered him the use of the bath, but he'd looked offended, so she hadn't tried again.

It was easier to make friends with the sheep as they munched all day long, keeping the grass as short as a crew cut. She supplemented their feed with a mix of home-grown oats and soya with minerals and yeast. They came running when she appeared with the bags to tip into the long, low feeders in the field. Even as the ewes got larger, they would waddle surprisingly quickly. She checked them over, taking particular care to inspect their feet.

She surveyed the land and drank in the space, the clean air and the freedom. She looked up to the sky, loving how it could change from indigo to arctic to cornflower then cobalt. She didn't even mind when it rained. There was an energy to the weather that gave her strength, and what most referred to as a bad forecast was, in her mind, a guarantee of colour to come. The cloud currently assembling above the Graig, the hill closest to the farm, was a case in point.

On a stormy day, the weather hovered between moods rather than colours. It could turn from mildly grumpy to downright furious in a moment, and it often sat in a state of smouldering threat, undecided on whether to unleash its anger.

'Without the rain, we'd be living in a desert,' she used to say to William, mainly to cheer him up. He could be as gloomy as the darkest of days, and she often wondered what he had lost in his life to make him so melancholy.

Gwen only hoped that Alex Roberts would appreciate the magic of this place. She felt impatient for the arrival of the new owner, hopefully in time for lambing. The ewes had been scanned and she could do with an extra pair of capable hands.

Jiffy had wandered to the border of the farmland and was sniffing along the hedgerow, his black-and-tan colouring standing out against the bare branches. It was the most active she had seen him since his master died, and she was relieved to see him acting much more like himself. He was having a lovely roll in the grass and, as he stood up, he shook himself from tip to tail. She hoped that grief was lifting for him, even if for her it would take a while longer. To add to her sadness, she was rattled by the uncertainty of her future at Tir Glas.

On the other side of the hedge, she heard the thunder of hooves, which meant that Dickon was exercising one of the few horses he had in training. Jiffy started to bark as the ground shook, but he was answered by a bark from Dickon's lurcher.

'Keep that bloody dog under control.' The wind carried Dickon's angry voice across the divide.

'Morning to you too, misery guts,' Gwen muttered under her breath, before calling Jiffy to her side. He trotted back with a look of innocence on his face and nudged her leg.

'You're a good boy, you are. You were only saying hello to that handsome lurcher, weren't you?' She reached down to fondle his ears and regretted it. He had rolled in sheep poo. She wiped her hand in the grass, which was less than effective.

Soon, Alex Roberts would be responsible for everything instead of her. There wasn't much time, as the letter she'd received a few days after Christmas said the new owner would arrive on 10 January. Gwen was torn. She had started to enjoy minding the farm, and she'd got used to spending time in the kitchen, only venturing out of it to go to bed in her annexe with a hot-water bottle and a full set of thermals. Jiffy had become more of a comfort, and they were helping each other navigate the emptiness of a world without William. But the new owner might not want or need a housekeeper, and Gwen herself might not want to stay.

She took Jiffy with her to the pub for an early supper and a chance to discuss it with Rhys. She could always rely on him to lend a good ear.

'I could put this Alex up here, if you want?' he suggested. 'The rooms upstairs will be free by then. The lot I've got in now are headed west to the coast tomorrow. That way, it won't be awkward, you know?'

'I guess he'll get the added bonus of central heating.' Gwen chuckled.

'That too,' Rhys confirmed.

As Gwen settled down to a hearty chicken-and-leek pie with vegetables on the side, Jiffy sat looking hopefully at the plate.

'He's got his appetite back then?' Rhys asked.

'And how.' Gwen blew on a chunk of chicken until she was sure it was cool enough before offering it up to Jiffy. 'He's on a winding road back to himself.'

'What about you?' Rhys enquired gently.

'Oh, I have my days. I'll get by.' Gwen sighed, feeling warmed from the fire and better than she had done for a while.

The bell on the pub door rang, announcing the arrival of a customer, and Dickon Jones strode in, followed by his unkempt but proud lurcher. He walked towards a table in the far corner and sat with his back to the room.

'The fun sponge is here. Good luck.' Gwen rolled her eyes.

Rhys greeted the skinny lurcher with a dog biscuit from the jar on the bar. He'd feed him a few more before he served his master with his regular Friday-night supper of lasagne. Rhys was pretty sure it was the one square meal either of them had in the course of a week. Both looked gaunt, and Dickon's face was turning greyer by the day. He looked much older than his forty years, and the bags under his eyes suggested a good night's sleep was as rare as any winner he trained these days.

'Same as?' Rhys said.

Dickon nodded. They had an arrangement whereby Dickon gave Rhys the odd racing tip; if they came in, the trainer ate for free. Rhys didn't bet much himself, but it was useful to pass on the information to his regulars.

The tips used to be for horses that Dickon had trained himself and, if they won, they paid out big. They were always at long odds, as the bookmakers consistently underestimated him. For a couple of years, the bookies had been fooled. Then he hit a lean patch, and Dickon started to tip horses trained by other people instead. Rhys didn't like to pry, but it was clear that Dickon didn't think he would have a winner any time soon. He was down on his luck, that much was clear, and he seemed more miserable than ever.

Rhys felt sorry for him and would have offered more, but Dickon only came once a week and ordered his lasagne, swearing it was the best he had ever tasted.

Rhys suspected it was really to do with how much it filled him up. He offered the lurcher another biscuit and would keep back the leftover chicken for him as well; Rhys wasn't about to let the dog go under-nourished.

Gwen had finished her chicken-and-leek pie and was draining a lime and soda as Dickon's lurcher came over to say hello to Jiffy. The two dogs were always pleased to see each other, even if their owners had been sworn enemies. The lurcher was a fine-looking beast, gunmetal grey in colour, with a shaggy top coat and a smooth head. He opened his mouth wide in a grin as he approached, wagging his whip-sharp tail. Jiffy jumped up and seemed to kiss his face.

'You're such a friendly boy, aren't you?' Gwen spoke to the dog and put her face closer to his ear. 'Not like your master. He's a miserable sod. Never says hello, never smiles. I don't know how you live with it.'

Rhys brought over the chicken, and Gwen fed it to Digby in small chunks. Jiffy took the odd handful but was happy enough to share.

'*Digby!*' The voice was so loud it made Gwen jump. Dickon had inhaled his food and was on his way out.

Digby turned immediately to follow his master. He was mercifully obedient for a lurcher, as long as he wasn't in pursuit of a hare or a deer. Then there was no calling him back.

'Bye, Digby,' Gwen said mournfully. She would have loved to get hold of him and give him a good brush as well as a decent meal. As for Dickon, he never said hello or goodbye, never even made eye contact with her and, apart from that brief appearance at William's graveside, it had been a long time since she'd seen him show any concern for anyone other than himself.

The trainer raised his hand in silent thanks to Rhys as he left to walk back along the unlit road to his yard. Ah well, Gwen thought, the cantankerous neighbour wouldn't be her problem at all. She could hand over hedgerow relations to Alex Roberts. Maybe he would do a better job of it.

CHAPTER THIRTEEN

On a grey and misty mid-January morning, Alex and Ethan set off together, heading west down the M4. They listened to Eighties music and sang at the top of their voices. The two had bonded over a shared love of music, especially the Norwegian band A-ha (they both fancied Morten Harket). They both loved dogs and shared an irrational fear of Wandsworth Common or, as they called it, Nappy Valley. They'd met during Alex's first week at *Rizz* magazine, when she was covering an event that Ethan was organizing. Alex was instantly drawn to the freckle-faced man-child who was constantly smiling. He had a buzz cut in those days, dyed white blond, and he was so naturally slim that he could eat whatever he wanted and not put on a pound. She had never felt so comfortable with a man to whom she was not related, and secretly, she felt more at ease with Ethan than with her own brothers. There was no sexual tension or competitive work rivalry either, so they could freely discuss love, loss, jobs, travel and parents.

Ethan was exactly the person she needed beside her for this trip. She glanced sideways near the Bristol turn-off as the traffic slowed and saw a man in a Range Rover laughing at them as they shoulder-danced to Spandau Ballet. She didn't care. She felt nervous, excited and terrified all at the same time, especially after the Zoom meeting she'd had a few days earlier with Davies and Davies Solicitors, during which it had been made clear she'd been bequeathed the farm on the condition she didn't sell it for five years.

'What?' Alex had asked. 'Can you do that? Leave someone something that they might not be able to afford to run? That's ridiculous.'

'Well, if you don't like the arrangement, I would suggest that you engage us to act on your behalf to contest the will. I can send you a breakdown of our charges, although I ought to point out that people usually contest a will because of things they haven't been left, rather than things they have.'

Alex had baulked at the mention of fees. She didn't want any of this to start costing her money she didn't have, so she'd just have to make this work for five years, one way or another.

In the meantime, if what she'd found on the internet was true, it could cost her everything she had and more. The article she'd read stated that this type of farm made on average a £10,400 *loss* every year.

Crossing the Severn Bridge, they felt the strength of the wind coming in from the west, seemingly funnelled by the Bristol Channel to hit them side on. The car veered off to the side, and Alex's heart rate increased as she battled it back into its lane.

They turned off the motorway at Newport and followed the signs to Raglan. As far as Alex was aware, she had never been to Wales in her life, let alone to this particular place, and yet she had a strange sense of familiarity.

She had found a pub online that had a room, but the postcode she had put into the satnav took them to a dead-end road in the middle of dark, foreboding trees.

'Must be a wide postcode area.' Ethan sighed as he searched on his phone for some sort of a clue. The signal only had one bar, barely enough for him to zoom in on the map. 'There are a couple of buildings on the other side of the river. Maybe it's over there.'

Alex took five attempts to turn the car around in the narrow lane, and they drove back two miles before they found a bridge that would take them to the other side.

An hour later than they had anticipated, they arrived at the Black Prince.

Ethan leapt out of the car and stretched after the long drive.

'Ooh I could murder a martini,' he exclaimed. He was wearing a pair of tight yellow jeans and an orange jumper that hugged his chest and admirably flat stomach. Alex had always wished she could eat what she liked and do no exercise like Ethan, without fear of gaining the pounds which seemed to creep on more easily these days. He had no idea how lucky he was.

She heaved herself stiffly out of the car, rolling her shoulders and shaking her legs to restart her circulation. She wasn't used to driving long distances and, despite the music and the warmth of Ethan's company, she felt exhausted.

'Gin and tonic for me,' she decided as she grabbed her bag from the boot.

They creaked open the front door of the pub and walked into a warm bar. A fire was roaring on the left-hand side, where one table was occupied by a gaunt-looking man, his lurcher at his feet. On the other side, there was a table in the bay window, surrounded by a few old armchairs and a battered sofa. Ruddy-faced men in woollen jumpers nursed pints while chatting, and a family tucked into plates of generously piled food.

The furniture all looked ancient, and the stone floor was worn with the imprint of countless heavy boots making their way to the bar.

Standing behind that bar was the biggest man Alex had ever seen. He looked like a superhero from an action movie with his thick beard and shoulder-length brown hair. Despite the chill of the evening air outside, he wore a short-sleeved T-shirt.

As she dithered and hesitated, Ethan strode confidently to the bar.

'Nice tiger.' He flashed his best smile as he pointed at the tattoo on the barman's arm. The diamond in his left ear glistened as the light hit it, and the barman nodded.

'You're clearly a man with good taste.' He laughed. 'What can I be doing for you both?'

'I've booked in,' Alex told him.

'Duw,' the barman said.

'No. Alex Roberts,' Ethan corrected him. 'There's no Duw.'

The barman laughed again.

'You're not from these parts, are you?'

Alex and Ethan shook their heads.

'It's just a turn of phrase. The name's Rhys.' He stretched out his hand towards Ethan. 'And you must be the mysterious Alex Roberts. We were wondering when you'd come by. Although I have to say, you're not at all what I was expecting.'

It was Ethan's turn to laugh. 'You've got the wrong one.' He pointed at his friend. 'She's Alex Roberts.'

The man with the lurcher looked up. He glowered towards them before looking down again.

Rhys stretched his hand out to Alex. 'Waw. Never!' he muttered. 'Well, this is a turn-up. Old Will was an enigma all right.'

He shook her hand. His accent was a variation of a strong West Country burr. She had heard similar in a friend who came from Herefordshire. She had expected a Welsh accent, but this was technically the Marches, the land of borders that straddled Wales and England.

'Alex Roberts, eh? Who'd have guessed?'

'Nice to meet you, Rhys,' she said softly, still processing that her name had been headline news in these parts, even if they had all assumed she was a he.

'Now then, you two lovebirds, you've travelled a long way. What can I get you?'

'We're strictly friends only.' Ethan winked at Rhys shamelessly. 'No benefits apart from good conversation and companionship, if you know what I mean.' He tapped the side of his nose. 'A martini for me, no ice. A gin and tonic for my lady *friend*. Oh, and I'm Ethan.' He presented his hand with a flourish and winked at Rhys again.

Alex dug him in the ribs and hissed, 'Stop it!' under her breath.

Rhys took it all in his stride, seemingly well used to admiring glances from the punters.

'A martini, eh? Haven't been asked for one of those since

99

James Bond dropped by. Lucky I got a delivery of olives this morning.' Rhys lifted down a martini glass from the furthest corner of the bar and started to mix the drink.

'Dry, wet or dirty?' he asked.

'Now, there's a question for a first encounter!' Ethan lifted his hand to his mouth in mock horror, and Alex just rolled her eyes at her friend's outrageous flirting. 'I want to say dirty but, as we've only just met, I'll keep it dry please.'

Alex noted that Rhys was coping exceptionally well with the incessant innuendo Ethan seemed to inject into every comment.

'We were going to head out to the farm today,' Alex explained. 'But we got lost, and now it's dark, so I think it's best if we wait until the morning, don't you?'

Rhys placed an olive on a stick and handed Ethan his dry martini. He started to pour Alex a double measure of gin. 'Best leave it till it's light, I'd say. Your car might not like the drive, and you'll need to see where you're going. Also, it'll give Gwen time to prepare.'

'Who's Gwen?' asked Ethan.

Rhys paused and considered his answer. 'Gwen has been the gatekeeper of Tir Glas Farm ever since I came here, and that was a good twenty years ago. She's had a bit more life experience than me, so she may have been around for longer than that. Anything you need to know about that place, she will know the answer. She's a good woman, is Gwen, and she loved that grumpy old stick William Griffiths like he was a part of her.'

Alex took a sip of her gin and tonic, feeling the cold liquid slipping down, and she took a deep breath.

'I thought William would do better by her, to be honest, and see her right,' Rhys added.

Alex hadn't considered other people at the farm. She'd only thought about the land and the animals and the business. Of course, there were people: how else would it all have kept running these last two months?

She hoped Gwen would not turn out to be a Mrs Danvers type, who would resent her presence at the farm. She lifted her drink off the bar and headed towards a battered sofa to sink into. The lurcher that had been sitting next to the solitary man came over to say hello.

She fondled his ears, and he immediately accepted what he saw as an invitation, clambering up onto the sofa beside her and asking for more of her gentle petting. She looked over to the bar to see Ethan tracing his finger over Rhys's tiger tattoo.

'It's magnificent,' he was saying.

Rhys started to regale him with the story of his grandfather in Burma and the history of the tiger in question.

The solitary man in the corner stood up to leave. He spotted the lurcher curled up on the sofa and let out a mighty roar. '*Digby!*' he shouted.

The dog jumped off the sofa as if a gun had gone off.

'Honestly, it was fine.' Alex was horrified. 'He just wanted a cuddle. I don't mind.'

'You might not mind, but I do,' the man explained, his face tight with tension, before slamming the door behind him.

'What did I do?' Alex turned towards Rhys and Ethan at the bar.

'Ah, don't mind him,' Rhys comforted her. 'He's like that

with everyone. They've been through a lot, him and Digby. Have another G&T, and this one's on the house.'

Alex and Ethan drank and ate grilled chicken in a chimichurri sauce, served with vegetables and a mountain of roast potatoes.

'Good food for the sticks, eh?' Ethan murmured.

'Oi.' The deep voice came from the bar. 'I heard that. We're not stuck in the Dark Ages, you know.'

'Sorry – didn't mean to offend,' Alex shouted back, giving Ethan a glare. 'It's delicious and we're very grateful. My friend hasn't done a lot of travelling.'

The other customers seemed friendly enough, smiling as they passed by on their way out. Soon, it was only the two of them left. They chatted with Rhys, making up for their earlier faux pas by asking a million questions about the pub, the local area, and the character of the mysterious William Griffiths. Ethan steered the conversation towards Rhys's life, at which point Alex left him to his personal enquiries and his gentle flirting. She walked towards the corner where Digby's owner had been sitting on his own, and took a closer look at the photos on the wall.

There were pictures of racehorses, a lot of dogs, and a few rugby teams in maroon and gold. In the centre of one of them she spotted the name she had been looking for: William Griffiths. She looked at his face, and again, that flicker of recognition came to her. She had seen this man before. Definitely. She had seen him with her father in a photo at her parents' house. She was sure of it.

'Right, time for bed, my friends.' Rhys nodded to the

clock. 'You're up the stairs and to the right. Twin beds, as requested.'

'And where are you?' Ethan whispered into Rhys's ear when Alex wasn't looking.

The room was clean and unfussy, with an en suite shower and loo. The curtains were on the thin side, so the light was bound to come through in the morning, but the nights were still long so that wouldn't be too much of an issue.

'You go first.' Ethan gestured towards the bathroom, knowing enough about life to understand that good friendship, particularly between a man and a woman, relied upon respecting boundaries.

Alex cleaned her teeth and inspected her face in the mirror. Her mother would 100 per cent tell her she looked tired, and this time, she'd be right. They swapped places in the bathroom, and Alex crashed out on the bed nearest the window. In less than thirty seconds, she had fallen into a deep and motionless sleep.

When Ethan had finished in the bathroom, he didn't bother getting into his own bed but instead silently slipped out of the room, satisfied Alex wouldn't notice.

Alex barely stirred when he crept back in just before the sun rose.

CHAPTER FOURTEEN

When Alex woke up the next morning, her heart was strangely aflutter with nerves. Most days of her life, she hit the mental snooze button, lying in bed pondering the day ahead, but today, on this frosty morning, her brain was racing because she was embarking on an adventure for which she was nowhere near prepared.

Breakfast in the pub was a help-yourself affair. There was good-quality yoghurt and granola, various cereals, and one loaf of bread to be sliced and toasted. Cooked options were available on request, with Welsh rarebit a recommended speciality and – joy of joys – they had oat milk as an option, which she could enjoy without suffering her mother's disdain. She noticed that Rhys positively glowed when Ethan descended the creaking stairs, this time sporting a scarlet pair of skintight trousers, with frayed rips below the knee and a white sweatshirt. He wore pristine white trainers on his feet, which she was sure were totally impractical for the day ahead.

'Looking bright this morning, fella.' Rhys smiled. 'Might want to save those trainers, though – it's not the cleanest place up there.'

'Ever on the lookout for me.' Ethan giggled like a teenager. 'If you've got a spare pair of wellies around, I'll happily borrow them. I don't own a pair myself. Never needed them. Even at

Glastonbury, I just went barefoot. Barelegged as well, to be fair.'

Ethan settled down opposite Alex and poured himself a cup from the teapot.

'I was out like a light last night.' Alex sighed. 'Apologies if you were after late-night conversation. You sleep OK?'

'More than OK.' Ethan glanced towards Rhys and winked. 'I had all the conversation I needed.'

Alex furrowed her brow. He couldn't have, could he? Night one in the depths of Monmouthshire, and trust Ethan to have already pulled. Bloody hell, men didn't hang about.

'You never fail to astonish me,' she teased him.

'Well, I hope I live up to that. Ever the practical one, I have brought you something that may help.' Ethan produced a hardback book from his man-bag. He presented it with a flourish.

Alex scanned the front cover. '*The Idiot's Guide to Farming*?' she exclaimed. 'Well, at least it's not a cookery book.'

'It's a start,' Ethan said as he raised his cup. 'Here's to the future and everything it may throw your way.'

She lifted her mug of tea to touch his. 'Cheers.'

'Here's to Wales and all its surprises,' Ethan replied. 'Cheers.'

'One Welsh rarebit.' Rhys arrived at their table with a plate of golden cheese atop a slice of bread, which he presented to Alex.

It tasted like the food of the gods. Better than anything she had eaten in the myriad fancy restaurants she had visited in London and overseas.

When she finished, she strolled back to the photo on the wall, gazing at it intently.

The deep-brown eyes of William Griffiths stared back at her.

'Who were you? And why on earth did you leave anything to me, let alone a farm in the middle of nowhere?' she asked the photograph.

After breakfast, Rhys offered them a lift to Tir Glas.

'It's better if I take you. The drive is full of potholes, and I'd hate to see you ruin your car on your very first visit,' he explained.

Alex let Ethan sit in the front so the boys could continue their flirting, while she sat in the back of the Land Rover, staring out of the window. There was a glow to this land that warmed her right through.

Rhys clunked through the gears and chatted away to Ethan over the throaty rumble of the engine. They turned into a narrow lane with high hedges on either side, and then off to the right, over a cattle grid and onto a rough drive. Rhys slowed down to negotiate the potholes.

'Do you mind if I get out?' Alex leant forward to make herself heard. 'Nothing personal – I just want to walk and take it all in.'

'Sure.' Rhys pulled to a stop. 'I'll just help you with that door. It gets stuck.' He leapt out of the driver's seat.

Rhys's tiger tattoo caught the dappled sunlight as he wrenched the door open; he put his arm out to help Alex down.

'Watch those shoes.' He looked at her trainers. 'They won't

last long. Gwen might have a pair of wellies that'll fit you down at the house. You sure you want to risk it?'

'I'll be fine.' Alex didn't care. 'You boys head on down and I'll be along in my own time.'

The Land Rover spluttered into life again and rumbled off down the drive, weaving comically from left to right to avoid the worst of the potholes.

Alex looked around her to take it all in. There was a water-logged field to the left and a wood to the right. The hills rose up behind, to the sides, and beyond her, creating a bowl in which the farm sat. The sky seemed vast, and there was not a house to be seen. She could see a pillar of smoke snaking its way into the sky, the first clue there might be a farmhouse over the rise.

A rusted-up tractor sat in the woods, abandoned long ago, and she could see more discarded machinery, randomly left, as if someone had just got off the seat and walked away.

The land around rose and fell, rose and fell. Clumps of trees, their branches bare of leaves, stretched out to each other with thin tendrils of black. The verges were wet, and deep tyre marks revealed the tracks of cars that had wandered from the hardcore driveway and got stuck in the red, claggy soil.

Dots of clouds on the hill in the distance raised their black heads to reveal themselves as sheep. It was a world away from the London life Alex knew.

She walked slowly down the drive, hearing the sheep bleating in the distance, trying to take in the enormity of the responsibility she had been bequeathed. That word. Responsi-bloody-bility.

A horse thundered up a hill on the other side of the hedge-line. It was being followed by a lurcher in full flow. Wait, it was the dog she'd met last night. Digby. That was his name. She smiled at the image of dog and horse galloping together.

As she reached the top of the sloping drive, the farmhouse revealed itself in the dip below. The smoke she'd seen earlier was rising out of a red-brick chimney that sat at the right-hand side of a sagging slate roof. The windows were misty with grime, and the white frames sported grey gaps or had large flakes of paint flapping in the wind. The red brick of the walls was in desperate need of repointing, and the ivy growing up it had caused cracks that looked wide enough for birds to nest in. There was an old digger in front of a barn door that was tied up with baler twine, and an ancient Land Rover on stacks of bricks, no tyres to be seen. The potholes in the drive had filled with rainwater; where holes had been topped with bricks or gravel, the surface was treacherously slippery and uneven.

Alex picked her way carefully across another cattle grid, making her way towards the house. The big door in the centre looked as if it hadn't been used for decades, with the doorstep covered in leaves and moss that had been thrown from the roof tiles by the birds.

She knocked on the door to the left, but there was no answer, so she raised the latch to let herself in. She discovered a long, narrow, chilly room, with coats piled high on hooks to the left, boots of various sizes caked in mud lying on the floor, and a large white butler sink with a ring of grey around it in the middle of the wooden shelf that ran along the wall.

109

She took her shoes off and left them next to the boots, feeling the cold of the tiled floor as she followed the sound of voices and opened the door on the right.

'Dear lord, don't take your shoes off!' a woman's voice greeted her. 'Your feet will get dirtier walking across the floor than if you walked down the drive outside.'

Alex lifted one foot to examine the underneath of her socks and saw the woman was right about that.

'I'm so sorry,' she said, flustered. 'Must be a London habit. Of course, I'll put them back on.'

She scurried back to the boot room and retrieved her shoes, feeling like a child who had been reprimanded.

'I'm Gwen,' she introduced herself, as Alex came back into the kitchen. 'I didn't want you catching your death of cold by foot, if that's such a thing.'

Alex assessed the woman who stood before her. She had a warm smile and the cutest button nose, but there was a sadness in her eyes that betrayed the grief she had suffered. Her hair was scooped into a tight ponytail held in place by an elastic band. It looked as if it was due a wash, and the state of her fingernails suggested that a long soak in a bath was a luxury she did not often indulge in. Gwen's accent was what Alex had assumed everyone would sound like – classically Welsh. She had a musicality to her voice, and the pattern of sentences ran into each other at a rapid rate. She rolled her r's and dropped the ends of some words.

'So you're Alex Roberts, eh?' She offered her a cup of tea. 'I gather from Rhys that we got it all wrong. I feel a fool, so I do, to have assumed that you must be a man. I swear to you

110

I'm not backward. I blame those fancy legal folk in Monmouth for making me think you was a man.'

Alex thanked Gwen for the cup of tea and assured her that it was an easy mistake.

'Sometimes, in my job, it's an advantage,' she told Gwen. 'I almost encourage it. It can be very useful if I'm trying to get an interview or an upgrade.'

Gwen nodded, although she had no idea what Alex was talking about. Could you get your grades improved at school if you were a boy? If so, that really wasn't fair.

Alex took in the state of the big kitchen, which served as a living room as well, with a large wooden table running down the centre that was scored with scratches on the top and down the legs. There was a battered sofa facing the fire, a faded armchair to the left of it, and a window on the right, offering a view of the drive. It had bits of newspaper and old cloth shoved into the gaps that had appeared between the frame and the sides.

Ethan had parked himself by the Aga, leaning against the oven doors for warmth as Rhys moved across to the open fireplace to lay some logs and light them. He paused to say hello to a dog on the sofa.

'Is that a Welsh terrier?' Alex asked.

'Don't get too close; he doesn't like strangers,' Gwen warned her. 'Most English folk think he's a small Airedale. You must know your dogs.'

'She'll always talk to the dogs first. Then the people,' Ethan joked as he lifted himself up to sit on the closed lids of the Aga hob.

111

Gwen was a woman who liked to see the best in people, and took a clear view early on as to whether they would be in her team or on the bench. If this Alex Roberts liked dogs more than people, then she must be an all-right sort. She would be on the team, and that was that.

'Be careful you don't cook your arse sitting up there.' Gwen turned to Ethan. 'We don't want a toasted rump cheek.'

Ethan offered Gwen his most dazzling smile. 'Oh, I promise I won't let that happen!' He winked and looked over to Rhys, who had finished laying the fire.

'So, what's he called?' Alex pointed at the Welsh terrier.

'Ah, that's Jiffy,' Gwen replied. 'Named after—'

'Jonathan Davies?' Alex ventured.

'Spot on. You know your rugby too?'

'Well, my dad was a player back in the day,' Alex told Gwen. 'In fact, I think he must've played with William Griffiths. That's the connection, as far as I can tell.'

'There's a pile of old photos you'll want to have a look at,' Gwen offered. 'In fact, I'd better show you around. Put your coat back on – it's colder in the rest of the house, mind.'

Alex coughed as they stepped out of the warmth of the kitchen, partly from the damp chill and partly from the dust that hung in the air. The house was bigger than she had imagined, with another door leading to an expansive garden. Peering through the window, she could see an overgrown lawn and out-of-shape box hedging, some of which had yellowed in colour, with a bed of big-headed seed pods that had been flowers and a lower set of bushes that looked like twigs but might yet transform into lavender. She could see a collection of what she imagined were fruit trees, and a greenhouse whose roof had caved in, leaving shards of glass on the floor.

'Garden's not my thing.' Gwen looked at her apologetically. 'William fancied himself as the Alan Titchmarsh of Monmouthshire, but he hardly had time and it's gone horribly wrong since he left us, I'm afraid.'

Alex looked at the three doors leading off the open hallway, which was dominated by a heavy oak staircase. There were five or six large frames leaning against the outside of the stairs and consequently a number of large squares on the wall where the paint was a different shade to that around it.

'Study, downstairs loo, junk room.' Gwen pointed at each door. 'I think the junk room might have been a dining room once upon a time, but you wouldn't know it. I got Rhys to help me take the pictures down because I couldn't reach them to clean and I thought they'd be safer on the floor. Everything's in a bit of chaos, to be honest.'

They started to head upstairs, and every step creaked with the weight of their bodies. The middle of the stairs was worn with the tread of over a hundred years of human footsteps, and Alex imagined a time when this house would have been full, with adults and children running up and down, with the constant flow of food, fun and laughter bringing its own warmth and sunshine to this otherwise cold and dark place.

Tir Glas Farm today was empty and eerie. She wouldn't have ventured upstairs at all if it hadn't been with Gwen beside her for protection and company. Alex didn't believe in ghosts, but she remembered a trip to Norway she had once been on.

She'd been reporting for *Rizz* on a new ice-bath boot camp that celebrities were raving about. They believed so firmly in trolls in Norway that they'd had to ask permission from the specific troll of the lake for the camp to be built there. She had laughed when the general manager told her about it and assumed he was joking. He had fixed her with a glare and said, with no hint of irony, 'This is no laughing matter.'

So no, she didn't believe in ghosts as such, but if there were trolls in Wales, she would kindly ask their permission to tidy up a bit before doing any work to the house.

In the main bedroom, the curtains were drawn. Gwen walked gingerly to the closest window and pulled them open. Pale winter light revealed a four-poster bed with a pile of heavy wool rugs across it. The pillow had a dent in the middle of it, as if the incumbent had only just got up.

Gwen hovered by the window, reluctant to move further into the room. She didn't often stand still, preferring to keep her hands and her mind busy.

'This was William's,' she said softly. 'I haven't been in, you know, since he left.'

Alex stared at the pillow. Her mysterious benefactor was the last person to lie right here. Atoms of him were still here in this room. No wonder she could feel the presence of someone. He was in the room, in every part of it. When it was just her and Gwen, she would ask her a million questions about William Griffiths. What mattered to him, what made him laugh, what angered him or piqued his interest? She was eager to know about this man who had bequeathed her his home and his life's work.

Ethan was on the landing when they came out of the main bedroom. Clearly, his curiosity had got the better of him.

'Tell you what, Alex, you could have some house party here.' Ethan whistled as he gestured around him and pointed down to the enormous hall. 'I would happily plan a gathering here. Maybe that's the answer for your birthday?'

'I don't think having a whole load of people to stay in a farmhouse with no heating and dodgy plumbing is a good idea,' Alex replied. 'We would have to delay until the summer and put them in tents in the field.'

'It'll be like Glastonbury!' Ethan smiled. He was never happier than when he had a party to plan.

Gwen led them into the other bedrooms, all of which were tidy enough, if a little dusty.

'You can stay in any of these if you like. It's yours to use as you wish.'

Alex shook her head. She knew Ethan wouldn't want to leave the pub, and she certainly wasn't ready to stay here on her own.

'I think we'll leave it for a while,' she replied to Gwen. 'I don't want you to feel we're pushing you out. You stay for as long as you like. I've got to work a few things out first, and of course, we need to talk about your salary.'

Gwen was embarrassed at the mention of money. She had never thought of her role at Tir Glas as a job. It was a calling, and the opportunity had come to her quite by chance when she had been doing part-time work at the pub. William's housekeeper had just left, she needed a place to stay, and it had all fallen into her lap. She had made sure she earned his faith in her by always doing something: cooking, cleaning, feeding the animals, washing, shopping and ultimately caring for him when he got ill.

Alex pulled her phone out of her pocket to take a few photos. She'd need to show her father so he could tell her what to do because he was always the practical one, but then she hesitated, because what if he didn't recover soon enough to offer advice? She looked at her screen and saw no sign of any signal.

'Oh, what's your Wi-Fi here?' Alex asked Gwen, who raised her eyebrows. 'You know, broadband. Does it have a code?' Alex continued.

'Wi-Fi?' Gwen pronounced the word as two distinct syllables, then laughed out loud. 'You're joking, right?'

Alex blinked. The pub had broadband, so it didn't seem that strange a question. How could anyone exist without access to the internet? Especially if they were running a business. Or just living a life. It was like not having central heating. You could clearly survive without that – Gwen was living proof – but living without the internet was an impossibility. Alex would never be able to do her job without it.

As they made their way back down to the warmth of the kitchen and the smell of freshly brewed coffee, Gwen explained that Will always took his paperwork down to the pub to use Rhys's Wi-Fi.

'That way, he could get a hand with his accounts if he needed it. Rhys is a dab hand with technology and he's not bad at numbers,' she said admiringly.

'Seems to me he's a man of many hidden talents.' Alex grinned.

'Too right,' Ethan murmured under his breath.

'Stop it,' she mouthed, shooting him a warning look.

'Does anyone have broadband out here?' she asked.

Gwen thought about it as Rhys handed her a mug. 'I can't think of anyone.'

'What's that?' Rhys chimed in.

'Wi-Fi. Broadband. You know, the internet. Has anyone out here got it?' Alex said.

'Dickon has,' Rhys replied. 'He needs it to do the entries for the horses. That's if any of them ever run in a race again. He's only over there.' He pointed out of the window towards the hedgerow.

It suddenly dawned on Alex that her nearest neighbour, perhaps her only one, would be the misery guts who shouted at his dog last night.

'Well, this will be an adventure.' She raised her mug of coffee to the group. 'Thank you, Gwen, for being so welcoming, and to Rhys for looking after us so well.'

'I'll drink to that,' said Ethan, his eyes twinkling.

CHAPTER FIFTEEN

Alex shivered, pulling her coat neck closed and making a mental note to visit the nearest Cotswold Outdoor. She might be able to get a discount if she promised them an article on rural chic, although there was nothing chic about her right now, garbed as she was in a borrowed pair of wellies and an oversized man's Barbour, so worn that there was no sign of waterproof wax and the pockets were hanging half open where the stitching had split. It smelt musty and of wet dog.

Ethan looked more stylish, with his tight red trousers tucked into Rhys's wellies and a short leather bomber jacket. He pulled on a black beanie hat to protect him from the wind and immediately looked as if he could jump into the pages of a magazine.

'I'm channelling David Beckham!' he chuckled as he strode out into the yard.

'I'm not sure David Beckham ever actually gets his boots muddy,' Alex joked. 'It's all country gent squeaky clean. I don't think the animals dare take a dump for fear of making a mess.'

Alex took in the yard, the massive barn with its doors hanging by one bolt and tied together with orange baler twine. There was more rusting and abandoned machinery, tyres left in random piles as if waiting for a purpose, a trough filled with rainwater and a caravan on bricks. The green mould around the windows suggested it hadn't been lived in for a while. At the far end of the farmyard, there was a blue Portaloo that had become a permanent feature. When she opened the door, Alex noted that the loo roll was being held on the wall by an old Pelham bit from a horse's bridle.

There was mud everywhere, and Alex felt completely out of her depth.

The wind suddenly picked up, and the buildings creaked. The giant door of the main barn flapped loose and banged against the wall. Alex was dazed by the scale of it. There was so much to do, and she didn't have the first clue where to start.

'Talk me through all the machinery,' Alex said, genuinely perplexed at how thousands of pounds' worth of farm equipment could be left to rust and rot like this.

'Same the world over,' Rhys explained. 'Farmers spend a fortune buying a brand-new tractor or baler or whatever. They use it and use it until it falls apart, and then they can't afford to get it mended and no one will take it away, so they leave it in a field or in a yard. It becomes so much a part of the backdrop that they no longer notice it.'

Alex could see at least ten machines here in the yard alone, plus the tractor she'd seen on the way in.

'Some of this stuff would go back to the early twentieth century, and that one over there' – he pointed to an ancient blue tractor with a rotting seat and no cab – 'if that was restored, it could go to one of the big tractor shows.'

'There are tractor shows?' Alex looked at him blankly.

'Oh yeah. There are vintage shows, tractor runs, ploughing competitions. All sorts. There's a whole world of rural festivals to keep us folk busy, so we don't drink ourselves to death on our own or turn to the sheep for a little extra company.'

'*Stop it, Rhys!*' Gwen cried. 'You'll have them believing all the old clichés. We do not, I repeat, do *not* do anything inappropriate with our sheep, and don't you let him kid you otherwise. It's just a tired old stereotype, and it's not fair.'

She may have been affronted, but Rhys merely chuckled.

'Oh, Gwennie, you always bite.' He laughed, enjoying the wind-up.

'Do you know much about farming?' Gwen asked Alex.

'Only what you're telling me now,' Alex said meekly.

'Oh right.' Gwen bit her bottom lip.

It was one thing for Alex to turn out to be a woman rather than the man she'd mistaken her for, but quite another for her to have no idea how to run a farm. Gwen had been hoping the new owner would come in with bundles of cash, a heap of new ideas, and be able to sort everything out, especially with lambing season around the corner. At the very least, she had hoped for a capable helper. Christ knew they needed it. If Alex knew nothing about farming, or indeed about William, she couldn't help but wonder why on earth she'd inherited the farm in the first place?

'Wait until you go to the sheep-shearing championships – now that's a testosterone-fuelled sports event if ever I've seen one. I expect you'll find some ancient shears round here that you can take along to show them. They'll be dead impressed with that.' Rhys turned to Alex, trying to lighten the mood.

'Is there money in sheep's wool then?' she asked hopefully.

'God no,' Rhys fired back. 'Your shears would be worth more than a thousand fleeces. There's no money in it at all.

121

But when the sheep-shearers hit town, you'd think a chart-topping rock band had arrived. They have the place buzzing, and I don't just mean with the shears.'

'Well, I'd better make a date to be back for that.' Ethan looked impressed.

'Right up your street,' Rhys joked. 'All white vests, jeans and leather boots, muscles rippling and egos exploding.'

'But do any of them have the chat? It's good conversation I'm after.'

'A man after my own heart,' Rhys flirted back.

Alex wondered about the night before and what had happened between them. Maybe they had just talked. Ethan always said he was looking for a man he could really talk to. It helped, of course, if they were handsome and could make a decent coffee like Rhys.

'You should come to the next one this summer,' Gwen suggested. 'The New Zealanders are coming over for that one, and it'll be a cracker.'

Although Gwen was petite, she was trim and surprisingly strong. She could flip a sheep onto its back with one hand, shift a trough or lift a bale of hay if need be. She enjoyed the physical side of farming and thought of it as a daily workout, which meant she didn't need to pay for gym membership or Pilates classes. This was exercise enough.

Gwen walked towards a bright-red quad bike as the other three made their way on foot out of the farmyard into the first of the fields.

'When will they have lambs?' Alex asked, looking to the sheep.

'Another month or so,' Rhys explained. 'This lot were serviced at the beginning of October, so any time from the twenty-third of February. A lot of them lamb within the same week, but lambing lasts about a month altogether. It's a crazy time. No sleep for anyone because they seem to pick the early hours of the morning. They come into the barn at night when they're close. William didn't like the risk of lambs being born out in the open, and if they're in, you can help with any difficult births. They're up on their feet soon enough and can't wait to get out.'

'Sorry.' Alex swallowed. 'What do you mean help with the birth? Doesn't the vet do that?'

Rhys laughed. 'God no. If you had to call the vet out every time a ewe was giving birth, you'd run out of money before the spring even started. You've got to do it yourself. It's a hands-on job, so I hope you're not squeamish.'

Alex tried to process the information. She was very squeamish, with a fear of blood, and the very idea of putting her hands anywhere near the icky, sticky mess of birth made her feel like she was going to vomit. She couldn't even watch *Casualty* or *Call the Midwife* because of the operations and childbirth scenes. There was no way she was ever going to be pulling lambs out of ewes' backsides. Never.

Gwen came through the gate behind them on a quad bike, with a trailer behind her. She was calling the sheep over and, like obedient, highly trained animals, they came running.

She dismounted and started filling low troughs with what looked like breakfast cereal. 'If they come when they're called, they deserve a reward.'

'So, what do they eat?' Alex checked.

'This is the good stuff. It's mainly oats with soya, minerals and yeast. They love it, and it keeps them full of milk for when the little ones come.'

Alex watched them munching their food, their muzzles quivering and their backsides seeming to shake and shudder with excitement.

Her reverie was broken by Gwen answering a question Ethan had asked about whether they had names.

'Some of the older ewes have names,' she said. 'But mainly it's done with numbers now. When the lambs come, we can't name them. Too many of them, and besides, it would be too painful if we got too attached. They'll all be gone by the end of August, and I don't want to be thinking about that.'

'Gone where?' Alex hesitated, although she feared she knew the answer to the question.

'To feed the nation,' Rhys answered quietly. 'They need to weigh about forty-two kilos and they'll fetch good money. Well, at least enough to cover what they've cost. Not enough to send you off on the holiday of your dreams, I'm afraid.'

Alex's head was spinning from machines she'd never seen before, language that was utterly foreign, animals she couldn't take for a walk, a house that needed a full renovation, and a business that she simply didn't understand. How could anyone ever make any money from this? On top of all of that, she was going to have to send animals to slaughter on a regular basis. She was living in her own horror movie.

Gwen watched quietly. She could see how overwhelmed Alex looked. How on earth would the poor girl cope? She had looked as pale as a sheet of white paper ever since they'd mentioned lambing.

Alex spotted a figure skulking on the edge of the field, up by the woods, a manic dog running around and looking at its owner with its tongue hanging out.

'Who is that?' she asked, alarmed at the sight.

'Oh, don't worry about him. That's Owen Odd Job. He lives in a caravan in the woods. You'll never need a security camera with him around. That dog of his can hear a noise from a mile off.'

Noticing Alex's frozen face, Rhys walked towards her and put a comforting arm round her shoulder.

'He's no harm, I swear. He doesn't talk much, but he'll be out here in all weathers, and he'll do any job you need. Just ask him and it'll be sorted. Same goes for me. You ask for help and I'll come running.'

Alex was reassured by his kind offer, but there was so much to take in and she was fighting an unfamiliar and over-whelming sense of anxiety.

Behind Rhys, the Black Mountains rose to meet the sky, and the shadows from the clouds chased across their slopes in the distance. Alex loved her London walks with Ethan, which regularly took them around Richmond Park, revelling in the huge space and the uninterrupted view from one side of it all the way to St Paul's Cathedral. They would dash for cover when a storm suddenly arrived, or buy ice creams on hot days, eating them at Pen Ponds while sitting on a bench to admire the ducks and swans. There was always someone else's dog to pet and other people's children running riot, to confirm her decision not to have them.

It wouldn't be like that out here. This was hardcore adventuring. She felt a sudden thrill of adrenalin.

'I think we should take up rambling.' She turned to Ethan, who tried to disguise his laugh as a cough. 'Imagine climbing up there!'

'What has got into you?' he asked. 'Richmond Park is one thing because we can still get a takeaway coffee or an ice cream. Walking up there is, you know, quite extreme. I'd need proper walking trousers and everything. Right now, I can barely make it across the field without chafing my inner thighs and getting blisters on my feet.'

'Oh, you'd enjoy it up there.' Rhys looked at the hills in admiration. 'It's well worth the yomp. The view is breathtaking. You'll feel like a grain of sand in the desert. How such a small thing as us can do so much damage to the world, I have no idea.'

'Didn't know you had a philosopher deep inside,' Ethan joked. 'There's more to you than meets the eye.'

Rhys bowed his head in self-effacement. 'Sorry. Did that sound a bit, you know, a bit high-falutin?'

'God no,' Alex jumped in. 'I know exactly what you mean – you pay no attention to Ethan. He's been splashing about in the shallow end of life for long enough. He could do with thinking a little deeper.'

'Rude!' Ethan exclaimed.

Alex broke into a smile. However out of her depth she was, seeing Ethan adapt to country life would provide some entertainment.

CHAPTER SIXTEEN

The sky had turned from benevolent to a dark, angry grey in the time Alex and Ethan had been walking across the fields accompanied by Gwen and Rhys. Big fat raindrops started to fall, faster and faster, drumming the ground and bouncing back up again. Jiffy barked and sprinted across the field towards the yard.

'Back to the house, quick as you can!' shouted Gwen from the quad bike. She zoomed back towards the farmyard as the three others ran back across the fields towards cover.

They were soaked before they reached the front door, from a storm as violent as it was sudden. Jiffy shook himself from head to toe, spraying water into the air as he did so. The humans shed their outer layers and took off their boots. Gwen, always aware of the changeable weather, had taken the precaution of wearing a fully waterproof boiler suit, so she was relatively unscathed. She looked at the Londoners, who were standing in two pools of water, drenched and shivering.

'There are dry clothes upstairs in the main room,' she told them. 'I haven't touched a thing, so find yourself a nice warm jumper – it'll all be a bit big for you, Alex, but pull on something and we can hang your wet clothes over the Aga to dry.'

Ethan and Alex headed upstairs while Rhys and Gwen stayed downstairs, stoking the fire and putting on the kettle.

'Seems like a nice girl,' Gwen said to him cautiously. 'Not a country type obviously. I assumed William would have picked someone who knew what they were doing and could turn this place around. She'll need to learn fast, otherwise we're doomed. There's a stack of bills in there that need paying, and I don't know where the money's going to come from.'

'She'll need your help, Gwen,' Rhys replied. 'She won't be able to manage any of this on her own.'

Gwen started brewing a big pot of tea. 'Her boyfriend will help her, won't he?'

'Boyfriend?' There was shock and a little humour in Rhys's voice. 'Ethan's not her boyfriend. He's not that type.'

Gwen poured milk into a jug, conscious that she should make tea the posh way. 'Oh, I see,' she said calmly, thinking a few things now made more sense.

Jiffy came to her feet, and she leant down to give him a dry biscuit. He cocked his head on one side, as if to listen to whatever it was she needed to say.

'Silly me,' she whispered as she ruffled the head of the Welsh terrier.

Ethan and Alex reappeared wearing a strange assortment of old clothes. Ethan sported a pair of faded old jeans pulled in at the waist with a worn leather belt. He had an oversized round-necked blue jumper with a large moth hole in the front. Alex had found some tartan pyjamas that she'd pulled in with the cord so that they didn't drop down from her waist. They looked brand new and were not ridiculously big for her. She put her hand on her hip and stood in the doorway, modelling the look.

'I found these still wrapped in tissue, so I guess they've never been worn,' she said, wondering for whom they had been intended.

They had been in the bedside chest of drawers of William's room. She had felt a little odd unwrapping a present that wasn't for her, but needs must. And they felt gorgeously soft against her skin, the best kind of sloppy joe outfit in which to sprawl out in front of the TV and while away a wet afternoon waiting for the storm to pass. Not that there was a TV anywhere. Probably no signal, she thought, amazed that anyone could exist without television or the internet.

Rhys and Gwen laughed. Alex really did suit the red flannel pyjama look, even with a pair of chunky socks hanging round her ankles. As for Ethan, he looked like a local and would fit right in at the pub dressed like that.

'Stick your clothes on the Aga, and we'll give them a chance to dry out,' Gwen instructed them. 'Then come and make yourselves comfortable. I've made a nice pot of tea, and we can all warm up in front of the fire.'

Ethan had barely lowered himself into the battered armchair before Jiffy leapt into his lap and was nuzzling into the jumper. The dog let out a little whine before making himself comfortable and falling asleep.

'Don't think you're moving any time soon,' Gwen placed a steaming cup of tea on the low table beside him. 'He could always smell William from a mile off in that jumper, and he's not letting that memory go.'

'Can I ask you about William?' Alex curled up on the sofa

and tucked her feet up under. She patted the space next to her and motioned for Gwen to sit down.

Not used to sitting and chatting, Gwen was hesitant. She was more comfortable if she was making food, clearing it up or generally tidying. She hovered and then sat. 'Fire away,' she said cautiously.

'Well, how did he end up here?'

Gwen shifted and made herself more comfortable. 'Oh, that's easy. His father, his father's father and the one before that. They all farmed here. They started small and then expanded. Then his grandfather overstretched himself so they had to sell off some land. That's when Dickon's lot came along. They bought it and turned it into gallops for the horses.'

Alex nodded. That's where the resentment would have started, she guessed. Old feuds, going generations back, born of protectionism and envy. 'And what was he like?'

Gwen smiled, her eyes a little cloudy as she summoned up the memory of the man she had spent the best part of her adult life rubbing along with. 'Oh, he was a fine man. He was always polite and kind to me, never anything but a gentleman, you know? He could be a bit quiet and off with other folk. He didn't have many friends, and I always felt there was something . . .' She paused and stood up again, turning the tea towel in her hands. 'Something a bit sad deep in there.' She pointed at her chest. 'Like he'd lost someone. He didn't talk about it, mind. Never talked about much, to be fair.'

Alex stared at the flames of the fire and tried to let the strangeness of the situation and of this place seep into her. She tried to imagine William here in this room, sitting where

Ethan was right now, in the same jumper, with Jiffy curled up in his lap. She had the weirdest sense of déjà vu. It wasn't the look of the place or even the smell, but it had an aura that she felt she'd shared before. She wouldn't say any of this out loud, of course. They'd all think her mad, but somewhere in her brain was a tiny seed of recognition.

CHAPTER SEVENTEEN

Alex had to drag herself away from the farm to go back to London five days later. Her job was calling and, within a few short weeks, her editor at *Rizz* magazine had commissioned her to write an article on the opening of a new restaurant in Dubai in February. It was a shock to be surrounded by holiday-makers and pushy business travellers at Heathrow airport after the quiet of the Welsh countryside.

Her flight was delayed and, amidst the fidgety children and harassed parents at the gate, she yearned for the peace of Tir Glas Farm. She tried to settle in her seat when they were finally able to board, but struggled to get comfortable. The offer of free alcohol on the flight was too tempting to refuse, and she drank herself into a sleepy state, eventually finding the escape she needed.

She was deeply asleep when the announcement came that they were coming into land. The stewardess shook her awake and asked her to lift her seat to the upright position. She felt as if she'd been drugged as she robotically obeyed the instructions, and dozed off again as the plane bumped onto the runway and taxied to its station.

She had anticipated sunning herself on the beach and enjoying the mixture of social events and sport, but that dream was shattered as soon as she emerged from the plane. Monsoon rain flooded the roads and the airport runway. The beach was deserted, and the hotel pool was closed because of the danger of slipping on the surrounding stone. With a glass of wine costing £22, she couldn't even drown her sorrows – if it wasn't at an event she was covering or with a source she was interviewing, she couldn't charge it to *Rizz* expenses.

The article she was here to write centred on the opening of a restaurant co-owned by an ex-footballer called Layton Brooks. He had teamed up with a celebrity chef to produce a glamourized burger bar, which showed a constant stream of live sport on huge screens. Gambling was not allowed in Dubai but, for an extra charge, those at the restaurant could predict a scoreline and enter a 'lottery'. The winning ticket would be picked out of those who got the score correct, and they would earn a free meal at the restaurant. It was a side-hustle that paid dividends, whatever the result.

Layton Brooks schmoozed the press, calling all the men *mate* as he slapped their backs, and all the women *darlin'* as he stroked their arms. A slick PR team of young men and women in black outfits moved amongst the guests at the launch party, plying them with his own brand of champagne, called Brooks Bubbles. They issued the journalists a one-page press release with quotes from Layton, the head chef and the manager of the resort. Alex looked at the words on the page, all of them oozing with fulsome praise.

'So fake.' She tutted to herself as she looked around the room at the invited journalists, the influencers, the models, the television personalities and the footballers who had been roped in to add stardust to make an otherwise rather standard sports bar seem more glamorous.

She could see, very clearly, the workings of the media machine, and she understood what she had long suspected: she was complicit in this too. She felt disgusted with herself for being part of it. She felt conflicted about what to do, knowing full well she couldn't be rude; she could not storm out, and yet this was not honest or real. Another top-up of champagne was offered, which she accepted in the hope that the alcohol would dull her senses.

Alex had chosen an all-in-one jumpsuit in the hope of avoiding unnecessary attention. It was deliberately androgynous and, she hoped, stylish without being sexy. Layton Brooks clearly had other ideas and, an hour into the launch, he slid into the booth beside her.

'Enjoying the grub?' he asked, leaning over her to reach a bottle on the far side of the table. He made an exaggerated stretch and placed a hand in her lap to steady himself. He gave her thigh a squeeze as he retrieved the red wine.

'Sorry darlin'. Must be losing me balance.' He smirked, knowing full well what he was doing. 'Top-up?'

'No thanks, I'm fine,' Alex replied firmly. 'And you're clearly not losing your touch. It's as heavy as ever.'

Layton gave a deep and throaty laugh. He was a large man, with a flop of dark hair that she suspected was kept chestnut-brown with the help of a special shampoo. He wore a flamboyant shirt with a pattern of black snakes on a cream background.

'That's my kind of gal,' he told her, before winking at her. 'Gives as good as she gets.' He glanced at her slyly. 'Royal suite, by the way. You know, for the after-party.'

135

Alex gave him what she hoped was a death stare. She had zero intention of going to one of his famed 'after-parties'. There were girls she had spoken to who had never recovered from the experience, yet they all knew they couldn't complain or report him because Layton would say they went of their own free will and knew what to expect.

'I'll leave you to it. I'm sure you have a lot of guests to entertain,' she said curtly.

'Suit yerself,' Layton muttered as he slid out of the booth. 'No sense of humour.'

Alex helped herself to the red wine because the only way she could afford to drink out here was if someone else was paying.

Her father was absolutely right not to like Layton Brooks. He'd taken against him during his playing days when he'd get sent off for rash challenges or violent conduct. She wished she could talk to her dad on the phone now and confirm that his prejudice had been well-founded, but despite her father now being at home, his speech was still limited and slurred.

Layton moved on to a younger female journalist and was soon stroking her bare shoulder. Alex pulled out her phone and pretended to be taking a selfie but instead pointed the camera at Layton and his latest attempted conquest. She took ten more photos that evening, and in each one he was leering over a different woman. She decided that would make a story of which her editor Sophie would approve.

Alex escaped soon after the unbearable speeches, in which each investor showered the other with praise and talked about wanting to create a unique space for shared experiences. It was just a bloody sports bar with ginormous TVs, she thought, serving over-priced burgers and triple-cooked chips. What was so special about it, other than the cost?

She made it back to her room, a little unsteady on her feet, and decided to write her review straight away, while it was all still fresh in her mind.

Best to strike while the iron is still plugged in, she thought as her fingers danced over the keyboard. *Lechy Layton won't know what's hit him.*

She made pointed references to the absence of his wife and children for someone who was now a self-styled 'family man', and attached the photos alongside her copy. It was sharper and more critical than her usual style. Sophie would be delighted, and yet she knew she was taking a risk. The PR blacklist was full of journalists who had broken the unwritten rule of never slagging off the host, but Alex had reached her limit and was committed to exposing the fakery.

Emboldened by the mixture of alcohol she'd consumed, her judgement clouded by anger and tiredness, she embraced the power of the written word. She was on a mission, a personal crusade to shine the cold light of truth on men like Layton Brooks and the saccharine, phony world of PR puff. Her mother might finally, perhaps, be proud of her if she ever read her column, which she didn't. Satisfied with her work, she pressed send.

Alex was relieved when she arrived back at her flat in London and shut the door behind her, craving her home comforts.

She allowed her shoulders to relax for the first time in twelve hours and poured herself a glass of wine, figuring she'd earned it after the PR trip had turned out to be such a dud.

Her phone rang – a number she didn't recognize – and she answered it in case it was the hospital and her dad had had another turn.

'Who the fuck do you think you are?' The voice on the other end was spitting the words at her. 'You fucking come over here at *my* expense, you drink *my* champagne, you accept *my* hospitality and then you fucking crucify me.'

Alex held the phone away, but she could still hear his voice shouting at her. Layton Brooks must have got her number from one of the PR team, and he was raging.

'You will fucking pay for this, I promise you,' he bellowed. 'You *bitch*. Now fuck off.'

He ended the call, and Alex stared at her phone. She hadn't said a word in response. Her hand was shaking, and her whole body shuddered with fear. The strength she had felt in writing her article, the bravery she thought she was displaying had disappeared in a flash.

She opened her app for *Rizz*, realizing that her piece must have been published straightaway and that Sophie had uncharacteristically not asked for any edits to it. It was not only live; it was the headline piece. She opened it and scrolled down to the comments, hoping for support and comfort.

'Oh my god,' she gasped, shocked at what she saw.

The comments were a stream of abusive messages, but they weren't directed at Layton Brooks: they were directed at her. He had put out a link to the article on X, but he had twisted it to make it sound as if she had written it in a fit of jealous rage.

This is what happens when you reject a woman's advances, he wrote. *Shame on @alexrobertswriter. She certainly ain't got no rizz.* He had added an emoji of a chocolate doughnut.

'The bastard,' she hissed.

Alex looked to the bottom at the notifications, and her eyes widened as she saw the number. There were hundreds of messages. She clicked on the bell and immediately regretted it. The torrent of abuse hit her like a jet wash. It was vicious, personal and physically threatening.

One of the conditions of working for *Rizz* was that she had to be active on social media, but this was surely beyond the pale. She called Ethan, but it went straight to voicemail. He must be working at a party. She needed to talk to her editor. Sophie would understand. She wrote a message to her, explaining what had happened and asking for permission to withdraw from X.

Don't be daft, came the terse reply. *This is the best reaction we've had to anything you've written. You should send Layton a bottle and a thank you letter.* She added three thumbs up and a crying-laughing face.

Alex sat back in her chair and held the phone at arm's length, not wanting to be near the poison it contained. This was not the response she had anticipated. She hoped a wave of women would come out in solidarity with her, having been subjected to his unwarranted advances, but instead she had invited upon herself a torrent of toxic masculinity. She read again the response from her editor and felt a deep sense of shame. It had been brewing, long before her friend Frankie had had a go at her, this feeling that she didn't like what she was being forced to become. She didn't want to be digging for dirt, to be mean about people or to help inflate the ego and the bank balance of men like Layton Brooks. This was not who she wanted to be.

CHAPTER EIGHTEEN

In the kitchen at Riverview Manor, Isobel felt the familiar bubble of rage in her chest. She knew she should do some breathing exercise or a roll-down or some such nonsense, but instead she started cursing under her breath and then getting louder and louder. This would work just as well, she figured.

She didn't often swear, but sometimes needs must, and since David had been home, she was finding it very difficult. When he was in hospital, part of her had yearned for her husband's presence in the family home, but part of her had enjoyed his absence. There were no extraneous noises to endure, no flinching at irrational shouting and no clearing up of unnecessary mess. She had missed the best of him, but the worst of him – she could happily do without that.

She stared through the window and saw the robin sitting on the garden wall next to where she'd positioned her husband for a while to give him some fresh air. David had lost weight in the weeks he had been in hospital, so she'd resolved to feed him up and get him out in the garden, as long as he was wrapped up warm enough. The bird cocked its head to one side and looked at her, as if judging her life choices.

'You can fuck off too,' she shouted through the glass.

Isobel's phone vibrated in her pocket. It was Kit ringing.

'Hey Mum, just checking in on things with Dad. How are you doing?'

Kit was the most attentive of her children and very much her favourite. She barely even bothered with hiding that view.

'That's sweet of you to call. He's getting there,' she lied. As she glanced outside, her husband looked a shell of his former self.

'Well, if you need any help, you just need to ask,' Kit promised her.

'Yup.' Isobel injected a burst of cheeriness in her voice to pretend she was coping just fine.

'Well, you sound in good spirits,' Kit said. 'And it'll be no time before he's back to normal.'

Isobel didn't respond. She wasn't sure what normal was any more. She didn't know whether she wanted 'normal'. She could hear the noise of another phone ringing at Kit's office.

'You'd better go, darling. You're a busy man,' she told him, not wanting to take up too much of his time.

'See you, Mum.' Kit ended the call.

Isobel went to bring David inside so that he could take his pills. Before he'd been discharged from the hospital, she'd had to have a difficult conversation about how things would have to be when he came home.

'I've been thinking this through, and there need to be rules.' She'd spoken slowly and calmly. 'If you have been prescribed pills to take, you take them. You do not shout at me if I remind you.'

David's eyes had widened, but he did not respond.

In her head, there were so many things she had wanted to

say. So much she thought she might get off her chest now, while he was not entirely incapable but at least captive.

One glance at David and she stopped in her tracks. He was just too . . . vulnerable. The way he had looked at her was pitiful. He needed her. Perhaps, for the first time ever, he was at her mercy, and she knew that it was her responsibility to care for him. Those were the vows she had taken all those years ago, the contract she had signed – and for all his faults, she wasn't about to turn her back on him now.

'You've got physio this afternoon,' Isobel reminded him when she'd settled him into his favourite chair.

'Try,' David said quietly, his forehead furrowed.

Isobel hoped that meant he would try, rather than score a try.

'I have to take Coco for her walk, but I'll be back soon,' she promised, feeling guilty for leaving him but knowing their beloved dog needed to get outside.

Coco trotted happily down the lane, sniffing every tree root and finally settling in for a long pee. At least she was content, and she was the perfect excuse to escape for a while. Isobel wondered whether she loved David purely out of habit or lack of imagination, and felt bad for questioning it when he was in such a bad way. She kicked a fallen branch in frustration.

'Dammit!' she squealed in pain. The branch was denser than she had expected and didn't budge. She leant down to lift it off the path and was struggling with the weight of it as Coco barked impatiently.

'Want some help with that?' Muriel called out, and Isobel

was relieved to see the familiar figure approaching, in her pale-purple anorak and a woolly hat, to help heave the branch out of the way.

'Haven't seen you for weeks and I've been worrying about you. How are things with David?'

'Fine,' mumbled Isobel. She really wasn't in the mood for a heart-to-heart and, much as she liked Muriel, it wasn't as if talking to her was going to change anything or help in any way.

They moved the branch together, and Isobel started to make her exit, trying to show she was busy, a woman on a mission with no time to stop and chat.

'Mind if I join you?' Muriel asked.

Honestly, the woman simply couldn't take a hint. Couldn't she see that Isobel didn't need or want company.

'That's not—' Isobel started to say.

'Lovely,' Muriel cut in, changing her own direction and falling in step with Isobel.

For fuck's sake, she thought, why couldn't people leave her alone? Then she berated herself for using the f-word again. Even if it wasn't out loud, it was still swearing. What was wrong with her today? She knew she'd been out of sorts ever since Christmas Eve.

'Penny for your thoughts.' Muriel smiled kindly.

Isobel kept her gaze straight ahead, searching for Coco in the undergrowth. Who said that these days? No one even carried coins any more, and if they did, it would cost a lot more than a penny to get Isobel to open up. This wasn't a bloody therapy session. Not that Isobel believed in therapy, of course. What a way to steal a living. Sitting there in a plush chair asking some poor bastard, 'What do you think?' instead of giving answers. It was completely fraudulent.

'It's good to talk,' Muriel added encouragingly.

Bloody hell, thought Isobel, *it's like she's swallowed a tea towel with trite phrases on it.* Next she'd be telling her to be kind to herself. Or to learn to dance in the rain or some other drivel that she'd read in a self-help book.

'Nothing.' Isobel shrugged. 'I am practising the art of thinking nothing.'

'Oh good!' Muriel was suddenly excited. 'You're taking up meditation. It's very good for you, you know. It has honestly changed my life to do a little meditating every morning. Got to concentrate on your breathing as well and then start to feel your body, every bit of it from the tips of your toes all the way up your legs into your body and right through your arms to the ends of your little fingers.'

Muriel waggled her fingers in front of her in demonstration, but Isobel ignored her and walked on, concentrating on each toe, moving through to her foot, and feeling grateful that she didn't have plantar fasciitis. Everyone else seemed to be getting it at her age, and it sounded awful.

'I'll get it,' Muriel said cheerfully when Coco squatted in the leaves, clearly about to do another poo. 'You concentrate on your breathing.'

Isobel started to get the poo bag out of her pocket.

'Don't worry!' Muriel produced her own bag with a flourish. 'I always come prepared.'

'But you don't have a dog.' Isobel was horrified. Why on

earth would you bring a poo bag on a walk if you didn't have a dog of your own? Was Muriel some kind of vigilante foot-path officer who cleared the debris, whatever it was and whoever had caused it?

'Oh, really it's not a bother. I quite often pick up things that might ruin a walk for anyone else. I think of it as a service to the community,' Muriel explained.

They walked on, thankfully in silence, before Muriel spotted a bin and got rid of the bag.

'The snowdrops are coming out,' Muriel said, pointing at a clump of white bells dangling downwards from green stalks.

'Won't be long before we get the crocuses,' Isobel found herself saying out loud, admiring the woods she loved so much for the way they changed throughout the seasons.

Coco busied herself chasing squirrels that shot up trees as soon as they heard her coming. She stood at the base of the trunk, looking hopefully upwards in case they dropped back down.

'It's been hard.' Isobel sighed.

'I know,' said Muriel, leaving a silence which Isobel then thought she ought to fill. She kept her gaze forward, looking out for Coco and appreciating the more frequent clusters of snowdrops.

'I know I should be pleased that David is home, but it's so difficult looking after him, and I don't know if . . .' She paused and dug out a tissue to blow her nose. 'I don't know if he'll make a full recovery.'

'I know,' Muriel said again. 'You feel helpless. Rudderless. Useless. And totally, utterly alone.'

'That's it.' Isobel stopped and turned to look at Muriel, surprised. 'That's exactly it. How do you know?'

'Oh, I know more than you might think. My Bill got cancer when he was only fifty, and he deteriorated so fast that neither of us could really adjust or even comprehend it. We didn't have time to even have one last holiday together.'

Her voice cracked a bit, and Isobel strained to hear as Muriel walked with her head down and coughed before she continued.

'So I do. I do know,' Muriel said. 'Why do you think I've joined every committee in Hampshire and do endless classes? I've got to keep busy to fill the time. Otherwise, I'd be alone with my thoughts, and that is a prospect that does not appeal. If I can fall into bed exhausted, then it's another day I've got through.'

She didn't say it with any bitterness or self-pity. It was just a statement of fact. This was an example of survival of the toughest test of all: grief.

They had turned back towards home on the circular route that was Coco's favourite.

'I told the robin to eff off, so I know I'm not coping.'

Isobel thought it rude to use the word in full. Muriel always made her feel as if she should be on her best behaviour.

'Oh, that is funny.' Muriel chuckled. 'We all need to let off steam, and I'm sure the robin has heard worse than being told to fuck off. I wouldn't worry about it.'

They had reached Riverview Manor, and Isobel opened the back door to let Coco back in.

'Do you want a coffee?' She invited Muriel in and actually meant it.

'Another time.' Muriel shook her head with a smile and continued her walk back to the village, raising a hand as she went.

For the first time in years, since well before David was ill or the children left home, Isobel felt her chest release a little and her heart have space to beat. Somehow, she would get through this.

CHAPTER NINETEEN

Alex stared at the raindrops running down her windowpane in West London. They mirrored her grey mood for the past week. She stirred her coffee and stood at the kitchen counter to check on her emails on her laptop. She had deleted her account on X and felt cleansed in part, as if she had climbed out of a cesspool.

The top email was from her editor. It would no doubt be an instruction to write more articles and to reactivate her social media. She hovered the mouse over it and double-clicked to open it.

There was no *Dear Alex* or enquiry after her well-being. Instead the email began:

> I'm sorry not to be able to see you in person to deliver the news that we are making adjustments here at *Rizz* and will be making increased use of the power of technology to enhance our offering.

Alex swallowed hard, knowing what was coming.

> AI allows us the ability to search the internet across all accounts all over the world at every hour of day and night. The advantage for us is that we don't need to ask you to work long, anti-social hours. The disadvantage for you is that we won't need as large a staff and, as such, we won't be requiring regular contributions from you at this time.

For all her distaste at what her job had become, Alex hadn't wanted to lose it completely. It would have been hard enough not to have a regular income if it was just the mortgage on the flat to cover, but now, with the farm to worry about as well, she couldn't afford not to work.

She read on, wondering if Sophie might offer some support in the face of the online abuse Alex was getting, but there was no mention of anything like that.

She slammed the laptop shut.

Well, that's one decision made for me, she thought, feeling shocked and then a little sick. Then anger started to rise in her. It was a shitty job that made her feel dirty and, after the lack of support from Sophie, she wouldn't work for them in the future even if they begged her.

She looked at her phone, wondering who to call for support, and saw that her mother had sent a message on the family WhatsApp group.

> Dad has another physio appointment today but is doing well so far.

There were no more details.

Alex should probably drive down to visit, although that would mean explaining her lack of employment and why she could suddenly take time off.

There was no notice to serve out, no way of contesting the decision; after all, her job security with *Rizz* had been non-existent, given she was a freelancer. It was effectively a zero-hours contract, even though she had been contributing regularly for them up to now. As long as she wrote content the editor liked and followed the rules of engagement, she would benefit from the glamorous work trips and the regular commissions. As soon as she didn't, she was ejected. She knew she had burnt all her bridges with the article in Dubai. No other publication would touch her while she was engulfed in the ensuing social media fallout. She was effectively cancelled as a journalist.

Her chest started to feel tighter, as if she couldn't breathe. It was a bubble of panic, and she didn't have the tools to burst it. She would have to find another job if she was going to afford to pay Gwen and Owen Odd Job. She would need much more if she was going to make much-needed changes to the farm.

Then there were the bills. Oh god, the bills. Gwen had shown her the most urgent ones when she'd been down there. Alex hadn't yet got around to paying them, but she knew it had to be done. For someone who'd always prided themselves on being free, Alex now felt the crushing weight of multiple responsibilities.

The oil for the Aga had tripled in price since Christmas, while electricity and gas prices had also gone through the roof. Then there was the feed for the sheep, the fuel for the quad bike, the vaccination costs and the vet's charges. At this rate, she'd need to start working shifts at the pub to earn enough to eat.

Yesterday, she had been Alex the journalist. She had easy answers to the first question anyone asked. What do I do? Oh, I work for an online magazine. You may not have heard of it. *Rizz*. Oh, you have? Yes, that story was mine. Yes, that one too. I know, it lost him his job and his marriage but, you know, that's not my fault, it's his.

Today, she had no way of describing herself, and everything felt up in the air and so uncertain. If someone asked her what she did, she had no idea. There was no subtitle to her biog. She was just another person in London living beyond their means.

It was too early to call Ethan. He'd sent her a message at two in the morning, so there was no way he'd be up yet after last night's event.

She ran through a list of names of other people she could call. Her school and university friends would be busy either with children or high-pressure jobs. They didn't have time for her morning crisis. Her brothers were both at work, her mother wouldn't want to talk, and her father wasn't yet up to proper conversation.

She drained her coffee and switched on the TV, where Deirdre, the agony aunt, was asking the audience to call in about their problems.

'It can be anything at all that's bothering you. Your relationship, your job, your children, your parents,' she said in a breathy voice.

'If only you could help, Deirdre.' Alex sighed at the TV. She knew that it was all too easy to sit down and be trapped by the screen, waiting for the newspaper reviews, the horoscopes, the healthy recipe and the awkward interview with an actor or a child who could mimic animal noises. Then it would be three hours later and suddenly lunchtime. Daytime TV was a bottomless pit, into which she did not want to fall, no matter how terrible she already felt. She pointed the remote at the screen and switched it off.

Ordinarily in life, she had been happier alone than with someone else. The closest she'd ever got to getting married was with Dan, who she'd dated in her late twenties. He was handsome and fun, which impressed her mother, and had a golf handicap of three, which impressed her father. Her parents thought she was lucky to have nabbed him. They made it all too clear she was punching above her weight. He agreed, which rang alarm bells.

'Ask me again in a year,' she'd said when he'd proposed to her after a few too many beers.

It wasn't a yes, but it wasn't a no either; the timing just felt too soon, and Alex couldn't imagine being tied down. A few months later, her answer had changed to a definite no after she'd walked in on him in bed with a woman she had thought was a friend. After that, she'd never let anyone else get close enough to be able to hurt or humiliate her.

Alex had often struggled with understanding men, except Ethan. Even with her own brothers, she wondered how she could be so different. Hugh was arrogant and deluded, while Kit was organized and efficient, but he was so ambitious he would step over a body in the road if it got him to the other side ahead of his work colleagues. Perhaps, if she was honest with herself, she could do with a little drop of Kit's ambition and a splash of Hugh's optimism.

She needed to go for a walk, clear her head and work out what to do next.

She decided to do a loop on the river towpath, down to

Chiswick Bridge and back on the south side, where it was wild and wooded along the edge of Barnes, and all the way up to Hammersmith Bridge, coming back past the pubs and the boathouses.

She smiled at the dogs she saw along the way – some running with their owners, some following bicycles, most walking haphazardly along the path. There was even one little Pomeranian in a buggy, its furry face poking out of the front.

She kept the pace quick enough to make herself feel as if she was taking exercise but not so fast that she was out of breath or sweating. She listened to her favourite Eighties music playlist to cheer her up and paced along to the rhythm.

Bouncing down the steps at the end of the ancient suspension bridge, she turned back to the west. A figure ahead raised a hand at her and waved. Alex looked around to see if someone behind was waving back and then raised her hand tentatively, not wanting to wave back at a complete stranger but also not wanting to be rude.

As Alex got closer, the face became clearer, and she couldn't believe it was her. She'd thought about her after the Christmas party and had even managed to find her on Instagram, but she'd decided it was too full on to start following her. It was a woman in a navy-blue donkey jacket, a faded baseball cap on her head with *NY* on the front.

'Wanna see my latest trick?' Mandy grinned, her smile accentuating her strong jawline and prominent cheekbones.

'Magic Mandy!' Alex beamed. Her shitty morning had just got a whole lot better. 'This is a nice surprise. How's the party circuit?'

'Not bad,' Mandy replied. 'Just on my way to a very nice house over there.' She gestured behind her, towards the row of huge river-facing houses on Chiswick Mall. 'They've got fifty children round for a four-year-old's birthday. It's going to be hard to keep them concentrating at that age, but they love balloons that turn into dachshunds so I'm going to do that. No point wasting the good stuff on an audience that won't appreciate it.'

Mandy laughed, and Alex noticed that her eyes scrunched up and little dimples appeared on her cheeks. She was startlingly attractive. Alex thought she must never be short of admirers. She started to write an article in her head about magicians being the new rock stars of the party scene.

'Pulling in the crowds.' That could be the headline, she thought, before she remembered she didn't have a job any more.

'What was that?' asked Mandy.

Dammit. She'd said the headline out loud.

'Nothing.' Alex recovered quickly. 'Just realized I left my pullover at home.'

'Pullover?' Mandy teased. 'Who even says pullover these days?'

'Oh god, I'm sorry. My mother has always said pullover rather than jumper, which could apply to a horse, or sweater, which she thinks is dangerously American. Pullover can be nothing but what it is, and it seems a quaintly British word.' Alex found herself babbling again, and she wasn't sure what power Mandy had over her to make her blither like such an idiot.

'I shouldn't tease you for trying to keep alive the ancient British quirks.' Mandy smiled lazily. 'We've got to hang on to our traditions, like having a magician at a children's party, otherwise I'd be out of a job.'

'Believe me, you wouldn't want that,' Alex said, feeling a pang in her chest.

They had paused outside the Blue Anchor. Alex contemplated asking Mandy if she wanted to go for a bite to eat but remembered she had the party to get to.

Mandy broke the awkwardness by producing a pack of cards from the inside of her jacket pocket. No wonder it was an oversized jacket. There must be loads of things stashed in there.

She motioned Alex towards one of the wooden tables outside the pub.

'Pick a card, any card.' Mandy held them out.

Walkers stopped momentarily, and suddenly a crowd started to assemble around them. Alex immediately grew uncomfortable, not enjoying being the centre of attention.

'Eyes on me.' Mandy clearly didn't mind. She wasn't going to be thrown by the gathering masses.

Alex reached for a card that was sticking out a bit before changing her mind and going for the card two to the right of it. It was the seven of hearts.

'Right. Remember that card. Or in fact, even better . . .' Mandy produced a marker pen from her pocket. 'Write your name on it. Anywhere you like, but I don't want any doubt about it. This is your card.'

Mandy turned her head away so that she could no longer

see Alex's hands and told her to put the card back into the pack. She asked one of the watching strangers to cut the pack again, while Alex cringed slightly at the attention they were drawing. Mandy shuffled the deck twice. She cut the pack in half and showed the picture side of the top half.

'Is this your card?' It was seven of clubs.

Alex shook her head.

'Close though, eh?'

She shuffled the pack again, cut it in half and showed her the bottom card. It was the seven of diamonds. Alex shook her head. The crowd sighed collectively in frustration.

Mandy had one more chance. She shuffled quickly and displayed yet another seven, this time the seven of spades. The spectators moved on with their walk.

'Bad luck,' Alex said softly, careful to find a tone that wouldn't come across as patronizing.

'Oh, don't feel sorry for me.' Mandy smiled. 'Happens all the time. I've got to go.'

'How was Christmas?' Alex changed the subject, trying to prolong the encounter.

'Pretty shitty. My girlfriend dumped me. You?'

'Well, my dad nearly died, my mum got fed up with me, and then just last week, I've been sacked.'

Mandy's face filled with concern; she reached a hand out to Alex's arm. 'God, I'm sorry. That really does sound awful. You win our pity party, hands down. I wish I could stay with you and talk it through but' – she looked at her watch again – 'dammit, I really do have to go to this gathering of spoilt children.'

She leant in towards Alex and gave her a hug before disappearing down the path.

Alex walked on into Chiswick, stopping off for a coffee. When she pulled her phone out of her pocket to pay, a playing card came out with it.

It was the seven of hearts – the card with her name scrawled on it. As she turned it over between her fingers, she saw Mandy's name and number on the other side in black marker pen.

How on earth had she done that?

Now that's a good trick. Next time I have a party, consider yourself booked.

As Alex walked home, she thought about her ideal of being free from responsibility and what it might have cost her. She didn't want to share her life with someone she didn't trust, someone who bored her or sought to control her. Ethan was the only man whose company she could tolerate for longer than an hour. Maybe her dad was right, and they could ignore the obvious problem, just get married and fit in, but Alex knew that wouldn't make her happy.

She might not know what she was looking for, but she hoped she'd recognize it when she saw it, being drawn to it like a masterpiece hanging in a gallery. She had seen a lot of paintings. Sometimes they blurred into similar images with the same brushstrokes and colours. She closed her eyes and found it impossible to recreate, accurately, the facial features of a lover she had genuinely liked. She disappointed herself.

For all that she had resisted responsibility, she had never intended to deny herself love.

She wanted a chance to reinvent herself.

She imagined Magic Mandy turning a bunch of paper flowers into a dolphin.

'Ta-dah!'

The kids' faces staring at her in wonder, asking her breathlessly how she had done it.

That's what she needed. Someone to wave a magic wand over her and transform her into a new person. She wanted to care about something, someone, anything.

That was it. That was the plan. She needed a change of scene, and Monmouthshire was the place she could start again. She needed to get back to Wales.

CHAPTER TWENTY

Alex bumped her suitcase down the stairs and dragged it to her car. She shed the three coats she was wearing and shoved them in the boot along with the case. Warm, practical clothes. That's what she had packed. No evening wear required, no fancy shoes, and just one smart daytime outfit with a decent coat, in case she took up the invitation to the races that she had accepted before she got fired from *Rizz*. The details still lingered in her emails.

She headed out to the motorway, towards her parents' house, unsure of whether she was fleeing or being evicted. Fuelled by adrenalin, her heart raced while her brain fizzed with conflicting thoughts.

She found her father sitting in a chair with his legs raised. Her mother had bought it in a January sale and had it delivered. David only had to press a button on a remote control to activate the panel below his calves and raise them into the air.

'That's great, Dad.' Alex grinned as she settled down on the sofa beside him.

He said slowly, 'Magic chair,' and gave her a lopsided smile.

'As you're here, I'm going to pop to the shops,' Isobel called, clearly grateful that she could leave Alex on supervision duty. 'Anything you need? Other than oat milk, of course.'

'Thanks, Mum. A small one will do. I'm only staying a

night,' Alex replied, surprised that her mother had mentioned non-dairy milk without a hint of irony.

Coco hopped on the sofa beside her and nuzzled her small, solid body to Alex, who obligingly stroked her.

'Where . . . are . . . you . . . going?' David asked Alex, the gaps between each word reflecting the effort he was making. It was difficult for her to see her dad still struggling with the simplest sentence. She'd taken his quick wit and his mobility for granted for so long, and now he was stuck.

'I'm heading down to Wales. To Tir Glas Farm. Ethan says it means blue land in Welsh, and it's full of sheep, which will be lambing soon. I don't know the first thing about any of it, but I want to learn.'

Her father was staring out of the window towards the river at the bottom of the garden, and for a moment Alex thought she had lost his attention.

'Messy,' David said, turning his head back towards her.

Alex smiled. She agreed with him. 'Lots of blood – you know I'm no good at that. I don't think I'm cut out to be a farmer, and I still don't know why I have been left this place. It doesn't make any sense.'

Her father raised his hand slowly, and he seemed to be pointing towards the bookcase. The shelves held a range of sports biographies, detective novels and travel guides. Her parents had always promised to spend their retirement travelling the world but, when it came to it, there was always a reason to stay at home and they'd never got around to it. On the top shelf was a picture of her parents at a fancy ball. Her father looked dashing in black tie, and her mother was radiant in a long silk gown. Alex figured it probably wasn't real silk, as her mother would have thought that impractical and too expensive. Behind them, his head turned slightly towards the camera, was a tall, good-looking man the same age as her father. He seemed to be looking at Isobel rather than at the camera.

'Is it a book you want, Dad?' she checked, trying to anticipate his needs.

He shook his head and kept his finger pointed at the bookcase. 'Will,' he said.

'That's right,' Alex replied. 'I was left it in a will. I know you've always said "where there's a will, there's a way" but I am up against it if I'm going to find the right way.'

Her father finally lowered his hand. 'Will,' he said again before closing his eyes, and within seconds, he was gently snoring.

Alex stood up from the sofa, taking care not to disturb Coco, and went to the bookcase to inspect the photo more closely. She had never before noticed the man in the background, and yet there he was, clear as anything, the same face she had seen on the wall in the Black Prince pub. It was William Griffiths.

So he definitely knew her parents, but they must have lost touch over the years. He had not been at their silver wedding anniversary party or either of her brother's weddings. His name had never been mentioned to her knowledge, but maybe he had just been busy with the farm. She could understand that happening with all that was going on there. What she couldn't work out was why, of all the people in the world, he had chosen to leave his farm to her.

'They didn't have oat so I got almond milk. Is that all right?' Isobel asked when she arrived back with the shopping.

'That's fine, Mum. Thanks for trying.'

'And there was a Clubcard offer on soup, so I've got plenty of that. It should be easy for your father to eat; he'll just have to hold a spoon in his left hand, as his right side is still weak,' her mother was saying.

'Good idea, Mum,' Alex agreed on autopilot.

With her father still asleep, Alex walked to the kitchen island with the framed photo in her hand. Something told her to take this slowly.

Her mum was busy packing the shopping away, so Alex flicked on the kettle. 'Coffee?' she suggested, and her mother nodded a yes.

Cupboards and fridge restocked, her mother placed the empty bag for life by the back door so that she wouldn't forget to put it back in the car boot. Alex knew there was no way she would pay for a new bag, not now they were thirty pence each.

Alex handed her mother her coffee and took a deep breath. 'Mum, we need to talk.' She beckoned for her to sit down at the kitchen table, but Isobel preferred to stay standing. Seemingly ready, as ever, to escape if need be.

'So . . . um . . .' Alex hesitated.

'Don't start a sentence with "so",' Isobel cut in. 'Everyone does it nowadays. Even the politicians. Especially the politicians. You're a journalist. You should know about correct grammar.'

Alex grimaced. Her mother had an uncanny ability to make her feel like she was still twelve years old.

'Yeah, well, about that.' Alex knew she hadn't started that sentence correctly either, but she was going to barrel on and not be deterred by her mother's prickliness. 'I'm technically not any more.'

'Not what?'

'Not a journalist.' She sipped her coffee, hoping it would fortify her. 'I lost my job.'

'Why?' Isobel asked her daughter. 'What did you do? This time . . .'

Of course, it had to be her fault. Alex sighed. It couldn't possibly be her boss, whom Isobel had met once at a birthday party in the first year of Alex working at *Rizz*. She was trying to impress, to make friends and keep them, so she'd asked Sophie to the party. Sophie had dazzled everyone, including her mother.

'I didn't actually do anything, other than write a piece that caused a bit of a reaction.' She looked down at her coffee cup, unwilling to meet her mother's eye. 'I didn't like what people were saying to me. Men in particular. So I shut down all my social media accounts, and that's not allowed if you work for *Rizz*.'

'Well, I don't see anything wrong with that. You can happily live without social media in your life. I have never had it, and it's not done me any harm.'

'I know, Mum, but your job didn't depend on it,' Alex said. 'Not that Sophie admitted it was about that. She just said they'd be using AI more in the future and that I won't get regular work any more.'

'Well, I think they'll miss you more than you'll miss them,' Isobel said defiantly.

165

Alex was taken aback. She hadn't expected such strong support from her mother. It was the sort of thing her father might have said, but not Isobel.

'Thanks, Mum.' Alex smiled, grateful for the backing.

'And what is it they're going to use instead?'

'Artificial intelligence,' she answered her mother. 'Chatbots. That sort of thing. It's taking over.'

AI could be employed to cover the bit of the job Alex had most enjoyed – the digging around on obscure feeds, checking tags on photos and finding information that wasn't intended to be public. When Alex had first started at *Rizz*, she hadn't believed she was getting paid to snoop on Instagram when her friends did that for nothing. AI could work all night ingesting, assessing, summarizing content from every social media app in the world. It could search across tens of thousands, if not millions of accounts, and if it was fed the right information about what to look for and which names to monitor, it could create an endless stream of articles.

'I've always told you the internet would be the undoing of us all. You'll have to find a job that can't be done by robots. A real job.' Her mother nodded sagely.

That took Alex's mind back to the farm, where she increasingly wanted to be. There was nothing to stop her now, so she had to make a go of it. She fiddled with the photo frame that was still in her hands. She needed to address the mystery of William Griffiths.

'Is this William Griffiths?' she asked, turning the photo so that Isobel could see it clearly and pointing to the man in the background.

Isobel gave a cursory glance to the photograph, then looked down at the floor. Alex could see she was preparing to be evasive, to dodge her questions once more.

'Mum?'

The noise made Isobel jolt. 'No need to shout. I can hear you perfectly well.'

'Not always,' Alex muttered under her breath.

'What? Oh never mind.' Isobel looked again at the photo, deciding it was best to play along. 'Yes, of course it is. Rugby club reunion dinner, 1988.'

'So you knew him too?' Alex asked, hoping that this was an acceptable use of 'so' at the beginning of a sentence.

Isobel moved to start unloading the dishwasher, turning her back on Alex. 'Not very well.' She clattered knives and forks into the cutlery drawer and stacked plates together. 'He was going to be your godfather, and then it didn't work out.'

It was all she seemed prepared to say, but Alex wasn't going to give up that easily. 'Why do you think this man, yours and Dad's rugby playing friend, chose me? Of all the people in the world, why leave his farm to me when I never knew him?'

Isobel kept her back to her daughter. Alex could see how tense her body was.

'I have no idea.' She sighed, then continued, 'Your father and he had a massive row about something – probably polit- ics or religion or money. It was one of the big three. Just before you were born, it was. They didn't speak again.'

Alex contemplated this information. She remembered her father's face when she'd shown him the letter from the solicitors. He'd been looking unwell before that, and she hoped that bringing up an old friend he'd fallen out with hadn't been the final straw that brought on his stroke. Maybe William had been making a point from beyond the grave – that he was the bigger man, he was the one who had forgiven, even if in doing so he had made sure that David could never, ever forget him.

'What time are you leaving?' Isobel asked.

'Keen as ever to get rid of me, Mum?' The change of subject didn't go unnoticed.

'No, Alexandra. Don't be defensive. That's not what I meant. It's just that the physio is coming today and the speech therapist tomorrow, so I don't want Dad to get tired out.' She added, 'When you're running the farm, you'll understand how annoying it is when people just turn up expecting to be fed.'

'Ow.' Alex rubbed her arm as if she had been injured. 'That stung. I'll get out of your hair today, if it's that much trouble.'

Alex put her empty coffee cup on the table a little too hard, and headed upstairs to gather her things together, the familiar frustration bubbling up. Her mother could be so understanding and supportive and then in an instant make her feel as if she was an unwelcome guest. It was discombobulating at best.

Alex had never planned to stay for long, but she had intended to be supportive to her mother and to help her father get back on his feet. The path to hell is paved with good intentions and all that.

If she wasn't wanted here, she might as well get on the

road. She could be in Monmouthshire before it got dark, rather than hang around getting on her mother's nerves.

She kissed her father and Coco goodbye.

'Farm,' said her father. 'Sheep.'

'Yes, Dad, that's right. I'm going to the sheep farm. Wish me luck!'

'Good . . . luck,' he said, gazing after her, a sadness in his eyes.

CHAPTER TWENTY-ONE

As she bumped her way carefully down the long, potholed drive at dusk, Alex looked out across the land and smiled. The space, the light, the clean air would restore her, she was sure of it.

She caught her breath. Lambing had begun. In the field closest to the farm on the left, she could see the first few lambs now, pulling hard at their mother's teats. The brave ones were playing together and paused briefly to look at the car before getting back to head-butting each other and leaping sideways. Stopping the car, she opened her windows and turned off the music so that she could hear them. The ewes were deep and throaty with the timbre of a tuba, the lambs light and airy like a piccolo, or insistently banging like a timpani drum. It sounded like an orchestra tuning up, each one hitting a different note, none of them in time or in harmony, but it still sounded like music to her.

One lamb decided to climb onto a bale of hay and leap off the other side. The others followed like . . . well, like sheep. As if performing for her approval, the leading lamb sprang suddenly sideways and then jumped off the ground on all fours. Alex laughed as all the others copied him.

As she parked up, Jiffy ran out of the open door, barking loudly in warning. As soon as he realized it was her, he looked slightly embarrassed and wagged his tail apologetically as he ran to greet her.

'Yes, my boy, hello to you too,' she said. 'I know, I know, I've come home. Yes, I have.'

Alex said it without thinking. London was a long way away now. For all its energy and variety, its history and beauty, it was often noisy and crowded. And even with all those people jostling for space, it could be the loneliest place in the world. This place, the farm she had unthinkingly and reflexively called home, had already filled a hole in her heart that she didn't know she had. Home. Such a small word that signified so much.

Gwen met her at the back door, took her bag out of her hands and swept her into the kitchen.

'I've put the kettle on,' she said warmly. 'Come on in and relax. You've had a long drive, and I've got lots to tell you.'

For once, Alex found being fussed over comforting rather than annoying. She was grateful to be with someone who didn't immediately tell her she looked tired or give a scathing assessment of her outfit.

'I lost my job,' Alex told her, coming straight out with it.

'Well, that's their loss,' Gwen said immediately. 'They clearly didn't value your talent. We'll put you to work soon enough, don't you worry. There's a million things to do, but all in good time. You get yourself settled in first of all.'

'I've missed this place,' Alex muttered.

'Hiraeth.' Gwen looked at her with a strange intensity.

'What?'

'Hiraeth,' Gwen said again. 'It doesn't have a direct English translation, but to me it means a longing for a place that feels like home.'

Alex said the word to herself and let it play on her lips, digesting its meaning.

Gwen put a cup of tea in front of her before announcing she was heading off to feed the ewes and check on the newest lambs.

'I've put a boiler suit on the hook out there for you, for when you come out,' Gwen said. 'It'll protect those nice clothes.'

Alex sipped the strong tea and looked around the kitchen with its array of mismatched crockery.

A shaft of low sunlight broke through the window and hit the kitchen table. Everything was damaged in one way or another. A burnt frying pan, chipped mugs, saucepans with handles that were wonky or insides that were scratched. She wasn't one for cooking, but even she could see they needed replacing.

She rinsed her mug out and put it on the draining board, stepped into the dark-blue boiler suit, slipped on a pair of wellies and pulled a beanie hat over her hair. Jiffy followed her out of the back door, keeping close to her ankles as if herding her.

'Now you look the part!' Gwen beamed proudly, beckoning her to the barn. 'Come and see.'

Alex peered over the gate and saw two newborn lambs lying in the straw, their bodies still wet and slimy.

'I'll give her a hand.' Gwen opened the gate carefully.

She lifted the lambs closer to the ewe, encouraging her to clean them. They started to wriggle, and in seconds they were suckling at their mother's teats.

'That's amazing,' Alex said.

'It's nature. It's part of farm life, but I never lose that sense of wonder. It's what makes it special.'

The big barn was divided into pens made of metal gates. They were about seven foot by four, and each one was laid with straw. Two buckets stood in the corner of every pen, one for water and one for food. Some of the lambs lay down next to their mothers; the ones who were hungry cried out for attention and stood on wobbly legs, wagging their tails as they found their mother's milk and sucked vigorously.

Alex stood, entranced by it all, listening to their calls and taking in the details. The black splodges on the faces of the lambs, their off-white, almost beige bodies, and the spindly legs, some of them black, some white. She couldn't believe these two in the closest pen had been born just that morning.

The last of the daylight rushed by as Alex ventured further into the farmyard, inspecting the abandoned machinery and taking photos on her phone. She could reinvent herself here and, as a first step, start a brand-new social media account. Farmer Al, that's what she'd call herself. She could post photos with funny taglines like *long-lost plough* and *look at the lift I got home last night*. It would distract her from the thought that the place looked like a scrapyard and, although it would take a while to build a profile, she would have different sorts of followers to before. That would be a good thing. A whole new identity: authentic, practical and kind.

She grabbed a brush and swept straw, mud and sheep droppings into neat piles, creating a clear path leading to the barn. She helped Gwen put feed onto the trailer behind the quad bike and followed her into the fields. The sheep came running, the heavily pregnant ones waddling. In the field closest to the house, the ewes ate quickly as their lambs played together. The bleating broke out when they'd finished, mothers and lambs identifying each other and reconnecting.

'They always find each other again,' Gwen explained.

An intense Border collie appeared from over the brow of the hill, followed by a man in a blue fleece and baggy trousers.

'A'right Owen?' Gwen waved.

'Right.' He nodded curtly in response.

The dog did a circle round Alex, and she reached a hand forward, trying to make friends. The Border collie ignored her and ran back to its master.

'Owen Odd Job?' she asked Gwen.

'The one and only. He's been brilliant helping us with the lambing, and his cousin has been lending a hand too.'

At dusk, she and Gwen, with Jiffy's help, herded the heavily pregnant ewes into the safety of the barn.

'Right. That's a good day's work. You must be exhausted. Let's get you back inside and feed you up,' Gwen insisted.

'I'll come in a second.'

Alex paused. She wanted a moment on her own to drink in the new landscape. She walked towards the big field behind the farm, the one that offered a view towards the setting sun. Jiffy stayed by her side, clearly smitten with her. She moved carefully into the middle of the field so that she was surrounded by open space. She breathed in deeply, filling her lungs with air that was sweet and pure. Better than a vitamin pill or a ginger shot. She felt as if she had plugged into the human equivalent of an electric charger.

As she walked back to the farmhouse with Jiffy at her heels, a murmuration of birds swooped and dived above them, creating waves of black in the sky, talking to each other. She watched them change direction, forming a different outline each time, as if mimicking the shape of various countries. Yes, we can do the outline of the Isle of Wight; now watch us change to Madagascar and now Italy. They created wave after wave, moving as one across a sky that was ripening pink. She marvelled at their skill. No collisions, no mistakes, not one of them getting left behind.

It was mesmerizing. A ballet of birds, all of them anticipating the next move and working as a highly trained, beautifully choreographed team.

'That's the secret,' Alex said out loud in a moment of clarity. 'I can't do any of this on my own. We need a team.'

Jiffy wagged his tail and trotted ahead, leading the way back to the farmhouse.

Gwen had made a large pan of chowder, thick and creamy and full of goodness. They shared hunks of homemade bread, spread with butter. There was soft cheese made from sheep's milk.

'Stick a bit of chutney on that and it really brings out the flavour,' Gwen recommended, passing it across the table.

'I'm not sure I like sheep's milk,' Alex started to say, trying to be polite, before Gwen raised her hand. She wasn't having any of this nonsense.

'You can have all the oat milk you like back in London – or

even at Rhys's pub, because he has to keep his customers happy – but if you're going to farm this land, you need to accept that milk and cheese come from cows, goats and sheep, and you need people to be happy to drink it or eat it.'

Alex reluctantly accepted the bread with a thick layer of cheese. She sniffed it suspiciously and then licked it. Gwen watched her as a mother would watch a seven-year-old child, trying to coax them to eat their dinner.

'Go on,' she said encouragingly. 'Give it a try.'

Alex finally succumbed and took a big bite. 'Fair play. That is delicious.'

Gwen smiled. There was nothing she liked more than providing people with food they enjoyed. She had done it for years for William, and she was happy enough to look after Alex for as long as required. She tried not to think about what might happen long-term and had put off talking about any arrangements.

'I saw these birds earlier on,' Alex told her. 'They were chirruping away and moving en masse, sweeping across the sky, making waves up and down, side to side. I couldn't believe they didn't crash into each other, not once.'

'That'll be the starlings,' Gwen said. 'They're super-fast when they get going. Over forty miles an hour, easy. They group together like that for warmth and for safety, so the peregrine falcon can't pick them off.'

'Working as a team?' Alex enquired.

'That's it. Best way,' Gwen said as she ladled another helping of soup into Alex's bowl. 'Now you eat some more of this,

177

because you're going to need your strength. There's a mountain of paperwork for you to get through.'

Alex swallowed solemnly. She had to find a way to repay Gwen for her kindness, but she couldn't even begin to do that unless she could get the farm back on track.

CHAPTER TWENTY-TWO

By eight o'clock, her tummy full and her body spent, Alex settled into the armchair by the fire. Her head kept lolling forward and, as she jerked it back, she made an involuntary snort like a piglet.

'Sorry,' she mumbled to Gwen. 'I don't know what's wrong with me.'

'I've made up a room for you,' Gwen replied. 'There's an electric heater in there if you need it, and I've taken your bag up. Go up now if you like. You've had a long day.'

'What about the lambing?' Alex asked.

'Don't you worry about that. Not on your first night. That's my job, and Owen and his cousin are on standby to help out if need be.'

Alex was too tired to argue. She nodded her thanks and headed upstairs. Gwen noticed that Jiffy followed her upstairs. He'd stayed close to Alex ever since she had arrived, which was odd. He was never usually like that with someone he barely knew. Alex was grateful for his company, any fear of strange noises or ghostly apparitions abated by having a guard dog, albeit a very cuddly one, by her side.

Alex had just enough energy to clean her teeth and pull on her pyjamas. She got into bed with Jiffy curled up at her feet, and she was asleep as soon as her head hit the pillow.

Gwen stayed downstairs, fully dressed. She had an alarm by her side and would get up every hour on the hour to inspect the ewes. Mostly, they got on with it on their own and she could just watch, checking they didn't lie on a newborn. Once in a while, there would be a breech birth or a larger lamb that needed help coming out. Occasionally, one would be born dead, and she didn't want Alex to see that. It was heartbreaking enough for the most experienced farmers to deal with, let alone someone who knew nothing at all. She tried to hide her disappointment that William hadn't chosen someone who understood farming.

As the sun rose the next morning, Alex's dreams were alarmingly real. It felt like someone was licking her face and nudging her chin. She put out her hand to push them away but was met with fur. She opened her eyes and found a face next to hers, gazing at her with devotion, desperate for her to get up and share the day with him.

'Jiffy,' she groaned. 'What time is it?'

She grabbed her phone from the bedside table. It might not be useful for anything else out here, but the clock still worked.

She had slept for nearly eleven hours.

'Good god,' she said to Jiffy. 'I need a pee, and you must be desperate.'

Gwen was making coffee when she got downstairs.

'Jiffy stayed with you all night, did he? He must like you.'

Alex nodded.

'What do you want to eat?' Gwen asked. 'I don't have the

range of breakfast options that you'd get with Rhys, but I can do eggs, toast or cereal.'

Despite the delicious meal last night, Alex ate as if she'd not been fed for a week. She was ravenous and figured it must be the country air.

Heading out to the farmyard, Gwen took her to see the lambs that had been born in the night.

'Twelve of them in one night?' Alex was shocked.

'Oh, that's standard. They were all pretty good, to be honest. Just two needed a little help.'

'So what do you do?'

'Well, I help, obviously.' Gwen laughed.

'They don't mind the interference? It doesn't ruin – you know – the smell of the lamb?'

'Not if you're quick. In fact, they seem to like knowing I'm there if they need me. It's the same as with humans – there's no point offering help unless they're ready to accept it.'

'Well, just for the sake of clarity' – Alex smiled – 'I will take any help you're willing to give me.'

She leant on the gate and watched Gwen quietly and confidently check over the lambs. A few of them cried insistently, like a baby wailing, begging their mothers for milk.

'You have to be careful lifting them,' Gwen explained as she leant into one of the makeshift pens and moved a lamb towards its mother's teats. 'Their ribs are very delicate when they're this young, so it's best to pick them up by the scruff of the neck, like you would with a puppy. Or by the front legs, like this. See?'

She lifted a lamb that was barely longer than her forearm, its back legs dangling downwards.

'How quickly are they up on their feet?' Alex was intrigued by this influx of new life.

'Within minutes. They'd have to be able to move fast in the wild, otherwise they'd get eaten as soon as they were born. Here, they're safe enough, and we'll keep them in the pens for a day or two before we put them outside.'

'The cold doesn't bother them?' Alex asked. Although the days were getting longer, there could still be an early morning frost and a sharp chill in the air.

'They're pretty tough, this lot. Heavy rain or snow might be a problem, but they can cope with the cold.' Gwen nodded with satisfaction as she finished her inspection. 'They all seem fine. Come out and see the ones that were born a few days ago.' She beckoned to Alex to follow her.

Twenty, maybe thirty ewes with two lambs each ranged over the field. The lambs looked sturdy and confident, a couple gently head-butting each other and another leaping sideways as if drunk.

'Do they always have twins?'

'That's the ideal,' Gwen told her. 'They have two teats, so two lambs can feed at the same time. If they have triplets, or even – and this is rare but not impossible – quadruplets, then I have to find a foster mother. The ones that have had a single or maybe had a stillbirth, they'll take on another. Have to be quick, mind, so I can rub the afterbirth from their real lamb on the adopted one. Then they know the smell and will take to it quicker.'

The ewes heard a noise in the distance and ran to the far

end, gathering in a large group, frightened by something. Alex watched them move, mystified and enthralled. They soon settled down again, the ewes biting hungrily at the grass, the lambs tugging at their teats as if pulling a bell rope.

'We should head down to the pub later,' Gwen suggested. 'I need Rhys to help file the accounts, and you can check your email. He'll be thrilled to see you. He's talked of nothing but you and Ethan since you left.'

Alex enjoyed the sense that there were people here who cared about her and who seemed to like her.

She left Gwen to her chores and walked to the boundary of the farm where it adjoined the gallops of the racehorse trainer next door. He was clearly not the friendly, supportive type and was going to be more difficult to win over. There was a gate in the centre of the hedge that was bound up with a double chain and lock. The padlock was covered in rust. She leant on the gate and surveyed the curve of the hillside. She heard the thundering of hooves from her right, and suddenly a horse was galloping by, making her instinctively jump backwards. The horse reacted to the movement and swerved off a straight line, its rider struggling to stay on board.

Behind the horse she saw the elegant figure of Digby the lurcher sprinting to keep up.

She waited until the horse and rider came back down the hill, eager to apologize and to check they were OK.

'I'm so sorry!' she shouted when she saw the outline of the horse, now glistening with sweat. 'Didn't mean to cause a fright.'

The man on board glared at her and, as he got closer, he

shouted at her. 'I could've broken my bloody neck thanks to you. Idiot.'

He turned his horse's head to the left and headed down towards a collection of red-brick buildings.

'Charming.' Alex rolled her eyes to Jiffy as they headed back to the farmhouse.

The Black Prince was busier than it had been in January when they arrived that afternoon. There was jump racing on the TV, and a group of men with beers in hand were following the action closely. A few walkers were taking a lunch break from hiking, and Rhys was busy behind the bar, asking them about themselves and offering food that would boost their energy.

He beamed at Alex as she walked in, coming from behind his counter to envelop her in a huge hug. 'The London lass returns,' he joked. 'On your own this time?'

'Afraid so,' she replied. 'Ethan sends his love. He also told me to tell you he's reading Philip Larkin on your recommendation.'

'Is that so?' Rhys grinned.

'I'm impressed you talked him into reading poetry. I've never known him take an interest before.'

Gwen joined them. 'Rhys can be very persuasive.' She chuckled. 'I'll have a lime and soda if it's OK. Alex?'

Alex held up her hand to signify that she'd have the same.

'We need your help when you have a moment,' Gwen added.

'Happy to serve in every way. Drinks first.' Rhys headed back to the bar.

As the men in the corner shouted at the television, cheering on horses they'd backed and banging the table at those that lost, Alex chatted with Rhys.

'This is just the warm-up,' he explained, pointing at the TV. 'The big week is coming up. Not long now until Cheltenham.'

'The Cheltenham Festival?'

'The very one.'

'I've got an invitation to that,' Alex told him. 'It was sent when I was still working for *Rizz*.'

'Was?' Rhys queried.

'Yeah. Not any more. Lost my job. Gwen says it's their loss and her gain. I think she was being kind. Anyway, I replied so early that I've just seen they've emailed me a badge and a car park pass.'

'Which day?' asked Rhys.

Alex checked her emails on the phone, searching for the details. 'The Tuesday.'

'Champion Hurdle day.' Rhys nodded, impressed. 'That's the best day of all.'

'If you say so. I don't know much about racing. I was only going because celebs always behave badly when they have too much to drink.'

'Well, all you need to know is that those tickets are like gold dust. Dickon's due to have a runner in one of the handicaps that day, so I'll be there too.'

Alex had been thinking it was all too much hassle and would be pointless without a story to write, but if Rhys was going to be there, it might be fun, and that's what she felt she needed right now.

185

'One of the few places that doesn't take half a day to get to,' Rhys assured her.

While she had signal on her phone, Alex sent a couple of messages: one to Ethan to check in on him, and another to Magic Mandy, just to say hello.

Gwen had set up in the corner table, using Rhys's laptop. She let out a sudden squeal. 'I've got an email from something called N, S and I Customer Services,' she shouted. 'It says I've won a prize.' She stared at the screen in disbelief before worry set in. 'Is it a scram?'

Alex took their drinks to the table. 'It's called a scam,' she told Gwen. She didn't want to be cynical, but experience had taught her not to trust emails that claimed to be offering a prize.

She looked at the screen, her eyebrows furrowed.

Gwen, you've just won! it read. *Thanks to your premium bonds, you've won a prize. Ready to check the amount? Have your holder's number to hand and click below.*

'Do you have premium bonds?' she asked Gwen.

'Yes. William left me some.'

'Well, this looks genuine. Do you have the number?'

Gwen fumbled with her phone. 'I've written it down here somewhere. Hang on a second. Yes, here it is.'

Together they entered the number to be greeted with what looked like fireworks exploding.

You have won £500! it said.

Gwen leant back in her chair. 'Well I never.' She sighed, her face breaking into a smile. 'I've never won anything in my life. Who'd have thought it? What do I do now?'

'Nothing. It'll go straight into your account.' Alex chinked her glass of lime and soda on Gwen's.

'You've always been a winner, Gwennie.' Rhys joined them. 'Good old William has left you something that will keep on giving you a thrill. You might not win every month, but that's the fun of it. Even better when you don't have to pay tax on it.'

Tax . . . A word that could invoke immediate nausea. Alex came back down to earth with a crash.

She had only ever dealt with simple self-assessment tax returns, needing to claim the obvious expenses like her laptop and recording equipment, stationery costs, printing costs, the occasional train ticket, but it added up to very little.

She looked at the pile of papers Gwen had brought with her. There were columns of numbers detailing various costs. They came to more than the value of sales. She puffed out her cheeks as the shock hit her. She was going to need someone to help on the business side. She had no idea how to manage all this.

'It costs about seventy pounds to keep a lamb,' Gwen explained. 'And if we're lucky we'll get upwards of one hundred and fifty when we sell them. The trouble is, a lot of them didn't make it last year.'

Alex looked at the screen. Thousands of pounds had gone out on 'disposal'. She pointed at the word. 'What does that mean?' she asked.

Gwen winced. 'That's what it costs to get rid of the dead ones. The ewes picked up a virus called EAE. Enzootic abortion. Most of the lambs were born dead, and those that survived birth were so weak they barely lived a few days. It was truly awful.'

Rhys put a protective arm around her shoulder.

'I've never seen William so upset.' Gwen shook her head. 'Every night it was like a crime scene. One dead lamb after another, and the ewes were so distressed. They knew what was going on.' She frowned at the memory. 'Then you have to pay to get someone to take the dead lambs away and incinerate them,' she said. 'It's like a never-ending nightmare.'

Alex felt tears prick in her eyes. It sounded awful, and another reason she didn't know if she was cut out for this.

'To be honest, I think the stress of it all got to William and made him ill. His flock was disappearing, but it wasn't just about the number or the money. He hated seeing them in distress.' She sighed heavily. 'Their pain was his pain – do you know what I mean?'

Alex nodded and leant closer to hear what Gwen was saying.

'I could see he was not well,' she went on, clearing her throat, 'but he wouldn't go to the doctor. I begged him to let me take him but he waved me away. Jiffy knew. He sat for hours by William's side, his head on his knee, just staring up at him. It was awful.'

Gwen took a sip of her drink, bending her head towards the table and almost whispering as she shared the memory she had tried so hard to suppress. 'When the pain got too much to bear, he took the tranquillizers that the vet had left for emergency use.'

Rhys was still standing over her, and she turned into him,

burying her face in his side. He hugged her tight and kissed the top of her head.

'It's OK,' he murmured. 'You did everything you could.'

Alex wiped her sleeve across her eyes. She didn't even know this man, and yet she felt his loss so keenly. She could see how much William had meant to her new friends.

'I should have dragged him to the medical centre,' Gwen mumbled.

'I know, I know,' Rhys said, over and over again.

He held her tight until her shoulders stopped shaking. Customers at the bar looked over, wondering why they weren't getting served, but Rhys stayed put. Friends before business – that was his rule. Alex silently got up and slid behind the bar, serving the two men whose pint glasses had been drained.

As she finished pulling the second pint, Rhys reappeared.

'Thanks, love.' He patted her gently on the arm.

Alex walked back to Gwen's table and sat down, waiting to speak till Gwen gave her a shaky smile. She didn't want to drag Gwen back to upsetting thoughts, but she needed to know about the illness that had killed so many sheep.

'How do you stop it happening?' Alex pointed at the figures for disposal.

'Well, we thought it must have come from some new ewes we'd bought and introduced to the flock. They were carrying a bacteria and it spread to the others. So all of them have been double vaccinated now – although that's expensive, mind.' Gwen pointed to another column of numbers. 'But it seems to have done the trick and, as you can see, the lambs are bonny and healthy this time around.'

'What's the tax situation?' Alex asked.

'Well. Whenever you make a profit on a farm, you put it into improvements, so there's never much to pay. The trouble is you haven't made a profit. It's a pretty heavy loss,' Gwen explained.

Alex was dazed by this new information.

'You've got to find a way to make the farm break even at the very least. Otherwise you may as well be pouring cash into those troughs for the sheep to eat.'

A big cheer erupted from the group of men watching the racing. At least someone was making some money, with their bets clearly coming in.

Alex leant back on her chair and stared at the ceiling. She had some serious thinking to do. She needed to turn things around, for Gwen's sake as well as her own.

Alex would need to invest. Not just money but her time, her effort and – biggest of all – her heart. If she was going to gamble, she might as well go all in.

CHAPTER TWENTY-THREE

Alex's body clock started to adjust to farming hours over the next couple of weeks, helped by the living alarm that was Jiffy. Every morning, as she opened her eyes, there he was, his nose in her face, his eyes imploring her to get up. He sometimes gently licked her chin or her ear, but mainly he just stared at her, his face inches away from hers. When she headed to the bathroom, he bounded off the bed, tail wagging, waiting to lead her down the stairs. He was well and truly attached to her, as if he had always known her. He was guiding her, encouraging her, welcoming her to this bizarre new life where no job was ever complete. Alex tried to fight the feeling of being overwhelmed by the sheer scale of problems that needed to be solved.

When she had been writing, Alex could research, write and file a story all in one day. She could make a list and tick things off, working through them until they were done. Here at the farm, the list seemed endless, and things could never be fully ticked off.

She made her morning coffee and looked through the cracked windowpane to the field beyond the ramshackle garden. In that one view alone, there were twenty things to put on the to-do list, involving repairing, painting, cleaning, trimming, weeding and a host of other jobs she had never done. She rubbed the side of her temple and tried to ward off the tension headache that was on its way. She thought of Mandy and her magic tricks. She could do with someone who could make things disappear, and she wondered if Mandy had read the latest text she'd sent her.

Even through the closed window, Alex could hear the music of the growing number of lambs. Just watching them now, cavorting in the field, was enough to lift her spirits. They were the funniest, daftest animals she'd ever come across. She didn't want to leave them or the farm. London seemed like another planet and, apart from Wi-Fi and the convenience of shops, there wasn't much else she missed about it. This place consumed her energy, her thoughts and her time.

For now, she would have to park the to-do list, because today, she needed to glam up and put on a show. She sighed. Where once she would have enjoyed dressing up for a day out at the races, now she just wanted to pull on her boiler suit and get on with what needed to be done.

She looked at the invitation to the Cheltenham Festival and had a word with herself.

'Get a grip, Roberts. This is a golden ticket to one of the sporting highlights of the year.' She looked down at Jiffy, who had his head on one side and one rear leg in the air. He was staring back at her, waiting for her next move. 'I know. I know. I've got to get changed. It'll be fun when I get there, won't it boy?'

Jiffy wagged his tail in encouragement.

She'd messaged Ethan last night to ask his advice on what to wear.

Tweed, darling! he'd replied.

That's all? Alex had expected slightly more detail.

Tweed is all you need to know. Doesn't matter if it's a coat, trousers, a hat or a shirt. As long as it's tweed, you'll pass.

The one smart coat she had packed was a navy herringbone. That would have to do. On the shelf above the downstairs loo, she had found an old trilby of William's. When it was brushed up, it would look pretty good, and if she wore it on an angle, she could get away with it being a fashion statement.

Her invitation was to a box. It promised minor celebrities saying stupid things. In her previous life, it would have given her valuable copy for *Rizz*. Now, it was just a place to get free drink and food, but at least it would be a change of scene.

Rhys had offered her a lift as he was driving the horsebox for Dickon, who had a runner in one of the later races.

'What time do you need me?' Alex had asked.

'Seven o'clock at Dickon's yard,' Rhys replied. 'Don't be late.'

After nearly causing him an accident the day she arrived, she was wary of the grumpy trainer, but Rhys had assured her that it would be fine.

'I'd be happy to have the company,' he implored her. 'Please come with us.'

She had swallowed hard and fixed on a friendly smile as she arrived in the yard, prompt at ten to seven and dressed for her day at the races.

She kept her distance as Dickon was leading a gleaming horse out of its stable towards the ramp of a horsebox. His hands were gentle on the rope, and he stayed at the horse's shoulder, persuading him forward rather than tugging. He was clearly better with horses than he was with people.

'Thatta boy, Skirry. There you go.' He encouraged the horse to take two giant leaps up the ramp and into the body of the ancient truck. She watched Dickon crawl under the bar and tie up the rope. Then he took what looked like a lump of mud out of his pocket and rubbed it on the horse's front legs, just above the top line of the hoof.

She noticed that the horse was trembling. Dickon stroked the front of his head and whispered something in his ear. He hopped down from the side door and flipped up the ramp.

Dickon clocked her arrival and nodded his head curtly. His face was set as a grim mask. She wondered if Rhys had even told him she was coming, and she nodded back awkwardly. It didn't feel right to speak to someone who clearly hated her and couldn't even muster a hello.

'Ah, well done, Alex!' Rhys beamed as he strode across the yard, a Thermos mug in his hand. 'You made it.'

He looked at his watch. 'And bang on time as requested.'

'It helps that Jiffy has decided to be my personal alarm clock.' Alex grinned.

'I hear he's got very attached to you,' Rhys said. 'Gwen says it's like he's always known you. Anyway, you hop in the front, and I'll just make sure Dickon's all set. He won't say much, just to warn you. He's always nervous as hell before a race. Best to let him be, I'd say.' He put his finger to his lips to signify that she shouldn't talk.

Well, this promised to be a jolly old ride to the races. A trainer who was so wound up she couldn't even speak to him, and a horse in the back who was quivering like a jelly.

They headed out of the stable yard and turned left onto the single-track road. The hill known locally as the Lump rose steeply to the right as they made their way up and over into the next valley. No cars came in the opposite direction, which was lucky as Alex had no idea how they would pass on such a narrow lane. They stopped in the village five miles away to pick up a young boy from outside the post office. Rhys explained to her that Dickon didn't have any staff, so he'd had to rope in a lad who had some experience with cows to assist today.

'He's not been around horses much, but it's the same sort of thing.' Rhys winked at her. His positivity knew no bounds, perhaps to counteract the deadening weight of Dickon's pre-race mood.

They arrived at the racecourse at 9.30 a.m. One after another, gleaming lorries rolled in, their sides emblazoned with bright paint detailing the name of the trainer as they unshipped six or seven horses. She noticed the leather interior and the plush seating area of the other horseboxes, more like giant motorhomes than animal transportation. Most of them, she reckoned, must have cost more than a two-bedroom house in Monmouth. Dickon's battered and bruised lorry looked like an ancient shipwreck alongside super-yachts.

Dickon clambered into the back of the truck and untied the horse, which was trembling as badly as ever. He stroked him along his neck and led him down the ramp towards the stables. Dickon didn't look at anyone; he didn't speak to anyone; his focus was solely on the horse.

'Hope they're still serving in the canteen.' Rhys turned to Alex. 'It's the best breakfast in the country.'

They walked up the hill towards the public entrance, and studied the people waiting for the gates to open. Ethan had been right. Everywhere she turned, she saw tweed. Tweed suits, coats, jackets, scarves, even tweed shirts. She had no idea there could be so many varieties of tweed.

Racing was something her father had always enjoyed watching on the TV, and she knew enough to understand how to read the numbers that signified recent runs and the letters that stood for Course or Distance win. She bought a racecard and opened it to examine the runners.

She heard a loud laugh in the crowd just behind her, and she felt as if a sudden chill had passed like a wave through her body. She didn't want to look up in case he saw her, but it was too late. She felt a large, looming presence, closer to her than was comfortable.

'All right, luv? You found any dead certs yet?'

She recoiled from the hand placed without invitation on her arm. It was Layton Brooks, the ex-footballer she'd savaged in the article for *Rizz* and who had then threatened her on the phone. She froze and kept her eyes on her race-card.

Thankfully, he did not seem to recognize her under William's old hat.

He wore a garish yellow and pink checked woollen suit with a large trilby and a pair of sunglasses. He looked like that character who used to run onto kids' TV and fall over. What was his name? *Mr Blobby – that's it.*

Alex tried to take a step backwards, but the white fence behind her prevented a retreat. She glanced up to search past him for a friendly face, anyone who could save her from Layton's lechy attentions.

He leant into her side, exhaling stale breath on her face and peered at her racecard. Keen to get rid of him, she decided to come up with a tip.

'This one will definitely win.' Alex put on a strong Welsh accent, jabbing her finger at a name in the second race. 'Number twenty. I know the trainer.'

Her father had tried to teach her the lingo. Now was the chance to put that learning into action.

'The Skirrid, eh? Why's it got a string of duck eggs next to its name?' Layton asked, making reference to the recent form which read 0000 for four unplaced efforts in a row.

Alex kept her eyes down on the racecard, to avoid looking directly at him in case it prompted any recognition during this hideous encounter.

'Oh, don't you worry about that, see.' She imitated Gwen's singsong voice. 'Poor love has been running all season over the wrong trip and on ground that doesn't suit him, just to get a decent handicap mark.' She hoped she'd got the terminology right. Pulling her hat a little lower over her eyes, she carried on, 'You'd better get down to the bookies while the odds are so good.'

Layton Brooks opened up his lurid jacket to reveal a wad of cash in his inside pocket. 'Lucky I've come prepared.' He smirked.

He walked away to get to the front of the line with the

gates now opened, shouting as he went, 'Don't worry! I'll find you again when we win so we can celebrate in style.'

Alex heaved a sigh of relief as she watched the yellow and pink checks move away into the distance. Mr Blobby rolling through the waves of tweed. At least she'd be able to see him a mile off and avoid any further unwanted run-ins.

The Skirrid was 100–1 and would be 200–1 by the time anyone saw him trembling like a jelly. She felt satisfied in giving him a tip that had no chance of coming in.

There was no sign of Rhys, so she made her way into the main grandstand, following signs to the hospitality area to which she had been invited. She helped herself to a coffee and a Danish pastry and studied her racecard.

The Skirrid's race had a huge number of runners. There were a couple of sentences below each horse and a star rating out of five to sum up its chances. The Skirrid had only one star and the review read:

Brave choice to enter from a trainer searching for his first Cheltenham Festival winner.

Brave. She'd used that adjective many times in articles she'd written and, she remembered fondly, it was the first thing Mandy had said about the children's awful singing on Christmas Eve. They were being polite about something that was clearly futile. Poor Dickon. He was on a hiding to nothing. She checked her phone to see that Mandy had replied to her message from last night. Alex took a selfie, showing her racing attire as best she could. Almost immediately, she felt her phone buzz and looked at the screen. Mandy had sent a laughing emoji.

Determined to make the most of her day out, Alex joined in the roar of the crowd as the first race got under way, and then rushed round to the winners' enclosure in time to see the victorious horse led back into the amphitheatre of joy. The winning jockey stood up in his stirrups to salute the crowd. A huge group were slapping each other's backs – there must have been twenty of them surrounding the horse, all wearing matching red and white scarves.

'And congratulations to the Spend Your Kids' Inheritance Syndicate!' the Tannoy echoed. They waved their scarves in the air and cheered.

Watching the races, Alex wondered whether she was a natural front runner, or was she just someone who plugged along at the back, chasing the pack as she tried to keep up?

She headed behind the weighing room, from where the jockeys had emerged towards the pre-parade ring. This would be the place the runners for the next race would gather. It had open-faced stalls with buckets of water at their edges.

'You winning, cariad?'

She had picked up enough of the lingo to know that 'cariad' meant 'darling' in Welsh. The friendly lilt hit her with the warmth of a roaring log fire. It was Rhys, on the inside of the rails closest to where she was standing.

'I'm having fun,' Alex replied. 'I saw a huge group of people celebrating in the winners' enclosure. How many people can own a horse?' she added, curious about the rules.

'As many as you want. Loads of people do it in partnerships these days.'

Rhys was clearly distracted, checking his watch, so although

Alex wanted to ask more, she would look it up instead. This wasn't the time to be bothering him with questions.

'This is it,' he exhaled. 'Time for The Skirrid to do his thing. Dickon's round the back here, sucking on a cigarette. He'd given up for a year, but that's all up in smoke now, if you know what I mean.'

Alex peered through the arch and caught sight of the rake-like figure pacing up and down, his right hand moving back and forth from his mouth, clouds floating above his face.

'Why does he even do it if it causes him this much agony?' she wondered aloud.

'That's a very good question.' Rhys contemplated the conundrum of a racehorse trainer who hated racing. 'I'm not sure he even knows. Just how it's always been, I guess. His father did it, his grandfather, his grandfather's father before him. Dickon never had a choice. It was his destiny. For a while, he was good at it. He had plenty of winners, a happy marriage and sweet kids—'

'What?' Alex interrupted. 'Dickon was married?'

Rhys nodded.

Alex had assumed Dickon was a loner who hated company and couldn't bear the sight of anyone apart from his dog, because that was certainly the impression he'd given.

'Abigail.' Rhys moved closer and whispered, because racing was a world awash with gossip, but he was not one for spreading it. 'He adored her. Would do anything for her and worshipped those kids, but then she upped and left with Bertie O'Reilly, the jockey who had ridden all their winners. Bertie has an inexplicable magnetism. I don't get it myself, but women fall over themselves to get near him, and even Abigail wasn't immune. I credited her with more intelligence or at least better taste, but I was wrong. That was that. Dickon fell apart, and he's never been the same since.'

Alex saw Dickon grind his latest cigarette butt into the grass and walk towards the weighing room. His skin was grey in colour, his dark hair lank, and he walked like a man older than his years, his legs slightly bowed and his back hunched. He nodded towards Rhys but didn't acknowledge Alex.

'I'd better go and check the horse is on his way,' Rhys told her. 'That boy from the village isn't the sharpest in the pencil case.'

As Rhys headed up the hill towards the stables, Alex felt ashamed for judging Dickon Jones from afar and making assumptions based on false information. It was perhaps a bad habit she'd picked up from *Rizz*, where she'd learned to see the worst in people. As for Dickon, being bitter and angry out of choice was one thing, but having bitterness and anger forced upon him because of a broken heart was a completely different matter.

Now she wanted his horse to win, even if it meant Layton bloody Brooks collecting on his bet.

Alex couldn't fathom what it was that distinguished one horse from another, other than colour. Most of those walking past her were brown, so that didn't help. They all looked fit and athletic and were beautifully turned out with shiny fur.

'Lovely coat,' the lady next to Alex said.

'Oh thank you.' She smiled, smoothing her herringbone

sleeve and grateful for the compliment, because she had made an effort to fit in.

'Not you.' The lady chuckled. 'Number five. Positively gleaming.'

Coat, that was it. Not fur. She remembered from that long-ago day as a girl at Newbury Races with her father. She nodded back at the lady, whose red lipstick looked strangely out of place on an otherwise make-up-free face.

'Yes. He does look well. No sweating between the legs,' Alex said confidently. 'I'm told that's a no-no at the races.'

She knew if she'd said that to her mates in London, or even down at the Black Prince pub, there would have been raucous laughter, but the woman next to her fixed her with a steely glare.

'Spot on.' She spoke in a clipped manner, finishing off her words with precision. 'Any sweating is a straight red line in my book.'

Alex spotted Dickon striding towards a stall with a saddle and a number cloth tucked under his arm. He scanned the remaining horses in the pre-parade ring and looked increasingly flustered. He checked his watch and stared at his phone.

'I've seen them all except number twenty,' said the lady who knew everything. She stuck her pen into the fur band around her head. 'Not that it really matters. The Skirrid has got no chance.'

'What if he doesn't make it in time?' Alex asked.

'Can't run. If he's not in the parade ring by the time stated, then the stewards will take a view.'

No wonder Dickon looked worried. The last horse in the

saddling boxes was having the final touches applied by its trainer, then being calmly led towards the parade ring. There was a clatter of hooves and – through the brick arch on the far side – Alex spotted Rhys running alongside a horse that was dripping with sweat, the boy from the village nowhere to be seen.

Rhys wrestled with an armband with the number twenty on it, trying to fit it over his bulging biceps. The sweating horse had straw in its tail and a piece sticking out of its forelock. Dickon threw on the thin grey numnah, the number cloth and the saddle. He was still tightening the girths when a man started shouting from the tunnel to the parade ring.

'You've got two minutes, Jones. Get a shift on.'

'Go! Go!' Dickon patted the horse on the backside to encourage it forward, and it leapt out of the saddling stall.

Rhys jogged alongside The Skirrid, his tiger tattoo stretched into roaring mode as his arms strained to keep a grip on the alarmed horse.

There had been no time for a brush or a calming pat as Alex had seen all the other trainers do with their horses. The Skirrid was a wreck compared to the other runners. Rhys ran into the paddock as the bell was going for the jockeys to be mounted. As Alex got to the rail, she saw a short, round-faced jockey make his way towards The Skirrid. He barely looked old enough to be out of school. Dickon ran in behind them, just in time to offer a hand in which the jockey placed his left foot. He leapt into the saddle before Dickon had any time to issue instructions.

As they passed Alex in the crowd, she saw the jockey lean

forward and heard him hiss to Rhys, 'Your trainer is a fecking joke. Can't even be on time at Cheltenham, for feck's sake. It's a shambles. No wonder his Mrs upped and left.'

Rhys kept his eyes forward and stroked The Skirrid with his spare hand, not acknowledging the comment. 'It's all OK. You're going to be just fine. You do your best, Skirry.' He removed the prominent wisp of straw from Skirry's forelock and tried to calm him.

The horse's eyes were out on stalks, and he was quivering. 'What's the name mean?' the jockey asked.

'The Skirrid?' Rhys looked up at him for the first time. 'It's a mountain near us. It's the land that shakes. They say the soil is holy, so we rubbed a bit on his feet this morning.'

'Well, if he so much as wobbles over a fence early on, I'm pulling up. I'm not risking my life for that useless Dickon Jones, Cheltenham Festival or not.' The jockey shook his head.

Rhys gave The Skirrid one last pat and unclipped the rope. The horse cantered away to join the rest of the field at the start. Alex had followed as best she could and was waiting for Rhys as he got back to the rails.

'I had to run all the way back to the stables,' he huffed. 'The boy had disappeared so I just slung a bridle on the poor horse and jogged him down as fast as I could. What a bloody nightmare. At least the owner's not here. Poor old Mr Thomas is on his deathbed. It would have definitely killed him if he'd witnessed this chaos.'

Rhys put his huge arms on the rail in front of him, and sank his head into them. Alex stood awkwardly next to him, giving him a rub on the shoulder, and turned to scan the crowds, looking for Dickon. Finally, she spotted him, halfway up the chute back to the parade ring, pacing up and down with a cigarette in his hand.

Alex's ears pricked up at the commentator mentioning Bertie O'Reilly. He was riding the favourite in this race, hoping to add to his record-breaking tally of winners at Cheltenham. Alex didn't know much about racing, but even she had heard of him. He was a multiple champion jockey renowned for his uncompromising, ruthless will to win. He was rare in the racing world for having an appeal that reached far beyond the sport, and his name was often in the gossip columns thanks to his unusual good looks, his love of fast cars and his rapidly rotating carousel of girlfriends. He had taken advantage of a ban for overuse of the whip to enjoy a skiing holiday and a stint of rally car driving. Bertie O'Reilly was admired and respected but not widely liked, so it must have stung for Dickon's wife to leave him for a man like that.

Alex looked across at the big screen and saw The Skirrid at the back of the group, swishing his tail and spinning round in circles.

'He looks upset.' She turned to Rhys.

'He's highly strung at the best of times,' he replied. 'And he hates things being done in a rush.'

The starter climbed the ladder, next to a long length of orange tape that stretched across the course. He called them forward, shouting at them all the while to take it steady, and then he released the lever.

The tape sprung upwards, making a loud twanging noise.

All the other horses leapt forward into a gallop. The Skirrid whipped round, turning so fast that his jockey had no chance of staying in the saddle. In one tenth of a second, he went from sitting on the horse's back to sitting on his backside in the turf, not looking amused.

'That's revenge.' Alex laughed. 'Serves him right.'

Rhys gasped and ran past her, dipping under the rail and running towards the racecourse. Security guards shouted at him, but he pointed at the band on his arm.

'It's OK,' he bellowed back. 'My one is loose.' An already shambolic day was taking a further turn.

CHAPTER TWENTY-FOUR

The Skirrid galloped free, following the runners and soaring over the first hurdle. Within a quarter of a mile, he had caught up with the field and continued to jump like a buck. As the field turned away from the grandstands, where Rhys had hoped he would make a dash for the stables and he might be able to catch him, The Skirrid followed the other horses and continued to race. He jumped every hurdle and seemed to speed up, looping round the entire field as they turned for home. He produced a spurt of speed to power over the last hurdle and up the hill in glorious isolation.

The crowd cheered ironically as he passed the post in front. With no jockey on board, it meant nothing, but Alex wondered if the horse himself had wanted to win against all predictions.

As for the race behind, which did count, the favourite, ridden by Bertie O'Reilly, and another horse with a jockey in red colours, were fighting out the finish. The red colours seemed about to pass when Bertie O'Reilly brandished his whip in his right hand and, as he lifted it, reached his arm out a little wider. As the whip came down, it struck the other horse in the face.

'Surely that's not allowed?' Alex exclaimed to a stranger now standing next to her. 'He's hit the other horse over the head!'

The shock of the strike was enough to throw the other horse off its stride. It lost all momentum, and Bertie O'Reilly pushed on to win by half a length. The punters who had backed the favourite threw their hats in the air in celebration. As far as they were concerned, their hero had delivered; whether it was by foul means or fair, he had won them their money.

Alex saw The Skirrid had slowed to a trot at the very top of the hill. The white fencing blocked his path, forcing him to stop. Rhys stretched out his big arms to prevent him galloping back down the hill. Dickon ran over to him and gently walked forward to grab the reins. He took off the saddle and handed it to Rhys, pointing him back towards the weighing room.

Even from a distance, Alex could see that any air that might have been in Dickon's body had been expelled, like a balloon being deflated.

Intercepting Rhys as he walked back with the saddle, Alex checked that the horse was all right.

'He's fine. Completely unscathed, and I think he quite enjoyed it without a jockey on board to mess around with him. Dickon, though – he's another matter. The poor man is broken.'

The journey here in uncomfortable silence had been bad enough. Alex wondered how much worse it could be on the way home. She told Rhys what had happened between the two horses fighting out the finish and asked him if striking another horse over the head was allowed.

'The stewards will have a look, no doubt,' Rhys explained.

'But O'Reilly will argue it was accidental. He's a sly bastard, and he's got a way with words.'

Bertie O'Reilly rode into the winners' enclosure, waving both his arms to the appreciative crowd. Alex noticed a slender woman with a long blonde ponytail greet the victorious jockey as he dismounted. He took her cheeks in his hands and kissed her on the lips.

'Marking his territory,' Alex said to herself. She had seen these signs of ownership before.

Out on the racecourse, Dickon was pouring cold buckets of water over The Skirrid's steaming body, glancing up at the big screen at the wrong moment to see his ex-wife and his former jockey in the midst of their very public display of affection. It was the final blow to a man already down on the canvas. His horse might have stopped trembling, but now Dickon couldn't stop his own body going into shock. He trudged towards the stables alongside The Skirrid, who had no notion of what had gone wrong.

'You got a fright, poor lad, didn't you?' He soothed the horse with a low murmur. 'Still ran your heart out, Skirry. Still ran your heart out.'

Alex headed back to the hospitality area high up in the grandstand to thank her host before heading back to the stables. On her way back down, the lift doors opened, and the brightly attired Mr Blobby-like figure of Layton Brooks emerged. He had a gang of male friends around him who were laughing at something he'd said. She tried to make herself invisible, but he was heading straight towards her.

She pulled her hat over her eyes and stared at the ground.

She held her breath and prayed for them to walk on past her. They were still laughing, and she heard one of them telling Layton what a legend he was. She slid into the lift and exhaled, leaning on the back wall for support. There was one other woman in there already. The doors started to slide across but, just before they met, they opened again. Someone had pressed the button outside.

Layton's frame filled the doorway.

'C'mon, Layton mate!' she could hear his friend shouting.

He started to back away, patting his jacket where the money was stored. He pointed at her and sneered. 'You owe me one, tipster girl, and don't think I don't know who you are. I never forget a face.'

He lurched sideways, and Alex jabbed at the close doors button. He was clearly pissed.

'Layton, the champagne's on ice!'

He turned his head and moved half a step away from the lift doors.

'Luckily for me, I had a saver on Bertie O'Reilly. The man's a born winner.'

He flicked a finger in her direction and muttered something incomprehensible as he staggered back towards the bar.

'Is he a friend of yours?' The woman in the lift arched an eyebrow.

Alex shook her head as she leant against the back wall for support.

She was breathing heavily by the time she got to the stables to meet Rhys and Dickon. She clambered into the front seat without saying a word.

Her working life had been full of social engagements, and she was used to being entertained, but now it left her feeling strangely hollow. Now that she didn't have a column to write, what was the point of hanging about with strangers, hoping they did something stupid? If she was to go racing again, she'd rather be involved and be useful.

The battered horsebox rumbled out of the racecourse with its sad and sorry load. Alex was sure The Skirrid would get another chance to shine but, as for Dickon, that seemed much less certain.

CHAPTER TWENTY-FIVE

Alex scrambled upstairs to change out of her racing attire when she arrived back at Tir Glas, desperate to get back to what she already regarded as normal clothes.

'Poor man.' Gwen sighed when Alex filled her in on what had happened. 'He's a strange one, that Dickon Jones, but he's due a change of luck, surely. And then that bastard Bertie O'Reilly kissing Abigail like that in front of everyone. I saw it on the telly. That was unnecessary.'

Alex also told Gwen about bumping into the odious Layton Brooks and what had happened in Dubai. She described in detail his garish attire and mimicked his voice as he revealed his pocketful of cash.

'Loadsa money!' Alex slapped an imaginary wad on the table.

It helped to laugh about it, and Gwen poured her a glass of wine. 'I hope you told him where to get off.'

'Better than that,' Alex replied. 'I told him The Skirrid was a dead cert.'

Gwen declared that if Layton Brooks ever came within a mile of Tir Glas Farm, they would get Rhys to dump him on the muck heap.

'That would teach him a thing or two. He can't go round insulting a respectable woman like you. Or indeed any woman. It's not on.'

Alex was surprised at how cross Gwen was getting on her behalf, because she normally seemed so calm and took everything in her stride.

She had made a stew and turned to the Aga to stir it. 'Needs warming up, but it'll be ready by the time I've done the evening feed.'

Alex tried not to imagine which cute little lambs from last year had provided the meat for the stew.

She stoked the fire and picked up a magazine from the pile beside the armchair. When Gwen came back from the evening feed, she found Alex with her nose in an old *Horse and Hound*. She quietly placed a pile of letters and bills on the kitchen table so that Alex could sort through them later.

'Should have read this before I went to the races.' Alex lifted up the magazine. 'Might have given me some good background.'

'That's the one with the article about Dickon taking over from his father,' said Gwen. 'He was a big deal, and the locals loved him, because he'd have at least one decently priced winner a month. I don't know what it is with Dickon, but he's just not got the knack these days. It started off fine, but now, since Abi and the kids left, he couldn't train ivy up a wall.'

Gwen spooned some stew into a shallow bowl and motioned for Alex to join her at the kitchen table. She brought the magazine with her.

'I was staggered when Rhys told me he'd been married.' Alex stared at a photo in the old issue of a smiling Dickon with his arm round a beautiful blonde woman. Two toddlers, riding pillion on a Shetland pony in front of them, grinned at the camera. 'They look so happy.'

'They were.' Gwen looked at the photo over Alex's shoulder and then pointed at the jockey on board a horse in another picture. 'Until he came along.'

There was the sharp, beak-nosed outline of Bertie O'Reilly.

'He was a snake.' Gwen tutted. 'He's charming when he wants to be, no doubt about it, and he coiled himself around her and the kids, taking advantage when Dickon was busy with the horses. He never saw it coming, poor man. I think that's what made it even worse. He felt like he'd been a fool and that everyone else knew before him.'

Alex knew from experience what that felt like. All your friends seeing things while you're left in the dark. It had happened to her with Dan, the boyfriend she had so nearly married. Knowing someone has been unfaithful is one thing, but everyone else knowing before you – that takes it to a whole other level.

'Did William never marry?' Alex asked Gwen.

'No,' Gwen said sadly. 'He told me once that he got close, but he didn't have any financial security, and it didn't sit well with him to impose that on someone he loved.'

Later that evening, as the fire slowly died in the grate, Alex felt calmer than she had done in months. Somehow, she could unwind here, in a way that she had never experienced either in London or at her parents' house. It was strange that she could feel so comfortable in a place she was only just getting to know.

Glancing out at a full moon in a clear sky, Alex offered to take Jiffy for his night-time walk.

'If he'll go with you, you're more than welcome,' Gwen said. 'I'll head off to bed and see you in the morning.'

There was no doubt about him wanting to go with her. Jiffy was infatuated, and the two of them were inseparable.

Alex pulled on a pair of wellies and an old padded jacket. She headed out into the cold night air. Jiffy trotted ahead of her, pausing to sniff and cock his leg here and there. Then he put his head on one side as if he was listening. There was the faintest sound of whining in the distance. The Welsh terrier darted ahead into the field where the sheep were grazing.

'Jiffy!' she called, jogging to keep up. 'Come back.'

He was headed for the hedge that bordered the farm. On the other side were the gallops and the stables. Alex turned on the torch on her phone just as Jiffy darted through a gap in the hedge.

'*Jiffy!*' she shouted helplessly out into the night.

She couldn't lose him. There was only one thing for it. She sank down to her knees and scrambled through the gap, collecting wet mud on her tracksuit bottoms and her elbows. Her phone fell onto the ground, and she scrabbled to retrieve it, but it was covered in mud and the torch was useless. She swore and shoved it deep in her pocket for safety.

She closed her eyes for ten seconds and then opened them again. It was a trick she had learned on a night navigation exercise, when she was doing her Duke of Edinburgh award. Her eyes slowly adjusted to the light available. It was a clear sky, and she had never seen so many stars. She could see geometrical shapes, a triangle of stars here, a division mark over there, and then a giant smudge of mashed-up stars like a brush of white paint on a black canvas, stretching horizontally above the hills.

The Milky Way. She'd never seen it before, because the city always had too much light pollution.

She could also hear the excited squeaking of Jiffy, who had found what he was looking for. He ran in circles around Digby the lurcher, who wagged his tail and crouched, ready to pounce in play.

Alex smiled at the innocent joy of their friendship.

When they headed towards the edge of a copse of trees, Alex saw a small glow of red. She could smell cigarette smoke. She saw the outline of a skeletal silhouette sitting on a fallen log.

'Oh, clear off home, Jiffy.' The voice was hoarse and cracked midway through the sentence. 'I'm not in the mood.'

She crept a little closer, making out the outline of Dickon's shoulders heaving and a shotgun leaning up against the log. Jiffy ignored the instruction to leave and leapt up next to him. He leant into Dickon's side and insisted on attention. Dickon didn't have the strength to fight. He flicked his cigarette butt away and accepted the affection. He put his arm round Jiffy and let the Welsh terrier lick his face.

Alex's eyes had adjusted, and she saw Jiffy offer comfort to a man who had never shown him any love. She marvelled at the ability of dogs to forgive and at Jiffy's natural empathy. It was as if he knew when and where he was needed.

She did not dare approach, knowing that the reassurance offered by a dog was far superior to anything she could say or do. Despite their journey to the races and back, she had never had a proper conversation with Dickon, and tonight, in the dark, when he had a gun by his side, did not seem the time to start.

'I know, Jiffy, you're right. I think you and Digby would

both give me sensible advice if you could only speak.' He ruffled the top of Jiffy's head. 'I know what you mean, though,' he said. 'I will. I'll call them now. And yes, I promise I won't sit out here on my own in the cold. I'll take the phone inside. Now go on, off you go.'

He got up from the log and picked up the gun. He snapped the barrel in half and carried it over his arm. It was no danger to anyone now. Jiffy ran back to Alex's side, and Digby followed his master towards the stables. Alex heard the beginning of a conversation.

'I need help,' she heard Dickon say into the phone.

She scrambled back through the hedge with Jiffy close behind, eager not to disturb any branches underneath, which would snap and alert Dickon to her presence. Her heart was pounding, her breath forming circles in the chilly air at what she'd seen. What if he had picked up the gun and attempted to do what she worried he was thinking of? How hard it must be to keep up a tough exterior, to present a brave face to the world when everyone you love has left.

When she got back to the farmhouse, Alex threw another log on the fire, put the ancient kettle on the Aga and curled up on the sofa to watch the flickering flames. Jiffy settled in beside her, studying her with his soulful eyes, and she fondled his ears. Still reeling from what she had witnessed, she wasn't ready to sleep, but she also didn't want to face the bills and the letters from the bank that Gwen had left on the table.

'I think you saved a man's life tonight,' she whispered to Jiffy. 'And I bet it's not the first time you've done that. Clever boy.'

CHAPTER TWENTY-SIX

A week later, Alex nodded off in the same armchair, too tired to climb the stairs after days of trying to learn the basics of farming. As the warmth of the fire faded and the early dawn light spread across the valley, she became conscious of unfamiliar noises. In her half-asleep/half-awake state, she rolled her head from side to side to relieve the stiffness in her neck and listened more carefully.

The farmhouse creaked. Outside, she could just make out the bleating of a ewe. She got up and pulled on a coat, seeking out the noise in case a sheep was in distress. Jiffy followed silently at her ankles as she made her way into the farmyard. She leant over the gate that protected the ewes who were close to lambing and, on the other side, she spotted a ewe in the far corner, hunched up against the wall. She was panting and looking towards her bottom.

'Oh god,' Alex said under her breath.

She thought about running to wake Gwen but, by the look of this ewe, there wouldn't be time. As she was dithering by the gate, she felt a nudge at her calf. She looked down to see Jiffy urging her forward. He stared up at her and let out a small whine.

'Get on with it. Is that what you're saying?'

She had watched Gwen on many an occasion, swinging into action to help out when required, but she had never done it herself. She took a deep breath, knowing that she needed to be decisive and confident, even if she didn't feel it.

She quietly opened the gate and grabbed a pair of long-armed gloves from the box on the inside. As calmly as she could, she walked towards the ewe, muttering soft words of encouragement as she got closer. She could see the hooves of a pair of legs poking out and, as she crouched down, the ewe looked at her with desperation.

'It's all right, I'll help,' she found herself saying.

She swallowed hard, hoping to suppress the churning in her stomach, and put her left hand on the sheep's backside, her right hand reaching for the lamb. In one swift movement, she pulled the legs, and the whole body slipped out. Oh god, it was slimy and messy. She turned and retched then, willing herself to hold it together, looked back at the lamb and wondered what to do next.

She cleared the afterbirth away from its face and, as she had seen Gwen do, picked up a piece of straw to clear its nasal passages. Then she lifted the lamb and placed it under the sheep's nose. She stepped back.

'Come on,' she whispered to the ewe. 'It's your turn now. Lick it.'

She waited anxiously.

'Come on,' she said softly again, willing the ewe to take over.

The button-like eyes stared back at her and, finally, after what seemed an eternity, the ewe started licking off the after-birth. The lamb sneezed.

'Oh thank god.' Alex sighed.

She jumped as she heard a cough behind her and, turning round, saw a man in a beanie hat watching over the gate. It was Owen Odd Job, who dipped his head at her. They'd been on nodding acquaintance, but he never came into the house, barely came near the farmyard when she was around and had never said a word to her.

She stared at him, alarmed at his proximity and unsure of what to do or say. Her mind was scrambled from the events of the night. She stood there, feeling like an idiot in her long gloves, covered in blood and slime.

The lamb made a noise, and the ewe nudged it with her nose, encouraging it to feed from her.

She glanced back at the lamb.

'Well done,' she thought she heard him say.

By the time she turned around, he had already disappeared into the night, leaving her alone in the barn again.

CHAPTER TWENTY-SEVEN

Jiffy let her sleep until 8.30 the next morning, needing a lie-in as well. When she emerged for her morning coffee, Gwen was in the kitchen.

'I heard you were a bit of a star last night.' Her voice was full of pride.

Alex was in a daze, still reeling from all the exhaustion of the week.

'You helped with the lambing?' Gwen prodded. 'Owen told me you were superb.'

Alex doubted whether Owen Odd Job had ever used that word, but she smiled gratefully. 'That's kind of him. But I don't think I'll ever make a full-time midwife.'

She took her steaming mug from Gwen and set it on the kitchen table, her chest swelling with a sense of achievement. She wanted to please Gwen in the way she'd wanted to impress her English teacher at school, especially because she knew Gwen had been alarmed about her lack of farming experience. This was the equivalent of getting an A star in her exam.

'Well, the little lamb is doing just fine this morning,' Gwen told her. 'You've clearly got the magic touch.'

Alex promised to come out and check on him later but, on her long list of things that had to be done, she had 'clear the study' at the very top, no longer being able to ignore the

223

letters that had been arriving from the bank and solicitor. She had to get on top of the accounts.

'William's filing system was not the best,' Gwen warned her.

Jiffy followed Alex into the study, sniffing at the skirting board and checking the wastepaper bin. There was a thin layer of dust on the windowsill, and on the large wooden desk that stood against the far wall. It had a central covering of leather, and the few spaces she could see in between piles of paper were cracked and worn. All around the edge of the small, square room were shoeboxes stacked on top of each other, like a child had been playing Jenga with cardboard shapes. She flicked off the lid of one of them to find more paperwork. Bills going back for years, as well as receipts for machinery and for the purchase of livestock. There were out-of-date guarantees, old insurance agreements and various letters from the National Farmers' Union. William Griffiths was not one to throw things away, which reminded her of her mother.

She'd need to spend a week in here to dispose of what was no longer needed and sort out anything essential. It was a mess but, now she'd lost her job, she had time. She also needed to work out the gravity of the farm's finances.

Jiffy was sniffing under the desk and wagging his tail. He pounced forward, and she saw a small brown shape move fast towards the corner. It had a bare, dark tail. A mouse, not a rat. It disappeared in an instant. Jiffy sniffed in vain at the tiny gap in the skirting, his claws scratching in the corner.

'It's gone, Jiff. Too fast for you.'

She would add investing in some ethical mouse traps to her to-do list. Then she could release it out into the wild. She needed to find a big diary, somewhere she could write things down easily and assign specific dates to all her tasks.

Maybe there was an NFU diary she could use, or an old ledger. She opened the top drawer of the large desk. There was no diary, but it was full of photographs, fading and curled at the edges. Not wanting to stay in the study long enough to discover whether the mouse had friends, she pulled out a handful of the photos, along with a batch of other documents to sift through, and took them back with her into the kitchen. Jiffy reluctantly followed.

There was Will in one photo, a tall, strong figure at a country fair. He was wearing a checked shirt and jeans, smiling at the camera. His deep-brown eyes creased at the sides into gentle lines, and his face was accented by a suntan that stretched into a clear V at his neck. In another shot, he was caught unawares, running his hand through thick dark hair. He had been a good-looking man back in the day.

Alex sifted through some of him holding rosettes with his sheep, until she got to one shot of a group of men and women at the races. She could make out a skinny boy with sallow cheeks who looked a bit like Dickon. They were clearly celebrating a big win. Will had his arm round Dickon's father.

In the middle of the pile, she found an envelope. Inside was a collection of small Polaroid photos. There was a baby with a podgy, round face. It was wrapped in a crocheted blanket and lying in a big Moses basket, just like the one her parents had. They were all the rage back then. Her mother

225

still had theirs up in the loft. She tried to lend it to her daughters-in-law, but they had already ordered their own new-fangled multipurpose baskets that converted to car seats. She remembered her mother nearly having a coronary when she found out the price of them when they could have had what she saw as a perfectly good one. Nothing maddened her mother more than money being wasted.

Alex smiled as she looked at the baby. It had a cute face.

There was another photo of a toddler dressed in an all-in-one romper suit. Alex had had one just like it when she was young. She remembered rolling about with Chippy, their Jack Russell terrier. Her father had adored that dog, but her mother used to get cross because he kept digging holes in the garden.

This toddler was holding its hands up to the camera and looked thrilled at the mess it had made. She turned the photo over and found a message written on the back in blue biro.

She loves the mud. Just like you.

Her heart stopped for a second. It was her mother's handwriting.

Alex hurriedly pulled out the remaining photos. She was frantic, flipping through them with a speed that defied logic. The toddler was now about four years old and was holding a dog in her arms. She smiled cheekily at the camera, and there was no mistaking it now. Alex stared back at the photograph of her childhood self.

She snatched up her phone and, calling Jiffy to her side, headed out of the back door. If she walked all the way to the end of the drive, there was more chance of signal. She strode furiously along the potholed path, taking care as she crossed the cattle grid. The sheep were bleating, and in the distance, she heard Owen Odd Job's Border collie barking. The sky was turning grey, a shower of rain not far away, but Alex didn't care.

As she reached the end of the drive, she saw that her phone had a rare and precious one bar of signal. She punched the keys and waited. The ringing went on and on until the voice-mail kicked in.

'Shit,' she said, before realizing this was now the first word of the message she was leaving. 'Mum. It's me. I really need to talk to you. Can you call me back as soon as you get this. *Please*.'

CHAPTER TWENTY-EIGHT

Isobel heard her mobile phone ringing. She kept it with her at all times now, in case of emergency. Her days had become a never-ending cycle of duties of round-the-clock care for her husband. She got David up, made him eat breakfast and take his pills. She settled him in a chair and turned on the TV. It was easier to keep him entertained if there was a cricket match in a foreign land or a golf tournament, so then she might get a bit of time to herself to clean the kitchen or briefly pop to the shops.

After lunch, they would go a steady walk down to the river and back, careful not to go too far. Their week was filled with appointments with the speech therapist and the physio. They kept saying they were happy with his progress, but to her it felt like a slow-moving glacier. She wasn't used to him being so utterly dependent on her; the weight felt like it would drag her below the surface at times.

When she finally got to her phone, she saw she had a voicemail message. She listened and tutted.

'Honestly, sometimes that girl can be such a drama queen.' She flicked the kettle on. 'We need to talk? Indeed, we do need to talk. I'll start with manners.'

She pressed the button to end the call and decided to leave it until later. She found it difficult to deal with her daughter at the best of times, and it was worse now that she couldn't rely on David as a buffer.

It was chilly in the kitchen. Isobel regretted turning down the thermostat but, as she repeatedly told the children, you can always put on another layer. She pulled a padded jacket out of the cupboard by the back door and sat in that, drinking her third cup of coffee of the morning.

She took Coco with her upstairs to help wake up David. She then guided him to the bathroom, helping him wash, clean his teeth and get dressed. The robin that was so often outside the kitchen window appeared on the ledge of the bathroom window. It nodded through the glass at her.

'Needs to talk,' she said out loud in the general direction of the bird, who was the only one listening.

It was typical of her mother not to answer, Alex reflected, as she shoved her mobile into her pocket. As she walked back to the farmhouse, she heard the ewes in the closest field bleating manically, and she could see one left behind in the far corner. She hopped over the fence and saw a flash of ginger fur and the white tip of a tail disappearing into the woods beyond her land.

Alex had seen plenty of foxes in London that were so unafraid of humans they barely reacted, especially on bin day, when they roamed the streets, flipping open the small green bins reserved for food recycling. This one had smelt her or heard her and had not wanted to hang around. She hurried across the field, wondering why the ewe was still not moving and why only one of its lambs was standing, forlornly bleating.

As she got closer, the crime scene was gorily apparent. The ewe had been attacked at her throat and her stomach. Her body was heaving, her breath getting shorter and shorter. She was not dead, unlike the lamb that lay mutilated in the mud, its innards ripped out.

Alex felt a knot in the pit of her stomach and retched.

The lamb that had survived the attack stood fifty feet away, wailing in terror and confusion.

This was something she knew she couldn't handle on her own. She needed Gwen. She ran as fast as she could back to the farmyard.

'A fox,' she spluttered. 'A fox has killed one of the lambs. The ewe needs help. What do we do?'

'That ruddy fox.' She shook her head, but that was the extent of her reaction, much to Alex's surprise. 'I'll talk to Owen Odd Job and see if he can take care of it before we lose any more. That fox had two last week, and he attacked a ewe as she was giving birth in the field. I'd not had a chance to get her in.'

Alex leant over, her hands on her knees as she struggled to regain her breath.

Gwen climbed onto the quad bike and started the engine. 'I 'spect you've seen more than you need to of blood and gore for today.' She headed towards the drive. 'I'll deal with it.'

The pain in Alex's chest was now emotional rather than physical, and she winced at the horrific image of that poor dismembered lamb. She wondered if the farm had a graveyard, as they had at her parents' home for their pets when she was younger, and she headed back into the house to carry on the endless task of sifting through bills and accounts.

'Did you save the ewe?' Alex asked when Gwen returned, already fearing the answer.

Gwen shook her head as she picked up the kettle. 'Heart

231

attack,' she said, as if describing the paint colour of the kitchen walls.

'Will we bury her with the lamb?' Alex asked.

Gwen paused in the middle of pouring hot water. Her hand hovered over the mug when she placed it back down again. 'Will we what, love?'

'Bury them together?' Alex repeated, aware Gwen was looking at her strangely.

Gwen continued making the tea and carried it to the kitchen table, sitting down opposite Alex, who was looking up at her earnestly.

'No, cariad,' Gwen said gently. 'We can't bury every lamb or ewe that dies. It doesn't work like that.'

'But what happens to them?' Alex asked, suddenly feeling foolish, as if she'd suggested a divorce party or something equally inappropriate.

'I'll call the hunt,' Gwen told her. 'They'll come and get the bodies and . . . Well, the kennel man will deal with it.'

Alex nodded, trying to cover up her naivety. Gwen's solution sounded brutal, but she trusted her with the same blind faith that she had Sarina Wiegman with the England women's football team. If she said that's what must be done, then that's what must be done. It was all part of her very steep learning curve.

Gwen chose not to add any more details about what would happen to the dearly departed ewe and lamb. Instead, she asked about the photos that lay scattered on the kitchen table.

Alex had arranged them in chronological order, and now she picked them up in turn, trying to work out from the background where they were taken. Most seemed to be at home in Hampshire, but in one, she was holding a lamb in her arms. She turned it to show Gwen.

'That's me as a child,' she explained.

'Looks like it was one of our lambs,' Gwen said immediately. 'See the blue number just poking out below your arm? That's our colour.'

Alex looked again at the photo and realized Gwen was right.

'I kept thinking this place felt familiar.' Alex sighed. 'Looks like I have been here before.'

'Makes sense. I don't think William would have left this place to someone he'd never even met. And that's why you're a natural with the lambs. You must've done it before.'

Alex didn't want to mention that her mother had studiously avoided telling her about any visit – or that she'd seen her mother's handwriting on a photo sent to Will. Their relationship had so often been strained that Alex knew she would struggle to get to the bottom of things.

Gwen didn't need to get involved in that, but when it came to the farm accounts, there was plenty to worry about. Gwen could help advise her on the ideas she was having to bring some money in.

'I was thinking of a mindfulness retreat,' Alex suggested. 'Or a literary festival. Or what about wild camping? Or – this one is good – an Eighties music celebration? We've got to come up with something, anything that can generate an income.'

She showed Gwen drawings she had done of where the stage might go, and she had sketched some triangles to represent yurts or bell tents in which people would stay.

'I'm going to carve wooden signs for the different

accommodation areas,' she explained. 'I'm going to call them things like "Space", "Time" and "Peace". Or maybe we could name them after different breeds of sheep: Cheviot, Herdwick, Badger Face Welsh Mountain. That one's a bit of a mouthful – it would need a bigger sign. My woodwork classes at school might not stretch to that.'

Gwen grinned at her enthusiasm. 'It's a nice idea, but don't you think it might be a bit remote for a festival venue, given that you and Ethan got completely lost when you first visited?'

'Well, that's true . . .' Alex couldn't deny it. 'But there are loads of festivals in remote rural locations,' she went on. 'Build it and they will come – that's what they say! We can lay on buses from the train station in Abergavenny or Monmouth to get them here. All my friends from London will come. I can have my birthday party at the same time. It'll be epic.'

Gwen stood up, her chair scraping on the stone floor, obviously keen to get on with her work. 'That sounds very nice, although I don't know that the sheep will appreciate the music. Nor will the racehorses next door.' Gwen was clearly trying to avoid crushing Alex's dreams entirely, but it was obvious she didn't think this idea was going to work. 'I think a silent disco might be more the thing personally, but I'll leave you to have a think. Diversification is probably a good idea,' she acknowledged.

Alex sighed as Gwen left the house. It wasn't just a good idea; it was utterly essential. She needed Ethan's help to come up with a business plan. After all, he had run a business of his own for years and made a success of it. She resolved to ask him to come down to Tir Glas when he next had a break so that she could pick his brains.

CHAPTER TWENTY-NINE

When Gwen had headed back outside to feed the sheep and check on the newest lambs, Alex dug out her *Idiot's Guide to Farming* and looked up 'diversification'. It listed the top five ideas, which ranged from setting up a farm shop to starting a bed and breakfast. 'Glamping and camping' caught her eye. That would involve less hassle and generate income all year round, unlike a one-off event. Maybe that was a better idea than trying to stage an Eighties festival, and she reckoned Gwen might have had a point about disturbing the tranquillity of their little corner of paradise.

Meanwhile, she would try to do something with all the machinery.

As she wandered through the yard, her mind was whirring faster than her phone could snap pictures of the battered blue tractor. She took close-ups of the tyres, the engine, the gear box and the worn leather seat. There was an ancient trailer behind the barn which must have transported sheep to the market at some point. Now, it was being used as a storage container and, as she lowered the ramp, she found it full of equipment.

A lot of it looked like medieval torture chains or stocks. An old set of rusty shears had been tossed on the floor. She picked her way through the narrow gaps and pulled back the protective cover on a wooden stand to reveal a saddle with two prongs sticking out of it and only one stirrup on the left-hand side. She knew from reading an illustrated copy of *Black Beauty* when she was young that it must be a side-saddle, designed for ladies to ride in skirts, maintaining their modesty while enjoying the thrill of riding.

Walking into the trailer was like stepping into Dr Who's Tardis. She was transported back through time. Everything around her had been handled and cherished by men and women hundreds of years ago. There were old shovels, pitchforks and metal buckets, a tool box full of kit, a couple of milk urns and a pile of animal rugs.

She picked up a heavy leather harness. It was a miracle it hadn't rotted, left out like this. She imagined it around the thick necks of two oxen dragging a plough through the deep, fertile soil. There was probably a museum of farming somewhere that might want it as a historic relic.

Underneath a large blanket, she uncovered a wooden crate. She used a flat-faced screwdriver from the toolkit to lift up the lid. Inside were piles of operating instructions for the machinery. There was a large brown envelope with *RACING* written on it.

Inside, she found newspaper clippings, photographs and racecards dating back to the 1960s. She could see Will in some of the photos and, from the feature she had seen, she identified the trainer as Gerald Jones, Dickon's father. She ought to take it all over to Dickon's yard and ask him about it, although she doubted he would speak to her.

'You all right in there?' Gwen came to check on her.

'I've found all this stuff. Do you think any of it is valuable?'

Alex was guilty of watching too many shows on TV where things found in the back of a cupboard or in a box in the attic were worth enough to pay for a new roof. She hoped she had stumbled across the junk equivalent of a gold mine.

'Ah, that's where William put the things he didn't want in the house. You'll find all sorts here. I doubt if any of it is worth anything, mind,' Gwen told her, as realistic as ever.

'I don't want to get rid of anything you think is important or has emotional value.'

'Oh, I wouldn't worry about that,' Gwen replied. 'Anything in here is fair game. There's plenty in the house that needs to go as well. You'll need a skip.'

The scale of the clearing operation was overwhelming, and Alex barely knew where to start. She needed someone to wave a wand and tidy it up, turning broken items into usable tools and making decrepit old tractors work again. Whenever she thought of magic, she always thought of Mandy, who was popping up in her mind more often these days.

Alex revisited the idea she'd had to make the most of her new profile on social media. She could post an Instagram story every day or two, charting her experience at the farm. She could post photos of lambs, fields, mountains and ancient farm machinery. It would be like a whole new identity and, if it took off, she could monetize it. Every penny of income was going to be essential. Keep creating content, she remembered. That was the mantra of the successful influencers.

She filmed the interior of the trailer, adding her own commentary.

'Have a look at this treasure trove. Let me know what you think this is . . . and this . . . and what about this little beauty?'

The rain started to fall in the afternoon and refused to stop, making any further filming impossible. She retreated to the house, taking the envelope of racing memorabilia with her. Along with all the photos and racecards, she found a document detailing shares that William had bought in a company she had never heard of. There was a note on it in capital letters saying, *DAVID RECOMMENDS MAXIMUM INVESTMENT.* The date was the year before she was born.

Gwen said William had put things in the trailer that he hadn't wanted in the house. This must be something he didn't want to look at but equally couldn't bring himself to throw away.

She arranged the various papers and photographs she'd found in the desk and in the trailer outside, and wondered about this man who had known her parents, met her as a young child but never as an adult, and had possibly accepted financial advice from her father. She looked again at the photos of herself as a baby and as a toddler, straining her memory for any recollection of meeting William Griffiths or coming here to the farm.

She was mentally and physically exhausted, but a plan was starting to form about how she could avoid bankruptcy. Getting the farm into a positive financial state was the ultimate aim, but she would need to take one step at a time.

She settled into his old armchair and yawned. She didn't have the energy to think any more. Pulling up a blanket, she succumbed to a much-needed nap.

CHAPTER THIRTY

Gwen woke Alex gently two hours later, offering to take her to the pub. Alex was starving, keen for food, company and Wi-Fi and, as the pub offered all three, she leapt at the suggestion.

Alex had got used to the notion that nothing was close by as they made their way down the dark, single-track road. When the locals said someone lived 'next door', they meant half an hour away. When they said they were 'popping out', they meant they'd be gone for at least an hour. In London, Alex had been able to walk down the road to get a carton of milk or a packet of biscuits at any time, thanks to convenience store late opening hours. Now, she had to plan ahead and make sure the cupboards were stocked. Soon, she'd be like her mother and have tins of unused beans going back years.

Up ahead, they saw the lights from the pub and from the few houses that surrounded it. The sign for the Black Prince swung in the breeze as they turned into the car park. Alex thought back to the first time she and Ethan had arrived here. It had only been a couple of months ago, but it felt like years.

She hurried through the big door, keen to see Rhys and to reunite with the outside world. Connecting automatically to the Wi-Fi, her phone started to ping with alerts.

She waved at Rhys and headed to the comfy sofa, scrolling through and deleting the unsolicited texts offering a free massage, the emails from companies trying to tempt her back into an order, the endless spam warning her that a non-existent subscription was about to expire, a phantom delivery had been attempted, prizes had been won, including a new coffee machine, an emergency kit for her car, a free mystery box from an outrageously expensive make-up company. It reminded her of that TV show where they had to remember items on a conveyor belt.

Delete, delete, delete.

'Jesus!' she said out loud as she deleted an email for penis enlargement. Maybe she didn't miss email as much as she'd thought she would; there was so much rubbish to sift through.

Alex posted her Instagram story and then scrolled through people she followed. Friends with their children, dogs, celebrities, clips from radio shows, from TV shows, from podcasts, and various adverts for diet plans and exercise routines that promised to give her a flat stomach in three weeks. She looked down at her midriff and wondered if she needed that.

'You OK?' Rhys asked as he brought over a gin and tonic.

She loved that he knew what she wanted without even asking for it.

'All good now.' She took a sip.

'I hear you've been delivering lambs.' He patted her on the back lightly in congratulation.

She looked up in surprise.

'News travels fast round here.' He laughed. 'This one's on the house. Think of it as a reward.'

He pulled up the chair opposite and sat down.

'How's Ethan?' Rhys asked casually.

'I've just had a message from him. Says he's keen to come down around Easter if there's room at the inn.'

Rhys's face lit up at the thought of seeing him in a few weeks' time. 'There's always room at the inn for him.' He smiled. 'Unless he wants to stay with you at the farm?'

'Oh, I think he'd rather be here with you,' Alex said knowingly. 'He likes central heating and good showers. And he says he wants Welsh rarebit for breakfast.'

'I'll do my best.' Rhys laughed.

Flicking back to her Insta story, Alex saw it already had a like from @MagicMandy. She started to text. *You should come and see the lambs,* she wrote.

The door of the pub opened, and Dickon ducked under the lintel, wiping rain off his shoulders. He was followed by a bedraggled-looking Digby, who shook himself violently and headed for the fireplace to dry off. Jiffy jumped off his favourite spot on the window seat to go over and greet his friend. Alex watched the Welsh terrier, knowing that he was also checking up on Dickon.

The trainer nodded at Rhys and glanced momentarily at Alex. She nodded her head at him and got a small flicker of acknowledgement in response. She thought about what she had witnessed the night of Cheltenham and wondered how someone could make themselves so thoroughly unreachable. He was like a magnet that operated in reverse. If he came close to people, he seemed to repel them. Rhys seemed to be someone he could tolerate, but even their conversation was fairly perfunctory.

'How's things?'

241

'Fine.'

'The usual?'

'Yup.'

It couldn't really be termed a conversation; it was more a business transaction. In the aftermath of his wife's betrayal, Dickon Jones seemed to have put up a massive and impregnable wall between himself and the other villagers. Having seen him in such a vulnerable state, Alex wondered whether he simply did not know how to breach that barrier any more, or just lacked the energy and will to do so.

It was typical of Gwen, whom everyone loved, that she seemed to be attempting to find a way to break through. She had found an old towel and taken it over to Digby to rub him dry. Dickon didn't stop her.

'Damned shame what happened at Cheltenham,' she said very quietly. 'I hope The Skirrid's recovered?'

Alex waited with bated breath to see Dickon's response, trying not to let on that she had heard Gwen's words and looking in any direction but theirs.

'He's got some talent, there's no doubting that,' Gwen tried again. 'One day he'll get it all together.'

'Thanks, Gwen,' Dickon muttered huskily, and took a hasty gulp of his pint.

Alex smiled inwardly. It would take time, but maybe he could be encouraged to dismantle that wall brick by brick.

Looking around the pub again, Alex wondered – not for the first time – how Rhys had made this place work. It was so remote, and yet there were always customers. The food was exceptional and reasonably priced, the bar was lavishly stocked;

he had rooms upstairs that she knew from experience were very comfortable, and she guessed word travelled fast that it was a perfect stop-off for walkers.

'It's seasonal,' he said, by way of explanation, as he placed a plate of steak and chips in front of her. 'We're rammed when the Abergavenny Food Festival is on – it's the biggest one in the UK. You wait until the weather improves: you'll see masses of folks coming this way to walk in the mountains or do Offa's Dyke. Then there's the stargazers and the history buffs and the paddle-boarders or kayakers. We've got a group of four due in tomorrow for the dark skies.'

Alex drank in this information, thirsty for more. She needed to know some of the tricks of the trade. If this area did get a lot of tourists, maybe the glamping accommodation could be a goer.

She cleaned her plate as if she hadn't eaten for a week and, keen to be helpful, returned it to the bar. She nearly dropped it in shock as Digby's nose arrived uninvited directly in her crotch.

'Digby! Manners,' came the admonishment from his owner.

Alex batted away the incident, stumbling over her words as she said it really didn't matter and that she knew it was typical lurcher behaviour. She was talking so fast it came out in a jumble of words that slipped and collided into each other.

'I can only apologize for my dog.' Dickon glanced up, speaking to her for the first time. 'He can get very over-excited when he's around women.'

Alex blushed beetroot red and didn't know where to look.

She couldn't work out if he was flirting with her through his dog or merely stating the obvious: all dogs liked her.

Dickon shouted a thank you to Rhys, patted Jiffy on the window seat and headed out into the wet and stormy night, Digby trotting along behind him.

'Someone's brightened up,' Gwen remarked as she came back from the computer, where she'd been checking her bank statements. 'Maybe he's had a win on the Preview Bonds as well. It's all gone into my account, so it's real. Let's raise a glass to William for his generosity. Cheers!'

Alex looked again at her phone, hoping for a reply from her mother to her voicemail earlier that day. There had been no response.

CHAPTER THIRTY-ONE

Fortified by a second gin and tonic and four bars of signal, Alex took matters into her own hands. She couldn't wait any longer. She dialled the landline, because then her mother wouldn't know it was her, and waited for the obligatory four rings as her mother got up from her chair, walked into the kitchen and retrieved the phone from its stand. Why she didn't keep it by her side, Alex would never know. That's the point of a wireless phone, she had told her. You don't have to leave it on charge all day, just at night.

'Riverview Manor, Isobel speaking.'

'Hi Mum, it's me. You heard my message?'

'Yes.'

There was an awkward pause.

'Yeah. I um, I just um . . . So . . .'

'No, Alex, there is no need for "so" in that sentence.'

Alex ploughed on. 'It's just that, er, I found these photos and they, uh, they're of me as a baby and a toddler. They were in William's desk.'

It was always so hard to talk to her mother. Isobel preferred to use phone calls as a means of making arrangements, rather than for proper conversations, and would chide her daughter for her grammatical mistakes in order to evade any questions she disliked.

'And?' Isobel's voice was clipped and efficient, as if she was a secretary taking dictation.

'Well, why did he have them?'

'I told you. He was going to be your godfather and then he and your father had a big row. I sent him the occasional photo just to keep him in the loop. A sort of honorary godfather, if you like.'

'Right.' Alex wasn't sure whether to mention the photo with the lamb in which it was clear she had actually gone to visit him as well.

'Now, would you like to talk to your father?'

Isobel held the phone to David's ear. He grunted.

'Hi Dad, it's Alex. How are you doing?'

'Good,' he said. 'Your mother is being very patient.'

Alex found that hard to believe, but it was uplifting to hear his speech so improved.

'I'm down at the farm in Wales. The sheep are lambing. It's very busy, you know, but it's good. I'm learning a lot.'

'Farm-ing,' he said deliberately.

'That's right, me farming.' She laughed. 'Or at least, I'm trying to. There's a lot to learn.'

Alex paused, waiting for him to respond.

'Are you OK, Dad? How are you feeling?' Alex tried again.

'Your mother is looking after me,' he said, fairly fluently.

'Oh, that's good. That's great news.' Alex knew he'd been having a lot of speech therapy and physio.

'Yes. She's doing a very good job. Farming is hard. It's a tough life,' he continued. 'You're in Wales, she said?'

'Yes, Dad. Monmouthshire.'

'I had a friend there once. A good man and a damned fine rugby player.'

Alex imagined him looking at the photograph on the bookcase as he spoke. His voice sounded a little dreamy, as if he was hunting for a memory.

'I let him down.' His voice suddenly cracked with emotion, and Alex thought she could hear him crying. Oh god, she didn't want to upset him and jeopardize the progress he'd been making.

'It's OK, Dad, don't cry. You don't need to worry or be sad.' She felt a huge surge of helplessness and pain that her father, who had been so strong and controlled his whole life, was such a wreck at the moment. She didn't know what to say.

'Do you want to give the phone back to Mum?' she suggested. She couldn't bear to hear him like this, and it hadn't escaped her notice that, as usual, her mother hadn't answered her questions properly.

'I love you, Dad, and I'll see you very soon.'

The phone was handed over, and she heard her father blow his nose loudly.

'I'm sorry, Mum. I didn't mean to say anything to confuse him or make him cry,' Alex said quickly.

'He'll be all right in a minute,' Isobel replied brusquely. 'He cries at all sorts now. The nurse said it's a side-effect of the drugs he's on, so I wouldn't worry. It's not you.'

Well, that was a relief, although the way her mother said it, Alex still felt as if she was being told off.

'Is he eating OK?' Alex checked.

'Oh, his appetite is fine, but he has trouble chewing things, so don't you be sending us any lamb.'

'Right. I'll bear that in mind,' said Alex, who hadn't thought for one second of sending lamb to her parents.

'Is that it?' Isobel's tone was brisk. 'It's just I've got to load the dishwasher and get your father to bed.'

Alex wanted to say more, but she wasn't sure how. She knew her mother was being deliberately evasive, but it was so hard to pin her down over the phone.

'You could come down here if you wanted to, Mum.'

The invitation tumbled out of her mouth but, if her parents did visit, the change of scene might help her father's recovery, and her mother wouldn't be able to avoid her questions.

'Don't be silly. I can't leave your father,' Isobel tutted.

'Of course not. You could bring him too. I'd help out. You know, to give you both a break and a change of scene.'

Alex glanced at Rhys behind the bar and pointed at her phone, mouthing 'my mother' to explain her end of the conversation. He nodded in mute support and lifted the gin bottle. She shook her head, having already had enough for tonight.

'Why would I need a change of scene?' Her mother batted back the invitation. 'Now, I'm sure you've got things to be getting on with.'

Alex was stumped. She couldn't think of anything else to say and, in the momentary gap while she tried to come up with a way to get her mother to reveal more, Isobel jumped at the chance to end the conversation.

'Well, thanks for calling. Bye.'

'Bye then,' Alex said as she stared at the phone. Her mother had already hung up, which confirmed Alex's suspicions that there was more here than met the eye. Her mother was surely hiding something, and her father knew more than he was able to articulate. There was some kind of mystery begging to be unearthed, but she still wasn't quite sure what it was.

CHAPTER THIRTY-TWO

Alex sank onto the big leather pub sofa, shiny in places where hundreds of people had sat, and called Ethan. He knew her mother, and he would know what to say to her to break through.

'You can't help someone who doesn't want to be helped,' Ethan tried to console her. 'But try to see it from her point of view. She's clearly at her wits' end with your dad and she can't process things properly. She certainly can't contemplate a long journey with him, and it's a good few hours' drive, after all.'

Alex sighed and leant back into the cushions. Jiffy jumped up on the sofa beside her, as if he knew she needed comfort.

'But I don't understand why she won't tell me what happened to make Dad fall out with William. He said he'd let him down, but I know Mum knows more than she's letting on.' She stirred her glass with the straw and took a sip through the ice cubes. 'It's all very odd. She's being even weirder than usual, and we both know that's pretty weird.'

Ethan's laughter on the other end of the line relaxed her. He was on her side. Even if he defended her mother, and often pointed out her strengths when Alex was seeing faults, he would always be on her side.

'I just don't get it.' She dropped her voice to an urgent whisper. 'It doesn't make any sense that he left me his farm. Even if he did meet me when I was a little kid and I came to the farm with my mum, it's a bit of a stretch to make me his main beneficiary. I'm not even a relative.'

Ethan raised his eyebrows. 'Have you considered the possibility that . . . ?'

'What?' Alex fired back. 'You're thinking that my mother really did know him. Like, know him really well?'

'I know you might not believe it, or certainly not want to believe it, but I wouldn't underestimate her,' Ethan said lightly.

Alex didn't know how to respond. It had of course crossed her mind as soon as she'd seen the photos, but honestly? She'd have believed it of her father, but not her mother. She just wasn't the sort. She had always been so proper, so very attentive to social rules and public opinion. There was no way Isobel, of all people, could have had an affair. No way.

'Very funny,' Alex finally said. 'If you want to ask her, be my guest, but I don't think I can even go there. It's too much of a stretch. I know my mother, and there is absolutely no way on this earth that she could have carried that off for all these years.'

'As I said, you may not see it because you don't want to, but I've always thought your mother has hidden depths – who knows what she may or may not be capable of? Anyway, as he *did* leave you the farm, it's just as well it's now. They're changing the rules for inheritance tax soon, though the government says it will only apply to farms above a certain value. A million, I think.'

'Hark at you, economics correspondent,' Alex teased him. Everyone always thought Ethan was a bit of an airhead because of his party-planning job, but he was one of the most clued-up people she knew.

'I even checked the value of the farm for you, based on similar properties in the area. I'm clearly lonely without you,' Ethan added.

'But I'm not allowed to sell,' Alex explained. 'That was a condition of the will. And anyway, I don't want to.'

'Really?' Ethan couldn't hide his surprise. 'You want to be a farmer?'

Alex looked down at Jiffy next to her and wished she had the confidence in herself that the little dog had.

'Well, I'll have to diversify to make ends meet, but I delivered a lamb last night.'

'You what?' he screamed. 'The woman who won't watch *Casualty* or *Call the Midwife* because she can't abide seeing childbirth – you delivered a lamb? What is happening to you, Alex Roberts?'

Underneath all the joshing, she could tell he was impressed.

'I don't know,' she said quietly. 'But talking of money,' she continued. 'I'm going to have sell the flat. I've got so many bills to pay that they'll make me bankrupt if I don't get some capital.'

'Really?' Ethan replied. 'Are you sure?'

She had been thinking about it, tossing the idea over for a few days now. Every time she looked out of the window, or stood in the fields, or walked down the drive, or watched the lambs playing, she had become more sure. She had to give this place a proper go.

'When you come down, it would be great to go through

the numbers and come up with a business plan. I know you're good at that stuff, and I could really do with the help.'

'Well, if you're certain, spring is always a good time to sell,' Ethan agreed. 'People feel more optimistic in spring, and the light is better, so your cosy top-floor flat won't look dark and dingy.'

'It is *not* dark and dingy.'

'I'm not saying it is but, if it was, even slightly, it won't look it in spring. You need to bake some bread.'

'What?'

'I know cooking is not your forte, but baking bread smells amazing. Fresh coffee too. That's what they recommend to make it feel homely for when people view.'

'Can't I get some incense sticks that smell of bread and coffee? It would be much easier.'

Ethan laughed. 'Now there's a business plan.'

'I hope you were serious about coming down soon and not just for financial advice.' Alex changed her tone. 'Rhys is very keen to see you again. I think he's smitten.'

'Tell Rhys I'll be down in April. Too many parties going on right now – stags, hens, birthday parties. It's all happening.'

'You're just too good at your job,' Alex teased him.

'I know and, on that point, babe, I've got to go. That magician you told me about who was so good – I've booked her to entertain the hen party tonight.'

She sat for a moment after he hung up, feeling a bit left out. Although she didn't want to be in London, she missed Ethan and was jealous of him seeing Mandy, when she wanted them both to be here with her.

CHAPTER THIRTY-THREE

Sunlight flooded through the curtains the next morning, waking Alex even before Jiffy had shoved his nose in her face. She was eager to get on with the day and the various chores she had set herself. She had a renewed sense of urgency and energy, fuelled by the idea of her friends and possibly her parents visiting the farm soon; she wanted to show it off in its best state, keen for them to love it as she now did.

Alex ventured back into the study to work her way through more papers, throwing away what was no longer needed and filing anything essential as she continued her mission to get the accounts in order. She had been carefully inspecting and discarding papers for nearly an hour when she came across a batch of letters. They were stored away in a folder at the bottom of the second drawer on the right. She recognized the handwriting as her mother's so started to read.

Dear Will,

It's been an age since I last heard from you. I hope all is well on the farm and the lambs are strong and healthy. David is away on a work trip so I'm home alone. The children are at school and seem to be doing well. Kit is top of his class and seems particularly good at maths, which he must get from his father because I was never any good with numbers.

Hugh got into a bit of trouble running a school betting syndicate. He's obsessed with racing and follows the horses trained by your neighbour. He had a big win the other week and got caught dishing out cash to his classmates. It's a shame you don't have a horse in training any more. I think he'd love to visit the stables.

Alex is not as diligent with her studies, but she loves sport and is so keen on animals that she wants to spend every spare moment with dogs or cats or horses. She's read Dr Dolittle and now she thinks she can speak to them all. She'd rather talk to animals than to humans, which reminds me of someone . . .

Maybe I should bring her down to the farm again.

Anyway, that's all my news. Please write back.

We miss you.

Love,

Izzy

x

Alex frowned and skimmed a few more letters. Her mother, so parsimonious with her texts and so abrupt on the phone, was more expansive when writing letters. She was surprised at the signature. No one ever called her Izzy, except occasionally her father. She was Isobel, and woe betide anyone who shortened it or spelt it incorrectly.

The pattern was repeated in the next letters she read, with news about all three children, the odd line about David, and occasionally the latest dramatic news on his older sister Diana's love life. It was like reading a memoir of her childhood. Every letter ended with a plea for him to write back and the line *We miss you.* So they were clearly much closer than her mother had admitted.

The tone was warm and familiar in the letters, the updates regular as clockwork. There was one every three months and then nothing. The letters suddenly stopped.

She looked at the dates at the top of each one. For twenty years, there had been no communication. How odd to keep up a running commentary and then stop when Alex turned eighteen.

She turned over the last letter, hoping to find something extra on the back. Maybe William stopped keeping the letters after that date; maybe it bored him, reading about children he never saw. She went back to the desk, searching through the drawer in case there was a postcard, a photo, a Post-it note. Anything. She came up empty-handed.

She turned her attention to the left-hand drawers. There were more recent documents in there. Bills, invoices and a doctor's letter asking William to make an appointment to review some test results. Buried underneath piles of papers, she found another envelope with her mother's handwriting on the front.

Inside was a letter dated from last year.

Dearest Will,

It was such a joy to hear from you after all these years. I am glad to know you're still at Tir Glas Farm. I often imagine you there, striding across the fields, surveying your kingdom. I cannot think of what might have been, as it will break my heart all over again. I will never understand why you did what you did, but I suppose we have both survived, in our own way.

Kit is flying high. He'll be a KC soon, I'm sure. Hugh is running some start-up tech company which I don't fully understand. You asked me for more detail about Alex, so I'll do my best, although she tells David more than she does me.

She is living in London, doing a job she hates, but it pays the bills. If I'm honest, I'd say she's in a rut. It's a shame, because she's got so much to offer if she would only believe in herself.

Alex almost dropped the letter in shock. Her mother had never once, to her recollection, said anything positive or encouraging to her face, and yet here in her own hand was a sort of a compliment.

She is funny, bright and, when she wears make-up and flattering clothes, not bad-looking. She writes well, even if it is for a dreadful magazine. You can find some of her articles online and I'd particularly recommend one from July last year which I thought was beautifully constructed.

Again, Alex was flummoxed. Her mother had never, ever given her any feedback on her work, and yet here she was, praising it, clearly up to speed on her articles for *Rizz*, which she didn't think her mother had ever read.

She has long-standing friends who adore her, but there's no one special in her life. Or at least, no one she has brought home.

Like you, she seems to be allergic to marriage. The one thing she knows she doesn't want is responsibility, which seems to be some sort of denial of duty. As you are well aware, I value a sense of duty very highly.

I hope she'll find an answer – either a person who loves her and allows her to be herself, or a job that is more of a calling, that makes her brain tick and her heart sing. It's a lot, I know, but I'm sure it's all out there for her if she'd just look in the right places.

I think you'd like her a lot if you met her properly. You have certain things in common.

With love, as always,

Izzy

Xx

P.S. I still miss you. Every day.

Alex looked out of the window of the study, from which she could see right across the fields. She felt a lump in her throat at what she'd read. She had hankered so much after her mother's approval, and here in these letters, she had proof that her mother did care about her well-being and her happiness. The seed that had already been planted in her mind, and watered by Ethan's suspicions, was now growing. She had to find a way of asking her mother without annoying her. That was going to be a challenge.

The sheep must have moved on because she couldn't see any of them along the hedgerow any more. In the distance, Owen Odd Job was cutting logs. She would ask him if filling in the potholes on the drive was something he could do, so that her guests would have a much better first impression of the place.

Alex wondered if her mother would be impressed with her now or whether she'd think she was out of her depth. The latter was probably closer to the truth. Alex knew she was taking on far more than she could handle, but she had no choice. Now she was here, she had to make it work for her own good, and for Gwen too. Even Owen Odd Job, strange as he was, needed her to succeed – for the first time in her life, people were relying on her to provide a living for them. It was a terrifying responsibility.

She vowed that by the time her mother visited, she would have cemented a plan to make the farm viable, if not profitable.

Then there was the line right at the end of the last letter. Not *we miss you* but *I still miss you*. There was definitely something her mother was keeping from her, and Alex was determined to get to bottom of it, even if it finally meant forcing her mother to open up to her, and doing so to her mother in return.

CHAPTER THIRTY-FOUR

The weather was warmer now April was here, and the bluebells sprinkled through the woods gave them a fuzzy sheen of deep indigo. That must be what Tir Glas refers to, Alex thought. Early in the morning, it looked like a misty pool of blue water. It was so beautiful it took her breath away.

She was still thinking about it as she sat in the study, going through the pile of paperwork in what had become a daily chore for the past few weeks. Her focus was shattered by a loud and insistent banging at the back door. Knowing Gwen was out in the fields, Alex leapt up from the desk to answer.

'Your fucking sheep!' Dickon shouted.

'Huh?'

Dickon gave her a disdainful glare before turning his back and shouting into the farmyard. '*Gwen!* Where the hell are you? Little Bo-Peep here has lost her sheep.'

Digby the lurcher sniffed around, looking for Jiffy as his master roared.

'What's the problem?' Alex stammered, having no idea why Dickon was so worked up.

'Those fucking sheep have trampled all over my gallops and are now making a right mess of my yard.' Dickon called Digby to his side. 'And if you don't sort it out pronto, then I will sue you for damage to my property, threat to the safety of my horses and whatever else I can think of. I've told Gwen before that fence needed mending.'

He stomped back to the Land Rover. So much for the short-lived improvement in his attitude. Alex looked down at Jiffy.

'He's a charmer, isn't he?' she muttered before heading back inside to change into clothing more appropriate for sheep rustling, which was apparently the next task on her to-do list.

Alex tramped across the field towards the gap in the hedge where she had scrambled through that time after the awful day at the Cheltenham Festival. Her mind flashed back to Dickon, sitting on the log in the dark with a gun by his side. She must try to remember that he was a vulnerable man, not just a cantankerous misanthrope.

Gwen and Alex frantically tried to herd the lambs back onto the right side of the boundary hedge. They had only recently been weaned and were seeking pastures new.

Alex ran from one side to the other, her arms outstretched, calling 'g'won, g'won' in a voice she hoped had authority. Gwen rode the quad bike, covering ground more effectively.

Dickon joined in, riding The Skirrid behind the flock and whistling at Digby to cover the left flank. The jittery racehorse seemed to enjoy the challenge and, every time he got close to a lamb, he lowered his head to gently nudge it forward.

'I think he likes them,' Alex observed. 'Especially that one.'

She pointed at a rotund, strong-looking lamb with the number 33 on its back.

Dickon cut her short. 'Don't be daft. I bet you read books

about talking animals when you were a young'un. You probably think they can be best friends.'

Alex smarted at his jibe. She might have been a Londoner for most of her life, but she had a connection with animals and she could see that The Skirrid needed a comfort blanket. She had read an article about a racehorse that had a sheep as a travel companion. It had gone to the races with him and had even kept him company in the saddling boxes, so she wasn't as clueless as Dickon thought.

Owen Odd Job and his Border collie also came along to help.

The Border collie ran left and then right, crouching down, its eyes switching from the lambs to his master and back again. Owen whistled and called one-word instructions, and the dog responded, hanging back when required and closing in a fast, smooth movement when commanded. It was a masterclass of sheep herding.

The leading lambs skipped over the puddles and back towards their familiar field. The others, as sheep do, followed. Digby and Jiffy might have helped a little bit, but the Border collie was in charge.

'Oh, Border collies are a breed apart,' Gwen said proudly. 'They were born to do this sort of work, and Gareth is one of the very best.'

'Gareth?' Alex queried. 'As in Gareth Edwards?'

'Or Gareth Davies, or Gareth Thomas. Take your pick.' Gwen laughed. 'Not that Owen ever calls him anything except Gee. Sheepdogs work best with short names.'

Once Gareth had successfully herded the flock through the

gate, Owen shut it behind them and waved at Gwen to go round the long way on her quad bike. There was no point risking another escape.

'You've missed one,' Dickon called over, interrupting their chat.

One lamb had detached itself from the rest of the flock and was standing underneath the stomach of The Skirrid. Dickon hadn't been able to see it, and it was only when it let out a throaty bleat that he twigged they still had a runaway.

The lamb tottered out from its hiding place, and The Skirrid lowered his head, nuzzling into its woolly coat.

'I think it's love at first sight,' Alex joked.

'Fuck's sake,' Dickon said crossly, after trying in vain to make the horse lift his head.

'Don't worry about it.' Alex's tone was light and conciliatory. He was talking, even if it was in expletives, rather than shouting. This was progress.

'I'll come back to get him later,' she offered. 'He's one of our orphans, so there's no mother to miss him.'

'OK, thanks,' Dickon muttered. With all his strength, he heaved the horse's head round to make their way back to the stables.

Alex watched him go and, as he disappeared over the brow of the hill, she saw the lamb trotting along behind The Skirrid.

'Animal instinct.' She laughed to herself. 'You can't fight it.'

Gwen had a stern word with the lambs about staying within the confines of their own land. She didn't want another twenty years of conflict between the farmer and the trainer, just like the generation before. Owen Odd Job was already on the case, mending the fencing again and blocking up any holes along the hedge line.

That afternoon, Alex walked across the field with a bag of sheep feed over her shoulder, deciding she could use it to tempt her lamb back home. Because he'd been orphaned a couple of weeks before, he was already weaned, and she knew he loved his food. It was certainly easier to make the trip now she could open and shut the big five-bar gate. Jiffy came with her, glued to her side.

As she approached the stables, she could hear music playing. It was the Pet Shop Boys, and she was surprised Dickon was another Eighties music fan, which meant they had something in common. The music covered the sound of her approach, but Jiffy ran ahead to find Digby, and they scampered off together across the lawn, which was in desperate need of mowing.

The house must have once been impressive, but the roof needed replacing, the windows hadn't been painted in decades, and the weeds growing in the flower beds outstripped any formal planting. There was more to repair and repaint here than even at her farmhouse. She could see a trampoline in the far corner of the lawn, its legs starting to rust from the non-stop rain. She imagined children playing and dens being built in the small wood behind the house. Once, it might have been filled with laughter and fun. Now, the only sound was Neil Tennant singing 'It's a Sin'.

She walked through the brick arch to the left into a small quadrangle of horseboxes. There were a couple of horses looking over their stable doors. One of them whickered a gentle greeting. She saw an open door, with a single chain across the front so the horse wouldn't escape. Inside the stable, Dickon was grooming The Skirrid. The tall, dark, majestic thoroughbred watched Alex approach, his ears flicking back and forth and his left eye following her every move.

'Hey,' Alex said awkwardly. 'Didn't want to disturb you. He's clearly enjoying it.' She nodded to The Skirrid, who had closed his eyes with his ears flopped slightly to the side, as if hypnotized.

Dickon grunted and started brushing the other side. Alex came close enough to stroke the front of The Skirrid's face.

'Watch it,' Dickon warned. 'He doesn't like strangers.'

Alex didn't flinch or back away. She rubbed her hand up and down the wide front of his head. She had never touched a racehorse before, and it was unlike anything she'd ever experienced. The ponies she had ridden as a child had a harshness to their hair. This was completely different. The hair was short and sleek, and his skin, on the side of his muzzle, felt like the softest velvet.

The Skirrid pushed his head towards her and settled under her armpit with his nose against her side.

'He seems very settled,' she observed. 'Maybe the lamb has calmed him down.'

'Huh.' Dickon kept brushing and polishing, brushing and polishing.

'I've brought some food to help tempt him away, but I can always leave it here if he wants to stay,' Alex offered.

The music changed to another Pet Shop Boys hit, 'Left to

My Own Devices' and, without thinking, Alex started to sing along.

'Bloody hell,' Dickon groaned. 'You are crucifying it. Are you seriously that tone deaf?'

Alex stopped singing and blushed. 'Sorry. I always forget that I really shouldn't sing out loud. I'll have to get some lessons from Gwen. Her voice is stunning.'

'Voice of an angel,' Dickon agreed. 'She can do any style. From Bonnie Tyler to Charlotte Church and everything in between. She's a rare talent, that woman.' It was the first positive sentence she'd heard him utter, but his good mood didn't last long. 'You, however. You would break a karaoke machine.'

There it was. The killer punch. Alex didn't know whether to laugh or cry, so she chose the former. She would take heart from the fact that they were having an actual conversation and Dickon was finally acknowledging her presence.

'When's he going to run again?' she asked, still stroking the horse.

'Bit of a tricky one.' Dickon sighed, keeping himself busy with the brushing. 'His owner – Percy Thomas – has just died, so there's no one around to pay the bills any more. Poor old Percy hadn't been well for a while.' Dickon stood up and stretched his back from one side to the other. He looked towards the ground and fixed his gaze on a piece of straw. 'I can't afford to train him without an owner to pay the bills, so that's that, I suppose.'

He stopped suddenly, and Alex wondered if he had revealed more than he'd intended. She looked around the yard and imagined how it must have been in the past, with twenty or thirty horses in training. Now there were just two, and the other one was recovering from an injury. The Skirrid was clearly Dickon's only hope; without him, he'd have nothing and would maybe even have to sell the place. Alex understood the financial dilemma more than she cared to admit. She was in the same boat with the amount of debt she'd inherited on the farm. They both needed to make things work business-wise, otherwise they'd be queueing up behind each other to see the estate agent.

'There has to be a way. There has to be,' Alex whispered, stroking The Skirrid's nose and hoping to come up with something to help both her and Dickon.

The silence was broken when Jiffy and Digby came tearing into the yard, knocking over a bucket as they chased each other in a whirlwind of tails and barks. Startled by the noise, The Skirrid flung his head up so suddenly he caught Alex on the chin. She was nearly knocked off her feet. The hard bone on his nose had caught the hard bone of her jaw and banged the back of her head violently against the wooden edge of the stable door. She'd bitten her tongue and could taste blood in her mouth. It hurt like hell. In a flash, Dickon was by her side, his arm around her waist to hold her steady.

'Breathe,' he said softly, taking deep breaths himself to encourage her to follow suit.

She counted to ten, determined not to show how much pain she was feeling. She didn't want to cry. Not in front of Dickon, who already thought she wasn't up to the job.

'Settle down, you two,' he commanded the dogs, who immediately obeyed. 'You bloody fools.'

He looked into Alex's eyes, and she struggled to focus. There were stars swimming in front of her pupils, and she thought she might faint.

'It's OK. I've got you.'

Those were the last words she heard before waking up on a sofa in a room she didn't recognize. Dickon was holding a cup of tea and encouraging her to drink from it. She took a sip and recoiled. It was so sweet it tasted sickly.

'The sugar will do the trick,' he said gently. 'My mother always said there's nothing that can't be fixed with a cup of sweet tea.'

He had propped her up longways on the sofa, with a heap of cushions behind her back and her head, so that she was supported. He crouched beside her and held the mug up to her lips again.

'I think—' Alex started to say.

'It's OK. You don't have to speak yet. I'll drive you and Jiffy back to the farm in a while. The lamb can stay here for the night if your offer still stands? He seems quite happy, and so is Skirry.'

Alex wanted to say more, but she didn't dare, so just nodded. Dickon was being so kind; she didn't want to break the spell because this version of him was much nicer.

She would not remember the next hour as he held a bag of frozen peas to the back of her head, where a large, throbbing lump was forming. Dickon drove her back to the farm and explained to Gwen that she'd suffered a mild concussion. She would need plenty of ice on the back of her head, and he advised that she should be checked every couple of hours through the night. Gwen took the instructions seriously. She had seen enough concussions in her time to know to keep a close eye on Alex.

Dickon popped in the next morning to check on the patient. He had intended to bring the lamb with him, but it hadn't worked out, he told them. The lamb had got so distressed when he'd tried to separate it and was bleating incessantly. The Skirrid had started to paw the ground and had then stood weaving his head from side to side.

'It was awful to see,' he explained to Alex. 'I fed them and left them together. It was the only way.'

'That's fine.' Alex smiled. 'Giving you a lamb is the least I can do to make up for the invasion of your property yesterday. I hope they didn't do any damage?'

'Nothing that can't be fixed.' He winked. As he did so, Alex thought how much younger he looked when he wasn't being miserable.

She made him a pot of coffee and gestured for him to sit with her at the kitchen table.

'Thank you.' Dickon perched on a scarred wooden chair. 'Skirry will be very happy that I'm not going to take away his new friend. I went out last night after I'd dropped you back and found him lying down with the lamb in between his front legs. He was cradling it and had his head on its back, using it as a pillow. It was very sweet.'

He smiled again, and Alex saw his eyes change. It was like watching dark clouds disappear when the sun comes out – all there in his face. The transformation was extraordinary. There was a human being under all that anger and rudeness.

'Oh yeah, and more good news.' He blew on the coffee before taking a sip. 'I got an offer for The Skirrid this morning. From an ex-footballer. Some bloke called Layton something.'

'Oh no,' she gasped. 'Is he called Layton Brooks?' She put a hand to the back of her head where she felt a sharp pain and rubbed it.

'Is that still hurting?' Dickon looked concerned. He jumped up and produced a bag of peas out of the freezer. 'Here.' He offered them to Alex. 'Keep putting those on to keep the swelling down. You need to take it easy today. Don't be rushing around doing all those jobs you think have to be done.'

Alex glanced at her kitchen table and saw she'd left the long to-do list in plain sight. She held the peas to the back of her head and enjoyed the cold sensation. 'So, is it Layton Brooks?' she repeated.

'That's the one.' Dickon nodded. 'He kept telling me how much money he had, but then battered me down when I named a price. It's well under what the horse is worth, but I can't afford to refuse it with the spot I'm in.' He took a sip of coffee and shrugged his shoulders. 'The Thomas family don't want a racehorse. They'd rather have the money, and I don't have any other options.'

'So will you have to train for Layton Brooks?' Alex asked.

'No. He says he'll take him to another trainer. One of the big boys. Someone who can make the most of his talent.'

'You can't let that happen!' Alex banged her fist on the table, surprising herself with her strength of feeling. She couldn't have Layton taking advantage of Dickon when he was at his lowest ebb. It just wasn't right.

271

'Steady there,' Dickon said softly. 'You need to take it easy for a few days.'

Alex could not stay calm. She could not let Layton bloody Brooks buy The Skirrid and take him away from Dickon, especially for a cut price.

If Dickon sold the horse, he wouldn't be a trainer any more, and then he'd have to sell the yard. The Skirrid was his only hope.

All day, after he'd left, she tried to think of ways in which she could help. She was convinced that somehow the fate of Dickon's yard and her farm were tied together; she felt that if she could save him, she could also save herself.

As she struggled to find sleep that night, the germ of an idea started to form. It might just be the solution for them both.

CHAPTER THIRTY-FIVE

Alex rubbed the back of her head. Two days on from what she would refer to as 'The End of the Ice Age', and it was still sore. The lump had grown to the size of a small potato, but the local doctor had assured her it was fine.

It was a minor price to pay, she reckoned, for the ceasefire that had been achieved between the warring factions north and south of the great hedge divide.

Dickon had offered to let her use his Wi-Fi whenever she needed it, which was a big breakthrough, so this morning she ventured out into the fresh air, which still had an edge to it even though the warmer temperatures of May were around the corner. She walked steadily across the field of boisterous lambs, which had graduated from playful ballet to head-butting.

'You're behaving like teenagers,' she admonished them as she made her way through the gate that Owen Odd Job had oiled and rehung. It swung easily now, providing access to Dickon's grass gallop, from where it was an easy walk to his stables. She recalled the gate she'd seen when she first arrived, chained and locked with a rusted padlock. Perhaps it was a metaphor for the reset in relations with her neighbour.

She could hear the music as she approached the yard. The electro-drum beat of 'Sweet Dreams' by the Eurythmics set a rhythm to her step. She saw Dickon with a broom in hand, nodding his head vigorously. His shoulders danced from side to side as he swept.

Dickon fell silent as she approached, turning the volume down.

'Don't let me stop you!' She laughed. 'That's one of my favourites.'

'It's a great album,' he acknowledged gruffly. 'The first CD I ever bought.'

The Skirrid whickered gently as she approached. The lamb was by his side, and he lowered his head protectively.

'It's OK, Skirry, I won't take him away from you. I promise.'

She reached out to stroke The Skirrid's nose, keeping a little further away in case he suddenly head-butted her again.

Dickon looked directly at her for the first time. 'So the lamb can stay here, can he?' he asked. 'There's no doubt he's a calming influence on Skirry, and it can only improve his racing chances.' They both stared at the unlikely duo. 'Not that it's going to help with the finances,' he said glumly. 'There's no real money in racing, not unless you're winning the big ones. If you come up with the answer, let me know. God knows, I need some sort of miracle.'

'Well, that's sort of why I came over.' She felt suddenly nervous as she pulled her phone out of her jacket pocket. She knew very little about country life or horses as it was, and she didn't have a clue about racing.

'I had an idea for a partnership or a syndicate,' she broached hesitantly. She looked up to check Dickon was listening. 'To buy The Skirrid. That way, lots of people could share the cost and share the fun, you know, if he turns out to be any good.'

Dickon raised his eyebrows.

'I've written an email.' She showed him her phone. 'I just need to run the numbers by you to check I've got it right. Then I'll send it to a group of friends, relatives, folks I know, and see what sort of response we get.'

She paused, hoping for some sort of a reaction.

'What do you think?' she prompted when none came, worried he'd jump down her throat.

He started sweeping again, more aggressively. 'It's a great idea, but it's too late. Layton Brooks is turning up with a horsebox this weekend. He's taking him away.'

Alex was shell-shocked. This was happening so much faster than she had anticipated. 'What about . . . the lamb? He'll take him as well, surely?'

'Who, Barry John?'

'Eh?'

'I know, I know. I mocked you for thinking you could talk to the animals, and now I've gone and given a lamb a name. I must be going proper soft. He's called Barry John after—'

'The legendary fly half,' Alex responded, knowing the answer.

Dickon was impressed. She might not know much about farming, but she knew her rugby union all right.

He looked towards the stable, where The Skirrid and Barry John were happily sharing the same space. His voice cracked slightly as he said, 'I'm going to recommend he takes Barry John as well because, without him, I don't how Skirry will react. Whether or not Mr Brooks will listen is another matter.'

Alex started to walk towards the house.

'Where are you going?' Dickon called after her.

'To use your Wi-Fi. We've got to move fast, so I'd better send this email straightaway.' There was no time to waste, and she didn't care whether anyone thought she was stupid; there were bigger problems to solve.

When they were sitting down inside, Alex showed Dickon the drafted email with the subject line: *An invitation to be part of a thrilling shared experience.*

> How many people get the chance to own a racehorse? This is a rare opportunity to be more than just a spectator at the most glamorous and exciting sport in the world – a chance to be at the very heart of it. Join the DJ Partnership and you will become an owner of a hugely talented young horse called The Skirrid, trained by the experienced and successful Dickon Jones.

'DJ?' Dickon scoffed. 'Are you promising them a disco as part of the deal?'

'No. It just stands for Dickon Jones. Sounds quite cool, doesn't it?'

'Not sure about "experienced and successful",' he said doubtfully. 'Experienced is true enough, but I can't remember the last time I thought of myself as successful. I think you might be overselling me there. And here's the key question – how much are you asking them to pay? There's no price on this.'

Alex was ready with an answer. She had estimated that to cover all training costs, travel to the races, entry costs to at least five races in a season, jockeys' fees, regular veterinary and farrier's bills would be £30,000 a year, so if she could get twenty-nine other people in the syndicate alongside her, it would be a thousand pounds each.

'I don't know if that's correct – or in the right ballpark' – she glanced at Dickon nervously – 'but if I can get enough people, it'll be about eighty-three pounds a month per person, under three pounds per day, which is less than I used to spend on my lunchtime sandwiches. The best bit is that my sandwiches were never going to win me any money back, whereas he might. If he won a race, or got placed, we'd be dividing the prize money between us.'

She was making notes in pencil on an A4 pad as she spoke to back up the maths and the research she'd done.

'I know that figure only includes basic costs and that if anything out of the ordinary happened it might be more, but is it close?' She hoped for a positive response.

'It's very good logic,' said Dickon. 'I wish I'd had you promoting my yard years ago – it would be full. The problem is the cost of the horse himself. The Skirrid doesn't come for free.'

Alex spun the pencil between her forefinger and her thumb. 'I know,' she said, lifting the pencil briefly to her mouth. 'I couldn't work that bit out because I don't know what he's worth. What has Layton offered you?'

Dickon looked over her shoulder at the numbers. It was a good idea, a creative solution. He wanted it to work because he didn't have a good feeling about Layton Brooks, but he wouldn't be able to keep going without the right sort of investment.

'Nowhere near what he's worth,' he answered. 'But the family are so keen to get rid of old Percy's assets, particularly any that are costing them money – and he'd had the vet out three times recently – that they agreed to accept eight thousand pounds.' He shook his head sadly. 'Honestly, he should be worth ten times that, but they want the money fast, and I haven't got time to run him again or to enter him in the sales, so it's the only offer on the table.'

'Give me an hour,' said Alex, with more confidence than she felt. It was less than she'd thought he would cost. 'I'll see what I can do.'

Adrenalin powered Alex through the afternoon, hunched over Dickon's kitchen table amidst a sea of unopened bills, similar to her own, although his fridge was covered by three children's crayon drawings of horses.

Alex focused on the matter in hand. She might not know the first thing about farming sheep or training racehorses, but she did have an extensive contact list, and she was prepared to use it. She found school friends, former work colleagues at *Rizz*, restaurant owners for whom she'd written good reviews, relatives, university friends, her old hairdresser, the dog walkers in Richmond Park – everyone and anyone she could think of.

She found a decent photo of The Skirrid in full flow, galloping with his ears pricked, and another of him jumping a hurdle, thankfully with a jockey on board this time. On a dusty wooden dresser in the corner of the kitchen, she found a framed photo of Dickon in the winners' enclosure, smiling broadly and patting a sweaty horse. She snapped it on her phone and turned the collection of images into a vibrant picture board to go with the email. She pressed send.

Now all she had to do was wait. And hope this might work.

CHAPTER THIRTY-SIX

Making a cup of tea in an unfamiliar kitchen can feel like rifling through a stranger's underwear drawer. The decisions you make over where you keep the teabags, the mugs, the teaspoons and the sugar are personal. The milk is easy, as long as the fridge isn't hidden behind an invisible door. Dickon's kitchen was rustic and old-fashioned, and although it might once have had charm, the grease stains on the surfaces and the rings where hot saucepans had left their mark marred its appeal.

Dickon had gone out into the stables, leaving Alex to wait for any bites on the line she had cast out into the ether. She walked slowly around the modest kitchen, taking in what was left of the furniture. Marks on the floor where the wood was paler offered clues that there had once been a rug and a sofa, a large table and dining-room chairs.

The absence of those items stood out more than what was left. She thought of something she'd heard a sculptor say once about the negative space between objects being as important as the figures that were there. This kitchen was all negative space.

She glanced over to one family photo that remained on a side table. Dickon's two children were clambering on their father. One was on his shoulders, the other upside down in his arms. All three were laughing. It was a perfect picture of happiness. This room and the contents of the fridge must've been very different when they were here. She understood how difficult it must be for Dickon to live in a house that was a shell of its former self.

She had a look at her Instagram account and posted some more photos from the farm. She also put up a shot of The Skirrid with Barry John the lamb standing between his front legs. It was very sweet and immediately got a like from Mandy, who seemed to be regularly across her feed. They had been messaging each other on text and WhatsApp nearly every day for the last few weeks. Nothing serious, just little comments and a bit of jokey back and forth, but already Alex felt dependent upon their regular contact.

Her phone pinged, and Alex glanced at the screen hopefully, although that was short-lived when she saw it was a message from her mother.

Your brother says you're buying a racehorse. Are you mad?'

News travels fast, she thought. She had the benefit of signal, so took the risk of dialling her parents' landline, because trying to sort out The Skirrid's future had added urgency to her approach. She couldn't keep pussy-footing around the subject of how her parents, and more specifically her mother, knew William.

'Riverview Manor. Isobel speaking.'

Alex could hear *The Chase* on TV in the background. It was so loud she could answer the questions in the cash-builder round and tell the host what she would do with the money 'if she was to win it' – she would buy a share in a racehorse. Bradley Walsh would like that.

'Mum, hi, don't want to disturb your quizzing, but I thought it was easier to ring and explain than to text back.'

'It's Alex. On the phone.' Her mother was clearly speaking to David. 'Do you want to talk to your father?'

'No, Mum. I want to talk to you, but it's a bit hard to hear you over the—'

'What?'

'Which Mexican artist . . .'

'The answer is Frida Kahlo. It's always Frida Kahlo if it's a Mexican artist. I can't hear you very well, Mum.'

'Speak up,' Isobel shouted back. 'I can't hear you at all. It's probably your signal.'

'MUM!' Alex was at full volume, trying to be heard over the TV. 'I found a load of LETTERS. I'm very confused because I think you LIED TO ME.'

She heard her mother get up from her chair and move away from the noise of the television.

'What are you on about? Why were you lying on a lettuce? And more to the point, what's this about you buying a race-horse? Kit says he's joining some sort of syndicate, and Diana just popped in specifically to tell me that she's buying at least ten shares and can't wait for the glamour of Ascot.'

'He's a hurdler, not a flat horse,' Alex pointed out. 'I don't think we're going to be dressed up in our finery and heading to Royal Ascot any time soon.'

Alex paced around the kitchen as she answered her mother's queries. She explained that The Skirrid was going to be bought by Layton Brooks and taken to another trainer if she didn't do something to help Dickon.

'But I thought you didn't like him. You said he was miserable and rude,' her mother pointed out.

'No,' she said to her mother, realizing how she'd misjudged him. 'He's just sad, and life has dealt him a rotten hand. I'm trying to help. Also, The Skirrid could win prize money, and that means it's an investment. You know what Aunt Di says: "speculate to accumulate". That's why she's so keen.'

'Yes, but she usually does that with men. Not money. Anyway, why didn't you ask me?'

Alex stopped and stood still. She glanced out of the window to see Dickon walking back towards the house. How was she meant to respond to her mother, who saved clingfilm and – until the new barcodes came in – had spent her life peeling off stamps to reuse them. She was hardly going to splash out on a racehorse, of all things.

'I knew you'd tell me it was a ridiculous idea and a monumental waste of money,' Alex admitted, keen to be honest.

She heard her mother huff on the end of the line. The faint music in the background told her that the Chaser had caught the first contestant.

'Well, I think you should have asked me. Your father might enjoy having an interest. He used to like racing.'

Her mother was an enigma. Just when she thought she knew her and could predict her reaction, Isobel threw her.

'How much do you need?' Isobel asked.

Dickon walked into the kitchen, his boots trailing bits of

straw. Alex pointed at the phone and mouthed 'my mother' at him. His face contorted into a mock grimace.

'It's a thousand pounds a share,' Alex said, fully expecting her mother to end the conversation there and then.

She put the phone on speaker and sat down at the table to inspect the list she was making of syndicate members. She added Kit and then Diana's name with a ten and a question mark beside it. Her mother's voice came through the speaker.

'Right. I think your father would like that. You can sign him up for one share.' She sounded like a businesswoman negotiating a deal.

Alex's eyes widened in shock.

'I'll transfer the money now, and I'll bring your father down at some point to see the horse. It will do him good.'

'Mum, that's – um – that's amazing. Thank you.'

'Got to go.'

Her mother ended the call sharply, as Alex knew she would.

Alex's hand was shaking as she held the pen over the page and added her father to the list.

'My god.' She looked at Dickon. 'I'm apologizing in advance for what you'll have to cope with.'

Dickon reached out and moved the list towards him, Alex noticing the bitten ends of his fingernails.

'Don't worry – I've dealt with some really terrible owners in my time.' He scanned the list. 'If it means The Skirrid stays here and we can look after him properly, then I don't care if they want a string quartet and a carpet of red roses every time they come to the yard.'

Alex checked the replies to her email and saw that Magic Mandy had reacted with a smiley face and a thumbs-up. She felt a strange sensation in her stomach, as if a miniature trampolinist was leaping up and down and spinning in the air at the thought of hopefully seeing her again soon. And with everyone who had expressed interest in joining the syndicate so far, this idea might just work.

CHAPTER THIRTY-SEVEN

Before Alex walked back across the fields, she stopped by at The Skirrid's stable. He came to the door to greet her, and she very carefully stroked his face, giving him a kiss in the softest part, the hollow side of his muzzle. He looked relaxed and happy, and leaning over the door, she saw the lamb happily guzzling his food in a low rubber bucket. It was a far cry from the nervous horse she'd seen going to Cheltenham, now with no hint of a tremor.

'How are you doing, Barry John?'

The lamb looked up briefly and let out a low, throaty bleat before resuming his munching.

Alex strode across the last field, having witnessed a magnificent sunset, with the sky turning from pale pink to a red so deep it looked as if there was fire behind the hills. The walk had given her the opportunity to mull things over, affirming that she wanted to be part of this team, here in Monmouthshire. She wanted to change the fortunes, not just of the farm, the pub and the stables but, most of all, the people who made them. Her head was full of plans of how she could possibly do that.

That evening at the Black Prince, Alex and Gwen were studying the list of names and numbers of everyone interested in buying a share of the racehorse.

'I want to use my winnings from the Preview Bonds to

buy a share,' Gwen announced. 'And William left me his shotguns. I don't need them, but they're worth a bit. I'll sell them and put that in too.'

'Are you sure?' Alex checked. 'Don't you want to go on a holiday or buy yourself a treat?'

'This would be better than a holiday, and it *is* a treat.'

'But you said Dickon was a sworn enemy of William's and he had no manners. If I remember correctly, you said he was a miserable bast—'

The door of the pub swung open. Right on cue, Dickon strode through the entrance, his faithful lurcher by his side. Digby's mouth was slightly open, his teeth showing in a broad grin as his long nose pushed against Gwen and then Alex in greeting. They stroked the smooth hair on the top of his head.

'Take it steady there, Digby,' Dickon instructed. 'Go on, you go and settle down with Jiffy. There's a good boy.'

Dickon looked at Gwen and Alex and hesitated. Ordinarily, he would have plodded to his table in the corner. Alex smiled and gestured that there was room if he wanted to sit with them.

'Do you mind,' Dickon asked, his voice unsure, 'if I join you?'

Gwen beamed at him. 'As you have asked so politely, Mr Jones, you may indeed join us.'

He pulled up a chair, the legs scraping over the stone floor.

'In fact,' Gwen continued, 'we were just discussing the syndicate Alex is putting together to buy The Skirrid.'

Rhys brought over a pint of beer for Dickon and set it on the table. 'By the way, I hope you've got my name on there?' He pointed at the list.

'Are you sure?' She lifted her pen.

'Am I sure? I've never been surer of anything. I'm not letting this happen without me. Count me in.' Rhys grinned, before returning to the bar to serve an older man with a face that had the changing weather of three hundred seasons etched into his skin.

While Gwen went to fetch another round, Alex talked Dickon through the names she had assembled and the revised breakdown of the financial plan, with him scrutinizing the numbers and making a few adjustments.

'You've got more here than we need.' He frowned, looking at the long list of names.

'Well, you said that Layton Brooks had knocked you down on the value of the horse,' Alex replied. 'This way, you can say we've outbid him – in case he gets nasty, which, in my experience, he is very capable of doing.' She took a sip of her gin and tonic to fortify herself at the thought of having to deal with Layton again.

'Thank you. I don't know why you're doing this, but thank you, and I hope I can repay your faith in me,' Dickon said quietly to Alex, wondering why so many people, especially the majority who he didn't know, were trusting him with their money in the most uncertain game of all.

Alex reached out and patted his hand. 'We all need a bit of help sometimes, that's all,' she assured him, before adding, 'And don't you worry – I have no doubt I'll be needing yours soon enough.'

Gwen returned from the bar with refills for them all and a soft drink for herself. 'I've been thinking about a name,' she ventured. 'You remember back a few months, at the end of the winter, when you first came down and saw that murmuration of starlings?'

'Oh my god, yes,' Alex gasped. 'I'll never forget it. One of the most beautiful things I've ever seen.'

Her memory took her back to the sweeping and swooping of that group of black birds, moving as one across the sky as they created different shapes.

'Well,' Gwen said meekly, 'they work as a team, protecting each other from the predator. They communicate as if by telepathy; it's a magical, mythical power to move independently but as one.'

'And?' Alex wondered.

'Well, what about the Starling Syndicate?'

Alex clapped her hands together. 'I *love* it!'

Even Dickon looked impressed. 'Better than DJ.' He rolled his eyes. 'I don't want to make it about me. The Starling Syndicate is much better. All we have to do now is ward off the peregrine falcon.'

'What do you mean?' Alex asked, worried.

'Layton Brooks.' Dickon looked solemn. 'He's due at the yard at the weekend. I need to call him and tell him the deal's off.'

CHAPTER THIRTY-EIGHT

Layton Brooks could be heard a mile before he arrived, his engine roaring obnoxiously with the intensity of a fighter jet. He turned into the stable entrance and skidded to a halt, sending gravel shooting sideways. Alex heard his approach as she walked across the fields, and she broke into a run towards the yard to get there in time to help Dickon ward him off. Jiffy ran beside her and then ahead, circling back as if it was a game.

'Not now, Jiff,' she panted as she ran across the undulating field. 'This is serious.'

Layton Brooks was striding across the yard as she intercepted him, putting on a final burst of speed and waving her arms.

'Wait!' It was the only word she could sputter, having completely run out of breath.

She put her hands on her knees and took big gasps of air as she tried to recover the power of speech.

'Not you again,' he spat. 'I know I make women breathless, but this is a bit much.'

Layton Brooks had the unnatural orange sheen of a man who spent the winter months seeking the sun, but had topped it up recently with a dose of fake tan, the palms of his hands betraying the evidence. Alex noticed their dark staining as he flourished a bright-blue handkerchief from his brand-new waxed jacket, which must have been his attempt at looking the part.

'Here you go, mop yer brow.'

Alex waved it away. She did not need his fake chivalry. Not now, not ever.

Before she could say anything else, she heard the rumble of a larger vehicle and turned around to see a large horsebox driving into the parking area. It was shining with the gleam of newness, the gold paint freshly applied and the black letters on the side saying *BROOKS BUBBLES*.

'But you can't . . .' Alex positioned herself in front of him, her heart thumping and her face flushed. She was scared of him, but at the same time, she felt almost reckless with the adrenalin of fury.

'Oh, I think you'll find I can.' He pushed past Alex to clear his path to the yard. 'You've caused me enough trouble.'

Layton Brooks looked around the quadrangle of stables and sneered. Alex recovered her balance, rubbing her arm where he had pushed her with unnecessary force, and followed him.

'What a dump,' Layton scoffed at the sight of two rugs hanging out on the line to dry, both crudely patched up with denim fabric from old jeans, and at the muck heap that hadn't been cleared in months.

Dickon had no staff to help him any more. He was just getting through each day, and Alex now knew that the endless cycle of feeding, mucking out, exercising, grooming, feeding again, doing the paperwork and paying the bills left him little time to do the extra jobs that required his attention.

Layton Brooks marched on towards the stable door that was ajar. Dickon was inside, grooming The Skirrid, who stood quietly, no need to be tied up to the wall.

'What's with the sheep?' Layton laughed. 'That coming too?'

'He has to be with The Skirrid, otherwise he panics.'

'Who panics?' Layton looked confused.

'The horse does. He needs Barry John to help keep him calm.'

Layton put his hands deep in his pockets and stood, legs out wide, his presence big and threatening. 'Well, he'll be calm enough when I have your so-called Barry John on Sunday with a pile of roast potatoes and some mint jelly.' He chuckled, delighted with himself for that one.

Dickon carried on brushing The Skirrid, whispering at him in a low voice. It sounded as if he was singing to him.

'All right, Jones,' Layton Brooks barked at Dickon. 'You making him look pretty for me?'

Dickon slowly walked round The Skirrid, stroking his neck and all the way down his back, across his quarters and down his tail. He faced Layton Brooks and said calmly, 'I left you a message last night. Did you not get it?'

Layton looked blankly at him.

'I told you not to bother coming this morning. The deal's off. I've had an offer superior to yours and, in the best interests of the late owner's family, I've had to accept the higher bid, which I'm sure you'll understand. I'm sorry you've come all this way, but if you'd listened to my message, you could have saved yourself the trouble.'

Layton Brooks had spent a lifetime working with football agents, managers, fellow players and latterly with restaurateurs. He puffed out his chest, set his orange face into a mask and placed his tinted hands on his hips. The classic power pose. 'You what?' he roared.

'You heard me.'

Dickon walked out of the stable and shut the door behind him, but Layton wouldn't be deterred, following him as he made his way out of the yard and back towards the house. Alex did the same.

'We had a deal,' Layton shouted after him. 'You accepted my offer.'

They reached the gleaming horsebox, sponsored by Layton's champagne brand. Dickon talked calmly to the box driver, explaining that there had been a mistake. The driver shook his hand and climbed back behind the wheel.

'*No!*' screamed Layton Brooks. 'You do not get to call the shots here. I made a deal with you. You agreed. That horse is mine, and I'm taking him away with me. Today.'

Layton squared up to Dickon and shoved him in the chest. He was furious. Alex had discussed this eventuality with Gwen and Rhys the other night, after she heard Dickon leave the message. She had been unfortunate enough to see Layton Brooks in action, knowing he could act erratically if things did not go his way, and if he got punchy, which he could, this was not a fair fight. Dickon was a bantamweight, and Layton liked to think of himself as a heavyweight.

'STARLINGS!' Alex called at the top of her voice.

The back door of Dickon's house opened. Out of it stepped

Gwen and Rhys. Layton had his fists raised, ready to punch some sense into this troublesome trainer who he felt wouldn't stick to his side of the bargain.

'Settle down now, there's a lad,' Gwen said as she walked into the middle of the fray. 'You don't want to be getting into a fight out here. Not where no one can call for an ambulance like.'

'Eh?' Layton kept his hands up, ready to swing.

'I mean it,' Gwen said firmly, pointing at Dickon. 'It's not him you need to worry about.' She turned and dramatically pointed at Rhys, who was wearing a tight-fitting T-shirt. 'It's him.'

Right on cue, Rhys crossed his bare arms across his chest and his muscles contracted, making the tiger tattoo ripple. He said nothing, but lifted the left side of his top lip, as if he was snarling, toying with his prey.

The driver of the horsebox started the engine. He had known Dickon from way back and was happy to accept his word that the deal was off. There was no point hanging around where he wasn't wanted.

'You've got no way of getting him out of here now. You can't be putting a horse in the back of that very expensive car now, can you? So let's play nicely and we can all get on our way. All right?'

There was something in Gwen's tone that reminded him of a teacher he had had at school who used to put him in detention. Layton was reduced to a nine-year-old boy again, failing his maths exam and being forced to do times tables over and over again.

His pride told him to argue. His shame told him to retreat.

'Well, if you want the useless animal, you can have him,' he snapped. 'He'll never win a race while he's trained in this shithole, and if you think having a bloody sheep by his side is the answer then you're more of a fool than me.'

'And that's saying something,' Gwen finished his thought process for him. 'Thank you for your time, Mr Brooks. Time for you to head off now, before we have to call the police and report you for loitering.'

Layton Brooks dropped his fists and spat into the gravel. 'You'll regret this,' he hissed at Dickon.

'And as for you.' He directed his gaze to Alex. 'You are a bloody nuisance. I thought I'd seen the last of you when I told your editor what a right royal pain in the arse you'd been in Dubai. I made sure she got shot of you so you'd get what you deserved.'

Alex recoiled as the words hit her.

'Then here you fucking pop up, in the middle of nowhere, getting involved where you're not wanted. What is your problem?' he added.

Alex was speechless. She thought she'd been hung out to dry by Sophie at *Rizz* after the fallout from her article, but it was even worse to hear that it was all done at Layton's bidding.

'She is not the problem,' Gwen stepped in. 'You are. And we've had quite enough. Now get back into your ridiculous midlife-crisis contraption and get out of here. G'won. FUCK OFF!'

Rhys uncrossed his arms and took a step forward, which

did the trick. Layton Brooks scurried to his car, revved it up and disappeared so fast his tyres left huge ruts in the gravel.

Alex let out the breath she didn't know she'd been holding. 'Thank you, Gwen. You were magnificent.' She hugged Gwen.

'I'm sorry I swore. Truly I am. I never use that word, but I thought it might be the only thing that got through his thick skull.' Gwen looked sheepish.

'There is justifiable swearing,' Rhys told her. 'Just as there is justifiable violence. I'm glad we only needed your sharp tongue and not my fists.'

The four of them stood for a second to make sure that the ear-splitting noise of the car engine had faded safely into the distance. They had each other's backs and, in the challenges that would undoubtedly come, they were stronger together than they ever could be apart.

'Right, Team Starling, I'd better exercise your horse.' Dickon smiled. 'He's not going to get any fitter standing in his stable, and we need to train you a winner.'

CHAPTER THIRTY-NINE

The following week, Alex walked outside to see Rhys's jeep pulling into the farmyard. 'I've got someone to see you!' Rhys announced. 'Hey presto!'

Ethan ran towards her, enveloping her in a hug so tight and warm that she felt slightly dazed as she pulled away. Then, from the back of Rhys's Land Rover, Alex saw two less familiar legs swing out. The jeans were turned up at the bottom, the boots hit the floor and, from behind the battered door, a vision revealed itself.

Her heart felt as if it had sprung right out of her ribcage, and her eyes were as wide as if she'd just seen a ghost.

'Magic Mandy!' she whispered. 'How?'

Mandy adjusted her leather jacket and casually waved with a powerful impression of complete self-assurance.

'I booked Mandy for the last hen party I did,' Ethan reminded her. 'And when I discovered that you two hadn't got around to sorting anything out about a visit, I decided to help out.'

Mandy walked slowly towards them. Alex didn't move, unsure of whether to hug her, shake her hand or turn and run.

'Hiya.' Alex waved awkwardly, as if she was a panellist on *Blankety Blank.*

All of a sudden, Mandy was right in front of her. Now

what? Oh god, she was going to hug her. As a reflex action, Alex's body went completely stiff. She kept her arms by her side and flung her head to the right.

'Ow!' Mandy yelped. 'I wasn't expecting a head-butt.'

'Sorry, sorry. I um . . .' Alex mumbled, berating herself for being such a prize idiot.

In the awkwardness of the head-butt, Alex inhaled Mandy's scent, which was a combination of cedar, bergamot and something citrusy – maybe lime.

'Have you got a cold?' Ethan asked.

'No. Not at all.'

'You're sniffing.' He frowned.

'Sorry. It's just that someone smells. I mean, someone smells nice. That's all.'

'Someone, eh?' he said. 'Uh-huh.'

Alex clapped her hands together and immediately regretted it. It made her look like a nursery school teacher. She was so thrown by not only Ethan's arrival but also seeing Mandy again, and she knew she had to get it together.

'So,' she said, 'tea?'

'Sounds good,' Mandy replied. 'And then you can show me round.'

The blue-eyed gaze locked into her, and Alex shivered, physically shivered, at Mandy's smile. As Mandy walked back to the car to retrieve her duffel bag, Alex wondered if she was experiencing a condition rather than an emotion. Was it something the doctor would be able to diagnose and prescribe antibiotics to cure? Had she picked up a dose of flu?

She had never in her life felt so odd. She couldn't speak, she could barely even move, and yet . . . And yet she knew that she had been looking at paintings all her life without ever seeing a great work of art, one that moved her soul. Now she had moved into a wing of the gallery that she had barely visited, and here in front of her, all of a sudden, was a masterpiece.

She bit her lip and looked at the ground.

'You OK?' Ethan whispered as they waited for Mandy.

Alex's mouth wasn't working, so she nodded her head.

'You seem a little out of sorts. I should've asked you if it was all right for Mandy to come, shouldn't I?' He hesitated. 'That wasn't fair to surprise you like that, but I thought it would be fine. She said you'd got along well at Christmas and she'd bumped into you since then and you'd been messaging a bit. I had no idea you'd react like this. I can always take her to the pub with me, rather than foist her on you.'

Mandy was coming back towards them with her duffel bag slung over one shoulder.

'S'fine,' Alex muttered. She turned towards the house and concentrated hard on making her legs move one foot in front of the other.

It took a full hour for her to regain the power of fluent speech. In that time, she listened to Ethan's version of booking Mandy for the hen party, and Mandy's version of the same story.

'Yes, so Ethan books me for this gig, then he pushes me into the room with all these drunk women on a hen night, and I'm meant to keep them happy. They were all too pissed to concentrate, and they couldn't remember whatever card they'd selected. It was hopeless.'

Mandy laughed, and Alex's internal trampoline bounced again into a full tummy flip at the sound. She bit down hard on her bottom lip.

'She was great.' Ethan had taken over again, so Alex turned her head towards him. She hadn't actually been listening to any of this story, apart from gathering that they had met a month ago and established that they wanted to visit their mutual friend in Wales. Alex felt a swell of pride that Mandy regarded her as a friend.

'Anyway, Farmer Alex,' Mandy teased, focusing on her when Ethan went off to look round with Rhys. 'What's this about a racing syndicate? I'd be up for that if there's still room.'

'You would?' Alex asked. 'Do you like horses?'

'I love them. I rode a fair bit as a kid, and my cousin is a jockey. She's based in Somerset. She's pretty good, to be fair, especially with the tricky ones. She's got a magic touch, they say.'

'Clearly runs in the family.' Alex spoke before she had a chance to think, and now she regretted it. 'Sorry. I just meant with the magic, you know. Not your touch . . . as such.'

She paused. What was she talking about? There was a hole opening up in front of her, and she was digging deeper and deeper. It seemed to happen every time she talked to Mandy, but nobody else made her this nervous.

'No offence,' she added unnecessarily. 'I'm sure that's magical too. Ha.'

She had turned into an imitation of a leery stand-up comedian. This was getting worse; she really needed to get a grip of herself.

'None taken,' Mandy said with a benevolent smile. 'I knew what you meant.'

Was that a wink? Had Mandy winked at her and, if she had, what did it mean? She had brought in her duffel bag. Did that mean she was staying the night? What would they talk about, what would they do? Her brain was scrambled.

If there was an actual doctor who could prescribe the antibiotics for this condition, Alex needed to see him right away.

'Can I ask you a question?' Alex asked tentatively.

'Sure.'

'What perfume is that you're wearing?'

'I'm not.' Mandy shrugged. 'I don't tend to wear perfume. It's too intrusive. I'm not going to march against it or anything, but I just prefer a natural human scent. Perfume stops anyone from knowing what another person really smells like, and that can be a shock.'

'Of course,' murmured Alex, who had never even considered not spraying herself with a smell that was nicer than her own skin. Maybe Mandy smelt naturally of cedarwood, bergamot and lime. Lucky her.

'So, do you want to show me around?' Mandy stood up, moving with an enviable, languid ease, while Alex felt like a Thunderbird puppet, her arms and legs stiff at the joints, her voice strangulated.

As Mandy put her teacup into the kitchen sink and started to rinse it, Alex told her she'd do it later and parked her own mug on the side. Mandy turned and Alex turned, and all of a sudden they were no more than an inch apart, facing each

301

other. Alex froze. She was going to have a heart attack, right now in this kitchen, and it would take ages for an ambulance to arrive. It wouldn't happen as quickly as in Hampshire with her father, and she would die this very afternoon and she hadn't even made a will so who would the farm go to then?

The thoughts were racing so fast through her brain that she barely noticed Mandy raise her hand, and then, all of a sudden, Mandy's forefinger was touching her lip. Alex stayed absolutely still.

'You've cut your lip,' Mandy said softly. 'Just there.'

She touched the sore bit on her bottom lip that Alex had created by biting it.

'Uh-huh.' She nodded. She wanted to say *it's your fault, you made me bite it*, but that would sound accusatory. All she wanted was for Mandy to keep her finger on her lip, to hold it there forever, even if that would make eating tricky. And speaking. Let alone farming. Yes, it might be impractical, but Alex didn't want her to take it away because she relished how close they were in this moment.

'C'mon. Let's see these famous lambs, and you can show me all that crazy stuff that's scattered around the farm.' Mandy changed the subject. 'I saw your photos of the tractor in the woods and whatever that thing was in the field. Then there's all that treasure in the trailer.'

'It's a lot of junk,' Alex warned her as they headed into the hall, where coats in all sizes hung off wooden pegs, and a range of boots, collected over the decades, were lined up along the floor.

'I don't agree.' Without prompting, Mandy pulled on a

boiler suit and selected some green rubber boots. Alex swallowed hard. This was unexpected in every sense, but here was a woman who could get stuck in without being asked.

'It only needs a bit of love and tender care, and it'll be grand again,' Mandy said.

Love and tender care were the words Alex latched on to.

'You clearly know what to expect.' Ethan gestured to Mandy's protective outfit.

'Oh, don't worry, I know my way around a farm – and how to protect the clothes I love.'

Love – there was that word again. Alex dreamt of being a favourite jumper, a jacket or a pair of socks. Oh, to be loved by Magic Mandy.

'You all right there?' Mandy called out as Alex tripped on a bump in the uneven floor.

Alex righted herself and waved cheerily. 'Yup, all good,' she said in a singsong voice.

Ethan and Rhys had just walked back in. Ethan glanced at Rhys and raised his eyebrows, wondering what on earth had come over his best friend.

'Has she been drinking?'

CHAPTER FORTY

Over the past few days, as if a spell had been cast, blossom had appeared on the trees, issuing in a riot of colour and an energy of new life. The birdsong was louder than ever, and the grass grew too fast for even the hungriest sheep to keep it shorn short. Even in the blaze of sunshine and bright colours, there was no hiding the disarray of a working farm. If anything, it brought the scrapyard vibe into clearer focus, and for all Alex's attempts at tidying up, it always seemed to revert to type.

'I'm really sorry about the mess.' She sighed, taking in the barn, the filthy farmyard, the muddy fields and the random, abandoned machines lying all around. All she could see were problems that needed solving, items on her to-do list that still needed to be ticked off.

'Jeez, don't worry. I've seen far worse,' Mandy assured her. 'And remember, I've seen your Insta stories, so none of this is a shock. The amazing thing is that it looks . . .'

Alex waited, her breath held, dreading the end of the sentence.

'So much better in real life. It's such a great space, and it has a force, you know, an atmosphere that's really powerful.'

'That's just how I felt when I first walked through it,' Alex agreed with a smile. 'Like it was pulling me in.' She stopped, unsure of herself again, worrying she sounded unhinged.

'That's a good way of putting it.' Mandy turned her head

slowly, like a camera panning across a stage, taking it all in. Her dark hair rippled in the breeze, and she put her hand up to tuck the sides behind her ears. 'I can help you shift the machinery, if you like.'

Alex stuttered that she would like that very much indeed and offered Mandy a percentage of the takings if they managed to sell anything.

'Don't be daft,' Mandy shut her down. 'It'll be fun, and you're my friend. You don't charge your friends commission.'

'Well, at least let me put you up,' Alex suggested. 'You can't be paying for a room at the pub and then helping me make money. That wouldn't be right.'

Alex hadn't intended to ask Mandy to stay and hoped it didn't sound too forward. Her mouth had engaged before her brain had a chance to catch up. Mandy nodded in a non-committal way. Alex wasn't sure if it was a yes or a no.

'Is this where they come to lamb?' Mandy asked, leaning over the gate to the barn.

Alex explained that they had put up separate pens during the weeks when the ewes were due so that they could each have their privacy, their own little cubicle. She took her tour group out into the field to see the lambs, which were now quite big. She pointed out Dickon's yard over the other side of the hedge and told Mandy and Ethan about the great escape. The lambs were now fully weaned from their mothers and it wouldn't be many weeks now until the time of their departure.

'That's the bit I struggle with,' Alex admitted. 'I try not to think about it, but every time we're feeding them or I'm watching them head-butting each other, I think that in a few months, they won't be here. Gwen says I have to consider all the people they'll feed instead and that I must see the contribution they'll make. She says I'll get used to it, but I don't know that I ever will.'

As if her ears were burning at the mention of her name, Gwen appeared over the brow of the hill on the quad bike, having checked the sheep further up the slopes. She drove towards the four of them, hair blowing behind her in the wind.

'She looks like Susan Sarandon in *Thelma and Louise*,' Mandy observed.

Rhys laughed. 'I tell you what,' he said. 'She'd sure as hell shoot anyone who tried messing with Alex here. I've never seen someone so naturally maternal to a girl she's not related to and hadn't met before this year.'

It hadn't occurred to Alex that Gwen was being 'maternal' towards her, but if that meant kind, protective, nurturing and educating, then yes, it was true she'd been lucky enough to experience all of those things from her.

'Hey Gwen!' she shouted.

Gwen jumped off the quad bike and hurried over to them. She was thrilled to see Ethan again and hugged him tight before kissing him on both cheeks.

'I'm so pleased you're back. We've missed you. Rhys especially,' she said, with a knowing wink.

It might have taken a while, but Gwen had finally cottoned on to what was going on between the two of them and wanted to make sure they knew that she very much approved.

'This is Mandy,' Alex introduced them.

307

Mandy stretched out her hand, but Gwen had already wrapped her arms around her, smothering her in Welsh affection.

'You must be Magic Mandy!' she exclaimed. 'I've heard a lot about you.'

Alex blushed. She didn't think she'd talked about Mandy that much, other than telling Rhys and Gwen about her magic tricks and how good she was with children, and she supposed she had told them about their messages to each other. That was it, wasn't it? Not much, really.

'See?' Mandy said when she emerged from Gwen's embrace. 'That's how you hug a person hello.'

They stood in the field, the five of them, with Rhys and Gwen pointing out the local names of the mountain peaks around them. As the sun began to get lower in the sky, lights were coming on in houses far in the distance. Gwen could name every one of the people who lived in them, and Rhys could tell Mandy what they liked to drink when they came to the bar.

'It's a friendly community then?'

'Well, everyone knows everyone's business,' Rhys explained. 'And we're all here to help one another. Apart from those who fall out, of course, but eventually they fall back in again. Just look at you and Dickon.'

'Oh, I never had a beef with Dickon Jones,' Gwen insisted. 'That was all William and his dad. Some stupid row over money, and then the row about the crops, and then that was it. Twenty years later, they still weren't talking. Dickon's all right, though, and Alex has thawed him out, haven't you?'

They all looked at Alex.

'To be fair, it took me cracking my skull to do it, but yes, the syndicate is to help him, so I suppose that's the spirit of this place rubbing off on me. He needs help, and we're his closest neighbours, so it makes sense we should offer first. Isn't that right?'

She wanted to make it clear that her need to help Dickon was based on friendship and community, not anything romantic, so that Mandy didn't get the wrong end of the stick.

'That's my girl,' Gwen said proudly. 'Spot on.'

'He likes to play music to the horses,' Alex explained when the distant strains of music drifted over. 'The Skirrid particularly likes The Eurythmics.'

'Good taste.' Ethan nodded approvingly.

Gwen turned to get back on the quad bike but, before she went, Mandy asked her. 'Have you heard of a farmyard sale?'

'Oh yes,' Gwen said. 'They have them every now and again round here. Why?'

'I figured it might be the answer to the abandoned machinery problem,' Mandy continued. 'Alex has got some great photos already, and we could advertise it the farming magazines, but also get the pictures out there online. There are folks all over the country who collect vintage farmyard machinery.'

'Really?' Alex looked doubtful.

'You wouldn't think it, but I promise you it's a thriving market. When my old grandad died, we had over a thousand people turn up over the weekend of the farmyard sale. We got rid of everything. Even the crap you think is unusable will get taken by the scrap merchants.'

'She's right, you know.' Gwen climbed back onto the quad

bike. 'I tried for years to persuade William to do it, but he didn't like the idea of strangers swarming all over his land.'

She started up the engine and shouted over the noise, 'So as long as you don't mind a crowd, it's a good idea. She's a bright one, that lass. You want to keep her hanging around.'

She tipped her head towards Mandy, who nodded in mutual respect.

'I guess I'd better take you up on your offer of lodgings.' Mandy turned to Alex as they walked back to the farmhouse. 'Seems like we have work to do, and you'll need me to stick around.'

Alex looked down at Jiffy, who was close by, as always.

'We'd like that, wouldn't we?' she said to the dog, trying hard not to give away the rush of joy she felt.

CHAPTER FORTY-ONE

Alex was astounded by Mandy's commitment to the cause. She was a woman on a mission, indefatigable in cataloguing items, pairing them with the relevant instruction manual, researching their history and accurately dating the build year of the various tractors from their serial numbers. She helped Alex draw up enticing sales pitches for each item, pairing them with photos and preparing each item for various online auction sites that specialized in farm machinery. She ran out to the farmyard with a head torch and a measuring tape to check the size of a chain harrow.

'It's 2,290 millimetres wide, 2,440 millimetres long,' she announced on her return. 'That's seven and a half feet by eight feet.'

'Bloody hell, that's good mental arithmetic,' Alex enthused. Was there nothing this woman couldn't do?

'Ah, it's nothing,' Mandy said. 'Wait till you see me sell. Then you're allowed to be impressed. If we are left with a single thing that we don't want, I will pay for it myself.'

Alex noted the use of 'we' and liked that feeling of being in it together.

Every time Alex made eye contact with Mandy, her tummy flipped. She didn't want to let her out of her sight, as if somehow that would break the spell, and yet she also didn't want to ruin it by letting Mandy see too much of her. She would only be disappointed. Alex was self-aware enough to know that she was not a woman of hidden depths, but she was confused by her feelings and didn't know how to voice them.

'Are you OK? You look worried.'

Alex weighed up whether to be honest or not. She walked towards the fire, desperate to do something to keep busy, laying the logs carefully and putting some kindling wood on top. There was no need to light it tonight, so she plumped up the cushions on the sofa and the armchair, tidying the magazines into a neater pile.

Mandy sat at the kitchen table, watching her. 'You can tell me,' she gently encouraged Alex. 'If I can help, I will.'

'I don't know how I'm going to cope, to be honest,' Alex said into cushions.

Truthful but vague.

'I've never felt like this before. I'm scared.'

Vulnerable and honest. So far, so good.

She turned back towards the kitchen table and saw Mandy looking at her with an intensity that was disarming.

'You can do this,' Mandy said firmly. 'I believe in you.'

Alex sat down again, and Mandy reached out, patting Alex's hand as if she were giving a dog reassurance. Alex didn't know how to make it clear that she wasn't talking about running the farm.

'We'll make this work, but right now I need sleep.' Mandy glanced at the clock on the wall above the Aga. 'It's not that late, but it'll be an early start and I'm knackered. Must be all that fresh air.'

She stood up and stretched. Alex tried not to stare as her jumper rode up to reveal a flash of her toned stomach.

'Gwen has taken my bag upstairs.' Mandy pushed her chair back under the table and made for the door. 'It's the second room on the right, she said?'

'That's the one. Bathroom is two doors beyond it. Don't worry, you don't have to share so it's all yours. No interruptions while you're sitting on the loo or standing in the shower. Ha ha!'

Mandy looked perplexed. Alex bit her bottom lip where it was already sore, the pain shooting through to her brain, which would, she hoped, prevent her from babbling any more nonsense.

'Right,' Mandy said. 'Good to know.'

She shut the door behind her, and Alex was left with Jiffy. 'I'm such an idiot.'

The Welsh terrier cocked his head to one side and looked at her, seemingly in agreement.

'What is the matter with me?' she asked him, wishing he could answer.

Alex had moved from a world of deadlines and word counts to what, exactly? That was the hard bit for her to fathom. There was no doubt she was working harder, felt more exhausted by the end of the day, but she was more alive, more present in every moment, keenly aware of the weather, the sounds of animals and what those sounds might mean.

She was hungrier and more sensitive to the flavours of her food. She was more reliant on others, more grateful for their support. She needed to succeed for them, but she also wanted

313

to be proud of herself. That was something she had never felt before. If this was what responsibility felt like, then she was strangely comfortable with it. In the midst of this gradual and yet sudden self-awareness, the one thing she wasn't looking for was love. Not looking at all.

And yet here it was, staring right at her.

'What am I going to do?' she asked Jiffy, who emitted a little whine. She reached down and ruffled his head. 'It's lucky you love me, Jiffy. C'mon – bedtime.'

The floorboards creaked as Alex made her way upstairs and across the top landing. She paused outside Mandy's door. She raised her hand, but she couldn't bring herself to knock.

She shut the door of her bedroom and sat on the bed, pulling off her jeans and her socks. Her heart was pounding, and her brain felt as if it was exploding. She had been attracted to women before, had even had the odd experimental kiss, but this was different. She had never entertained the idea of falling in love with a woman. Even though Ethan, her best friend in the whole world, was gay, she had always thought her future lay with a man as a partner, and it had certainly been drummed into her enough by her mum that she should settle down and find a nice husband. She examined the evidence of her failed relationships, her lack of commitment and her resolute refusal to let any man get close enough to cause her pain.

'How stupid,' she said to Jiffy, who was now curled up in a tight circle in the middle of the bed. 'How can I not have known I was looking in the wrong place?'

CHAPTER FORTY-TWO

Over the following days, Alex still couldn't seem to speak in coherent sentences whenever Mandy was nearby. Her body wouldn't function properly. She dropped things, tripped over her own feet, fumbled with knives, forks, a pen, a gate latch. She was in a permanent fluster.

'Get a grip,' she kept telling herself. She knew she could be a chump at the best of times, frequently saying the wrong thing or laughing inappropriately at what she thought was a joke, but this was beyond anything. Her brain was either not sending the correct messages to her limbs or they were somehow getting scrambled en route.

The good news was that the farm machinery was getting positive responses online. Various offers had been made, and Alex had arranged for one big collection day, which she would combine with a farmyard sale. If she could get people here to pick up one item, they might well decide to buy more.

After staying for four days, Mandy had to return to London for a job. Alex hugged her awkwardly and struggled to find the words to say goodbye.

'Yeah, well – um – thanks for everything,' was the best she could manage. 'See you soon, yeah?'

Mandy looked a little perplexed as she clambered into the Land Rover for a lift to the station with Rhys. She waved out of the window and put on an Arnold Schwarzenegger accent as she shouted, 'I'll be back!'

Alex watched the Land Rover all the way down the drive, thinking, *I hope so.*

Ethan didn't need to return to London yet, so was making the most of his time with Rhys, slowly getting to know him and share his world. He had also helped Alex draw up a business plan which would make best use of the farm's assets.

He put an arm round her after seeing Mandy drive away, knowing his best friend would need a distraction, and led her back into the kitchen to help her with the paperwork. Their goal was finding any diversification that wouldn't require a huge investment. They both decided that it was best to make use of the natural surroundings to offer a break to people who wanted to switch off from technology and the incoming buzz of text messages, emails, WhatsApps and social media.

The money from the machinery sale would help keep the bank from her door for now and, as soon as she sold her flat in London, she could invest in a few yurts and the basic essentials that would be necessary for a remote rural retreat. She might even be able to persuade Dickon to incorporate equine therapy into the deal. He had room at his stables to house retired racehorses, and there was loads of evidence that working with and around horses helped people with addiction issues, anxiety or post-traumatic stress. Maybe, she thought, there was a way of combining their resources in a way that could benefit them both.

'You know you talked about walking up one of those peaks?' Ethan ventured as he made them both a coffee.

Alex looked at the mountain of paperwork she needed to get through, unsure of whether he was being serious.

'We should do it today,' he suggested.

It was a lovely spring day. The weather forecast was good, the temperature warm but not too hot for a hike, and Rhys had already prepared a picnic for them.

'I mean it. We could drive over to the car park at the bottom of The Skirrid. After all, that's the hill we should climb. We've bought the horse named after it, so we should get to the summit and see what the view looks like.'

Alex fought the instinct to say she didn't have time, there was too much going on, too many tasks on her to-do list that needed to be ticked off.

'I know,' he said when Alex gestured towards the paperwork. 'There's a lot to do, but I think we could do with a bit of fresh air and to see the world from a different perspective. Come on – it will do you good.'

He chivvied her into submission and, as soon as they got out of the car and started the beginning of the climb through the moss-clad trees, she knew they had made the right decision. It would be lovely to spend the day just the two of them.

They were too short of breath on the way up to talk much but, after rising above the trees onto the bare sides of the hill, following the well-worn path and taking big strides up some stone steps to the top, they paused to take in the view. They could see the farm down in the valley and Dickon's gallop rising up to the woods.

'I've got an idea.' Alex wanted to test her theory. 'I think we could develop a retreat for people who want a digital detox.'

Ethan encouraged her to expand.

'I can put them up on the farm with basic accommodation and cold-water showers, that sort of thing. Pretty hardcore but not uncomfortable.'

'I'd prefer a warm bath.' Ethan bent down to retie his shoelaces. 'So I'll stay at the pub, thanks very much.'

'It's not for you!' Alex countered. 'I'm thinking we could combine walking with some farm work and, if Dickon likes the idea, maybe develop an equine therapy centre with retired racehorses at his place.'

'I love it!' Ethan took a swig of water before motioning up the slope, encouraging Alex to keep walking. 'I can help you draw up a business plan, if you like.'

'I would like.'

They continued their ascent, exchanging friendly greetings with a group of schoolchildren making their way down.

They pushed on, and after about an hour, they reached the trig point. Leaning on it for support and to catch her breath, Alex took in the panorama. The breeze was stronger up here, and she was grateful for its cooling effect. It had taken about an hour to get to the top, but boy, it was worth the effort.

'Oh my word, look at this,' she called over to Ethan, turning in a circle with her arms stretched wide. 'Look at all of this!'

They could see for miles in every direction. Ethan got out his Ordnance Survey map, Rhys having insisted he bring one just so they wouldn't get lost, and helped identify Sugar Loaf Mountain, the Black Mountains, Bannau Brycheiniog, formerly known as the Brecon Beacons, and the beautiful Usk Valley.

Looking to the south past Newport, they could see the sun glistening on the water of the Bristol Channel and, with the help of the map, they identified the Mendips in Somerset beyond the inlet. Scanning round to the east, they could see across the border into Gloucestershire and, turning to the north, they spied Herefordshire. In the immediate foreground, the slopes of the hill ran down into wide fertile fields divided by hedges into neat rectangles, squares and an occasional rhombus.

The walked along the long ridge and came to a couple of stones either side of a muddy path. There were lumps and bumps in what seemed a more ordered circle.

'Ah, this must be St Michael's,' Ethan told her. 'Rhys told me we'd find this. It's why it's called the Holy Mountain.'

Alex felt as if she was flying high above the land below and wondered how on earth they'd ever got a congregation to come all the way up here.

'It dates back to medieval times,' Ethan explained. 'But they used it as a hideaway place for Catholics to worship during the Reformation. You know, when old Henry VIII was smashing down the monasteries. It was useful to be out of the way.'

'This is pretty extreme,' Alex said. 'They wouldn't have got found up here, that's for sure.'

She sat down on a tufted lump of grass and patted the space next to her. Ethan followed suit.

'There was supposedly a landslide here.' Ethan pointed over the northern edge where the mountain fell sharply down to the valley below. 'At the very moment Christ was crucified. Skirrid comes from the Welsh for shaking or trembling.'

Alex nodded. It made sense for both the mountain and for the horse, although he was shaking less violently these days, thanks to Barry John, and she hoped the comfort the lamb gave him would galvanize Skirry into fulfilling his potential.

'It has a certain magic about it, don't you think?' she said.

Ethan agreed. Some places had a special aura, a sense that the space between here and somewhere else was very thin.

'Talking of magic . . .' he ventured gently, hoping to give Alex the opportunity to open up. Having observed Alex's recent odd behaviour and more frequent tendency to say the wrong thing, he could only put it down to her being nervous around Mandy.

'I don't know what's got into me,' she confessed. 'Mandy has this weird effect on me. Every time I look at her, I blush and I get this strange lurching sensation in my stomach. What is going on?'

'You've never had tummy flips before?' Ethan looked amused.

Alex shook her head. She had had many boyfriends – a few had even developed into serious relationships, and she'd briefly contemplated the idea of marrying Dan – but she had always been in control. Her guard firmly in place, a protective layer of armour that prevented her from getting hurt.

'I don't know why it's happening now.' Alex tried to reason her way through the strange reaction she had to Mandy. 'I kissed a girl once in school – everyone did – but I didn't think I was gay. I thought I just hadn't met the right guy.'

'And let's be honest, you've tried plenty!' Ethan interjected.

'Rude.' She elbowed him in the ribs.

Alex looked out at the view as Ethan unpacked the picnic, offering her a sausage covered in honey and mustard.

'Did you always know?' she asked him.

His mouth full with an egg mayonnaise sandwich, he nodded vigorously and then tried to reply. 'Uh-huh,' he muffled. 'They teased me at school and called me a fairy, that sort of stuff, but then I found the Pet Shop Boys, Erasure and Boy George, so I lost myself in all that.'

He finished his sandwich. 'It was so much easier when I got to London,' he added.

Alex had looked hard for love and hadn't found it. She had come here alone and was happy to make friends with people like Rhys and Gwen and even Dickon, who had thawed so much since his horse had tried to knock her out. If she was honest with herself, though, as nice as her new friends were, it did feel like something was missing from her life.

Alex remembered how entranced she had been by Mandy, the first time they met on the cold winter night at Aunt Di's party, and then again when they bumped into each other by the river in London, but it was only when she arrived here in Wales that she'd properly felt the ground shake, like the mountain up here. When they had started talking, she hadn't wanted the conversation to stop. Like a box set on Netflix, she wanted to watch one after another after another.

'What's making you smile so wickedly to yourself?' Ethan asked.

Alex blushed. He could always read her mind.

'I was just thinking that she's like a new box set I want to keep watching on repeat. You know, sort of addictive.'

'Please,' Ethan said sternly. 'Do not repeat that to Mandy. She will not appreciate being compared to a box set. You may think it is a compliment, but I assure you, it is not. And don't start talking about slippers either. No one wants to be compared to a comfy old pair of slippers. It just makes them think of smelly feet and verrucas. Ugh.'

They laughed together, friends who could be honest with each other about their own faults and inadequacies. Ethan passed her a sandwich, knowing she would like it.

'This is delicious,' she murmured approvingly, after taking a chunky bite.

'I know. Rhys can really cook. I said I'd help him with some theme nights to pull in the punters,' Ethan filled her in. 'That place deserves to be overflowing every night of the week, not just for Six Nations matches and the Abergavenny Food Festival.'

Alex smiled. She was so pleased that Ethan was investing proper time in someone and, in return, Rhys seemed to treat Ethan well, which hadn't always been the case with his previous dalliances. She reached out and punched him playfully on the arm.

'Get you,' she joked.

They could see rain in the distance, but it was being blown away from them. In the gap between, a glorious rainbow reached down towards the valley she now knew as home.

'Hope that hits the farm.' She sighed. 'I could do with a pot of gold right now.'

Ethan would let her talk about the farm and its finances on the way down, but right now, he wanted her to focus on her heart. If she could find genuine love, it would be worth more than any hidden treasure.

'So what do you want to do? About Mandy?' he asked, not letting her get away that easily.

Alex wasn't altogether sure. 'I just, you know, I hadn't ever thought I might be gay,' she said slowly, trying to process her thoughts. 'And now I'm annoyed with myself for all the years I've wasted. I can do all the talk about being brave, being different, having fun and enjoying the freedom of no ties, but here I am, nearly forty, floundering around trying to work out whether or not I am in love with a woman for the first time in my life.'

Ethan leant towards her and took her hand. She tried to resist the urge to cry.

'Don't overthink it,' he advised her. 'When you know, you know. Take me and Rhys. All right, I admit initially it was just a physical thing. The man is a god. But then we talked all night and I told him things I've never told anyone in my life. We have talked so much since then, and it's made me realize how special it is to find someone – anyone – with whom you can be utterly and completely yourself.'

Alex squeezed his hand back. She was so pleased to see him happy and settled and that someone liked him for who he really was.

'It's like I don't have to put on a show for him,' Ethan expanded. 'He has this way of making me feel like I'm the most special person in the world just as I am. It's amazing and – let's be honest – it's got to be, to make me drive all the way down the interminable M4. Those roadworks are doing my head in, and the train's not much better.'

Alex hadn't bothered going back to London since she'd left. There was too much to do on the farm, and she loved watching the lambs growing fatter and stronger every day, even if it meant they were getting closer to their inevitable departure.

'So how do I tell her?' Alex asked tentatively. Ethan was the expert. He'd know.

'Can't help you there, my love.' He shook his head. 'You'll cock up anything I suggest, and if you try and play it like a film scene or learn a script, it'll just come out wrong. You'll find the right time and, if she has even half an inkling of what's going on, you'll be fine.'

He took a big swig of water and started to pack up the picnic. 'And you can congratulate yourself on being part of the most popular trend of the moment.'

'What's that?' Alex asked.

'You're a LOL.'

'What? A laugh out loud joke?' Alex was offended.

'No,' Ethan clarified. 'A Late Onset Lesbian. It's all the rage, darling.'

She punched him on the arm again, harder this time, and scrambled to her feet. She felt lighter on the way down, as if she'd been carrying a rucksack for years and now it had been lifted off her back.

CHAPTER FORTY-THREE

Dickon was rejuvenated by the knowledge that The Skirrid was staying in his care. The Starling Syndicate had been officially registered, with Alex as the syndicate manager, so she was in charge of all the communication with the syndicate members. As long as Dickon told her what was going on, she could tell the members and, although she could have done without yet another job on her to-do list, it kept her connected to people she cared about.

With Ethan gone, Alex settled back into her routine. Over the next few weeks, her forays across the field to Dickon's stables became more frequent as she checked in on both the horse and him. Although Alex was no expert, even she could tell that The Skirrid was growing stronger and fitter by the day. He was also significantly calmer. Barry John the lamb was always there by his side, either in the box or when they were turned out in the small paddock that Dickon had created on his overgrown lawn.

'Saves on mowing.' He shrugged.

Alex took photos and little videos of The Skirrid. She sat in Dickon's kitchen and sent them to the other syndicate members, along with the latest plans for his next race. While she was on his Wi-Fi, she checked her emails, most of which were spam, and had a brief look at social media. Her thumb moved through the posts, but she didn't stop at any of them.

It wasn't as interesting as what was happening here, right now, and she realized she hadn't missed how she previously spent so much of her time.

'He'll be ready for a run fairly soon,' Dickon told her. 'There's a race at Chepstow that I think will suit.'

Alex wondered how many of the syndicate members would come.

'It's only down the road, so not too far for him to travel, and I know the clerk of the course so I'll ask permission for Barry John to be in the stables.' Dickon sat down to attack the bills he had now arranged into a neat pile.

'Thanks to you, I now get a few of these paid,' he murmured. 'I've got the kids coming this weekend, so it'll be good to have it sorted. Honestly, this is a lifeline. I can't thank you enough.'

Alex's face lit up, enjoying the feeling of having been useful. 'Now I've got to tackle my own problems at the farm,' she said, standing up to leave.

'You'll work it out.' Dickon looked up. 'I know you will, but if you need anything from me, anything at all, I'm here to help.'

Alex knew he meant it and was grateful for the unexpected friendship that had formed between them. She had only cautiously mentioned the idea of equine therapy; it seemed he was interested, but he'd suggested it should be a longer-term project. They had other priorities to focus on first.

She walked outside, calling Jiffy back from his hunting exploits with Digby, and made her way back across the field to her farmhouse.

Gwen helped her advertise the farmyard sale on the Farmers' Facebook page and across all the other relevant websites. The items that had already been sold online were marked with a red ribbon and a tag carrying details of the person who had bought them.

'It'll be quite a turn-out,' Gwen warned.

She wasn't joking.

At 6.30 on Saturday morning, the first cars started to arrive. Dickon had brought over sawdust and straw to lay in the field they had designated as a car park. He had also agreed that the sheep could graze on his land for a few days to keep them away from the crowds.

Their visitors had come from all over the country, and there was nothing they didn't want to examine. They bought the items they wanted in cash or transferred money direct into the farm account, and by ten o'clock, the place was heaving. Rhys had turned the kitchen into a makeshift café and was doing great business selling sausage and bacon rolls, egg butties and fresh tea or coffee.

Alex was staggered at how many people had come. There were a lot of locals – people whose faces she recognized but whose names she didn't yet know – but there were plenty she had never seen before as well. There was a buzz about the proceedings, with so many people having farming in common. Even the locals who had come mainly out of curiosity had ended up hanging around for a chat.

'She hasn't got a clue what she's doing,' she overheard a female voice say.

She paused at the corner of the house, just out of sight, but in range to hear the rest of the conversation, which was the first whiff of negativity she'd come across.

'Another bloody Londoner coming out here with big ideas. She won't last a year, I bet,' a man sneered.

Alex's face flushed with humiliation at what some of the locals really thought. She only half heard the man's voice as it disappeared out of range.

'Layton could help us finance it all. Looking at the state of it, it's only a matter of time until the farm goes bust, and when it does, it will go for a fraction of the price it should. That could be our opportunity to swoop in and snap it up. We could have some set-up here if we play our cards right,' the voice said.

Horrified by hearing Layton's name, Alex emerged from her hiding spot to see the back of the couple who had been speaking. The woman was slender with a long blonde ponytail, while the man was shortish and lean, his legs slightly bowed. He turned his head to one side, and she saw the glittering dark eyes, handsome face and beak-like nose, curved like a peregrine falcon. It was Bertie O'Reilly and Abigail, Dickon's ex-wife. They must have dropped off the children next door and then come here to have a poke around.

A surge of anger and determination coursed through her body as she saw them walking back towards their car. She had to protect her patch and warn Dickon, because he wouldn't be able to cope with the man he hated more than any other moving in next door.

By the end of Sunday, they had managed to sell more than either she or Gwen had ever imagined they would – even the broken-down car with no tyres had gone to a round-faced local who wanted it for storage.

'Better than a shed.' He ran a paint-stained hand over its roof. 'It's got four doors, see. Well, five if you count the boot, so it's perfect. It's watertight, it can be locked easily, and it's not going to need varnish every few years. I can keep all sorts in there.'

Alex didn't ask what sorts of things you would keep in the shell of an abandoned car because, much to her delight, it had gone, and that was the main thing. So had the old tractor, the ancient shears, the contents of the trailer and a pile of bricks left over from the building of Gwen's annexe.

'It's like the locusts have attacked.' Alex surveyed the scene as dusk fell. The yard was transformed; there was so much more space than before.

'I told you it'd be busy.' Gwen closed the gate of the field after the last car had gone. She walked back towards Alex with a huge grin on her face. 'I wish William could see you now. He'd be so proud.'

Alex was relieved that the first part of her plan had worked, but she knew this was just the beginning. While the cash they had raised would certainly help, she'd need to do much much more.

Despite the huge success of the day, she had been left with a slightly bitter taste in her mouth. The words she had over-heard still stung. She needed to prove she wasn't playing at being a farmer. She wanted to do it properly, and she could not afford to fail, not if people like Bertie O'Reilly were after her land, and perhaps Dickon's as well. It wasn't just her future that was at stake: it was that of her neighbour, and Gwen too. Jiffy whined gently and pushed his nose against her leg in sympathy.

'C'mon. There's a bottle of wine in the fridge, and I think we deserve a glass in celebration.' She turned to Gwen, forcing a smile.

Jiffy settled into the armchair as the two women sat together, Alex making note of what needed to be done next and expanding on the idea of a rural retreat for families. Gwen listened, occasionally questioning or offering practical adaptations.

'That could work,' she said a few times, filling Alex with confidence that she could improve the finances of the farm. 'I like the idea of yurts and, if being off grid is part of the appeal, they can't complain about there being no signal.'

Alex told Gwen that she was contacting estate agents to put her London flat on the market.

'It'll give me the capital to invest and a chance of making a go of it.' Alex knew there was no point sharing what she had heard Bertie O'Reilly and Abigail discussing because it would only put Gwen on edge. If she could make her plans work, their nasty little scheme wouldn't matter.

The proceeds from the farmyard sale would tide them over for a while, and the lambs would be gone by the end of August, hopefully making a decent profit.

'You don't mind me wanting to change things?' Alex asked, aware that her ideas might be disruptive.

'William knew what he was doing when he picked you. I told him that we had to move with the times, but he was scared of losing what he had. He often said he wished he could go back and do things differently. He must've known you'd be bolder than him,' Gwen assured her.

Alex digested this news but wondered how William had guessed she would be able to do any of it, given that she didn't know herself. At least if she failed now, it wouldn't be for lack of trying.

CHAPTER FORTY-FOUR

Alex's heart lifted when she got a message from Mandy, who asked if she could come down for a couple of days to check in on The Skirrid, having committed to being a part of the syndicate.

'I want to keep an eye on my investment,' she said. 'Otherwise you could be conning me into some sort of Ponzi scheme. I don't want to lose my hard-won fortune while you disappear to a Caribbean island to drink rum and smoke whacky-backy.'

Alex laughed and promised she would do no such thing, but told her she'd be very welcome to visit. She just hoped that – this time – she would be able to get her words out and be less flustered around her.

When Mandy arrived on the last Sunday in May, they went straight over to Dickon's yard to be greeted by a knee-high bundle of laughter and blonde hair, which cannoned into the two women as they came through the arch. Instinctively, Mandy lifted up the child under the shoulders and swung him into the air.

'And who are you, young sir?' she asked, gently returning him to ground level.

'I'm Benjamin Jones,' he said. 'I'm four and three quarters years old, and when I grow up, I'm going to be a racehorse trainer. Who are you?'

Mandy raised herself to her full height and put her hands on her hips. 'My name is Amanda Cox. I am thirty-eight years old and, if I ever grow up, I will let you know. Right now, I can show you the best trick you've ever seen.'

She squatted down on her haunches and reached behind the little boy's ear with her right hand.

'Let's see what you've got hidden back here. Could it be an insect, could it be a little bird, could it be a rabbit?'

'There's nothing there!' he squealed. 'I promise you I washed this morning especially because we were coming to see Daddy! There's nothing . . . *Oh!*' His face lit up with shock.

With a theatrical flourish, Mandy revealed a multi-coloured butterfly made of the thinnest tissue paper. It was a thing of beauty, so delicate and fragile that it wasn't going to last two minutes in the hands of the boy who was now running with it to find his sister.

'Beth! Beth!' he shouted. 'Look what was living behind my ear!'

'Ben! Do not run in the yard. You'll scare the horses. And you know the rules about shouting,' a woman's voice called out firmly.

Alex and Mandy walked into the yard, towards the voice they had heard and the stable that Alex knew contained The Skirrid and Barry John the lamb.

'Hello?' A figure revealed itself from the tack room. She wore jodhpurs and knee-length black boots, which accentuated her long, slender legs and a blue fleece gilet over her long-sleeved shirt. Her long blonde hair trailed down her back.

Alex recognized her immediately from the day of the farm-yard sale.

'Can I help you?' she asked, pulling her hair into a thick, bouncing ponytail.

'Hi. I'm Alex. I'm Dickon's neighbour over there at Tir Glas Farm.' She pointed in the general direction of it.

'And you must be Madame Butterfly?' she said to Mandy, her tone dismissive and her expression stony. 'My son now thinks you are a magician.'

'I sort of am.' Mandy stretched out her hand. 'Pleased to meet you.'

'Pleased to meet you both as well. I'm Abigail.' She ignored Mandy's hand. 'I'm Dickon's wife . . . I mean ex-wife.'

She walked back into the tack room to retrieve a crash helmet. She put it in a large bag that already contained various bits of riding gear.

'I left a few things behind,' she said, by way of explanation.

Alex watched Abigail walk back towards the house, wishing she could wear a shirt tucked into a pair of jodhpurs and look that good.

'Might see you later,' Abigail called out. 'But if not, nice meeting you.' She waved dismissively over her shoulder as she called out to her children to get themselves ready and say goodbye to Daddy.

'I don't like her,' Mandy whispered.

'I don't either, but gosh she's pretty,' Alex said, not meaning to voice her thoughts.

'Do you think so?' Mandy asked. 'I don't. She looks too much like a prototype. You know, what AI would create if it could make "rural mother of two" – an impossibly perfect Disney princess. There's no life in it.'

Alex didn't like the 'life' that was appearing in her face with every passing year, and more recently from the stress of taking over the farm. She yearned for the smooth, crease-free skin of her teenage years.

'Imagine if you looked around here at this landscape and every hill looked the same?' Mandy waved her arms theatrically. 'A perfectly rising curve of smooth land that dropped down on every side with the same gradient. That wouldn't be so exciting, would it? It wouldn't be so enticing or endlessly fascinating. You want a bit of irregularity to create originality.'

Alex didn't know whether she fell into the 'original' category, or whether she could ever hope to have a face that was 'endlessly fascinating'. She did not dare ask or look at Mandy.

They walked to The Skirrid's stable door to find the racehorse lying down at the far wall with Barry John sleeping soundly between his legs.

'Ah, a power nap.' Mandy chuckled softly. 'He's a sensible boy.'

Barry John woke up and bleated. The Skirrid shifted fractionally, nuzzled the lamb, and then they both settled back down again.

'The lamb is meant to be a comfort to the horse,' Alex explained. 'Even if it looks the other way round.'

'It's like all good relationships,' Mandy said. 'Gotta to work both ways. Fifty-one per cent to forty-nine per cent, and the one with the upper hand keeps changing.'

'Seems like you know a lot about relationships.' Alex stared at The Skirrid, amazed at how calm he looked in his role as protector.

'Had enough go wrong to work out a few things,' Mandy said cryptically, turning from the stable door. 'Now let's leave these two to their sleep.'

Alex wanted to ask who Mandy had loved and how it had gone wrong, but didn't want to seem too intrusive. She was deliberately dialling down the volume and trying to play it cool, but it was so hard as she was desperate to know more.

Inside Dickon's house, at Ben's insistence, Mandy did more tricks for him and his sister.

'Abigail is taking the rest of her things,' Dickon explained when they heard the clattering of drawers.

Alex made use of the Wi-Fi to check her emails, seeing an update from the estate agent informing her that there were plenty of viewings booked for the flat and he was hopeful of a firm offer. She started to do some calculations in her head about how much she could save if it was sold quickly, and how much she needed to spend.

'The Skirrid looks happy,' Mandy said from her position on the rug where she was building a castle for magic butterflies, having produced a few more from behind the children's ears. Now they were demanding that the animals had five-star accommodation.

'Look, Daddy, it has a bathroom here! See?' Beth showed Dickon as he joined them on the floor.

'And in the garden,' Ben said, 'we need to build a trampoline for the frog.'

Ben ran to the kitchen drawer to find some cling film.

Dickon helped him stretch the cling film across a cereal bowl. 'There! A trampoline fit for a frog,' he said, grateful to Mandy for distracting his children while their mother crashed about upstairs.

'Who's going to ride The Skirrid?' Mandy asked.

Dickon dangled a matchstick in the air, ready to place it in position. 'Now there's a good question. The jockey who fell off him at Cheltenham has refused to ride for me ever again.' Dickon sighed.

'My cousin is decent rider,' Mandy offered. 'She's only starting out, mind, but she's good. My mum tells me that she's getting a reputation for being able to tame the tricky ones. I'm not sure it's the sort of reputation you want in jump racing. Seems to me it's an invitation to A & E, but she doesn't mind.'

'What's she called?' Dickon asked.

'Lucy Maynard.'

'I know Lucy Maynard!' He was so excited he spilt the bowl of jelly beans they were using as the soft play area for the imaginary insects.

'Daddy!' Ben wailed as he scooped them up. 'Careful. You can't make the balls dirty, it will give the butterflies a virus.'

'Sorry, Ben. Butter fingers,' he mumbled before continuing his conversation with Mandy. 'I've been watching her ride for the last two seasons. She's fabulous. She's got great timing, can see a stride a mile out, she's a good judge of pace and, most important of all, horses run for her. She's going to be an absolute superstar, as long as trainers give her a chance.'

'If you want her to ride The Skirrid, I can ask,' Mandy

suggested. 'She can't ignore her favourite cousin, especially now I'm a part-owner of the horse.'

Not only could Mandy keep the children entertained with ease, she could also perform a real-life miracle and get a jockey for The Skirrid.

That bastard Bertie O'Reilly had spread damaging false-hoods about Dickon, and his reputation was in the mud after what had happened at Cheltenham. Now, none of the top jockeys would ride for him.

'Would she need to come here to ride him on the gallops?' Alex asked. 'To get to know him?'

'Ideally, yes,' Dickon agreed.

Mandy pulled her phone from her pocket and started typing a message. 'Leave it with me. I'll get her over here by the end of the week and let's see how they get on.' She looked up at Alex from her phone screen. 'Is it OK if I stay a few more days?'

Alex said yes so fast that even Mandy looked surprised, but she gave her a beaming smile.

CHAPTER FORTY-FIVE

It rained solidly for the next two days, so Alex couldn't take Mandy on the long walk she had planned to show her the view from on high, wanting her to fall in love with this landscape as she had done.

What Alex wasn't in love with were the bills that were mounting. The farm was leaking money like a rusty old trough. She paid what she could with the money they had made from the farmyard sale, and she transferred a lump sum into Gwen's account to make up for the months she had kindly held off on being paid while Alex sorted things out.

She sat at the kitchen table poring over the paperwork. As she held her head in her hands, muttering numbers out loud, she felt Mandy's hand on her back.

'It's OK.' She rubbed gently between Alex's shoulders. 'We'll sort it out. Just try not to think of it all at once. We can take it one chunk at a time.'

The knock on the door was so loud Alex jumped and knocked the coffee cup. She swiped at it with her sleeve, leaving a streak of brown on her clothes and on the table.

'Shit.'

'I'll deal with it.' Mandy picked up a cloth and wiped the stain away.

Alex opened the front door to find a bedraggled Owen

Odd Job. She beckoned him to come inside but he shook his head, rain spraying from his beanie hat. He pointed up at the sky as the rain continued to hammer down.

'Roof,' he said.

'What about it?' The panic in Alex's voice betrayed her fear.

'Collapsed in the barn.'

'Oh God! Was anyone hurt? Is Gwen OK? Are you OK? Are the sheep . . .'

Her words came out in a flurry.

Owen shook his head and turned away. Alex took that to mean that people and animals had survived unscathed.

She felt as if she'd been punched in the chest. She would need to inspect the damage and of course there would be the cost of repairs. She went back to the kitchen where Mandy was studying the paperwork and making notes on a large pad.

'We have another problem.' Alex delivered the news as if reading it on the 10 o'clock bulletin. 'The barn roof has collapsed.'

Mandy nodded, seemingly unruffled by the disaster. She looked up at Alex for more detail.

'No one was hurt. That's the only good news.'

'Right. Well let's add to the list.' Mandy jotted down a figure that had more noughts on it than Alex cared to think about.

'It's all too much.' Alex sat down again, and her head automatically sank into her hands. 'I'm already borrowing more than I can afford and the interest is ridiculous. I can't afford to wait until the lambs sell, and no one's put an offer in on my flat yet. It's a disaster.'

342

This farm she had never wanted, this life she had never imagined had grabbed her heart, and now she was terrified of losing it. She didn't want to have to go back to London, she certainly didn't want to beg for her old job back, and she knew she wanted more than anything to be here, preferably with Mandy by her side.

'You might have to drop the asking price for your flat,' Mandy advised. 'If you bring it ten grand lower, it'll be just below the threshold people set when they search online. That'll mean more interest and hopefully an offer sooner.'

Alex was grateful, but reluctant to slash the price too much. She needed as much as she could get, but she also couldn't afford a long, drawn-out sales process. If Bertie O'Reilly and Abigail got a whiff of her financial insecurity, she knew they'd be in like vultures to pick at her carcass. She couldn't let them or anyone else take the farm.

Once the rain slowed, Mandy and Alex went out to inspect the damage to the barn roof. The back section of it had caved in, leaving a damp pile of rubble below and a gaping hole above.

'Good for ventilation.' Mandy joked.

'Not funny. Not even slightly.' Alex dug her in the ribs but smiled shakily. Then she started to laugh. Mandy joined in. Other than crying, it was the only possible response. She didn't know how things could get any worse.

'C'mon.' She said. 'Let's go and see Dickon. At least we can help him even if I can't help myself.'

Later that morning, they walked across the sodden field, their boots sucked down every other step. Alex nearly lost her balance as her foot started to come out of the left boot, which remained firmly trapped in the mud. She shrieked and reached out to Mandy to help her.

'Steady there girl.' Mandy held out an arm.

Alex regained her balance, trying again to extract the boot from the mud.

'Follow me.' Mandy navigated her way across the drier sections.

'Happily,' Alex responded, before adding under her breath, 'Anywhere.'

They found Dickon in the stables, tacking up The Skirrid in readiness for his first encounter with his new jockey, Mandy's cousin. Barry John looked up as Alex and Mandy approached, but quickly decided his breakfast was more interesting. The Skirrid stood in his bridle, facing out. His ears flicked back and forth, and he reached his nose towards Alex in greeting, seeming much calmer.

'All right, girls?'

Dickon moved smoothly and efficiently, picking up the saddle with its padded saddlecloth already beneath it and placing it carefully on the horse's back, sliding it down from the withers so that it sat in the slight dip. He worked from the left-hand side, the near side of the horse, letting the girths drop onto the far side and reaching under the tummy to grasp the thick elasticated fabric band and gently attach it to buckles on the nearside.

He lifted the sleek racehorse's hooves, one at a time, picking out any dirt or compacted droppings with a hoof pick. He checked for any heat in the tendons of the horse's legs. When he finished that job, he went back to the girths and put his fingers under the strap.

'Naughty boy always puffs his tummy out when I first put the saddle on. Have to give it a second go.'

He gently but firmly notched the girth buckles up two holes.

'Don't want your cousin sliding off him because I haven't saddled up properly.' He patted The Skirrid on the neck and spoke directly to him. 'New rider for you today, Skirry. So just you behave yourself. None of that whipping-round malarkey. OK?'

Barry John let out a throaty bleat as if in agreement. The Skirrid flicked his ears back and forth, as if he had heard and understood the instruction from both master and friend.

Lucy Maynard arrived at eleven on the dot. She walked into the yard with a calm confidence, and immediately, Alex could see the family resemblance. She had expected Lucy to be short – she was a jockey, after all – but as she watched Mandy give her a hug, she saw that they were roughly the same height. About five foot seven, she guessed, but where Mandy was softly toned and slender, Lucy was sharp and angular, as lean and muscular as a greyhound. She had the same piercing blue eyes as Mandy but no dimples.

'Hey there.' Lucy waved as she strode towards Alex. 'Mandy has told me all about you. Sounds like you've got a lot going on.'

Alex blushed. The idea of Mandy talking about her to her cousin was thrilling. But what did she mean about a lot going on? Was it a reference to the farm, to herself or to the two of them together? Did Mandy think there was something going on there? If so, that would mean it wasn't just in her head, and that was, well, that was bloody terrifying actually.

Imaginary relationships were much safer, with no chance you could mess it up, like the one she'd had for years with Kate Winslet, who had been her 'best friend' since she was about fourteen years old. They had long conversations, with Alex providing both sides of the dialogue. Whenever she was in a pickle, had a tricky decision to make, or a challenge lay ahead, she would ask herself: 'what would Kate do?' The answer was always braver and more decisive than she would have dared on her own.

Right now, Kate was telling her to stop trying so hard.

'Yeah. Hi,' she said in a voice that was an octave lower than usual. 'I've heard a lot about you too. All good. Ha-ha!'

Her laugh sounded so strange that Mandy looked over with concern.

'You feeling all right?' she whispered.

Alex nodded. Maybe it was safer not to speak at all. What she would give for the nonchalant ease that Mandy possessed so easily. Where Mandy and Lucy were elegant ballet dancers, she was a clown wearing oversized shoes and talking in a funny voice.

Mandy introduced her cousin to Dickon, and they nodded a polite hello. Digby shoved his nose between Lucy's legs and, instead of recoiling in horror, she patted his head and laughed.

'Now this is the one I really need to meet,' Lucy said after exchanging a few words with Dickon, placing a hand gently on The Skirrid's neck and moving it slowly in stroking motions. 'What a handsome boy you are. And this must be your friend?'

'That's Barry John,' Dickon replied without any sense of irony. 'He's the best assistant trainer I've ever had. Skirry loves him, and he's calmed him right down . . . Now all we need is a jockey who understands him,' Dickon continued, putting his head on one side. His expression was full of hope.

Lucy had stopped stroking The Skirrid, and the horse looked round expectantly, nudging her gently to continue.

'Looks as if he likes you already.' Dickon grinned.

'Well, the feeling is mutual. I'm quite taken with him,' Lucy replied.

Dickon led The Skirrid out of the stable door, with Barry John following obediently.

Lucy stepped in between Dickon and The Skirrid and put her left hand on the reins, bending up her left leg to offer her shin. Alex watched in wonder as, in one smooth movement, like circus performers, Dickon helped her spring up and into the saddle. The Skirrid flicked his ears back and forth, but stayed still as Lucy patted him on the neck and started talking to him softly.

Dickon led them towards the arch and out into the open space between his yard and Alex's farm.

'I'd take him for a trot up the side of that hill. See the track over there?' He pointed to the edge of the woodland. 'Give you both a chance to get to know each other and then, when you're ready, the stiff gallop is six furlongs, starting down there.'

He pointed to a section of white railing at the bottom of the hill. Lucy nodded and carried on talking to The Skirrid as they trotted off.

'Let's see how it goes!' Dickon gestured towards his Land Rover, and they climbed up onto the seats, the interior of the cushions clearly visible through the holes in the vinyl.

They watched Lucy trotting The Skirrid in the distance and then walking him back down the hill to the start of the gallop.

Dickon positioned the Land Rover three quarters of the way up the hill and leapt out, binoculars in hand, to watch horse and jockey set off steadily, building up their pace. By the time they came past the group of three, The Skirrid's hooves were thudding in a fast drumbeat. Digby looked up as he heard the noise, and he took off as if chasing a hare, flying up behind the galloping horse. Lucy was crouched low over his neck, her back flat and her hands sitting on the base of the neck, near the withers, barely moving. Her core strength kept her aerodynamic, and she didn't move her head at all, even to glance at the dog now upsides her.

Dickon's binoculars were trained on horse and jockey as they steadied the pace half a furlong before the end of the gallop and slowed gently to a jog. They turned back towards the Land Rover, Digby alongside with his jaws open in a wide panting grin. Lucy was also smiling as she patted The Skirrid again and loosened her reins to let him walk freely back down the hill.

'How was that?' Dickon shouted as they approached.

'Bloody brilliant!' she hollered back. 'He's got so much power. I love him!'

Alex looked at Dickon and, for the first time, saw confidence come back into his body as he stood up a little straighter. He had endured a torrid time, facing the shame and the pain of his wife leaving him, the guilt of not being with his children and the desperation of his business falling apart.

'That's great. Just great.' He beamed at Lucy. 'Wanna have a pop over a few hurdles?'

'Just try and stop me,' she replied.

Mandy climbed into the front passenger seat, while Alex leant forward from the back so that she could hear her discussion with Dickon. They were both elated.

'She just needs a chance on a good horse,' Mandy told him.

'And he just needs a jockey who believes in him,' Dickon replied.

'It's a match made in heaven.' Mandy smiled in satisfaction. There was magic, and then there was real-life magic. This was the latter.

After the schooling session, which went better than Dickon had dreamt, they stood in the dusty kitchen discussing the next steps.

'His jumping is so accurate,' Lucy gushed. 'Honestly, I didn't have to ask him once. He knew what to do. If you run him at Chepstow, that line of hurdles in the home straight will suit him just fine, and I reckon he'll be OK going round the tight turn away from the stables. He's so well balanced, it won't be a problem.'

Dickon couldn't stop smiling, his careworn face transformed by the delight that someone else could see and feel the potential in Skirry.

'We'll have to keep you away from my Aunt Di, though, if the syndicate members come to see him run. She'll fill your face with vape steam and try to give you instructions on how to ride.'

'Oh don't you worry – I'm used to all sorts telling me how to ride.' Lucy laughed.

'Well, I won't be making that mistake,' Dickon promised her, not sharing the view of the more traditional racing folk that female jockeys weren't as competent as men. 'I've watched you enough in races to see that you know what you're doing. It'll take time for you and Skirry to get to know each other, so I'm not expecting miracles, but this is a long-term project.' He hesitated, suddenly unsure before checking, 'That's if you're up for it?'

'Up for it? Are you mad? Of course I am,' Lucy enthused. 'I've watched his previous races, and also I managed to get the aerial footage of the Cheltenham race, so I could see exactly what he was doing out there in front.'

Dickon looked impressed. That was a level of homework he hadn't expected.

'I think he's a natural leader,' Lucy continued, 'so if it's all right with you, and as long as the others don't try and go a crazy pace, that's what I'll try to do.'

Dickon and Lucy moved their chairs closer together as he pulled out the printed list of entries for the proposed race at Chepstow for them to discuss.

Mandy caught Alex's eye and mouthed at her, 'We should go.' Best to leave the professionals to it.

'Anything I can do to help, just say.' Alex retreated towards the door.

'We need someone to look after Barry John,' he said. 'He'll come in the horsebox, and they've agreed he can be in the stables, so I thought you'd better be the one to, you know, to look after him, seeing as he's technically yours.'

Alex had not envisaged her first outing as a syndicate manager to be one in which she was in charge of a sheep, but if that's what it would take, that's what she would do, because she wanted it to be a success. It was at least one ray of sunshine because, as Alex trudged back to the farm, she was jolted back into her now near-constant state of impending doom, wondering again how on earth she was going to stop everything from falling apart.

CHAPTER FORTY-SIX

David was slowly recovering, his speech improving and his strength returning every day. Isobel had been patient to a point, but she was increasingly frustrated at the lack of variety to their life, so Alex's email couldn't have been better timed.

The Skirrid was going to run at Chepstow in three weeks, and there was no reason at all why she and David shouldn't go. Muriel offered to dog-sit so that they could stay the night before at the farm to break the journey up, and Isobel had put off a visit for long enough.

As Isobel turned the car into the long drive to Tir Glas Farm, she remembered the last time she had been here, well over thirty years ago. The pain of what might have been, the life she might have lived, hit her like a physical blow. She caught her breath, trying to recover herself, because she couldn't afford to fall apart now when she had been strong for so long.

Her mind drifted back to the trip she and Will had taken to France. They had been so young, so naïve and so very much in love.

He hadn't proposed to her. He didn't ever use the word 'marry' or 'wedding'. He simply said, 'So will you?'

She had replied, 'Will I what?'

'Will you grow old with me?'

She had laughed, wondering why he would fast-forward their lives to old age.

'Course I will,' she eventually replied, and she had meant it.

Sadly, that future together had never evolved.

Isobel drove slowly round the potholes, glancing briefly sideways at David to check he was OK, but he was still dozing. He had slept for most of the journey, which was a relief. He had steadily improved over the past couple of months, his muscles getting stronger from his daily walks and his speech expanding into full sentences. He took his pills faithfully every day and had not raised his voice or even seemed short-tempered. Maybe, she considered, the stroke had transformed him.

She parked outside the farmhouse, the place she had once dreamt of calling home.

A week after they had returned from Paris, Will had abruptly told her that he couldn't see her any more. There was no explanation, no further communication. Her heart, so full of love and hope, had been smashed into a thousand pieces in the most brutal fashion.

Now, she sat in the car, waiting for her husband to wake up, thinking back to the way he had scooped her up. She had fallen off a cliff, and David had caught her. He had been there and hadn't let her out of his sight, offering her comfort and a dazzling array of generous gifts. Out of gratitude, grief and desperation, she had married him two months later.

For years after they married, she had waited for Will to call her or to write. If he had asked her to come to him, she would have dropped everything, but he never did.

She turned off the engine but still couldn't bring herself to get out of the car. Being back here was too strange, the memories too overwhelming.

She had no time for those people who said 'everything happens for a reason'. It wasn't true. Shit happened and you had to deal with it.

She woke David up and helped him out of the car.

Isobel heard a dog barking from within the crumbling walls. They needed repointing, and the windows needed sanding and painting too. One glance up at the roof confirmed that it ought to be retiled – another huge expense. It had all aged ungracefully, but then, so had she. The exterior was bad enough, but when Alex opened the door to let her parents into the general dumping area that had once been an entrance hall, Isobel was truly horrified.

'God, you're going to need to do some work to this place.' She sounded sharper than she intended.

'Lovely to see you too, Mum.' Alex sighed, reaching past her to give David a hug and a kiss. 'I'm so glad you could both make it.'

'That's Jiffy. He's a Welsh terrier,' Alex explained, pointing at the small dog wagging his tail in excitement at the visitors. She took David's arm and led him towards the kitchen.

'He was a great player.' He looked at the dog.

'Spot on, Dad. You're on the ball. You'll be warmer in here. Let's make you comfortable.'

'Thank you.' He looked around the room. 'Love what you've done with the place.'

Isobel followed behind, noting the deep indents in the

stone floor where heavy feet had trodden over decades. She flinched at the stained and chipped painted walls and the window, its cracks stuffed with newspaper.

She moved slowly, as if in a trance, because the place she remembered had not aged well. She picked up the chipped mug that sat on the sideboard. It had been Will's favourite. It was covered in a map of the United Kingdom, Ireland and Iceland, with the shipping forecast areas marked out around the coastline. They had tried to learn them in sequence.

'You have to start at Viking,' he would say. She could hear his voice again here in this room, picture him sitting in that armchair where Alex was now settling David. He was all around her, and the pain was unbearable.

'Viking, North Utsire.' She would start their Shipping Forecast memory game.

'It's not pronounced like that,' he corrected her. 'It's oot-seer-ah.'

'All right, clever clogs. I don't listen to Radio Four as much as you do. Viking, North OOT-SEER-AH, South OOT-SEER-AH.'

'Forties, Cromarty, Forth.' He did the next three. 'Cromarty would be a good name for a dog, you know.'

'It would, but don't distract me!' Her voice was lighter then, before her heart broke and never quite healed. 'I like this next bit. Tyne, Dogger – you couldn't call a dog that – Fisher, German Bight.'

'Humber, Thames, Dover.' His brow furrowed. 'Oh, I always lose my way down here. Dammit. I'm going to have to look.'

'That's cheating!' She nudged him. 'It's Wight next. The Isle of Wight is down there.'

She ran her thumb over the crazed glaze of the old mug, and her eyes prickled with tears which she blinked back.

'You OK, Mum?' Alex interrupted her thoughts. 'You look like you've seen a ghost.'

Isobel started. She was miles away, or rather right here in this room but lost in the past.

'Yup, I'm fine. Just a little tired after all that driving. It's always further than you think.' She moved towards the kitchen sink to wash her hands. Alex had noticed the use of 'always', and alarm bells were ringing in her head.

Isobel splashed cold water on her face, hoping the shock of it would help her recover her senses.

'You'll have to show me round the farm,' she said in the cheeriest tone she could muster.

'Oh, that's Mandy,' Alex explained, clearly spotting her mother's bemused expression at the sight of a tall athletic woman in a blue boiler suit striding across the grass.

'Mandy?'

'You met her on Christmas Eve at Aunt Di's party. Magic Mandy – the magician? She kept the kids entertained all evening. Remember? You liked her,' Alex prompted her.

'Ah yes,' Isobel said, picking up on the eagerness in Alex's voice, which made her wonder why it mattered whether she liked her or not.

Mandy came into the kitchen, now out of her boiler suit, stretching her hand out to greet Isobel.

'Lovely to see you again, Mrs Roberts. I hope you had a smooth journey. The M4 roadworks are a bit of a pain.' She stepped carefully towards the sofa and extended her hand towards David. 'We haven't met before, Mr Roberts. My name is Mandy.'

She did not take her hand away when David did not immediately respond, giving him time to lift his right hand slowly and meet hers. She shook it gently, looking him in the eye.

'You have very blue eyes.' He winked at her.

'Yes, she does, Dad,' Alex interjected. 'And you're clearly back to yourself. You old flirt. Wait until you meet Gwen. She's very much your cup of tea and more age-appropriate.'

David's eyes twinkled, and Isobel could see Alex's relief to find her father much more like himself.

Despite his obvious improvement, Isobel suggested they gave him time to recover from the journey, so they left him in the armchair while they headed off on their tour of the property. The weekend sale had helped the place looked less like a scrapyard and more like a functioning farm, and all the ewes had been recently sheared.

Isobel didn't strictly need a tour, remembering the place well, but she followed obediently, watching and listening. She noticed that Mandy knew a lot about the sheep and the running of the farm. She seemed very at home.

Alex was equally relaxed and settled. Her descriptions of the landscape and the animals were poetic. She shared details of the characters of individual lambs – the cheeky one, the timid one, the greedy one, the slow learner – and she imbued the landscape with personality, telling Isobel about the legends of the mountains and fanciful myths of wood nymphs.

'It's like the trolls in Iceland,' Alex explained.

'Or in Norway,' Mandy added. 'They must be appeased.'

'You want them . . . what's the best way of putting it?' Alex paused.

'On your side,' they said together, in perfect harmony.

Isobel noted the look that passed between them as they came up with the same expression at the same time. She saw it like an electric current flow from one to the other and back again.

She had felt it once too, here with her first love, William.

CHAPTER FORTY-SEVEN

That evening, Mandy left for the pub where she was booked in for the night so that David and Isobel could have plenty of room at the farm. David had gone up to bed, leaving just Isobel and Alex downstairs in the armchairs.

'Oh god, do you really want to know?' Alex sighed when her mother asked about the state of the farm finances. 'It's horrendous. I can't begin to tell you. I've got bills up to here' – she raised her hand to her chin – 'and everyone's demanding their money now. I was looking into a loan from the bank, but the interest rates have jumped up, so it's just a nightmare.'

Isobel was shocked to see her daughter so exasperated and desperate, and realized it was clearly a hugely complicated business.

'Everyone has been so helpful.' Alex's voice cracked. 'They all want me to succeed, and I don't . . . I don't want to let them down.'

Isobel couldn't remember the last time she'd seen her daughter be so upset, let alone cry. Her heart was pulling her in one direction, her head in another, as she wrestled with herself.

'Let's go through the options,' she said calmly. 'I'm sure we can work this out, if we go through the finances together.'

'And there's another p-problem.' Alex nearly choked on the

words, her whole body heaving. 'The vultures are circling. I overheard Bertie O'Reilly and Abigail talking, just waiting for me to fail so they could sneak in and buy it.'

She stopped to blow her nose, and Jiffy looked up from her lap, whining softly.

'I know, boy! You hate it when anyone is upset,' she said. 'But what are we going to do? The flat in London hasn't sold yet, so I've got no capital. I've already borrowed money to pay the bills and all the other money I found out was owed, besides putting in my share to Skirry. It was all a bit of a mess, and that's before we even get to the the barn roof. If I was being sensible, I'd get them to do the roof of the house as well because that will cave in sooner or later but it's all a great big money pit. The more I chuck in, the more it consumes.'

Isobel stared at the fire, the heat rising in her cheeks. 'I thought you were talking about diversification?' she ventured.

'It all costs money.' Alex shook her head. 'I can't afford to diversify because setting up a rural retreat would have big costs, yet I can't afford to stand still. The money from the farmyard sale has papered over a few cracks, but the whole place is falling down, and I can't save it.'

Isobel chewed the inside of her cheek as she deliberated what to say. Neither of them had noticed the third person in the room, standing silently by the door, having crept down the stairs.

'The will says I can't sell for five years, but I'll be bankrupt well before then,' Alex continued. 'The last thing I want to do is sell up to those toerags Bertie and Abigail, but I don't

362

see what choice I have. I can't do any of this – I just don't understand why William left it to me.'

The sound of a gentle cough made Alex jump.

'Why don't you tell her the truth, Izzy?'

Isobel leapt off the sofa and took David by the arm. 'You shouldn't have come down the stairs on your own, darling. You could have slipped and fallen on those uneven steps.'

She tried to guide him back to bed, but he stood firm, surprisingly strong in his resistance.

'Come on, sweetheart,' Isobel tried to cajole him, her panic rising. 'You're not making any sense. Alex doesn't want to see you like this now, does she?'

Alex caught her father's eye, and she could see that he was perfectly lucid. He knew what he was saying, and he wanted to say more.

'Let him sit down, for god's sake.'

Isobel was backed into a corner.

David sat down heavily, falling back on the cushions and letting out a sigh. 'That's better.' He smiled at Alex.

'What do you mean, Dad?' she asked, leaning forward. 'What truth?'

David looked at Isobel, challenging her to say something. She stared at her lap, twisting her hands back and forth. Heat spread up through her chest and her neck, and her throat felt completely dry. She tried to breathe slowly, just as Muriel had taught her, but still, the anxiety was overwhelming.

'Your father is not himself,' Isobel tried. 'He doesn't know what he's saying.'

David shook his head and heaved himself up straight. He

put his right hand over the top of Alex's and looked her straight in the eye. 'I love you,' he said gently. 'I have always loved you, and I will always love you, even if you . . .' He paused to gather his breath. 'Are not mine.'

'What?' Alex moved, her heart thudding.

She turned to look at her mother, who was staring intently at a far-off spot on the wall, her eyes seemingly glazed over.

'I don't understand,' Alex murmured, looking back at David. 'If you're not my father, then who is?'

Isobel still wouldn't or couldn't speak, so David filled in the blank that was so obvious to everyone.

'William,' he said.

Alex stood up so violently that Jiffy tumbled off her lap.

'Sorry, boy.' She reached down to scoop him up again. 'I didn't mean to do that. It's not your fault.'

She felt such a fool. She and Ethan had talked about the possibility, of course, but she'd never seriously believed it.

'What happened?' was all Alex could manage.

'My fault,' David said. 'Bad investment.'

Her father looked exhausted from the effort of it all, and was incapable of further conversation.

Isobel stood up slowly and helped lift David off the sofa. 'You knew?' she whispered to him, and he nodded to her.

'Mum, you've got to talk to me,' Alex pleaded. 'You can't leave me in the dark any longer. I know you've changed the subject whenever I mentioned William, but I deserve to know the truth.'

She hated herself for begging, for sounding whiny like a

teenager again, but her mother brought out the worst in her, and she knew she'd been avoiding talking to her.

'I'll come back, I promise. Let me just get your . . .' She stopped herself. 'Let me just get him up to bed.'

Jiffy whined again, and Alex took him to the back door, needing some fresh air too.

'You need a pee, and I need a bloody drink.'

She poured herself a large glass of wine, called Jiffy back in and waited for her mother to reappear. She got angrier by the second, feeling robbed of experiences and understanding, furious at being lied to all these years.

Her mother finally returned, as promised.

'Now, there's no need to be overdramatic about all this.' Isobel sat at the furthest end of the sofa, with Alex sinking into Will's old armchair. Isobel fought the memories of him sitting there, eyes sparkling as they laughed together and planned their future.

'I do not think it's over-fucking-dramatic to be a bit shocked that the man you thought was your father your whole life is actually not.' Alex tried to stop herself from sounding hysterical, but her words were coming out quickly and at a higher than usual pitch. 'And I do not think it's over-fucking-dramatic to perhaps expect your mother, who would actually know that information, to have shared it with you sooner. And do not, please *do not*, tell me not to swear!'

'Fine,' said Isobel, who had been about to say just that, hoping to deflect attention.

'So,' Alex challenged her. 'Do you want to tell me what the hell has been going on?'

'It's a long story,' Isobel said feebly.

'Well, it's my life story and I'm all ears, Mum.' Alex clasped her hands together in her lap.

Isobel told Alex how she had met Will when they were in their twenties. They had fallen head over heels in love, and felt even closer after a big journey across Europe. They had travelled cheaply, and it had felt like a five-star experience because they were together. They had walked when they could, or hitched lifts, occasionally taking a train. They stayed wherever they could find a room or occasionally slept on a beach or in a log cabin up a mountain. It had been the best adventure of her life. She was young, free and in love.

They were comfortable in each other's company; he made her laugh and brought out the best in her. When Will had asked her to spend the rest of her life with him, she was so happy she could burst.

'I think Dad always knew,' Alex mumbled. 'What he said tonight about a bad investment? I found some papers. He advised William to put his money in a company that went bust. He'd been trying to make enough money to keep you secure, but he lost it all. That's why he dumped you. And that's why Dad was there immediately to save you. He thought it was all his fault.'

'I loved William so completely that it hurt when he broke things off; it was like a part of me had died,' Isobel admitted. She pulled out a handkerchief from her pocket and dabbed at her eyes, then blew her nose.

'Go on.' Alex's heart was pounding. She needed her mother to keep talking because – finally – she was opening up.

'David was there,' Isobel explained. 'He was suddenly right there, as if he knew I needed him. He saved me.'

Alex chewed the inside of her mouth.

'He said he would look after me and care for me. My father adored him, thought he was "the right sort of chap". I had an inkling I might be pregnant when I married him, even though I tried to tell myself I could have missed my periods because of grief or stress. But deep down, I knew.

'You were late, thank god.' Isobel allowed herself a small chuckle. 'Some things never change. I told your . . . I told David you were early, and I hoped he wouldn't know the difference. Was that terribly wrong of me?'

Alex didn't know what would have been the right course of action. All she knew was that she felt completely flabbergasted by this information. She had never heard her mother talk about herself or her feelings. She had always been so emotionally in control, so contained, which was why Alex had always found it hard to talk to her, because her mother never opened up. That was at the heart of their discordant relationship.

'You've always been different from the boys, you know,' Isobel continued, meeting Alex's eye for the first time. 'There's something in your eyes that is him. I almost can't bear to look sometimes because it hurts, here.' She prodded at her chest. 'He's there in you but he's never been here with me.'

'You brought me down here. Why?' Alex asked, thinking back to the photo she'd found of her as a young girl holding a lamb on this farm.

'I needed him to see you,' Isobel explained. 'I thought he

would see himself in you as I did so clearly. If he did, he didn't say.'

Will had been polite and kind, had shown her the lambs and let Alex hold one, but he had not asked them to stay as Isobel had hoped.

She would have stayed forever – if he had just asked.

A firm knock at the back door surprised them both. Alex glanced at her watch. It was nearly midnight. Who on earth would be coming at this hour?

Alex opened the door to find a tall shadowy figure, beanie hat in one hand, other hand raised in a semi-salute to the long hairy brow that stretched in an unbroken line above his eyes.

'I'll come,' Owen Odd Job muttered.

She asked what he meant, and he mumbled, 'Barry John. T'morra. I'll do it.'

He immediately backed away from the lights and disappeared into the darkness.

When Alex returned to the kitchen, she found her mother had slipped away to bed, leaving her alone with a Welsh terrier and a thousand questions.

CHAPTER FORTY-EIGHT

The next morning, Jiffy nuzzled into Alex's neck then licked her face to wake her. He had a knack of being right there when she needed him most. Dressing fast, she was up before her parents, and relieved not to have to talk to them as she genuinely didn't know what to say to either of them, but particularly her mother. How could everyone else have known this massive secret and kept it from her? Why hadn't they been honest with her right from the start? In fact, why hadn't Isobel told her years ago, so that she could have chosen whether or not she wanted a relationship with William Griffiths.

Maybe she also wouldn't have made such a total arse of herself her whole life, talking about inherited traits from a man with whom she didn't share an ounce of DNA, or feeling weird because she didn't understand her brothers. Of course she was different. She'd been different her whole bloody life, but now the pieces had fallen into place. She was furious and curious in equal measure. The revelation had explained a lot, but it had also left so much unanswered.

She needed time to process all this, and it might need more than one long walk with Ethan to make her feel better, but right now she tried to focus on her most urgent problem: the triple threat of Bertie O'Reilly, Abigail and the hateful Layton Brooks. She had to stop them from taking her land and from trying to destroy Dickon as well.

Alex had been surprised by the enthusiasm with which the syndicate members had embraced the idea of a day at Chepstow races. Everyone was coming, even though she'd told them that The Skirrid was running for experience and had no real chance of winning.

Ah, it'll be a fun day out, her brother Kit had replied when she'd messaged an update.

Rhys was driving Gwen and Mandy, picking up Ethan from Newport station on the way. Her brothers Kit and Hugh had both, to her complete shock, taken the day off work and were treating it as a family outing. Aunt Di was using it as an excuse to show off her latest outfit and the new boyfriend who had replaced Orlando. Then of course there were her parents, although she didn't much want to talk to them.

Dickon's fingers drummed on the steering wheel of the old horsebox. Alex sat alongside him, staring out of the window in a daze, and next to her was the biggest surprise attendee of all – Owen Odd Job. He had scared the living daylights out of her the night before when he'd turned up on the doorstep, offering to come and help today.

It was the most she'd ever heard him say, and he hadn't added to it since, remaining stoically silent this morning. Alex assumed that Gwen must have talked to him and that he was happy to take care of the strong, fat lamb while the race was in progress.

'I hate this feeling.' Dickon let out a huge sigh as they queued to enter the horsebox park.

'What, the nerves?' Alex asked.

'Worse than that,' Dickon replied. 'The hope. The dream that this time it might work out better.'

Alex knew that one horse would not be the answer to his dilemma. He needed a yard full of decent horses to make a living, but she hoped that if The Skirrid ran well, it could be a good advert for his talent with sensitive horses. A bit like Lucy Maynard was developing a reputation for being able to ride tricky horses, Dickon could re-establish himself as the maverick who could train them.

The arrived at the stables in plenty of time, and on this occasion, Alex would be the one to lead up The Skirrid. Dickon knew he would be far more likely to relax with someone he knew and liked, giving the horse the best chance of running well today.

As they calmly got ready, Alex found the concentration on simple tasks therapeutic, stopping her mind from whirring. She did not need to talk to her mother or anyone else; she just needed to focus on the delicate thoroughbred in her charge. Whenever she had gone to Dickon's yard to use his Wi-Fi, she had paid him back by doing some mucking out and tidying up in the stables, so she had got very comfortable around The Skirrid, as he was with her.

The horse had never looked better. His coat was gleaming, his eyes were bright and alert, and he didn't show even the hint of a tremble as Alex led him towards the racecourse. Owen Odd Job stayed behind with the sheep, ignoring the stares being thrown their way by the stable staff from rival yards. Neither man nor sheep cared what anyone else thought, so Owen was perfect for that job.

Alex walked The Skirrid steadily round the circular path in the pre-parade ring, talking gently to him as she went.

371

He looked inquisitively at the new surroundings, his ears gently flicking back and forth, but he didn't sweat, staying perfectly relaxed. It was so quiet down in the bowl that you would never have realized there was a crowd or a racecourse anywhere near.

Dickon and Lucy had been in constant contact, speaking every day about how they should approach the build-up to the race, the race itself and the immediate aftermath, meticulous in their preparation. It was important that The Skirrid had a good all-round experience so that he would want to run again. They anticipated that the transition from the pre-parade ring to the main paddock could be the trigger point for his nerves. Lucy rode horses for lots of different trainers, but Dickon was impressed with her attention to detail and the amount of effort she was putting in for him.

Alex had the earplugs in her pocket that Lucy had suggested to shield the horse from the noise of the crowd, and Dickon planned to fit them when the time came to saddle.

'How is he?' Lucy asked, when Dickon went to collect the saddle from the weighing room, stopping for a brief chat.

'All fine so far, touch wood.' He tapped his fingers on the wooden rail between them. 'Barry John was good as gold, and The Skirrid never moved a muscle. He went into the stables grand, and he seemed happy enough to leave them because, just like at home, he knows he'll be gone for less than an hour and then he'll be back with his boy.'

'That's perfect.' Lucy nodded. 'Phase one complete. I'll just grab the colours and weigh out so you can get him saddled nice and early.'

She disappeared back into the changing room and re-emerged wearing the colours that would clearly identify her in the race. The thin silk-like fabric had poppers down the front, which she was doing up as she walked out. The shirt was green with black, bird-like shapes on it. The cap was bright yellow.

She grabbed her saddle and weight-cloth from the valet in the men's changing room, checked her weight on the practice scales and then came forward to the clerk of the scales for the official weighing out.

Dickon watched her, admiring her lack of nerves. He chewed on his forefinger as he waited for her to hand him the saddle.

'All present and correct, number twelve. Thank you,' the clerk of the scales pronounced.

Lucy carried her saddle to Dickon and placed it in his arms.

'See you in the paddock,' she said, before she disappeared back into the changing room.

Dickon could hear the commentator describing the action as the first race of the day got under way. He was vaguely aware that Bertie O'Reilly was riding in it, but he tried to dismiss any negative thoughts. The Skirrid was a hypersensitive horse, and he could pick up on other people's energy, so it was important for Dickon to stay calm. It was also why he'd asked Alex to lead the horse round before the race and to help afterwards. She was good with animals, and she had a naturally upbeat and supportive way about her.

Alex let The Skirrid walk at his own pace round the circular ring, and chatted to him as they went, explaining all about the race and the other runners and how many hurdles he

373

would have to jump. She told him to take his time and find his own rhythm, to listen to Lucy and to gallop up the hill at the end as fast as he could. His left ear leant towards her, as if he was listening to every word.

Dickon saddled him slowly and precisely, tightening the girths and stretching out his front legs to check nothing was pinching. Alex handed him the earplugs, and The Skirrid bowed his head to help him fit them. They had a long piece of string attached so they could be pulled out before the race was under way, as the rules stated.

Dickon stroked the horse's neck and admired the gleam of his skin. If this was a showing competition, he'd win by a mile as he looked so well.

'You show 'em what you're made of, Skirry.' He patted him one final time.

He nodded for Alex to take the horse up to the main parade ring. The owners were gathered in a group in the centre. Aunt Di was holding court, dressed in a beautiful blue dress and coat. It would have fitted in perfectly at Royal Ascot, and was far smarter than what anyone else here at Chepstow was wearing. Kit and Hugh were laughing at a story she was telling. Their wives stayed on the outside of the paddock with the children, who shouted out hello to Alex as she led The Skirrid past them. Rhys, Ethan and Gwen joined the group in the centre, not knowing how to act as owners. Her parents were there as well, but she couldn't look at them. Her heart lifted when she spotted Mandy chatting happily with the group.

Then Alex spotted a large, loud figure in a garish checked

suit. It was Layton Brooks. He owned the horse who was the hot favourite for the race that The Skirrid was running in.

The other runners were led from the pre-parade ring, and soon the paddock was filled with horses and people. The jockeys emerged from the weighing room, shooting like slender arrows in different directions as they found their respective trainers.

Lucy Maynard walked out last, and Alex admired the colours the syndicate had chosen. The main body of the silks was green, to represent the hills of the valleys around the farm, the black shapes like a flock of starlings and the bright yellow of the cap for the sun.

The wait for the race to begin seemed interminable, but now time suddenly sped up and, within seconds, Dickon had walked towards her with Lucy beside him. He legged her up and touched her knee briefly.

'Good luck,' he said. 'Do your best.'

He patted the horse on the neck one last time. Alex led him out onto the course and detached the leather leading rein. She watched Lucy and The Skirrid canter down to the start on the far side of the course, then walked back to the paddock. She could watch the race from there with the rest of the syndicate members, eyes on the big screen opposite.

'He looks marvellous!' Aunt Di gushed as she hugged her. 'What a thrill this will be.'

She introduced Alex to her boyfriend.

'You remember Dr Khan, darling,' she said. 'He treated your father at the hospital.'

Alex nodded politely, secretly marvelling at Aunt Di's

ability to attract younger men, even if she didn't know how to respond to the word 'father' right now. Nothing made sense any more.

The runners had all arrived at the start, and the commentator was name-checking them and assessing their chances.

'And the big outsider here is The Skirrid,' he echoed over the Tannoy. 'Hoping to redeem himself after the fiasco at Cheltenham for local trainer Dickon Jones.'

Alex detached herself from the group of owners so that she could watch on her own. She felt a presence behind her, and a voice suddenly sneered in her ear, 'You'd better start packing.'

She spun round, coming face to face with Layton Brooks. She shuddered at the sight of his white teeth sparkling in the sunshine and his flop of brown hair.

'Last-chance saloon.' He leered towards her. 'I hear you're skint. What a shame.' His voice dripped with sarcasm. 'I expect you'll need someone with real money to bail you out.'

In an instant, Rhys and Mandy were by her side. Rhys positioned himself so that he was protecting her.

'Back off, Brooks.' He flexed his arm muscles, standing up to his full height.

Layton Brooks looked amused. 'Got your personal security guard here again, have you? Don't bring him when you come running to me to take that farm off your hands.' He laughed and headed back towards the other end of the paddock, shouting over his shoulder as he went, 'I'll see you after my horse has won.'

Alex felt Mandy's hand on hers, which made her legs feel even more like jelly.

'It's OK.' Mandy squeezed her hand. 'We've got you.'

'*And they're off!*' The commentator narrated the action.

The Skirrid started well, and Lucy allowed him to bowl along in front. His ears were pricked, and he covered the ground easily, meeting the first hurdle on the perfect stride. They swung down the hill and left-handed into the straight, where all the runners skipped over three more hurdles and passed the winning post for the first time. The crowd cheered as The Skirrid maintained his lead, negotiating the tight left-hand bend away from them and up the hill again to the far side of the course.

'The Skirrid still leads.' The commentator sounded surprised. 'He's enjoying himself today, but the main contenders are lining up behind him ready to make their move.'

Alex could barely look at the screen. She felt faint and grabbed Mandy's arm to steady herself.

'I can't look,' she croaked, her throat constricting.

'It's fine,' Mandy comforted her. 'Lucy is letting him bowl along, and he's so well balanced he doesn't mind the hills. Must have got used to them at home, I suppose.'

Bertie O'Reilly moved into second on the horse owned by Layton Brooks.

'Champagne Supernova is waiting to pounce.' The commentator's voice was rising in tone and urgency, and the crowd started to respond as they turned away from the back straight and back down the hill again. 'Bertie O'Reilly is sitting pretty. Just three flights of hurdles left and then that long gallop to the line. The other runners are struggling with this pace. The Skirrid is still full of running as they come downhill and into the straight. Three hurdles left, but here comes Champagne Supernova.'

Alex felt herself swaying, as if her legs couldn't support her any longer, and her vision blurred.

'Oh god,' she muttered before she fainted.

CHAPTER FORTY-NINE

'Alex, it's all right. I'm here. I'm right with you.'

Mandy's was the only voice Alex heard as she came round. She had never fainted in her life and didn't know what had happened or how long she'd been out for.

'Take it easy. Just sit up slowly. You'll be fine,' Mandy promised her. 'Rhys and I caught you before you hit the ground.'

Alex sat up slowly and shook her head. 'What happened?' she asked, her voice barely a whisper.

Dickon appeared at her side and gently took the leather lead rein from her hands. 'I'll go. You stay here,' he told her, before running towards the racecourse.

'The Skirrid!' Alex mumbled, remembering where she was and what she was doing. 'What happened?'

She glanced towards the group of her friends and family, and saw them all jumping up and down, hugging and cheering, slapping each other on the back. She looked to Mandy for an explanation.

'He was amazing.' Mandy grinned.

'He couldn't have. He didn't, did he?' Alex asked, not daring to think the impossible.

'Skirry just took off. After the last hurdle, it was like he'd found turbo. It was amazing,' Mandy said excitedly.

Alex looked up at the big screen to see the replay of Bertie O'Reilly on Champagne Supernova coming up alongside

Skirry and giving him a deliberate bump, trying to throw him off course with his usual underhand tactic. She could see Lucy not even lose her balance, staying crouched over his neck, encouraging him with hands and heels all the way to the line. Passing the winning post, she didn't stand up in the stirrups, but she took one hand off the reins and patted him on the neck, as if he had just finished a gallop at home.

Champagne Supernova finished second, still some way clear of the rest of the field but a long way behind The Skirrid.

'That was as impressive a performance as we've seen all season,' the commentator admitted. 'What a result for local trainer Dickon Jones and for the up-and-coming Lucy Maynard. They've got a star on their hands here.'

Bertie O'Reilly's face looked like thunder as he guided Champagne Supernova into the area reserved for second place. He snatched the saddle off the horse's back and stomped his way to the weighing room. Layton Brooks was thankfully nowhere to be seen, now he couldn't lord it over them.

'A big cheer for your winner!' the commentator encouraged as Lucy trotted back. 'He's caused a big upset today, ladies and gentleman. Owned by the Starling Syndicate, it looks like the sky's the limit for THE SKIRRID!'

The cheer was so loud that The Skirrid's head shot up, and he stopped in his tracks. Dickon patted him on the neck, and Lucy encouraged him gently forward.

'You'll have to get used to this, Skirry.' She coaxed him into the winners' enclosure.

Mandy guided Alex into the centre of the celebrations. Despite her caution to the others about his chances of winning, the other syndicate members had all taken advantage of the generous odds offered by the bookmakers. In doing so, they had handsomely supplemented the winner's prize money.

As Lucy took her saddle back to the weighing room to weigh in, Rhys picked up a bucket of water and threw it across The Skirrid's back to cool him off.

'Watch out!' shrieked Aunt Di, as the water splashed her designer outfit. It was too late, although she was too happy to care.

Alex was still feeling a little dizzy, but the euphoria of the group was more effective than any medicine in bringing her back to her best. She had hoped The Skirrid and Lucy would start to build a decent partnership, that he would jump and gallop for her and perhaps finish fourth or fifth to show some progress. But to win today and, in doing so, to beat one of the most promising hurdlers in the country, with his devious jockey, was so far beyond her wildest dreams that she was struggling to take it in.

'Is this real?' Alex turned Mandy. 'Or am I still unconscious?'

'It's real all right,' she said, squeezing Alex's hand gently.

Rhys took over the duties of leading The Skirrid back to the stables so that the others could receive their trophy and celebrate, before continuing the festivities when they got back to the Black Prince.

'Drinks are on the house,' he promised.

The commentator welcomed the Starling Syndicate to the podium to collect their trophy.

Alex glanced up to the weighing room and saw that Lucy had been delayed on her way back by the menacing figure of

Layton Brooks. He was leaning over her, saying something that was clearly upsetting her. Lucy manoeuvred herself out of his path and ran down the steps and up onto the small wooden stage as her name was being announced.

'What did he want?' Alex whispered in her ear.

'Not now.' Lucy waved her away, not wanting to spoil the moment. 'We can talk about it later.'

Having agreed to meet everyone at the pub later, Alex and Dickon went to find The Skirrid, who had been happily reunited with Barry John in the stables.

As they prepared to take them home, there was a kerfuffle around a huge monster of a horsebox in the car park. Alex went out to investigate. The gold horsebox had the glossy black lettering of *BROOKS BUBBLES* along its side. A police car was parked in front of it, blocking its exit. Two police officers were asking the driver to lower the ramp. Layton Brooks came running towards them, shouting furiously. Alex watched on.

'We have received a tip-off sir,' the police officer said. 'And we would like to search this vehicle. Obviously if you have nothing to hide, then you have nothing to fear.'

Layton started swearing. He was bright red in the face, and now he was trying to prevent the police officer from walking up the ramp. As he was warned about his behaviour, he lost control of his temper and swung a punch at the police officer. Alex heard the crack as the police officer's jaw felt the full impact of Layton's fist. Within seconds, the other officer had handcuffed Layton and was reading him his rights.

'You are under arrest for assaulting a police officer,' he said firmly.

CHAPTER FIFTY

The celebrations that night were, even by Ethan's party-planning standards, epic.

After Alex and Dickon had returned The Skirrid and Barry John to the safety of the yard, they joined the others at the Black Prince, where the race was being watched on repeat.

Rhys handed Alex a gin and tonic. 'I've made it weak, mind,' he told her. 'You probably need to take it easy tonight. Go and sit over there with your parents.'

She looked at the space on the big leather sofa where her parents were, but hesitated, not feeling ready to talk to them.

'You OK?' Mandy enquired, pulling her to one side. 'You still look a bit pale. Have you eaten anything?'

'I'm fine,' Alex snapped, her tone harsher than she meant. 'Leave it,' she added with a sigh.

'Fine,' Mandy said, clearly taken aback. She walked away to the furthest end of the room and concentrated on talking to Ethan.

Alex had immediately regretted her sharpness – Mandy was the last person she wanted to upset. She didn't know what to do or say because Mandy had a disorientating effect on her. Alex's head was in a muddle; although she was thrilled with how the race had panned out, knowing that the syndicate would all get a share of the prize money, it still didn't solve the problems facing her.

383

She found Lucy at the bar ordering a Diet Coke. 'What did Layton Brooks want?' she asked, concerned. 'I saw him, and it looked as if he was threatening you.'

Lucy hesitated. 'Oh, he's just a classic bully.' She shook her head. 'He said if I rode for Dickon again, he'd make sure I was finished.'

Alex was horrified. 'What did you say?'

'I told him that I'd rather be finished than do his bidding.' Lucy looked defiant. 'I used much coarser language than that to make sure he understood, but you get my drift.'

Alex was impressed by her bravery but worried about the impact it would have on her career, not wanting her to jeopardize that for one horse.

'Oh and then,' Lucy added, 'and this was the weird bit – he told me to tell you that he'd be picking up the keys to your farm soon enough.'

The bastard. He was threatening her as well as Lucy. Fortified by the adrenalin rush of anger and fear, she spun round and rushed for the door. She needed fresh air.

'Woah there,' Dickon said, as she swung right into him. 'You set off at that pace and you'll never get home. Take a leaf from Lucy's book – she's the perfect judge of pace.'

His eyes sparkled as he smiled at Lucy and, buoyed by their victory, they headed into a corner together to plot the next steps for The Skirrid.

Alex didn't know where to turn. She had offended Mandy, she didn't want to talk to her mother, and she was no longer in the mood to celebrate after hearing about Layton's latest threat. Jiffy looked up at her and whined gently.

'Do you want to go out for a pee?'

She stood outside and let the chill of the evening air hit her, stepping away from the lights of the pub so that she could see the sky more clearly. She looked up into the darkness and, as her eyes adjusted, she started to see the stars appearing. Hundreds of them, thousands, twinkling in a clear dark sky.

'Pretty, isn't it?'

She had company.

'So pretty, Dad,' she replied, still looking up as a tear slid down her face.

David put his arm round her, and turned her into his body so that her face was resting against his heart. He held her as she sobbed, the emotions she'd tried to hold back all day finally escaping. He stroked the back of her head as Alex took huge gulps. She felt Jiffy's paws on the back of her legs as he jumped up gently to check she was all right.

'I love you, Ali. I loved you from the moment I first saw you.' David spoke slowly, meaning every word.

'I love you too, Dad.' Alex sniffed into his chest.

'I always thought he might come and take you away.' David sighed. 'That you and Mum would leave me. But he was too – oh, what's the word? Polite. That's it.'

Alex took a step backwards and gently released herself from his embrace. She reached down to stroke Jiffy, reassuring him she was OK, and then looked up at the night sky, and the stars all those millions of miles away, and at Venus glowing brightly. She could have lived a different life on what felt like another planet, been a completely different person. Here she was, made up of DNA that she did not share with the man opposite her, and yet he was the one whose comfort she sought and whose guidance she wanted, and that would never change.

'You're my father,' she told David. 'You will always be my father and, right now, Dad, what I need is your help. I've got to sort it out before "that dreadful footballer", as you call him, takes it all away.' She sniffed again and wiped her nose with the back of her hand.

'I think Layton Brooks has problems of his own,' David said. 'From what I hear, he won't be around to make trouble for quite a while, thanks to someone making an anonymous tip-off.' He tapped the side of his nose. 'I had a chat with some of my old financial friends, and it seems your nemesis isn't very keen on paying his taxes. I also hear he likes a bit of the old Charlie and keeps it hidden in his horsebox, so that's what they were looking for. Once he punched the police officer, he guaranteed himself a night in the cells. I suspect he's going to have a lot of legal expenses ahead of him.'

Alex shook her head. She hadn't known that her father was even aware of her problems with Layton Brooks. She hugged him tight.

'Here.' David offered his oversized hankie. 'You can't have Mandy seeing you like this. Not your best look.'

Alex blew her nose hard and wiped her eyes, cleaning up the mascara that had attempted to make a run for it and feeling so much better for their heart-to-heart. She put her arm through her father's, and they walked towards the pub together, Jiffy trotting behind them.

'Don't be too hard on your mother,' he said softly, as they reached the door. 'She only did what she thought was right.'

When they opened the door, the recording of The Skirrid's race was being played again. Alex could watch closely this time as he jumped the last three hurdles. The group booed theatrically as Bertie O'Reilly tried to bump him out of contention, and roared their approval as Lucy coaxed him for that last superb effort.

Having not seen it at the time, Alex still couldn't quite believe that The Skirrid had crossed the line first and had given them all a fairytale start to their new adventure as a team. As she looked around the room at the faces of her friends, so full of warmth, love and delight, she realized that she was not going to give up. She was even more determined than before to make a success of her farm, and to help Dickon to flourish as well. She still had a mountain to climb, that was clear, but today's victory had been a start.

She walked to the corner of the room where Dickon used to take himself on his own, and stared at the photo of William Griffiths, arms crossed, sitting in the front row of a rugby team.

'Penny for your thoughts,' a voice said softly in her ear. Isobel was now fond of the expression she had learned from Muriel.

'Jeez, Mum, you gave me a shock. Don't creep up on people like that!' She was so surprised that she momentarily forgot how cross she was with her mother. 'Sadly, I'll need a bit more than a penny to save the place he loved.' She pointed at the photo.

Isobel followed her gaze. 'But you'll do it. You're more like him than you know.'

They both looked at the photo again.

'Gwen knew,' Isobel said.

Alex looked surprised. 'How?' she asked.

'It was Jiffy. She said he gave it away when he jumped on your lap and looked so comfortable there. Who needs a DNA test when you've got a Welsh terrier? '

'William was a handsome devil.' Alex conceded. 'I can see why you fell for him.'

Isobel murmured something she couldn't hear about the energy it takes to love completely, which Alex decided not to press her on.

'On that,' her mother spoke louder. 'I remember you talking once about knowing a work of art when you saw it. I think that's how you put it.'

Alex nodded, wondering where the conversation was going. 'I did. And I looked at a lot of paintings.' She tried to be flippant, not wanting to get into something so deep as her personal life with her mother. They'd done more soul-searching and had more honest conversations in the last twenty-four hours than in the last thirty-nine years.

Isobel pointed at Mandy, who was deep in conversation with Lucy and Dickon. Jiffy had settled himself at her ankles, and she was casually fondling his ears.

'I think you were looking in the wrong galleries, love,' she said softly. Then she carried on, matter-of-factly, as if debating the rising price of cheese. 'I've always thought you might be gay – is that the right word, or would you rather I say lesbian. Is that an adjective as well as a noun?'

Alex felt faint again and grabbed the back of a wooden chair to steady herself. This was all too much. Discussing her sexuality with her mother had not been on her to-do list for today.

'Mum!' she tutted. 'Honestly.'

Isobel was not in the mood to be stopped. 'Well, I think she's a very impressive girl. Or woman. Or whatever it is I should call her. And Jiffy certainly approves. If you love her with all your heart and she loves you back, make sure you do whatever it takes to hold on to her. Do you understand?'

Alex nodded her head in mute submission. Her mother was again making her feel like a teenager. This was more familiar ground for the two of them.

'Don't make the same mistakes I did and let it slip away. Now go over there and make it up with her before I have to smack you.'

'No, Mum, that's not allowed these days.' Alex rolled her eyes, laughing.

She left Isobel to look at the photos on the wall and walked towards the group of three who were studying the racing calendar and plotting the route ahead after The Skirrid's summer holiday.

Alex didn't say a word but took Mandy by the hand and led her outside into the chill of the evening. Jiffy followed them.

'Are you kidnapping me?' Mandy asked.

Alex didn't reply but kept walking to furthest end of the car park.

'I'm really sorry for how I snapped at you earlier.' Alex sighed, trying to find the words and not turn into her usual blubbering idiot around Mandy. 'There's something I found out from my parents that I'll tell you about another time.'

'That's OK. I could tell something was up. But I don't want to talk about your parents.' Mandy smiled.

'So back to your question about kidnapping,' Alex laughed. 'Sort of.' She cleared her throat to find the courage. 'If you'll stay.'

She looked up to face Mandy, her heart pounding faster than was probably healthy. If she was going to die, she thought, she hoped it didn't happen before she had the chance to kiss her.

Everything in her head was exploding, as if the electric current she'd felt between them since their first meeting was creating fireworks. Mandy's blue eyes focused on her unwaveringly, making Alex feel nervous as much as exhilarated.

Mandy took her face in her hands and kissed her tenderly, like a butterfly landing on her lips. Jiffy gave a bark of joy. He jumped up at them both, tail wagging, dancing on his back legs in delight at the smile on Alex's face.

'I thought you'd never ask,' Mandy said quietly.

Alex's tummy did a triple flip, and this time she knew why. She kissed Mandy on the side of the neck and inhaled her scent, that intoxicating combination of aromas that was so familiar and yet new and exciting. This was what falling in love felt like. This was what home smelt like.

All her life she'd felt it. Hiraeth. That word Gwen had told her about, which meant longing for something that was missing. She'd never known what it was, and yet now it had arrived, she knew.

She had finally come home.

ACKNOWLEDGEMENTS

This has been a labour of love that took a whole year longer than planned, so a massive thank you to HarperCollins for their patience and their professionalism. The writing experience is a solitary quest and yet there is a whole team that makes the book come alive.

Every time I sat at my desk and started typing, I was transported to Monmouthshire and I could see, hear and feel the farm and those within it. That's because it's based on a real place and real people. One of my dearest friends, Sue (to whom the book is dedicated), lives in a beautiful farmhouse at the end of a potholed drive with a wood to the right, a waterlogged field to the left and hills all around. I could see it all, and having been there to stay with her and her husband Ed (who was a beautiful and talented writer, as well as a solidly magnificent man) on many an occasion, I knew I wanted to write about the place and the people. Sue has been unfailingly supportive and introduced me to her friends Colin and Tracey Evans who have a sheep farm down the road. They were so generous with their time and their knowledge, answering so many daft questions from me and correcting mistakes – a massive thanks to them. Any errors that remain about the demanding and complex business of farming are mine alone.

But it wasn't just their knowledge I wanted to capture, it

was the way they have wrapped Sue up in a bundle of love, food and family when she has needed it most. I have witnessed and have tried to represent what rural friendship is all about – whether providing food, rounding up stray sheep or mending a fence, the best neighbours help out without even being asked.

I may joke that this is all Jilly Cooper's fault, but my thanks go to the author who shaped my teenage years and then told me to knuckle down and write fiction for adults.

There is no one better to have on your side than my literary agent Eugenie Furniss, who was a driving force, constantly telling me that I could and should write a novel and securing the team at HarperCollins who could help me achieve my aims.

They let me get on with it, offering support when needed. Thanks to Lynne Drew, editor extraordinaire, whose judgement I trust completely, to Katie Seaman who was ruthlessly efficient in cutting unnecessary waffle, Pen Isaac and Katie Lumsden for eagle-eyed copy editing and proofreading. Also to Charlie Redmayne, Liz Dawson, Jo Kite, Alice Brown, Holly Martin and the sales team, to Fionnuala Barrett for help with the audiobook and everyone at HarperCollins who has believed in this book and helped me get it into your hands.

The theme of love and friendship is the beating heart of this book, and for that to be written authentically you have to know what it feels like to fall in love with the person you want to spend the rest of your life with, and how love grows with every experience and every day. For that I have to thank Alice, not just for being the love of my life but also for packing me off to the study to write, listening to me as I debated plot lines, characters and themes, for reading the first draft before anyone else and for being brutally honest in her feedback. So I went away and tried again, eventually finessing Alex into a friend we would want to hang out with.

It's a very scary thing to create characters, weave a story and then put it out there into the competitive world of books, so a huge thanks to you for picking this book up and for reading it. I really hope you've enjoyed the ride.